THREE SISTERS

A TALE OF SURVIVAL

By

NIKKI LEWEN

Amy~
Hope these books
help get you
through your
days. Enjoy!
Nikki Lewen

DEDICATION

Dedicated to my husband, who unfairly, gets neglected while I write. Thank you for supporting me in every way, spoiling me rotten—even when I don't deserve it—and putting up with all of my obsessions. You make all *this* possible.

ONE

Hearing her name, she freezes mid-step as the hairs at the base of her skull stand alert and goose bumps cover her arms. It's an eerie feeling after all these years, and been so long since it's been spoken, she's nearly forgotten its sound. Looking around, it's unbelievable — all the signs she missed. Trampled patches of undergrowth and a trail of broken earth, clearly evident, speak volumes. She's been careless, unfocused even, which is unacceptable and extremely dangerous. Disappointed by her lapse of attention, suddenly she's unsure of what to think. Letting her guard down is a crucial mistake and how costly it may be, will depend on what happens next and her ability to think logically.

Dropping into a defendable position with her crossbow drawn, she scans the redwood forest. Staying in the open is another error, so cautiously, she tucks behind a tree, while attempting to control the thoughts and questions penetrating her mind as she glances toward his direction. "How can this be?" she thinks. He doesn't move. "Where'd he come from…what the hell's goin' on?"

Nothing stirs but her mind. A bombardment of uncertainties mixed with vivid images from her past, make things even more challenging for her to decipher. Attempting to figure out how he found her, suddenly her thoughts shift in an entirely different direction. "Maybe, he wasn't looking…maybe it's…only coincidence?" With a shake of her head, the notion gets disregarded while she concentrates on circling the area, moving from one cover to the next. After verifying that no one else is around, she steps into the clearing for a better look.

"Damn it," she mutters aloud, trying to concentrate while stepping around a bloody mess and two motionless bodies.

It isn't the first time that death has surrounded her, but still, it's unnerving. Unexpectedly hearing her name and then seeing whose lips it came from makes it all the more uncanny. After a quick survey, she makes her way back towards him. He's slumped against a tree, filthy, and covered in a mixture of dirt and blood. What clothes he wears are threadbare and hang from a thin frame. His hair is long, matted in clumps, and he hasn't shaved in years. As for his face, it's badly beaten and blood drips from both his nose and a cut above the eye.

"Caleb," she says, lightly shaking him before trying again, "Caleb…you hear me?"

He's unresponsive and she realizes that gasping her name was the last thing he did. He's barely recognizable, but somehow the instant she heard her name she knew who it was, and a powerful gut reaction—something she trusts—confirmed it. What isn't trust worthy is the debate raging between her sense of self-preservation and her instinct to help. Her initial response already pulled her closer, but a sense of safety keeps yelling for her to hide and get away.

Checking his vitals, she's shocked by Caleb's presence. He's breathing, albeit very shallow, and from the look of things an intense battle just ended. He's bleeding from a serious wound in his side, and from what looks like everywhere else, which makes her concerns grow. Between the grime and blood, it's hard to tell exactly what injuries he suffers, let alone where they're located. What's immediately obvious is the rope burns cut deep into the flesh around both his wrists. She's wrong. This wasn't just a recent fight but something that dragged on for some time. Apparently, Caleb was held captive and the extent of his injuries won't be known until she can get him cleaned up. "But not here," she thinks. "It's not safe."

She leaves Caleb's side to take a more thorough look around. The other two bodies are obviously those of Splitters. All the telltale signs are present: the military uniforms, the guns and ammo, even a gas-powered, rugged, all-wheel drive, quad. The ATV is beat-up and old, but loaded with supplies. It was never military issue, but knowing how the Nation operates, she assumes they simply confiscated it along their way. In terms of her personal safety, she also assumes others will come looking, and more than likely, there're already more in the area. She hasn't been this far in a long time and can't believe the quad's engine noise went unnoticed, which means they must have ridden in during the storm. It's the only thing that would've covered the sound.

Of the two Splitters, the one closest to the four-wheeler has a hunting knife stuck hilt-deep into his heart, leaving no possibility he's still alive. As for the other, he's face-down only ten feet away and hasn't moved. If that one's still alive, she hates thinking of what needs to be done. There's no way he can remain living, especially if more of his comrades come looking. Walking towards the body her pulse races and an uneasy feeling grows. With heightened senses she closes the gap, looking for signs of life. She hates violence, but the world hasn't been safe in a long time and unfortunately, sometimes—killing means surviving.

Stopping only inches from the man's feet, she draws an arrow, aims at his head, and gives the body a sharp kick. No movement, none. She holds aim and kicks harder. Still nothing. Carefully, and with extreme caution, she grabs one of the outstretched arms and rolls the body over, exposing the throat. It's cut deeply, and his lifeless eyes have rolled into the back of his skull. The sight is unsettling, but a sense of relief washes over her with the realization that he's dead and it wasn't by her hand.

After a brief pause while contemplating her options, the problem at hand surfaces. An unconscious man, badly wounded, needs attending to, and there are two dead Splitters who obviously didn't die of natural causes. She's at least a half day's journey away from her nearest shelter, and then another two days away from her main quarters, which she calls home.

In terms of personal preservation, she should have left long ago. Thinking of it now, her conscience won't allow it. As the notion gets dismissed, a faint moan from Caleb gains her attention, re-affirming she can't leave him to die. Their paths have crossed once again, and why, she can't say. How he got here, why the Splitters held him hostage, and how he managed to not only escape, but also kill them, is a mystery she needs to solve.

Back at Caleb's side, she decides the first thing to do is slow the bleeding from his side wound. She runs back to the quad and rummages through the supplies strapped to the back cargo hold. She finds a small, basic first-aid kit and quickly inspects its contents. It's extremely old and doesn't offer much: a few gauze wraps, a couple rolls of medical tape, and some antiseptic wipes. She rips open his shirt where blood oozes, getting a better look at the injury. It's deep and needs stitches. Using the remaining material from his shirt, she wipes off as much blood as possible. Then, using the wipes, she cleans the area before covering it in gauze and wrapping it up. The dressing should temporarily do the trick, but it's going to require better care.

A much more complicated dilemma faces her now. "How...am I gonna get him outta here?" she wonders. Caleb's much thinner than she remembers, but he's still heavier than her. The four-wheeler can easily carry them both, but its use could attract others. Besides the noise it generates, the quad can't even get them to where they need to go. These mountains are rugged and steep making it surprising the Splitters even made it this far. They must have followed the old logging road up the ridgeline, which abruptly stops at the overlook. The only options from here were either turning back the way they came or continuing on foot.

Her land isn't very accessible by vehicle, especially from this side, which is one of the reasons she's felt safe staying there. Besides being difficult to access, her intimate knowledge of the area also gives her an advantage, and—the redwoods are home. She grew up in these mountains, spent her life exploring and hiking the valleys, canyons, and ridges. But things have drastically changed since her childhood and the days of peaceful explorations are long gone. Now it's purely survival, and it dictates everything she does. Each day brings her new challenges, but what today presents is especially difficult, creating uncertainty with how she'll manage it.

Contemplating her options, she decides the real dilemma is figuring how to either carry or drag Caleb. The enormity of the task is overwhelming, especially with her underlying fear of being discovered. Thinking logically, she rechecks the supplies latched to the quad, along with what the two dead men carry, and starts a small pile of salvageable items. There's a good amount of rope, two rifles with plenty of ammunition, food rations, a single canteen of water, an old army mess kit, a pack full of clothes, one tarp, two bed rolls, and a couple cans of fuel.

Pulling the hunting knife out of the dead guy's heart and wiping it clean on his clothes; it too, gets added to her mound of goods. Looking between the pile and Caleb's unconscious body, a strategy slowly emerges. There's no way to move all that's gathered, so scouting the area, she finds a stash sight for the guns, ammo, and fuel while deciding to return another time to retrieve them. Satisfied with the hiding place and cover up, she turns her full attention to the remaining items.

Knowing that dragging him is the only viable option, she vaguely recalls a Native American technique used for hauling things behind horses and has a vision to work from. Using the tarp, bedrolls, and rope, she gathers several sturdy redwood branches and builds a makeshift stretcher. It'd work better with two people, one at each end, but since she's solo—as always—it'll have to make do. It's the only way. Pulling it will leave an obvious trail, so she'll have to continually retrace their route to cover the marks. The only positive aspect of this plan is their destination is mainly downhill.

With a few trials and errors, she eventually finds a sturdy enough design for the task. She rolls Caleb onto the stretcher, uses one of the bedrolls to cover his body, and securely latches everything down. She refuses to cut good rope, so instead, the extra length gets bundled and tucked into the bindings while the rest of the supplies get squeezed into her backpack. Sitting back to inspect her ingenuity, a small surge of pride develops, but it quickly fades as the dragging begins. Only seventy-five yards away, she's already dripping with sweat. Looking back from where they've come, a clear path anyone could follow is visible. She tucks the stretcher behind an outcrop of rocks, uses fern fronds to camouflage Caleb, and goes back to cover their trail.

Back at the clearing, she still needs to figure out what to do with the two dead Splitters. Standing at the edge of the cliff, which ends abruptly, dropping straight down several hundred feet, she looks out. It used to open to an incredible view and on clear days you could see for miles, until the line of the horizon eventually met with the distant ocean. Now, the site below is heart-wrenching and serves as a reminder of terrible times. What used to be some of the most fertile agricultural land in the country is gone; swallowed by the ocean. Then, making things worse, it turned too acidic, killing just about everything except a few species of sea grass and jellyfish.

Originally, checking the view brought her out this far, but looking now, she isn't sure what was hoped. The rainfall from the other day was so surprising that a part of her thought it might be a sign of change and maybe things were improving. The last real rainstorm hit over five and a half years ago, and since then, only a few light drizzles have broken up the monotonous, grey marine layer permanently hanging over the woods. She's lucky, though—at least the fog brings moisture. The last she's heard, this was one of the few places left with any water, although she's no longer sure what's happening in the rest of the world or at least—in what remains of it.

After gazing out at the dismal dead ocean and seeing things remain the same, she returns to the bodies. Once again inspecting the quad, she finds a short, blood-stained rope attached at the back. It's obviously what they used to tie Caleb as they pulled and dragged him while traveling. Searching the back cargo area, she discovers two detachable metal sections and realizes they're removable ramps, which explains how they navigated the quad this far.

Still unsure of what to do, she observes her surroundings. From the looks of the clearing, they hadn't been there long, so she decides to hike down the old logging road and scout further. It's easy to track the four-wheeler's route, and it's obvious where the Splitters either drove around, or ramped over logs.

Staying close to the tree line, she proceeds with extreme caution not wanting to run into any more of the brutal militants, especially any still alive. Traveling further down the road, she realizes the effort taken to get the quad this far. In several places it's hard to tell that a road even existed—it's so thick and overgrown. Coming this way was chosen with some purpose and she needs to learn why. They must have traveled for weeks, and possibly even months, to make it this deep into the mountains, and wanting to figure out where they came from, she finds it hard to comprehend.

When she finds where they camped, no effort has been made to hide their presence or clean the area. She's survived this long by hiding her existence, blending in with the surroundings, and covering any and all tracks. The condition of this site is a slap in the face to her careful habits. They intruded into her domain and had the audacity to leave it a mess. Their lack of caution sends a deep shudder through her. Checking around the camp, she inspects their fire ring, debris, empty food pouches, and then, her fear grows. Off to the side, a crumpled mass of bloody cloths lies sprawled about and beyond those, a naked body.

Creeping closer, to her horror, reveals it's a man who's been tortured to death. His body has been grossly abused, his fingers and toes are missing, and it's difficult to make out any facial features: they're too swollen and misshapen. He wasn't a Splitter and must have been traveling with Caleb, making her wonder why they only killed him.

At this point, she's seen enough, turns around, and heads back to where she found Caleb.

Along the way, she forms a plan of action. Back at the clearing, she drags the two bodies to the ATV and places them upon it. Using a small section of tubing, she siphons most of the gas and fills one of the empty fuel cans, but leaves just enough to start the engine and drive it a short distance. At the halfway point between the clearing and where they camped, there's a section of cliff that has recently collapsed. The ground is still soft from the recent rain, making it the perfect spot.

Getting off the quad, she uses the short piece of bloody rope to keep the throttle on. Standing next to it, she releases the brake and lets the ATV go. It starts moving parallel to the cliffs edge, before slowly angling directly towards it. The farther it travels the closer to the edge it gets. As it nears, the ground gives way, and the four-wheeler, along with the two bodies, disappear. If anyone comes looking for these two, she hopes it'll look like an accident. It's the best she can do, especially since time's working against her.

Heading to where Caleb's been left, she knows there's no way to get both of them back to shelter before dark, which means, they'll have to remain overnight in the woods. The thought is anything but thrilling. For her, the cover of night is always spent hidden in a shelter, but tonight she's stuck out in the open. Not looking forward to the fast-approaching darkness, she stays alert and hopes they're not discovered.

Returning to Caleb's side, she checks him over and attempts dribbling water down his throat—knowing keeping him hydrated is going to be a challenge. She drinks, eats one of the Nation's MREs, and then looks for a better place to hide for the night. She adjusts the fern fronds covering him, and climbs up the rocks the stretcher butts against. It's not the best location, but it's high enough to see in every direction and there's a crevice big enough to tuck into and hide. Crawling in, she decides another stash of supplies needs to be hidden in this area. It'll add to her growing resources of shelters and caches that cover these mountains.

Settling in, she's tired, and fights the urge to sleep. Even though there haven't been any more signs of Splitters, she can't allow her guard to drop, especially since they're so close to the clearly-evident murderous scene. Getting comfortable for the night, she wraps a blanket around her body and keeps the crossbow loaded. The woods grow dark and soon only her hearing can be relied on. Sitting in the darkness, her mind grapples with the day's events. Concerned with what's to come, suddenly she's unsure of her hiding place. They're too easy to find. Dismissing the negative feeling, she replaces it with another.

If he lives—she's no longer alone.

TWO

Jerking awake, unaware of having falling asleep, it's hard to tell whether she slept for minutes or hours. It's still dark, but clearly becoming lighter. Listening long and hard before climbing down, her fatigue forewarns of the long day ahead and the effort needed to get Caleb to safety, where his wounds can be properly treated. Quietly heading back to the clearing, she checks if anyone else has come this way. Thankfully, all seems okay. Returning to Caleb and finding his forehead warm — a symptom that deepens her worries — she trudges along.

It's slow, tedious work moving them both along, and at this rate, it'll take most of the day to travel a distance, that's normally covered in hours. By mid-day and only halfway to her destination, a rhythm of sorts develops. It consists of dragging the stretcher for about an hour, taking a long, replenishing drink of water, checking Caleb, and then retracing the clearly obvious marks, that weighs heavily on her fear of being discovered. Jogging back and forth without him, she covers the evidence knowing his survival depends on how fast she moves. Determination drives her forward as every muscle aches, but — relentlessly — she pushes on.

The canteen taken from the Splitters has long been empty, and she's down to the last of her supply. She drinks more than usual, but under these circumstances, it's needed. Sweat soaked through all of her clothes hours ago, and her hands, even though calloused from years of hard work, have begun to blister. They burn with pain and she swears never again to forget gloves when patrolling. She travels these woods constantly, day in and day out, going from shelter to shelter, keeping each site maintained, observing any changes in the mountains, looking for signs of intruders, and scavenging for food and water.

Routines keep her alive and provide the sanity needed to survive. Each outing gives her a reason to get up in the morning and move on. Often, she stays longer in her home shelter because of its comforts, but getting complacent is dangerous and she always forces herself out, sometimes patrolling for weeks at a time before returning. She lives, surviving alone, and wonders about the meaning of it all, but like now, she perseveres with each step, each minute, and each grueling hour. It's what she knows, simply—keep going, but as the day lengthens, she's forced to stop.

Even though they're nearing her destination, she's so exhausted that tears threaten to break free. "Why's life so cruel?" she laments. She's been alone for years, and now, finally finding another, someone she knows even, he's in terrible shape and may not survive. She's practically killing herself trying to save him and the enormity of it is overwhelming. Losing control, sobs rock her body. Curling into a little ball of sorrow, her bleeding hands ache and fatigued threatens to end her attempted rescue. The heavy stretcher's been dragged through rough mountain terrain for eight hours and she's unsure if she can continue the grueling trek.

Lying on a side, feeling sorry for herself, she allows her mind to wander. She misses her dad, she misses her husband, and she misses what life used to be. After a few more minutes of self-pity, she forces the nonsense to stop by sitting up. She eats another confiscated ration and verbally berates herself for acting like a fool. Standing, she rubs her neck, straightens her back, and refocuses the effort. She's a survivor and needs to act like one. Looking at her bleeding hands, she decides to use what's left of the gauze and medical tape to protect them from further damage. The plan was to save the supplies for Caleb's wounds, but what's the point if she can't get him there?

Hours later, and only a few hundred yards away, she stops again, but this time out of caution. She never approaches any shelter the same way and practices extreme patience. No one has ever discovered any of her hideouts, and even now, the same care that's kept her alive is what she'll use. After collecting a few dead branches and fern fronds to tuck him beneath, she starts a perimeter inspection. Relief washes over her, as all looks well, and she can approach the site. She's made it; and never, in all of her life, has it been so difficult.

The spot holds a special place in her heart and the first time she visited, was as a little girl with her father. He'd known about the location all along, but let it be a surprise for his kids. When it first came into view, they ran ahead to check it out and explore. Back then, the small cave-like structure—about seventeen feet wide and eleven feet deep—felt like a fortress. It formed when a mudslide had broken off an enormous slab of rock, which settled across two huge boulders, butting against the base of a cliff.

Her dad had known it would excite them and over the years, the cave became their secret hideout deep in the woods. They played there for endless hours and with every visit, they brought tools and supplies to work on it. After cleaning the rubble out from the front of the opening and digging the floor deeper, they could easily stand inside. Her father, a skilled tradesman and talented engineer, who could build or repair just about anything, played a huge role in its remodel. He split logs and formed timbers to help support the roof, added a wooden floor, then cut and chiseled shelves into the boulders along the sides and back wall.

Their cave became a special place and sometimes they'd camp overnight. As they got older, the kids would hike to it by themselves, spending weekends or holidays tucked away. For the final touch, her dad constructed a wall in the front with two small doors. One door sat against the boulder on the right and the other against the left. Between the doors he made a small sliding panel that could be opened for either light or air.

In those days, she never imagined her childhood play-place would turn into something so important. Now it's an essential part of her survival, especially since its existence is completely camouflaged by a huge fallen redwood. When the tree fell, it'd taken several others with it, making a considerable mess. Seeing the tangle for the first time, she thought the cave was destroyed. Upon further inspection, she discovered that, not only was it still intact, but by climbing over and through the mess, access was still possible.

Crawling inside now, she leaves her backpack and heads back to Caleb to finish the job. She struggles through the last of the remaining distance and when close enough, she grabs a few things from inside and returns to work. She unties Caleb from the stretcher and carefully peels off his filthy clothes and blood-soaked bandages. He's covered in cuts and bruises and besides the nasty side wound, it looks like his ribs also took a brutal beating. She uses the cave's emergency water supply, almost an entire bottle of hydrogen peroxide, and every iodine swab she has to clean him. After scrubbing out the wound, she inspects it thoroughly. It looks terrible, but not as deep as she first thought. The rest of his cuts and bruises aren't life-threatening and should heal just fine.

Unpacking the rest of the shelter's first-aid supplies, she opens a suture kit and bites a bottom lip, as her hands shake. The past day has physically, mentally, and emotionally drained her. Now, on top of that weariness, she needs to sew up the side of a man she never again expected to see, and do so, without much confidence in her medical abilities. Taking another deep breath, she steadies her hands, and dives in. As she snips off the remaining thread, she sits back, inspecting the stitches. They're not quite even, but they'll hold, allowing the wound to heal. Finishing, she covers the area with a sterile bandage and checks Caleb's ribs. They feel intact, but she's not sure. There could be fractures, so using an elastic bandage and struggling immensely, she wraps his torso, providing the area with some form of stabilization.

While still outside, she decides to trim his hair and beard, in order to better check his scalp and chin. Both are caked with blood and she wants to make sure nothing serious lurks beneath. Using the scissors in the emergency kit, which aren't designed for cutting hair, she attempts to keep the cuts even, but it's pointless. With all the dreadlocks and matted tangles removed, she pours the remaining water over the area, carefully checking for more injuries.

Combing through his remaining hair, she finds several small cuts, along with a few on his chin, but most have already stopped bleeding and don't require additional care. As for his clothes, they're too filthy and torn to put back on, so instead, she digs through the bag taken from the Splitters and finds an old long-sleeved t-shirt and a pair of sweat pants. Having him clothed again immediately makes her more comfortable.

As it gets later, she stands at Caleb's head, bends over, and lifts from under his armpits. Part lifting and part dragging, she moves him closer to the fallen tree. She has to get him over it and then under a second to get to the cave's entrance. At the first log, she props him up and places his arms over it. From behind, she pins him against the tree while trying to get one of his legs up next. Every time she tries, his body slips. Her method isn't working and after several attempts, she gives up and sits down by his side. They're so close to safety, yet the last few feet seem impossible.

Completely exhausted and utterly frustrated, she sits contemplating a solution and decides on trying the rope. She loops it under his arms and around his chest and back. This time, she climbs the log, keeping tension on the rope. Once over, she wraps it once around the next fallen tree and returns to his body. Getting Caleb's arms over the log, she pulls out the slack. The rope keeps him in place while she continues lifting from behind. When she gets his waist to the top, she climbs over.

While deciding on the safest way to proceed, she leaves his limp body lying over the log, head dangling towards the ground. When she starts to pull him the rest of the way, Caleb begins slipping. Even though she's trying hard to be careful, she loses balance and his body collapses on her.

"Great," she murmurs out loud, wedged between two logs and pinned under his dead weight.

Trapped and ready to be done with the whole ordeal, she wiggles and pushes until able to get free. Unwrapping the rope from the log and using what strength she can muster, she drags him inside, grabs a water kit, and immediately returns outdoors. She just wants to collapse and sleep, but first, she needs to clean the mess left behind and make sure they stay supplied. She gathers his old clothes, bandages, and hair trimmings, and then, walks away. Although, it's getting dark, where she's heading is close by. She works quickly and returns to the shelter, where she simply shuts the door and falls, face first, into a deep slumber.

THREE

With fluttering eyes, she gradually comes to her senses. She slept soundly, maybe too much so. Usually, when away from home, the slightest sounds wake her, but last night she didn't move from the position she started in. Normally up before sunlight, she can tell it's no longer dark as a tiny crack near the doorframe allows a sliver of light to penetrate the interior, illuminating the dust particles floating by. It's just enough to signal the arrival of day. Rolling over onto her side, all the soreness from yesterday's exploits take hold as she detects another's breathing. She sits listening, before sliding the panel open.

Even with it open, not much light filters in, so she opens each door without making much sound. As the cave brightens, she peers around the dwelling she keeps maintained with precision. All the shelves are organized, packed tightly, and kept with enough supplies to last them both. There's plenty of food and the water can be replenished, but contemplating today's challenge, leaves her with more uncertainty.

Moving over to Caleb, she's relieved knowing he made it through the night, but if he's to survive, items not among the cave's shelves, are needed. He's feverish, pale, and has lost a lot of blood. Worried about his inability to fight infection, she knows what's needed. Quickly she packs, grabs the crossbow and an empty water jug, and leaves the enclosure.

Once out, she scurries under the first obstacle and hides underneath the brush before climbing over the massive log. It's later in the morning and this task should've already been done. Carefully scanning the area, she circles around before getting to the first collector site she regularly uses and maintains. Several old growth redwoods, with branches extending all the way to the ground, are kept trimmed so they never touch the forest floor but hang twelve to sixteen inches above it.

Before sleeping last night, she wrapped the clear plastic collection bags around the ends of several branches. In the dark, she hadn't done the best job of keeping the tree's vegetation from touching the bags' insides, but, still, they were successful. The ends of each bag, furthest from the ground, contain fasteners that secure them in place.

Opposite the fasteners, small stones weigh down the bags, and as condensation collects on the plastic, it flows to the bottom. She lifts the small pools of water that have collected and empties them through a drainage valve.

Normally, by this time of day, she would've already gathered the water and removed the evidence of the collectors' existence. Although her system works best during daylight, she rarely accepts the risk of someone seeing them. Today, the kits have been out long after sunrise, which means they're a little fuller than normal. Going from one to the next, she fills an entire jug. With the water stored, she repacks the collectors and moves on grateful they weren't discovered.

A growling stomach reminds her to eat and that Caleb's also going to need nourishment. Accompanying her thoughts of food, a rustling along the forest floor draws her attention. Remaining still, she determines its direction, sees a small bird hopping among the ferns, and quietly loads a slingshot. As the small creature carelessly hops closer, she releases the shot with deadly accuracy, and it falls to the ground.

"Thank you, little one," she says softly, bending to pick it up before leaving in the opposite direction.

With the patrol finished, she feels comfortable enough to head back. Along the way, she cleans the small bird and rubs it with a pinch of salt. Back in the shelter, the tiny morsel gets further prepped for cooking. She tosses all the skin and bones into a pot of water, along with dehydrated mushrooms and a single packet of seasoning. While waiting for it to cook, she eats another ration while preparing a list. When the soup finishes, she adds a few crushed aspirins to the broth before letting it cool. Then, painstakingly careful, with Caleb propped up by blankets, she dribbles it down his throat.

She knows, the only way to save his life means leaving him and getting to her main shelter, which contains everything she needs. There's no way to get him there and she never wants to drag that stretcher again. Besides the time it takes, the distance's too great and requires cautious travel up, and over, several steep ridges. She's uncertain about how long it'll take and the ridiculousness of what she'll face with this next feat is worrisome.

It's nearly two days of travel one way and she's not sure whether Caleb will hold up that long in her absence, but staying at his side would only mean watching him slowly slip away. She's going to have to get there faster, and at least it's a route she's traveled since childhood. Her worry is for her body and she prays it can take another toiling expedition. She packs a small, light bag and debates carrying the bow. She never leaves the weapon behind, but knowing it's faster traveling without it, she makes a decision. Instead, she grabs the recently acquired hunting knife and takes a good climbing rope from the shelter's supplies.

She re-checks the cave, and even though it's improbable he'll stir, she sets things up in case Caleb wakes. Tying a piece of twine to the nearest door handle, she loops the other end around his hand. In the other, she places an emergency LED light and a full canteen within his reach. If Caleb wakes in the dark, he'll be able to open the door, and at least be able to see around the cave's interior. She dribbles another few sips of water down his throat, examines his bandages, and leaves. Even though time is against her, she still pauses, carefully listening, before leaving the protection of the fallen trees. She decides on the most direct route and takes off at a trot. Her body revolts at the movement, but ignoring it, she hopes it'll get better as her muscles warm.

At her current pace, she attempts calculating how long it'll take, as jogging should considerably reduce the travel time. Running is something she usually finds too noisy, but thankfully, the recent rain has softened the duff along the forest floor, so it's not as crunchy. The uphills are slow, causing her pace to reduce to a fast walk, but she makes it over the first ridge rather quickly, feeling confident. The downhill, although faster, is where she's forced to concentrate. It's easy to lose footing and fall, and if she has an accident, it could kill them both.

Traversing the mountainside, she pushes forward focusing on controlling her breathing while looking ahead. When she thinks about the distance still left, it's depressing, and affects her confidence. Instead, she creates small goals, setting her sites on upcoming trees or rocks. When she reaches the designated object, she scans ahead for the next, trying to ignore the pain and fatigue increasing with each step.

Three hours in, she really starts to struggle. Tired, thirsty, and hungry, she slows to a walk, drinks slowly and deeply, and feels the heat generated by her thigh muscles. Eating, she stops, and drops the pack and rope. Having the weight off provides some relief, while she contemplates what's next. The more direct route, which allows for a quicker arrival, has its risks. The slopes are steeper and harder to navigate, and in her current location, impossible to hike down. Forced to repel instead, she fashions a harness, finds an anchor tree, and starts the descent.

At the bottom of the nearly vertical slope, and grateful to be there, she releases from the rope. The only way back up will be using the same line, which requires leaving it for her return. It's a necessary risk, and hopefully no one will come by in her absence and discover it. She allows herself to walk for thirty minutes before picking up the pace again. Her muscles scream, but she forces them to work. Hours later, and knowing the destination is getting closer, she slows. She never likes leaving her home, but staying put isn't safe.

Even though she's been pushing a relentless pace all day, and is ready to rest, safety is still, and always, a priority. Instead of using the main entrance, she uses one of the hidden tunnel accesses and finally gets to where she calls home. Inside the bunker, she drops everything, starts heating both food and water, and strips out of her sweaty, smelly clothes. She stinks and needs to wash, but first priority is replenishing the calories she burned and the water she lost. With this accomplished, the next task begins with her flipping through reference materials and taking notes.

As soon as her research is complete, she settles into a hot bath. Heating plenty of extra water is a treat usually reserved only for her birthday, and then again at the new year, but knowing an important aspect of survival is keeping a healthy mental state, she decides that a good soak is what she needs. The bath is a tremendous relief to her sore muscles and more importantly, it boosts her morale, which at this point is a huge help. The past couple of days have been taxing, and thinking on what she's accomplished, she's amazed. She scrubs, washes her hair, and uses the last of the hot water to rinse.

Out of the tub, she swallows a few aspirins and goes straight to bed for some much-needed sleep. She can't stay in bed long, but any rest is wonderful. When the little wind-up alarm goes off, it feels like her eyes just shut. Slapping at it while rolling over, she lies still, cherishing a few more moments of comfort. Getting up, she isn't sure if her body will allow movement.

Her knees, ankles, and hips throb. The muscles in her legs are so sore and stiff that each step feels impossible. She can't even bend over to put on clean socks without pain. Instead, she eases down into a chair, and slowly lifts each foot. On top of that, her hands are still torn up and ache from dragging that damn stretcher. Besides all the muscle soreness, her stomach feels unsettled and queasy from lack of sleep, and a substantial headache has settled in. She's a mess, but the thought of him possibly dying, alone in the cave, is a strong incentive to force her forward.

Making some hot tea, she checks the notes and collects everything Caleb will need. She adds a few things for herself and a couple of other luxury items. With everything gathered, she sets about making a large breakfast. With a full stomach and another tea, she begins packing. Even with the movement from prepping, her body won't loosen up. It hurts, and the trip back is daunting. She barely made it here and now, she has to repeat the journey while experiencing greater pain, carrying a heavier backpack, and attempting it without enough sleep.

She shouldn't be thinking so negatively, but she can't help it. Sitting down for a moment, she wishes for help, but as always, is alone. Contemplating her predicament, she makes a choice. First, she rubs ointment into every sore muscle, then, she re-checks the medical references and goes back through the supplies. Finding what's needed, she unscrews the lid, and shakes out two pills. After hesitating for a moment, she washes them down with the last of her tea and reluctantly decides to put a few more in her pocket.

It's still dark, but she goes outside hours before the sun even comes up. She hates using any type of light in fear of being found, but without one, it's impossible to see. Turning the red light from her headlamp on, she walks at a brisk pace. Within thirty minutes her muscles began to loosen and by an hour into the trek, the pills fully kick in. Feeling great, and full of energy, she quickens her pace. As the sun comes up, she drinks half of her water and takes another dose. A surge of energy courses through her veins.

Before long, she's back at the rope and attacking the slope with fury, fascinated at the drug's effects. At the top, she coils the rope, replenishes her body with more food, water, and another round of meds, and then takes off, feeling unstoppable. As the day lengthens, the distance to the cave shortens. Nearing its area, she tries being cautious, but with the amphetamines still coursing through her veins, it's hard to slow down.

Back inside, she notices that Caleb still hasn't moved. He looks terrible—extremely pale, and hot to the touch. She fumbles through her bag and unpacks hastily as her heart pounds and her hands shake uncontrollably. She closes her eyes, taking several deep breathes and with each exhale, relaxes. When steadied enough to work, she opens her eyes, reviews her notes, and begins.

Afterward, she knows she should lie down and rest, but the drugs are making her jittery. Instead, she finds herself walking the area's perimeter. About halfway around, she gets sick and pukes what little food remains in her belly. With it emptied, her stomach continues lurching until there's nothing but dry heaves. By the time it stops, her sides ache, and the trembling begins. She really did a number on herself, and it takes every ounce of remaining strength to get back to the cave, where she literally crawls the last few yards, barely making it inside before collapsing.

FOUR

Waking full of anxiety and concern, she bolts up. The sudden movement intensifies a throbbing headache as she worries about someone discovering the vomit she left uncovered. With a disgustingly-dry mouth, she traces a swollen tongue over both her lips and teeth in an attempt to generate some saliva and return some moisture, but the only thing she accomplishes is discovering a horrid taste.

Grabbing a water bottle and gulping a huge amount only ignites the burning sensation at the back of her throat. Feeling utterly miserable, she realizes the punishing pace from the past few days has caught her, and she suffers for it. Sliding open the window panel, reveals that it's once again daylight. It wasn't dark yet when she crawled in yesterday, which means she slept for a solid twelve to fourteen hours. With that amount of rest, she should feel refreshed, but that's not at all what her body is telling her.

After taking another long drink, she eases over to Caleb. He doesn't feel as hot and some of the color has returned to his face — indicating the IV and meds she administered seem to be helping — but there are still signs of fever. After switching the empty drip bag out to start a second, she moves to cleaning his bandages and checking the stitches. Caleb's wound doesn't smell bad and the tissue shows indications of healing, so she re-bandages it and then gives him another dose of penicillin. A few rounds of antibiotics, over the next couple of days, should eliminate any infection and ensure his recovery. At least, that's her hope.

What look worse are his ribs. Her struggle with getting Caleb over the log and then into the cave might have caused more damage. Dropping him, and then trying to escape from under his weight, probably hadn't helped either. Using her fingers to palpate the area, she still doesn't detect any fractures, but knows that doesn't mean the bones aren't damaged. Since there isn't anything that can be done for them, she settles on re-wrapping the area and hoping for the best. He needs time to heal.

With Caleb all squared away, her focus turns inward. In sorry shape, she drinks more water, eats, and then exits the security of the shelter to cover the evidence of last night's purge, making sure no one found it and is now looking about for who left it. Still jittery and unable to keep track of all the aching body parts, she finds her every movement takes too much effort. Fatigued, sore, hurt, and a little sick, what she really needs is a long, restful recovery day. As she approaches the spot where she puked, terror takes over. Her vomit's gone—and it's the right place because she can tell where the ground's been disturbed.

Shifting into combat mode, she loads the crossbow and tucks behind a tree scanning for any movement. The only sounds come from a light breeze moving through the canopy. Gradually slipping from tree to tree while keeping cover, she checks the perimeter. Even though all seems normal, she watches and listens for hours. Eventually, she grows too miserable to stay out. At this point, even though she's troubled about the missing puke, it's rest she needs. She heads inside, sits intently for a bit longer, and then allows sleep to take hold.

Throughout the night, she wakes repeatedly, worried that the Splitters are nearby. Each time, she sips a little water then tries relaxing enough to fall back to sleep. Hours before sunrise, and finding sleep futile, she gets up. Her body still hurts everywhere, but at least her headache's gone, and she's starting to feel a little better. The missing vomit still isn't sitting well with her, and her fear of discovery continues to grow. Needing to confirm they're still safe, she waits for the approaching day then goes out to patrol.

The hunter and survivalist in her take over and she moves like a creature of the forest. Picking a place to hide that offers a view of where the puke was, she settles in. Just before the sun fully rises, she detects a movement among the foliage and it kicks in her instincts. Her ears strain and eyes focus. She zeros in on the sound, while maintaining peripheral vision, making sure no one sneaks up from a different direction. It's getting lighter and easier to see, but nothing's in sight. Maintaining her position and continuing to listen, her senses sharpen.

Detecting the sound of steps, when they stop, and then creep forward, she prepares for more Splitters, as they get closer. From the noise, it sounds like only one person. Seeing the two dead bodies a few days ago, shook her deeply and at some point she knew there'd be more. It was just a matter of time. With an arrow loaded, and prepared to stop any threat, she aims in the direction of the disturbance, and waits for a visual of the target.

Even though she's been in similar situations before, an uneasy feeling takes over. She calms herself by breathing deeply and tries to block past images clouding her mind. The noise intensifies, but to her relief, a small raccoon appears. She should have known it was an animal, or at least thought it a possibility. It makes complete sense, as it sniffs around the area looking for anything else to scavenge. She's gotten all worked-up and allowed fear to take hold. Disgusted by her lack of judgment, the disappointment in herself quickly fades to amusement as she watches the little coon.

It's young and not quite full-grown—a good sign, she believes. It's been a long time since she's seen a raccoon and the discovery of this little one means there must be others. She cherishes the sight, while weighing her options. As the raccoon pauses, she re-raises her weapon, taking aim. It's simply survival, but with it sitting in her crosshairs, she lowers the bow. Even though she's an expert hunter and killing for food whenever the chance arises is a necessity, today she can't do it. The fresh meat, although tempting, just doesn't feel right at the moment. She watches until it wanders off, and slowly, she returns to the cave.

Checking Caleb once again, and seeing that he's okay, she decides to take a full day of recovery. She curls up in a blanket and pulls out a book from one of the shelves. Reading's an enjoyable pastime that takes her mind off of troubling fears. She naps a little as the morning turns to afternoon, and with evening approaching, she's out once more checking the perimeter. She always patrols; it gives her peace of mind and allows her to gather the resources needed to stay alive. These mountains are full of food, if you know how—and where—to look.

Out foraging, a noticeable difference fills the air. The temperature drops, and at first, the moisture's barely detectable. She starts back to the cave as it turns to a steady rain and then to a heavy downpour. Hurrying inside, she grabs the water collector kits and a stack of buckets kept in the corner. Back outside, she works quickly to adjust the collectors to catch the rain falling between the logs blocking the shelter's entrance. She switches out the first bucket as soon as it fills and strips down. It's cold, but she needs a shower, and as she lathers up with haste, the cold rainwater rinse sends a deep chill through her.

Naked but wrapped in a towel, she steps back inside, dries off, and puts on clean clothes and rain gear. Her work continues until all the buckets are filled and returned inside. She also partially fills several collector bags and hangs them from the supports inside. The cave's a little crowded, but they're fully stocked. With the wet gear hung, she sits, listening to the rain's soothing sound that conjures memories of days when rainfall was normal and water was abundant.

For most of her life, water surrounded these parts. The mountains were full of creeks and streams. Every winter, they'd swell with the rains and run-off would flow down the steeper sections, accumulating in drainage arteries, creating seasonal waterfalls. Thinking back to those days, it feels as if it were a lifetime ago. Now, it's nothing but memories long gone. Saddened by the thoughts of days past, she returns to the present, reminded to be thankful for what's falling. At least she's fortunate enough to have water.

This is the second rain in a week, and she hopes it's helping bring back the world. "Maybe the planet's beginning to heal," she thinks. The days, which are growing shorter, indicate that the winter months are near, and maybe with them, the rainy season shall also return. She offers a silent prayer, hoping these two miraculous rains are only a hint at what's to come. As she continues listening, her mind wanders to Caleb and the two dead Splitters. The images of their dead bodies linger with her as she outlines her next steps before turning in for the night.

The following morning, she starts with a mission. Her body, although definitely still sore, feels ready. She's still not completely recovered, but at least she feels good enough to get done what's needed. Getting up and briefly stretching, she starts by checking Caleb over, changing the IV bag, and administering another dose of penicillin. He seems better, but it's worrisome that he's yet to wake. Changing the bandage dressings, she systematically examines his body, observing the various stages of healing his bruises and cuts are in. Their colors and appearance provide a timeline of all he's suffered.

Tracing her fingers along their edges and shapes, she deciphers the clues of what abuses caused such horrific damage. An outline of a shoeprint in one, and possibly a fist impression in another, are visible. Wondering how long he suffered at the hands of the Splitter Nation, her head shakes in disgust as anger rages inside. Unfortunately, she's no stranger to Splitter brutality, and an onslaught of images surface. Fighting them back, she re-covers Caleb's torso and refocuses her energy on the day's agenda.

After a quick, simple breakfast, she prepares the needed supplies, makes sure all is left as intended, and heads out for the day. The outside air helps clear her mind and has a calming effect. Thoughts of the Splitter Nation always produce an unhealthy effect and lately they've filled her mind. The forest though, smells refreshing, and hiking among its scents is medicine for her soul. With each step, her body warms and her spirit lifts.

FIVE

Caleb's first thought is that he's blind, and trying to find his vision, he blinks several times, but everything remains black. Unable to make anything out in the darkness, it doesn't help not knowing where he's at and what's happened. Lifting a hand to his eyes, Caleb grows even more concerned when something tightens around it. Immediately believing he's been re-captured, something feels odd about the scenario, but he doesn't quite comprehend what's causing the sensation. After another attempt, he finds that his hand isn't restrained at all and it easily slips out from whatever had bound it. Moving the opposite hand, he feels something hard near it. Fingering the object, his finger happens to hit a button and the LED light clicks on. He can see!

Still confused, but relieved with finding his sight, his mood brightens. He moves attempting to sit-up, but stops abruptly with the intensity of pain. Breathing cautiously, as a mixture of faintness and nausea wash over him, Caleb tries to remain calm. Flashes of what put him in this condition explode across his mind, but the images fail to link together all the events. As his fuzzy memories grow clearer, he uses the small light to scan his surroundings, growing even more disoriented.

Hoping to figure out his location, he tries taking it all in. Buckets surround him, plastic bags with water hang from log supports, and the walls and ceiling are made of stone. Slowly, he moves the light's beam around in an effort to determine whether he's in an old mine shaft, or some type of bunker, but his limited range of motion makes it challenging. It isn't a very big space and from what he can detect, both the back and sides don't have any outlets.

At his feet, the structure's material changes, and it's the only section not made of stone. Its entire length is constructed of wood and the twine he discovered around his hand is attached to what appears to be a door handle. Caleb grabs the string, pulls cautiously, and the door opens a bit. As he pulls harder, it swings the rest of the way, allowing light to penetrate inside and the entire space to be seen. He notices, with surprise, the IV in his arm, the clothes he's wearing, and the bandages on his body. His beard's been trimmed, and scratching at his scalp, he's also surprised to learn that his hair has been cut. It all adds to the mystery and confirms how discombobulated he is to have not noticed before.

Everything leads him to the same conclusion. Someone brought him to this place, cleaned him and provided medical attention. An image of her walking in the woods flashes across his mind. It's only a fleeting image, but it's definitely his last memory. Bleeding in the woods all alone, Caleb knew he was dying and fought to stay conscious. As he felt it slipping away, he'd seen her approach, a picture of beauty, moving among the forest like one of its creatures, appearing suddenly at the hour of his greatest need. Now, he's unsure whether the vision was real or if his subconscious conjured a comforting image to ease him through what seemed a certain death.

Thinking about it, Caleb knows she's always been in the back of his mind, even if he never admitted it. Looking around, he wonders if she could have done all this. He slowly scans the various items stocked on the shelves, then seeing the canteen lying near him, reaches for it. Caleb attempts to lift his head further, but an intense pain shoots through his ribs. After it subsides, he tries again and manages to drink some of the water. His stomach rumbles in response and seeing food stored among the shelves, moving to it becomes his focus.

Caleb takes another careful drink and tries to self-assess. His head feels dizzy, his body weak and broken, and even his eyes ache. He tries swiveling around to see the entire shelf behind him, but realizes everything can't be seen while lying on his back. Straining with exertion, he painfully tries a seated position, but it takes too much effort and his body refuses to respond. After several minutes of recovery, he tries another tactic. Caleb rolls over onto his stomach and slowly gets to his hands and knees. In this position, he crawls slowly to the back wall, and using it for support, raises his torso until he's balancing on both knees.

The amount of effort it takes affects him immediately. His forehead is drenched with sweat, and his breathing is erratic, causing more pain. Caleb knows he's in bad shape, but he's grateful to be alive and in what looks like a safe place. He starts inspecting the shelf along the side nearest him, and slowly, staying on his knees, starts searching the longer back shelves. Without the energy to thoroughly search and take everything down, he simply goes for the obvious food. Because the IV is still in his arm, Caleb can stretch only so far before it tugs tight. The bag still has fluid left, so he decides to stop and not risk pulling it out—since, he's found sustenance.

Slowly, Caleb returns to where he started, and eases back down to all fours. From there, he manages a seated position leaning back against the wall. Trying to control his breathing, to lessen the pain, he sips from the canteen while wiping his forehead dry. He struggles with opening the container he removed, as his fine motor skills refuse to cooperate, but after several attempts, the lid comes loose and he inspects the package's contents. It contains a few days' worth of food, and without hesitation, he tears open a pouch, and attempts using the flameless heater accompanying the meal. Managing to get some water into it, he fumbles reclosing and setting down the package. Once it's situated, Caleb forces himself to wait while the water activates the heater and warms the food.

After what seems forever, the food is ready and assumedly safe enough to eat. Realizing he didn't retrieve any utensils, and deciding he's not moving to get any, Caleb sticks in a couple of fingers before cramming them in his mouth. Either the food was too old, or his preparations poor, because the first bite isn't too great—and, it's the same with the second. After adding mouthfuls of water to soften the meal and make it more palatable, he manages to get it down. He's extremely hungry and has no idea how long he's gone without eating. There're two empty IV bags nearby and Caleb assumes that the one still attached is probably the third, but his assumption still doesn't help establish a timeline.

He finishes the meal, drinks more water, and opens another package taken from the shelves, in hopes that it contains something for pain. The throbbing emanating from his ribs is barely tolerable, but it's the sharp stabs induced with any movement that are crippling. Obviously, there are medical supplies here, which make Caleb think he's got a good chance of finding some form of relief. As he searches through the container, the only thing he finds is an old bottle of aspirin. He hoped for something stronger, but settling on it, he swallows a few, and carefully returns to a lying position.

The little bit of movement has been exhausting and he's incredibly weak. The food and water should help him regain some of his strength, but the pain won't go away. Tired, he tries ignoring it, and by staying still and controlling his breathing, it's almost manageable. After a while, he begins to drift back to sleep, and deciding it's for the best, he shuts his eyes and welcomes the break.

When Caleb wakes, it's still light outside, and finding the door left open, he knows he should have been more careful and closed it. He looks up, notices the empty IV bag, and decides to remove it. With minimal movement, he pulls it from his arm and tosses it aside. Still curious about the shelter, its location, and exactly how he got here, he painfully returns to hands and knees, cursing with each shift of his body weight.

On all fours, he pauses, while recovering from another bout of pain, and contemplates lying back down, but curiosity takes over. Crawling out the door, only to find a giant log, he discovers there's enough space to go under it, so he does. On the other side, another log blocks the path, so, placing his hands on it, he pulls himself up. Caleb's wobbly and dizzy from the effort and the pain nearly knocks him over. Looking around, he learns that the shelter is deep in the woods and that the two giant logs, along with a gnarl of broken branches, hides it.

Unable to imagine how he got here in the first place, especially in his current condition, Caleb finds he can't get his body over the last log, let alone figure how she might have managed, if—it was even her. Caleb has questions, but no answers, and the only thing he knows is that whoever helped is still gone, and it's starting to get dark. Taking another controlled breath of fresh air, he decides to return to the safety of the shelter. First, though, there's another need to address, and leaning on the log, he relieves himself.

Gradually, and with excruciating pain, Caleb makes it back inside. Since the IV no longer restricts him, and since he's partially up, he decides to check the rest of the cave's supplies. He moves about, taking his time to look through various containers. He's amazed at the organization of all the supplies and finds it's stocked well enough for numerous weeks without having to worry about finding food or water. Actually, there's more water around than he's had in a long time and it eases his mind. Fatigue sets in before he finishes the inspection and his pain continues to intensify. Caleb stops what he's doing, manages to shut the door this time, and tries to find a comfortable position.

He knows his path to complete recovery will be a long ordeal, but at least there's security in his surroundings. Each movement serves as a painful reminder of his condition and reinforces his notion of needing to rest. Even the ache behind his eyes increases, until the point, he has to keep them shut. The real trouble, though, is with his ribs. Every movement, no matter how subtle, hurts. With the amount of suffering they cause, Caleb knows they're broken. He gently settles flat on his back, realizing it's the position he'll be spending a lot of time in.

Lying down, he breathes through another painful sensation, finding the pain brings escape from his thoughts and the memories that continue to take shape in his mind. Visions from the recent events become clearer and keep flashing across his brain. Their hands brought this suffering upon him, and he can't shake the horrible images. Eventually, his body will heal, but psychologically, he's not so sure. Never again will he be the same, and he'll never be able to undo, what he was forced to do. With this realization, tears roll down the sides of his face.

He squeezes his eyes tighter as an overwhelming sense of sadness, frustration, and anger settles in. He's completely and utterly miserable, both inside and out. A sob rocks his body, sending waves of intolerable pain through his torso. The physicality of it snaps his attention back to his body and away from the horrible images. Clenching the blanket, he lies perfectly still, wanting only to sleep and forget.

SIX

Returning to the clearing before mid-day, she finds suitable cover to observe from. Everything looks the same as she left it, there are no indications of anyone else's presence, and most of the signs left by the struggle that took place here days before were erased in yesterday's downpour. Finding the area secure, she continues to where she sent the two Splitters over the edge. A larger section of the cliff has collapsed, and the only safe way around it, is through the trees. Continuing to search the area, she collects a couple wild mushrooms while creeping along the tree line, until an overwhelming stench nearly knocks her over. It's terrible, and she knows what it is before seeing the horrible evidence. The smell of death and decay lingers heavily in the air. She's upset at her negligence and partly to blame for leaving the body when she first discovered it.

Nearing the site, the stench becomes overbearing. The body—what's left of it—has been scattered about and the buzz of insects assaults her ears, as she tries to stomach the site and smell. From the look of things, an animal tore the body open and ate a large portion of it. The entire rib cage sits empty and a few limbs have been ripped off. The whole thing is terrible and she feels an obligation to correct it. If something had been done, when she first found it, then this wouldn't have happened, and the poor man's remains wouldn't have been desecrated further.

She doesn't have the right tools for a proper burial, or the time to perform one, and it's too risky to leave evidence of a fresh gravesite. It'd draw the attention of any more potential intruders. Thinking about options, she says a prayer while spreading out a small blanket on the ground near the cliff's edge. Then, picking up what remains of a leg, she sets it on the cloth. Each time she bends over to collect a piece of him, her stomach churns and bile rises in the back of her throat. Using the remnants of his bloody clothes, she gathers what remains and adds the parts to the pile.

She gathers everything but his torso and head, which is, by far, the largest and heaviest piece. Unable to pick it up, and carry it at arm's length like the others, her only solution is dragging the partial carcass by the one attached arm. With most everything collected, she adds several stones, ties the edges of the blanket around the mass, and silently wishes him peace. Then using a long, sturdy branch, she manages to push the remains over the edge and into the ocean below.

As it tumbles over, she falls to her knees and vomits. It's too hideous and wrong. This poor man suffered, and his remains were scattered like those of any slaughtered animal. She sits for a moment, trying to think of what else to say or do. Never being very religious, she finds it's still appropriate to offer some type of condolences. Finding another branch, she breaks it into two pieces and rips the last tattered piece of his clothing into strips. Using these materials to construct a cross, she offers a small prayer, and then, it too gets tossed over. It's a rather dismal sea burial and after another moment of silence, she makes a last check of the area and covers any signs of her presence.

She continues traveling in the direction the Splitters came from, drawn to find out what they're up to—and, especially, how many more may be around. Coming upon another clearing, she cautiously skirts its edges before freezing behind a fallen tree. With the detection of movement in the nearby brush, she stays hidden while patiently waiting. A small group of quail is moving about, and occasionally, she catches a glimpse of one before they disappear again.

When a few of them jump up to perch on an old fence timber, she loads her slingshot with a homemade version of birdshot, and creeps forward. In unison, the quail turn their heads and she fires just as they take flight. The first quail falls before it even makes it into the air. Two others, thrashing about on the ground, were knocked out of the air only inches above the fence. Getting to them quickly, she instantly snaps their necks. With the dead birds in hand, she whispers a heartfelt apology for causing any suffering and offers her gratitude for their sacrifice.

Returning to the safety and cover of the woods, she cleans the birds, and even though hungry and looking forward to fire-roasted quail, she decides it's safer to head back to the cave. It'd take too much time to find enough dry materials to build a fire and its smoke would be a beacon leading straight to her. Instead, the quail get tossed into her game pouch, and even though her hope was to explore more, she wants to return before dark and put this gruesome affair of cleaning up the man's remains behind her.

As the sun begins to set, she draws nearer the shelter and does a shortened perimeter check. She approaches the entrance at last light, and without making any sound, opens the door, enters, and immediately detects change as her foot bumps into something. She crouches low drawing a knife, and listens intently. Hearing breathing, her heart races, even though it has to be Caleb's—but still, she's careful. Slowly using a hand to feel about the ground, she tries to figure out what's there. Just as her hand touches a box, a light hits her eyes. She lurches to one side, crashing into more items scattered about. With knife raised, she prepares to defend or attack.

"Sadie?"

Her heart races, and for the second time this week, shock comes with hearing her name. Frozen in surprise, she slowly lowers the weapon. Once again, Sadie can't believe, that something so simple as her spoken name can affect her so deeply. As the light shifts towards the ceiling, allowing her to see, she's overwhelmed with emotion—first, it's relief, then joy, and then an uncomfortable awkwardness. Nervously, and a bit hesitant, she makes her way over to Caleb's side.

Sadie goes straight into first-aid mode and begins by checking him over, trying hard not to make eye contact. All this time, she's been alone and now that he's awake, she's shy and a little embarrassed. His staring doesn't help, but Caleb can't believe what he's seeing. Sadie's alive, she's the one who saved him, and now, she's within reach and examining him. He wants to touch her, but remains still. He's afraid she'll disappear and he worries that it's still his mind playing tricks on him. The spell breaks when she checks his ribs.

"Ooowww!" he forcefully exhales through a tightened jaw with both fists clenched.

"Sorry, I think you've got a few broken ones…" she trails off, unaccustomed to speaking to another and affected by the absurdity of it being Caleb. She swallows, then, continues, "I'm not sure how many. You're gonna have to let me know as I check 'em. Okay…Ca-leb?"

She feels odd saying his name and stuttered slightly pronouncing it. Mentally, she chastises her foolishness. "What the hell is wrong with me?" she thinks. "I gotta get it together." Sadie takes a breath, regains her composure, and looks Caleb in the eyes.

He's a shadow of the man she remembers, but he's alive. Sadie starts working her way down his ribs on the good side first, slowly examining each one and watching his reactions. As she moves to the other side, Caleb grows apprehensive. She knows it's going to hurt and tries to be delicate. Each time she presses into a broken rib, Caleb inhales sharply and grimaces. She stops, letting him recover.

"Only a couple more...then we're done. Ready?"

"Yeah, go ahead," he responds through gritted teeth.

"Well, at least now we know what we're dealin' with. Three... maybe four, are broken, and the others...badly bruised." She drops her head slightly. "Caleb, I'm sorry."

He's flabbergasted. "What are ya talkin' 'bout?"

Still looking at his torso she continues, "I caused more damage to your ribs when I brought you here. I tried to be careful, but..."

He cuts her off, "Sadie...if it weren't for you, I'd be dead. How'd you even find me?"

With his question, she looks up, "Find you? I thought you might've been lookin' for me."

Caleb, confused, looks at her long and hard, but the throbbing in his ribs isn't helping him think clearly. Sadie notices his discomfort and decides they can talk later. She moves back to the other side of the cave and busies herself with putting away items. Caleb, unsure of the meaning in her sudden change of actions, watches her clean up the mess he left and wonders what she's thinking. Following her every move, and still feeling fuzzy, he's unable to comprehend the situation. He wants to get up, but it's too uncomfortable, and the pain is intolerable. He closes his eyes, attempting to take his mind off the throbbing, but it's impossible. Caleb hears Sadie moving about, and when she returns to his side, he opens his eyes.

"Here, drink this," she says, bringing a metal mug toward his lips.

He lifts his head just enough to get some of its contents into his mouth. It's warm, and soothing, and swallowing a few mouthfuls, he wants more, but it's difficult to drink in his current position. Sadie realizes this and helps prop him up. The movement causes shock waves of pain, which ease only slightly when he finally settles. With him in a better position, she hands him the mug and returns to the other side of the cave. Caleb, happy to go back to watching Sadie, sips on the hot tea.

Returning to his side, she starts explaining: "So far...I've given you three bags of saline, a few doses of penicillin, and a couple aspirin. You were out…'bout five days…and ran a fever that worried me. I stitched the cut in your side, but…I'm not sure what we can do for your ribs. I'm hopin' this will ease the pain and let you sleep." She holds up several little glass containers as he strains to see what they could be.

"What is it?" he asks.

She turns the vials around in her hands and answers, "It's morphine. It should ease the pain. I got a little bit, and…planned on usin' it with the drip, but…since you pulled out the IV…we'll have to go to plan B." She lifts a sterile, medically-wrapped item.

When he looks more closely, the hypodermic needle is easier to identify.

Sadie keeps talking, "I'd prefer the drip, but…this'll work." She flips through her notes, completely ignoring him. "There should be enough to help you…through the worst of it…for several days." Finally looking back up at him, she asks, "You allergic to morphine?"

It takes him a while to answer, "I…I don't think so. But…I'm not sure."

Sadie returns to reading her information. When she finishes, she closes the notebook, and stands up, "Okay, let's try a small dose and see. Any bad reaction will show up pretty quickly…so…we can counteract it with this." She holds up another small glass vial.

Caleb has difficulty taking in all the information. He simply nods his head and lets her continue. Sadie ties his arm with rubber tubing, picking the left this time, since the other she used for the IV. Tapping her fingers along the inside of his elbow, she feels for a good vein, "Make a fist." He does so. "Open and close it."

She prepares the injection, making sure to get all the air out of the needle. Then, she cleans the area with an iodine swab before inserting the needle, weary of going completely through the vein. Pushing the depressor, they watch as the liquid slowly disappears. When she finishes, Sadie re-packs the items leaving them closer to his side. His body relaxes and his eyes grow heavy.

"Just rest," she says, watching him.

Caleb slips into sleep while she monitors him. When all looks okay, she tucks him in, and then goes back to her side of the cave. The thought of it being "her side" elicits a soft chuckle as she lies down to rest. Another long day is ending, and Sadie falls asleep listening to Caleb's breathing, finding comfort in its sound.

SEVEN

Sadie's running through the woods, but her body and legs won't respond. The harder she tries to speed up, the slower she becomes, and the worse it gets. Sensing them getting closer, she knows they're going to catch her. Suddenly, Sadie realizes she's carrying a small child in her arms. Glancing down at the infant, her fear deepens. It's not just her they'll get. Hugging the infant closer, she wills her feet forward. When she looks down again a new terror grips her.

In her arms, a rotten, decaying, human leg appears. The stench permeates the air and overwhelms her senses. The flesh starts peeling off and falling away in grotesque chunks. It's covered in convulsing and throbbing maggots, creating the illusion of movement across the muscles. Sadie drops the leg and frantically tries brushing them away. Her panic rises and the harder she brushes, the more maggots appear, until they bore into her flesh. She falls to the ground and rolls around in an effort to crush them, but nothing works. She can't get away from them, and it feels hopeless.

Sadie's eyes fly open. Breathing hard and drenched in sweat, she tears the covers off to examine herself. She can't resist the urge to check, even though she knows it was a nightmare. Starting at her face, she uses her hands to works down the rest of her body. As she reaffirms her safety, Sadie's breathing calms, and her heart rate slows. Nearly back to normal, she takes a drink, then another.

Staying in bed, trying to sooth her mind and relax, she attempts to fall back to sleep. Eventually, Sadie gives up the notion. Her mind is too restless, and the images from the nightmare, and from yesterday's mess, won't leave, but it's the overwhelming sense of hopelessness conjured by her dream that really bothers her. It hangs over her now and she can't escape its grasp, so quietly, Sadie leaves the cave.

Outside, the cold air fills her lungs as she sits in the dark, listening. It's too cold to stay still for long, and since it's still too dark to patrol, she heads back inside, grabs a portable shovel, and steps back out. Sadie moves as far away as possible between the two logs and starts digging. For the first hour, she digs in near darkness, using only the faint, red light, that emanates from a small headlamp to aide in her work. She piles dirt underneath the log closest to the cave, and whenever the shovel strikes a rock, the vibrations travel up her arm muscles. It's slow, but the work takes her mind off all the grisly details she's trying to forget.

As the sky begins to lighten, Sadie can see well enough to clean up her dig. She squares the hole and continues making it deeper. When its depth reaches her thigh, she stops. It should work well enough. She removes her gloves and checks her hands. Two blisters have torn open, and the others look terrible, but she prefers their pain to the visions of the nightmare and her haunting memories.

Sadie goes back inside, washes her face and hands, grabs her patrol pack, and heads out. She's been staying near the cave for longer than normal and wants to make sure all is still safe. Usually, she spends only a night or two in the area before moving, but Sadie knows Caleb's in no shape to travel and needs lots of recovery before it's safe for him to move. She just isn't sure how long they have until another group of Splitters appears. If they find the cave, her and Caleb are trapped. These thoughts worry her, but there aren't any other options, as he needs to stay put and heal.

Patrolling a little longer and traveling further, she pays close attention to every detail of her surroundings before turning back. When she returns, Caleb's awake and trying to get up. He rolls over and gets to his hands and knees as Sadie goes to his side, noticing his difficulties. He places his hands on the back wall and slowly makes his way to a kneeling position.

"Caleb, you need something?"

He looks at her and shyly answers, "I need to use the bathroom. Could you help me outside?"

Sadie finishes helping him up and then stops. "Wait a second," she takes a lid off of one of the smaller containers and removes its contents. She steps outside, but returns almost immediately. Back inside, she opens another container, grabs an item, and returns to his side, "Here, I'll wait outside."

Before Caleb can respond, she leaves again. He looks at the small container handed to him along with the roll of tissue. He can't believe it. Besides medical supplies, food, and lots of water, she has toilet paper! "God, she's amazing," he thinks, wondering how Sadie came to be so prepared. Her hideout is stocked well and looks to be out in the middle of nowhere. He checks the small bucket she handed him, finds a thin layer of dirt inside and discovers that it's sturdy enough to support his weight. When he finishes, he snaps the lid back on, and then, a little embarrassingly, calls out to Sadie.

She enters and without saying anything, grabs the bucket and takes it outside. A few moments later, she returns, sets the bucket back down, and busies herself. He looks at her, unsure of what to say. Sadie, sensing his uncertainty, stops what she's doing and turns to him. He's still standing, and thinking his upright position is a good opportunity to clean his bandages, she goes to him.

"We should change these dressings. Can you lift your arms a little?"

Caleb does so without saying a word, and Sadie carefully unwinds the wrap from around his torso. When she removes the bandage covering his stitches, she pauses inspecting the wound. He already feels awkward about her taking out his bucket of waste, and now she's close enough that he can feel her breath on his skin. Dependent on her, there's so much he wants to say, and ask, but he's not sure where to begin. Still amazed that Sadie's even there, he keeps thinking that he'll wake up only to realize it's one long, strange dream.

"Sadie...I...umm...what...I mean is...well..."

She stops what she's doing and looks directly into his eyes.

He continues to stutter, "I think...th-th-that...ahhh...well..." he can't wrap his mind around his thoughts, and nothing comes out right. He takes a deep breath, looks down, and finally, the words come. "I really don't know what I'm tryin' to say, and...I don't really understand how we ended up findin' each other, but...I'm glad to be here...with you. You've gotta...unique home...and I appreciate you sharin' it."

The smile spreads from her eyes to her lips and he detects a hint of amusement. "Caleb, this isn't my home, but I'm glad you like it. When you're better I'll take you there." She finishes rewrapping him and satisfied with the effort continues, "But for now...we need to get you set...so you can manage on your own."

Hearing her words, a sense of worry pangs him. He's almost afraid to ask, but does so anyways. "Wha d'yah mean...manage on my own? Are you leav-ing?" he tries not to sound too distraught, but the crack in his voice gives him away.

She didn't mean to hurt his feelings, or frighten him, but the mood between them shifts.

"Please…don't worry. I'm stayin' all day…and tonight…to make sure you're okay, but…I have to check a few things, and…make sure we're safe. I've been on my own for a long time, and…I'm…really…" Sadie finds herself at a loss for words. She tries gathering her thoughts, "It's nice to have company and…I've got tons of questions…I hope you can answer." Still detecting his apprehension, she tries returning to a lighter mood, "How 'bout I make some breakfast, and…we spend some time together."

He nods, and she helps him settle into a position in which he can eat. Even though Caleb doesn't complain about the pain, Sadie knows it's bad. She contemplates giving him more morphine but decides to wait until later. Instead, she hustles about preparing a meal. When she pulls out a small electric burner, he looks at her sideways. "What the heck?" he thinks with his curiosity peeked.

She sets it down and plugs in another item. Then, wrapping her hand around a small handle, she repeatedly pulls the retractable cord. Sadie knows Caleb is watching her every move. Generating electricity is simply one of her routines and she forgets how unusual the process must look, so she turns the device so he can get a better look.

"It's an electric hand generator. This one uses a pull-cord. I've got others that charge by turning a crank handle. Once charged, it'll produce twenty to forty minutes of continuous electricity, depending on what's plugged into it."

His jaw drops and when he shuts his mouth, it's only to reopen it to speak. "Sadie, that's the most amazin' thing I've ever seen. Where'd you get it?"

Sadie smiles, "My dad. This," she says, holding up the unit, "was originally invented to power laptops." She sets it back down to continue preparing their meal and after grabbing a few more things, finishes the explanation. "A non-profit company designed 'em for super durable laptops. Their goal was to spread education to kids livin' in third world countries by providing access to the Internet…even if they didn't have access to electricity. My dad saw a TV special 'bout the project and became…fascinated. It took him a while, but…eventually, he tracked someone down who sold him a few cases. When they arrived, he tinkered for months."

Sadie's enjoying herself, and finds it wonderful having someone to talk with. While getting the last of what she needs, she shares more about the devices.

"He thought they could be adapted for anything electrical and couldn't believe the technology existed and people didn't know. My dad...mastered its design, improved the capabilities, and created a few models. He planned to market them as the latest green technology...a world saver, but...he never got the chance."

She stirs the pot while the food cooks and Caleb watches as she goes about making breakfast. It starts with hot tea for two, followed by a hearty bowl of oatmeal that spreads both comfort and warmth through his body. She even serves it with a cup of milk! It's from a powdered mix, but it washes down the last of his meal nicely. Caleb leans back against the wall, feeling content for the first time in—well—he can't remember. What a turn of events! He never would have thought he'd be here with Sadie, but he is, and it makes him happy. While trying to move from the position he's in, a stabbing pain stops him. Sadie finishes what she's doing, comes over to his side, and helps him lie down while asking if he'd like more of the pain meds.

Caleb can only nod, with clenched teeth. Sadie gives him another round of morphine and watches as his face relaxes. For the first time in a long while, he doesn't worry about a thing, starts falling asleep, and then his body jerks slightly as he opens his eyes.

"Go ahead and sleep." Sadie encourages. "I'm goin' outside but... I'll stay close."

He looks at her and thinks about fighting to keep his eyes open.

"It's okay, Caleb. You need to rest. I'll be here when you wake, we can talk more then."

His response is more of a grunt than a clearly spoken confirmation, but she senses his acceptance and realizes they have lots to catch up on.

EIGHT

Caleb's first sensation upon waking is hearing a strange, rhythmic sound. The noise, coming from the pull-cord of the electric hand generator repeatedly being worked by Sadie, pulls him from his drug-aided slumber. As his level of consciousness returns, the aroma hanging in the air makes his mouth water. He struggles, trying to change positions, and once again, she's instantly helping. Sadie's strong, yet gentle, helping him through the worst of it. Then, without saying a word, she goes right back to what she was doing.

"That smells really good," Caleb's stomach grumbles, echoing his words.

He's hungry and thirsty. While waiting, he grabs the canteen that stays at his side. It's been refilled and taking a long drink, Caleb appreciates the life-saving liquid. God, he loves the refreshing water. Continuing to drink, he reflects on how things have changed over his lifetime. For most of his existence, water was taken for granted and wasted. People simply let it run down drains and wastefully used it for tasks such as hosing driveways and sidewalks clean. He was just as guilty, but now, Caleb can't fathom wasting such a valuable commodity.

"Careful, it's really hot," Sadie warns, leaning over and handing him a large bowl.

Caleb inhales deeply as he brings the dish towards his nose. He closes his eyes, letting the steam swirl around every feature of his face.

"It's quail and mushroom soup...there's plenty, so eat up," Sadie says, smiling and watching his reaction.

As his bowl nears empty, she's back at his side refilling it. He turns and their eyes meet briefly. When he finishes his second serving, she quietly takes the bowl and starts cleaning up. Caleb uses the time to look around, noticing Sadie's been busy. Not only did she return the items he'd left out, but she also rearranged the entire cave. Everything he might want, or require, is within reach. Her words from before come back to him. "So, you can manage on your own." He guesses that soon, he'll be finding out what that means. Before Caleb can finish his thoughts, she comes over and sits next to him.

"Caleb...I need to know about the Splitters, and...how you got here."

He sees the concern in her eyes, but there's more, it's something— else. It takes him a moment, but he finally realizes it's not just concern Sadie's feeling, but a tinge of fear, covered carefully by her gritty reso- lution. Caleb can see she's prepared for anything he might say and he too, is curious to find out about her, but from Sadie's look, he knows he'll have to wait before learning anything from her. She wants info from him, and that's what's going to happen. He takes a deep breath, trying to collect his thoughts, and decides that the only place to start is at the beginning.

"I was livin' in San Diego when the Tri-nami hit...but, luckily...I was away in Tahoe...a group of us met there...to stay at my friend's cabin, and...enjoy the slopes. The first couple of days, everything was...idyllic...but...then the news started arriving."

Images and sound bites from that day bombard his mind. The cataclysmic, global phenomenon astounded the scientific community, and the world, as it changed the face of the planet. Caleb's feelings of despair return as the memories take hold.

"We sat glued to the TV, watchin' in horror...and feelin' helpless. All of us...had friends, and family, livin' in areas where the Enders hit. Those first tidal waves...the images...." he pauses, remembering those behemoth monsters annihilating everything in their paths, "As things got worse, we grew desperate...each of us frantically tried con- tacting loved ones, only to be frustrated by the lack of responses, or busy signals. As the horror spread, our situation became serious. We talked about where to go, and realized...we were already better off than most. At least we were alive, and above the disaster line. Our plan was to stay...at least...until things got better, but...they never did."

He pauses, taking a drink. "We ran out of supplies pretty quickly, and...went into town...we were shocked at the changes. Mayhem fol- lowed the panic. Everything was overrun...people scramblin' to get whatever they could...the store shelves emptied, people were looting restaurants, hotels, resorts, and homes. Every building became a tar- get, unless guarded by their owners...or...people layin' claim to 'em."

He falls silent as an image dashes across his mind. It's of a woman running hysterically with her small child. She's in such a panic—she doesn't realize she's going in circles. Caleb can still clearly see her desperation as she tried finding food. He blinks, trying to get rid of the haunting image, before returning to where he left off.

"We managed to get enough to last a while, but…it was ugly, and our behavior…and actions were…" He pauses again, this time at a loss for words.

He never imagined he'd be caught in the mob mentality, but it happened, and he finds it shameful. Sadie hesitantly places a hand on his arm, understanding, and feeling his remorse.

Eventually, Caleb continues, "We holed-up in the cabin for the rest of the winter and watched the influx of refugees trickle in. As the snow melted…and spring returned…the number of survivors comin' into Tahoe…dramatically increased. My buddy, who owned the cabin, was a true outdoorsman. He owned several rifles and taught us to hunt. Food was scarce, so we foraged in the woods, and began growin' whatever we could."

"By the following winter, the city's water supply was nearly empty, and…things got worse. People fought to live…and killed to survive. At the arrival of snow, people melted it, and celebrated having water, but…quickly it became a curse as many froze to death. All the hotels, ski resorts, casinos, and vacation rentals were full…of refugees. There weren't enough rooms and…camps sprung up. The picturesque, mountain paradise of Tahoe was transformed into a dirty, rough shantytown. The massive food shortage forced people to strip the land of resources. Any and all animals were regarded as food… even birds became scarce. Gunshots could be heard frequently, and… it wasn't just animals being killed…there was complete…lawlessness."

Finding some comfort in sharing his tale, Caleb continues providing details for Sadie. "At first the local authorities tried to intervene, but they were outnumbered and out-resourced. It simply became… survival of the fittest. People formed packs, protecting one another and their supplies. Some groups retreated to boats…tryin' to avoid the worst of humanity, only to find that it was just as bad out on the lake. We lost two friends the following fall. They were murdered… over two birds and a handful of peanuts."

His discomfort resurfaces, but he doesn't stop, "No one felt safe… and we had to kept watch at the cabin. It was during this time, that I…I had to…" he swallows, closes his eyes, and finds the courage to continue. "A small band of men attacked us while I was on watch and…I saw them run towards the back of the cabin. I fired a warning shot… but they didn't even slow. They smashed a back window…climbed in before I could get to 'em…and by the time I arrived…. they…they had…" Caleb's eyes threaten to water as he struggles, controlling his emotions, "They stabbed my girl and…killed two of the other women."

Caleb grows quiet, and Sadie just waits. When he recovers enough to talk, he finishes. "By the end…we killed three of 'em, but the others got away. For the first time, I had blood on my hands, and I realized…I was changed…forever."

Caleb clears his throat and goes on, "My girlfriend died later that night…the next day, we buried the bodies. We took shifts, switchin' between diggin' and guarding each other. Our group was shattered, and…as another winter arrived, things grew even more dismal. We lost two more friends to a combination of sickness and starvation. Thousands died that winter…and bodies were stacked in what little snow covered the ground. When spring arrived there wasn't enough manpower…or strength to bury everyone. Bodies were burned en masse, or left to rot. As the seasons changed, more people arrived searchin' for water. The three of us left, decided…stayin' in the cabin was no longer safe…we packed what we could carry…and disappeared into the mountains."

Caleb shifts positions, trying to get more comfortable, and Sadie helps adjust his bedding while waiting for the rest of his story.

"Just as we moved out, the Splitter Nation arrived. At first, we thought they were gonna return order and some form of organization. They came in long caravans, with forces greater than we knew even existed. We watched from afar, trying to decide if we should return or not. They settled their troops along the shore and began policing the water. They set up barricades and…as people tried to get to it…they were turned away…or shot."

"Skirmishes broke out everywhere…people fought to get to the lake's edge. The Splitter solution was eliminating any and all resistance. As we traveled south around the lake…we witnessed the complete annihilation of survivors and the horrors the Nation brought. We kept moving. Not wanting to spend the upcoming winter trapped in the elements…we searched for someplace safe to hole-up, and… one day…stumbled upon a lone man huntin' in the woods."

Caleb shifts again, settles quickly, and keeps talking, "The tension was nerve-racking, as we stared each other down. We kept our rifles aimed, and…he did the same. Eventually…we exchanged words, and then…gradually, we lowered our weapons. For the next few days, we traveled together, gettin' to know one another."

Caleb, still not comfortable, tries ignoring it. "We gained his trust, and…eventually, he took us to a safe location…where he shared all the preparations he'd made. He'd spent the last twenty years of his life stockpiling food, water, and supplies, with a plan to make sure his family and friends survived…if anythin' ever happened. He didn't just want to survive, but…be in a position to help others. We met his family and the rest of the group at his compound. A majority of it was below ground…in bunkers. For the next few years, we lived as a part of their community and helped in any way we could."

Caleb remembers those first days fondly. It was such a relief, and at the time, life seemed to be getting better. He takes a sip from his canteen then returns to his tale. "Even though the compound was self-sufficient…the ongoing drought made it difficult on the water supply…and…the well produced less and less…then…San Andreas erupted."

Sadie shudders at the mention of the earthquakes. It brings up terrible images, and she tries pushing them out of her mind so she can focus on what Caleb's saying.

Caleb, not noticing, keeps talking, "Considering the strength… and intensity of the quakes…the compound held up fairly well. One bunker cracked and partially collapsed…but…the well went dry and the only water left, was what remained in storage. We estimated…if we were careful…six months of water…but…we needed to find a new supply. So…we sent search parties, travelin' in different directions. They'd carry enough supplies for one month and then return to report what they'd found."

"Four parties of three, set out. The three of us that left Tahoe were grouped together and sent there. We returned to see what changed and…if it was safe to return. But…the Nation had been busy. They militarized the entire area, and we were shocked at the lake's level. I never thought it possible, but…it was nearly gone. We tried findin' a place to get close enough to get some water, but the entire area was heavily guarded and under constant surveillance."

Sadie shifts, this time. She balls up her jacket and places it in the small of her back.

Caleb waits, before continuing. "We returned, just after a month, to share the news of our discoveries. Of the four groups that ventured out, only two returned. Besides us, the other team brought back a stranger...with news...that's when we learned how bad the earthquakes had been."

Images from the quakes once again flash across Sadie's mind and a deep sadness fills her.

This time Caleb notices and he stops his tale. "You okay?"

"Yeah, I'm just not used to sittin' this long," she lamely replies, standing up to stretch her legs. Sadie turns so he can't see her face. "I need to go to the bathroom anyways. You okay taking a short break?"

Caleb can sense Sadie's emotional change and isn't sure how to act or what to say. "Sure, it's not like I have anythin' else to do," he responds with a grin, trying to brighten her sudden mood shift. "Besides, I need to go, too."

Sadie steps outside and walks away. She stops fighting back the tears and lets them fall. Sometimes, her emotions well up so suddenly, and with such force, that it surprises even her. She starts on a short hike, realizing she's forgotten her crossbow, and cursing herself for being so careless and distracted, she returns to the cave. Inside, she grabs her bow and the bucket Caleb was using as a toilet, and heads back out. She returns just as quickly with the bucket and sets it back down near him.

"I dug a latrine," she states, a little too abruptly. "It's near the door on your side of the cave, further down between the logs. I piled the dirt nearby...to use as cover up...when you use it. It'll keep the smell down."

He stares at her, a little confused, and Sadie realizes she needs to back track.

"Sorry, that came out...kinda...gruff. When I'm here, it doesn't bother me to take out your bucket. I'm just lettin' you know, so...when I'm gone, you can take care of it."

He doesn't even try to hide his fear of being left alone, and Sadie realizes once again her mistake.

"Shit. Caleb...I'm sorry. I'm doing a terrible job of communicating, and the last thing I want to do, is make you worry. I've been really concerned…'bout those two Splitters I found with you. I'm used to stayin' on the move, and patrolling regularly, makin' sure no one sneaks up on me. Since I brought you here, I've neglected my normal patrols and…it's makin' me…a little…apprehensive."

She comes to his side and sits down. It's getting later and she's hungry again. Caleb still hasn't said anything and she feels bad about it. Wrapping her arms around her legs, she pulls them close, and rests her forehead on her knees. Sadie can't find the words, and he can tell she's struggling.

Leaning towards her, Caleb lightly places his hand on her arm, "It's okay Sadie."

This time, her eyes water, but with her head down, they're hidden from him. They sit together not saying anything until a rumble from his stomach brings her back.

Lifting her head, she asks, "How 'bout…I make us some dinner… then, you finish your story." He nods in agreement, as she moves away from his side. "Hope you don't mind leftovers," she says, pulling the generator's cord, grateful for the distraction.

NINE

After finishing the last of the quail soup, a sly smile crosses Sadie's lips. "You want dessert?" she asks, knowing her question peeks interest.

"Of course!" He tries to see what she's up to, but Sadie turns her body blocking what's being prepared.

When she comes back, Sadie hands him the bowl he'd eaten from earlier. Caleb looks into it and his mouth waters.

"Chocolate and peanut butter!" He tosses the first piece into his mouth fighting the urge to chew. Instead, he slowly lets it melt. Caleb moves his tongue around until every surface of his mouth is coated in the melted, gooey combination. "Yuuummmm...I can't believe... mmm...you have choc-ohhh-let."

He tosses another morsel into his mouth, while licking his fingers, making sure none is wasted, as it's too rare. The two of them take their time enjoying the treat and afterwards, Sadie makes them both a hot cup of tea as they settle to finish what they started earlier. They sit in silence, sipping from their cups, until Caleb is ready to continue his tale. Setting down his tea, he clears his throat and begins.

"When we returned from our search...I shared all we learned about Tahoe, the lake, and the Splitters. When our group finished... everyone anxiously turned to Gus, the newest arrival...the man who returned with the other search party, the one...who had actual news and...came to offer help. It was his firsthand account of the earth-quakes that everyone was anxious to hear."

She nods her head silently, understanding the feeling of being anxious. Sadie's been without news for so long, she finds herself hanging on Caleb's every word. The more she hears, the longer her list of questions grows, and Sadie finds herself fighting the urge to blurt them out and demand answers.

Unknowingly, Caleb continues, "Gus was a smoke jumper...he parachuted into forest fires to fight from positions the ground units couldn't reach...he...was stationed in Yosemite when the tsunamis came. His team was called to help with the rescue efforts. They flew in and out of the Monterey Bay area and then moved north to San Francisco. The coast guard was pullin' people out of the water as fast as they could, but there were just too many...all-available helicopter units were asked to assist. His team set a grueling pace...worked 'round the clock, only stoppin' long enough to refuel and drop off survivors."

"There was too much destruction...and too many people. The efforts couldn't keep up with the demand. Gus described it as tryin' to stop falling dominoes. One piece after another of the rescue strategies failed. Eventually, Gus and his crew were sent back to Yosemite...grounded by lack of fuel...since...every agency in the country demanded what was available."

Sadie recalls hearing the activity in the sky all those years ago. She couldn't always see the helicopters, but she heard them overhead as they headed over the mountains and along the coast. Caleb pauses again, sipping his tea, and she grows impatient.

"Gus told us that, after the rescue efforts failed, his crew stayed in the park. It was one of the few safe places left, and most of 'em didn't have homes to return to anyways. They continued helpin' those they could...and, even though it took a while, they managed to find more fuel. It was used sparingly...flying only to find resources to aid their survival. Whenever they headed out, they'd return with any survivors who wanted to join 'em. They set up a rescue camp...built a community of people willing to work together...grew food, hunted, and eked out a civilized colony."

"Their numbers grew and...as the drought lengthened, the park's streams, rivers, and lakes dried...then...the forest began to die. Eventually, they decided to use what fuel remained to find possible places to relocate. During earlier excursions, Gus noticed the coastal redwoods...up in the mountains were still thriving, so...they decided to start there. On the first flight back in the air, the earthquakes struck, and Gus...had a bird's eye view...of...the whole thing."

Caleb pauses to scratch his leg and pull up his blanket. Sadie can no longer resist. It's too long a pause and she blurts out a bunch of questions.

"Lake Tahoe's dry? How many people live in the colony? All of them need...relocating? Is Gus's crew comin' back here? He saw everything? From the air? What'd things look like?"

Sadie, breathing harder, can't believe what she's learning and needs to hear more. Caleb's eyes widen. Momentarily confused by the flurry of questions, he loses his train of thought.

"Aahhhhh…" is all he lamely replies while trying to digest all she's asked. "Yes, Tahoe's almost dry…more…like dead." He wants to answer all her inquires, but he's lost track and struggles. "Ummm… I'm not sure how many are in the colony. It was still growin' when I arrived. A lot of 'em want to stay…but…who knows what's happened since I left."

Caleb stops unable to recall what else was asked. Sadie, watching him struggle, realizes she's caused him to lose his place. Still trying to control her patience, she attempts to jog his memory with a single question.

"Exactly what did Gus see?"

"Oh, yeah…he saw everything…and when he spoke about it…we hung on his every word. Getting legitimate news is rare, and what he witnessed…silenced us all."

Caleb now gets a sense of how Gus must have felt when he'd told them. The look in Sadie's eyes says it all. She's hanging on his every word, just like they did then. It's amusing, in a way, and he finds a touch of enjoyment as he continues.

"Gus took it as a sign…he believed he was up in the air, at that moment, for a reason. He witnessed the quakes like no one else… waves of rolling land…then…it all…sank and…completely disap-peared." He pauses, letting his words settle.

Sadie squirms with anticipation. "Caleb! What already!" She says, getting to her feet. "What happened? Wha d'yah mean disappeared?!"

Caleb, surprised at the force in her voice, doesn't think it wise to delay any further.

"The earthquakes were worse than any of us thought. When San Andres went off…huge chasms opened as the plates shifted. What wasn't destroyed by the floods…sank, and disappeared…while other landmasses rose. Gus was in the air in time to see the first major quake. He watched the landscape change in front of his eyes as after-shocks continued to shift the terrain. When it finally ended, he landed to check on the colony and evaluate the damage. The next day…he went back up tryin' to see what options for relocation still existed."

With a pounding heart, Sadie begins to relive her earthquake experience as adrenaline courses through her veins. Remembering that horrible day, she recalls how violently the trees shook as the tops of the redwoods were snapped off. Trees kept falling, as the ground convulsed and vibrated, making it impossible for her to stay on her feet. Sadie's thoughts betray her, and she realizes Caleb's stopped talking and is starring at her.

She barely whispers, "I was here when the earthquakes struck."

Her face grows pale as the terror runs through her for the second time today. Caleb wants to ask, but thinks better of it. He gives her a few moments, and then decides to continue.

"The Tri-nami devastated the world and rearranged our coasts... and the Global Flood...made it worse, but...the earthquakes...finished the job. California's...gone."

Sadie's attention snaps back to Caleb. "Wha d'yah mean gone? We're here now."

"Sadie, with the tidal surges and floods, almost half the state vanished under the ocean...Southern Cal pretty much disappeared. What was left, the earthquakes tore apart or sank. The ground kept opening, and...with each quake, more and more disappeared. All that remains are a few segments of land and...what's thought to be a scattering of islands."

Sadie's face freezes with shock. In total disbelief, she's unable to picture what he's describing. As hard as she tries, it's just not comprehensible. Caleb understands her confusion. It put him in a similar state when he first heard and it took seeing it to fully grasp the changes. Now he's the messenger trying to explain the unimaginable. He tries painting a better picture.

"You're on an island," he blurts, "and...it's not that big."

The truths of his words slap Sadie across the face. She knew in her gut that things had drastically changed with the earthquakes, but she pushed it aside. His words tug at something deep, something she's neglected, and it leaves her reeling. How could she fail to realize? She should have explored further, instead of limiting herself to her patrols and perimeter checks.

Thoughts and questions fill her mind and she can't slow or stop them. Caleb notices her confusion and is at a loss. He was overwhelmed when he first heard the news, and at the time, he was living on the largest remaining portion of the state. He can't imagine how she's dealing with the realization that what once surrounded her, is gone, and that she's living isolated on a tiny speck of land. Suddenly, she's on her feet, exploding with more inquiries.

"Scattering of islands? How many? How big is this one? How far away is the next one? How much land is left? Wait a minute...how did you get here? And...what about those two Splitters? Where'd they come from? Are there more of them!?"

Caleb's taken aback as Sadie's body language sends a shiver down his spine. The look in her eyes also sends a clear message. Sadie's not someone to piss off, especially when she wants answers.

He regains his composure and voice, "I'm not sure how many islands there are. Gus wasn't able to explore in depth and...the marine layer out here makes it difficult. Your island...as far as I know...sits by itself. It was hard to locate...I was surprised we even found it in the first place. It's kinda small."

Caleb reaches for his tea wondering; "Why does it feel like I'm being persecuted?" The intensity in Sadie's eyes hasn't softened, and he doesn't risk making her wait any longer.

"Gus dropped us off here...in a small clearing, on top of a summit. I'm scoutin' for places to relocate the colony."

Sadie's eyes narrow, which causes him to worry.

"The reason we're considering this island is because...it exists. It's still green, seemed uninhabited, and might be easy to defend."

Sadie doesn't even blink. "Wha d'yah mean, easy to defend?" Her hands become a part of the conversation and when they rest on her hips, Caleb nearly flinches. "Who's us? Are there more people here?"

He responds quickly, "Flying here, we saw some of the land before the fog filled in. The shoreline has steep cliffs and...the terrain looked rugged and steep...making flights by helicopter the only way. There were only two of us, but...he..." His voice trails off thinking about his departed friend.

Sadie, realizing the body she found was indeed Caleb's partner, is a little embarrassed by her insensitivity, and her demand for information. Living so long without others has diminished her sense of social interaction, but images of finding Caleb remind her of how bad it must have been for him.

"Caleb, I think I found your partner. I...ummm..." she struggles finding a way to tell him. "I buried him at sea. It wasn't too great of a funeral, but...it was...somethin'. I made a small cross and said a few things. I'm sorry."

He's surprised and at a loss for words. He never expected to hear about his friend from Sadie. Everything about her is astounding and it takes a while to let it settle before he can say anything more.

"The two of us were long-time friends. It was his cabin in Tahoe."

Caleb stays quiet, and Sadie lets him take his time. He drinks the last of his tea before he's ready to share more.

"We thought the island was empty...and...from the small clearing...where we landed...we headed out to explore. Our plan was to scout for resources and determine if people could live here. We followed an old logging road and...near the west side of the island, it Ts. We stopped to rest, debating whether to turn north or south...but... before we settled on a direction, we were ambushed. I was struck from behind, and...the next thing I remember is wakin' up with a terrible headache...with my wrists and legs bound."

"Both of us were taken captive and...the Splitters...were ruthless. They thought we were from here and tried to beat information out of us. I think they came from the north side and assumed we were from the south. After a while, they tied us to the back of their ATV and... dragged us along. I wasn't able to learn much about 'em, but some of their conversations made me believe there were more of 'em around."

Her fear and worries intensify. There are more!

"How many days were you with 'em?" she asks.

Caleb really doesn't want to talk about it, but he doesn't think it's an option. "Three. They...tortured...him...makin' me watch and listen. They wanted answers we didn't have and used him to get to me. They...kept..." he can't finish and Sadie understands.

She saw the body and doesn't want to think about having to witness such cruelty. Caleb doesn't talk again for a long while and Sadie can see the anger, sadness, and guilt that torment his soul. She gets up, makes them another cup of tea, and returns to his side. They drink in silence, but halfway through their drinks, Caleb finds his voice.

"I decided...I'd make those two pay for what they did. As we traveled...I observed their every movement and waited for my opportunity. I worked the rope loose, and...when one of 'em was distracted... gettin' supplies off the quad, I attacked by grabbing his knife and slitting his throat. The other guy had wandered off to pee and when he returned...he knocked the knife out of my hand as we fought."

Caleb shifts his weight but doesn't stop, "It went back and forth... and...when I got to the knife, I was near exhaustion and not sure if I could continue. I lost a lot of blood and knew it had to end soon. He lunged towards me, and...luckily I was able to bury the blade into his chest. I was lightheaded, and my vision started to blur. I sat against a tree, tryin' to find the strength to get back to the quad, where I knew there were some supplies. It was at that point...I saw you."

He turns to look at her, "I thought you were a hallucination, a last dying image. When I woke up here...alone...I still wasn't sure if you were real, or if you had anything to do with my rescue. You'll have to tell me the rest."

He looks at her with such intensity that it scares Sadie and not sure how to respond, she feels drained.

"Caleb, it's late, and you should rest. Tomorrow, I need to leave early, but I'll return before dark. When I get back, we'll talk more."

She can tell he's disappointed and also in a lot of pain. He keeps trying to find a better position and Sadie moves to help him.

"I think more painkillers would help ya sleep. Yeah?"

He nods in agreement, and she prepares another injection. As she slips the needle out of his vein, he closes his eyes and visibly relaxes. Sadie pulls the covers up to his chin and whispers goodnight. Caleb smiles, then mumbles something incoherent, as she moves over to her side of the cave and curls up. Even though she's tired, it takes a long time for sleep to come.

TEN

Sadie can't stay on her feet as the ground ripples. With every attempted step, she loses balance and is forced to settle on crawling. She hears yelling and tries to reach him.

"Sadie, NO! Get to the barn!"

Trees and branches crash all around, creating a constant barrage of noise and obstacles. He's struggling too, and as a branch strikes his shoulder, he falls further behind, but she manages getting closer to hear his words.

"Keep going! I'm right behind you. Get to the barn! Get in the doorway!" he yells, worried about his wife's safety.

She turns as a disturbing crackling sound draws her attention. A huge redwood collapses and the impact vibrates through her entire body. The trees, still standing, sway with such force that it's surreal. The ground continues trembling and even on all fours, she struggles. Making it to the barn, Sadie clings to the reinforced, metal framework of the doorway, but she can't see him. There's too much debris, and more keeps falling. Overtaken with panic, the ground finally stills, but another shock wave hits just as she stands. An orchestra of cracks, pops, and smashing trees follows with such intensity that the atmosphere takes on a war-like quality.

As it falls, a tree smashes into the back corner of the barn. On the way down, it knocks down two more redwoods, partially crushing a steel beam supporting the structure. One tree falls to the side and another toward the barn's front. They're falling in every direction, and her only chance is to wait it out and hope he'll make it. Her arms and hands ache with the effort of hanging onto the metal supports for what seems an eternity. Each time the ground stills, another aftershock rocks the earth. When finally able to stand and look around, she barely recognizes the area.

"Markus! Markus!" she screams.

He never made it to the barn, and frantically searching, Sadie continues yelling his name while climbing among the debris. Then, suddenly, she falls, wailing uncontrollably. He's trapped under a fallen tree and only his legs are visible. The right one twitches, making her believe he's still alive. She tries with all her might to move the tree but it won't budge. Running to the barn and desperately searching for the log roller, panic overcomes her with each passing second. There's no one to help, and she's his only hope.

Spotting the handle of the implement, she grabs the simple tool designed to provide leverage for one person, but no matter how hard she tries, the log won't budge. It's too big, too long, and too heavy. She leans a shoulder into the wooden handle with such intensity it digs deep into her flesh. Ignoring the pain and gathering her might, Sadie makes another attempt. Both arms strain with the effort, and her legs jerk abruptly—waking her.

Sadie's heart races, "Ohh...Markus," she murmurs.

Her body shakes with sobs she can't control. It's a terrible dream that's haunted her for years, and still, it robs her of sleep. The image of her husband's twitching leg remains, as it always does. It lingers, with a mixture of guilt and shame still carried from leaving him behind, even though, Sadie knows that blaming herself, isn't healthy. Lying in the dark, she recalls the days, weeks, and months that followed, along with the depression she barely survived.

For hours, she stayed at his side, trying to move the tree. Eventually, Markus's leg stopped twitching and she didn't know what to do. Unable to get him out, an irrational fear took over, and Sadie worried animals would eat him if he was left alone. Tired and delirious, she headed to the barn, and returning with a chainsaw she'd never before used—due to a fear of them—Sadie checked the gas, adjusted the throttle, and pulled the cord.

It took several attempts, but finally, it started. Looking back on the memory, Sadie knows it was truly a poor decision. At that time, she was in a terrible state and shouldn't have attempted using such a dangerous tool. Making it even worse was her lack of experience. Beginners typically start with a manageable-sized chainsaw and small diameter logs, but Sadie's first attempt was with a massive redwood using a forty-one-inch bar.

She could barely hang onto the damn thing, but once it dug into the wood, she committed to the task. Sadie struggled, to say the least, and nearly got the entire cut done before the bar's tip caught on the ground and bucked so hard, she almost lost her grip. The chainsaw died and stuck in the log. For hours, she used wood wedges, pry bars, and even a hammer to try and free it.

Finally, it loosened, and once it was out, she could inspect the damage. Striking it on the ground ruined several teeth and loosened the chain, but after several adjustments, Sadie got it restarted. There was only a few inches left to cut, but it took a tremendous effort to finish, as the dull chain struggled. On the final push, she slipped and nearly cut her leg.

With a section cut from the tree, Sadie tried the roller again. Her strength vanished rapidly, but the fallen redwood moved just a bit. It was enough to give her hope and renew her determination. While manipulating the roller, she wedged rocks underneath the log, creating just enough space to slide a five-ton tractor jack below. With it in place, she worked the pump action handle until there was enough space to drag him out. Pulling Markus from under the log, Sadie saw what was left of her husband.

The memory causes the image to appear again and another wave of sorrow strikes Sadie. What remained of Markus was a whole new horror. He was smashed and lost all three-dimensional shape. His insides had squished out and she couldn't stomach the sight. She dry-heaved, repeatedly, with eyes clenched shut. When recovered enough to move, she retrieved a blanket to cover him, but struggled wrapping his body. Once finished, she fell to the ground and passed out.

Sadie faded in and out of sleep, and eventually, the smell finally got her off the ground. He needed to be buried and it took her an entire day to dig the grave. Afterward, Sadie mounded rocks over the site so animals couldn't dig him up. When she lifted the final stone and set it in place, emotions overpowered her, and Sadie slid to the ground, curled into a ball, and cried herself to sleep.

In the days that followed, Sadie could only weep and lie about. She locked herself into their home bunker and mourned. Unable to stomach the thought of food, she grew weaker by the day. Several weeks later, she could barely stand and was plagued by a constant headache. Everything around her conjured memories of their life together and she allowed grief and loneliness to take over.

She slipped in and out of consciousness, ready to succumb to death, when an old photo caught her attention. It was stuck between two shelves and was only visible from the angle she happened to be positioned in. For hours, she stared at it. The picture was of Sadie and her father, at the beach, on a day they spent kayaking and picnicking. It happened to be the day her father invited both Sadie and Markus to live with him, on the family property. He talked about building a small place for himself and giving them the house.

Markus wandered down the beach, leaving the two of them to talk in private. She knew, at some point, they'd move to the property, but at the time, they weren't ready. Sadie tried to explain it, and eventually her dad came to terms with her choice. He settled on the notion that, at some point, they'd be back living together on the family's secluded property. He realized, pushing too hard might keep them away altogether and it was the last thing he wanted.

It was her father's fear of losing Sadie that pulled at his heart. He lost his wife and sons in an accident and felt that he failed at keeping them safe. Now, all the family he had left was his daughter and he constantly feared for her safety. He worried about the future and the struggles it held, yet he couldn't find a way to reach Sadie about his concerns without sounding like a lunatic.

Even now, she hears his voice. "Sadie, promise me two things."

The look in his eyes held enough conviction. She knew the accident had torn him apart, and afterward, his behavior was worrisome. Fearing he was losing his senses and that his habits were becoming obsessive, she hoped time would heal him.

"First, promise…if anything goes wrong, you're lost or…not sure what to do, you'll come home."

Sadie looked carefully at her dad, knowing how important his request was. She always knew that, if trouble arose, she could count on him. At the time, she thought he just needed reassurance, so she gave it. Their conversation and how she responded, continues to replay in her mind.

"Dad, I know I can count on you…for anything I need." Her reply wasn't enough and his face grew grave.

"Sadie, I need to know you'll come home. I mean it. Promise me." He was fighting fear and Sadie hadn't fully understood it at the time, but agreed anyways.

With her promise, he relaxed slightly before continuing. "Second…" he'd taken her hand, "promise that, whatever may happen… to me, to…everything around us…you'll always find the strength to go on…and…live."

Sadie jerked her hand away with his alarming words, "Whatever happens to you! What are you saying?"

"Nothin's gonna to happen to me. I'm sorry. I ...didn't mean to scare you. I just want to know you'll always be strong. You'll choose to fight and never give up. You'll...survive."

He gazed so imploringly, as a whirlwind of thoughts, concerns, and questions raced through her mind. Sadie really didn't know how to respond or what to think. At the time, she thought she was losing him.

"Sadie, it's important to me. It'll give me peace of mind. I need this. Please...promise me."

Solemn and near tears, she could feel his heartache and Sadie knew she was all he had left. If her word eased his suffering, it was the least she could do, so she promised.

Looking at the picture, Sadie's promise, nearly forgotten, surfaced. Slowly, she crawled from her position and went to the photo, feeling dizzy and forced to stop several times to keep from fainting. With it in hand, she clutched it to her chest. She lost her mom, her brothers, her dad, and her husband. She was alone, and it hurt, but she'd given her word and wasn't going to fail her dad.

Finding the courage to continue, she crawled to get water. After a long drink, Sadie tried standing, but was unable. She was so feeble that even lifting her head took too much effort. Barely able to move, Sadie realized she needed food to regain her strength. Painfully slow, she made it to the food stores and grabbed a jar of peanut butter from the bottom shelf, since it was the easiest item to reach.

Sadie struggled with the lid, but once it was off, she jammed a finger into the jar and then into her mouth. Lying on a side, she resembled a child sucking her thumb. She didn't even have the strength to find a spoon. She forced herself to eat and as the peanut butter melted, she swallowed. Little-by-little, and in between mouthfuls of water, her only focus was on eating and drinking.

It took a while, but she managed to eat a quarter of the container. Several times, Sadie's stomach tried refusing and the urge to vomit was intense. When she just couldn't take any more, she slipped into sleep. Awaking hours later in the same position, she ate more, and still unable to stand, she continued forward on all fours. Over the next few days, her battle continued. She could consume only small amounts and at times, even chewing felt too arduous.

Days turned into weeks, and weeks into months. She stayed in the security of the shelter, but gradually returned to some form of normality. Every day was a struggle and sleeping filled most of her hours, but small tasks, such as brushing her hair and teeth, returned to her routine. Once Sadie regained her physical strength, she found ways to distract herself from the loneliness, but she refused to venture outside. Grief damaged her mental state and she feared leaving the bunker's security. After several more months, she knew, in order to survive, she had to get out. Determined one morning to overcome the fear, Sadie willed her feet forward and opened the door.

Outside and leaning against the door while repeating the mantra, "I can do this. I can do this," she took her first step.

As the distance from the shelter increased, so did her fear. Overwhelmed with feelings of insecurity, a squirrel running up a nearby tree, nearly frightening her to death. Sadie scrambled back inside and locked the door. With heart racing, she cursed repeatedly at such foolishness. She grabbed her crossbow and arrows, demanded self-discipline, and went back out. From that moment on, Sadie carried the bow, as it provides a sense of security and the courage to face what's left of the world.

ELEVEN

After lying in the darkness, emotionally spent from her recurring dream and the thoughts that followed, Sadie's unable to fall back to sleep. She gets up and moves about, trying not to disturb Caleb. Quietly, she prepares for the day ahead as he rolls over and painfully sits up.

"Sorry, to wake you...I couldn't sleep," she whispers, making tea.

"That's okay...can I have some, too?" Caleb asks.

He's actually been up for a long time. Sadie's nightmare woke him long before tearing her from slumber. He's been lying still listening as she fought to gain control of her sobbing. Her sorrow affects him deeply, digging up his own feelings of guilt. Long ago, he too, brought pain into Sadie's life and has never made things right. Time passed, he pushed it aside, and then the world flooded and survival took priority.

Being in her presence stirs up a lot of old feelings and regrets for Caleb. He's having enough difficulty grasping their current situation without any former baggage clouding his judgment. When he woke and heard Sadie crying, he had to fight the urge to crawl over and wrap his arms around her. He wanted desperately to comfort her but wasn't sure if she'd accept the gesture, or if it was even appropriate. Instead, he remained still pretending to sleep.

"Here," Sadie whispers, handing him a hot cup.

They sit in silence until Sadie begins rearranging and packing her bag.

"Caleb, I'm headin' out for the day. I'll be back by nightfall. After that, I'm gonna be gone, a lot...longer. I need to digest all you've told me...and...check a few things out."

He keeps his gaze on her, but says nothing. Sadie's barely there, her mind's elsewhere, and when she speaks, it's still faint. The nightmare's changed her demeanor and she's doing a poor job of hiding it.

"But first...I'll make us some breakfast."

Before he responds, she already starts. Sadie makes them a meal of re-hydrated eggs and cheese, accompanied by a glass of milk. They eat in complete silence and afterwards, she cleans up, grabs her stuff, and turns towards him.

"You okay?" she asks, pausing at the door.

"What can I say?" He thinks, nodding as she disappears through the door. Caleb leans his head against the back wall and shuts his eyes. He's such an idiot, and now that he's got a chance to make amends, he can't even figure where to begin. The best thing to ever happen to him was Sadie, and in his miserable state, Caleb has nothing but time to reminisce about his mistakes.

A lifetime ago they shared something most people never experience and the memories fill Caleb's mind. He remembers locking eyes with Sadie, and literally, everyone else disappearing. He was close to earning his college degree when a terrible car accident killed Sadie's mom and younger brothers. She went home for their funerals and Caleb stayed. It was too close to graduation to fall behind and Sadie thought that at least one of them should stay on track. Besides, she needed time to mourn, and felt compelled to stay with her dad after the tragedy.

Her dad blamed himself for the accident, which wasn't healthy, so Sadie took the rest of the semester off with plans of regrouping the following year. At first, Caleb talked daily with Sadie, then, only every other day. He missed her deeply and at night, when her scent drifted up from the sheets and pillows, it drove him nearly mad. Gradually they spoke less, Sadie's smell washed away, and his focus shifted to his own life—and needs.

He remembers talking to her about flying to visit over spring break, but at the last minute, he changed their plans. Several of his friends wanted to go camping as a last outing, before graduating and going their separate ways. He chose them, as Sadie started slipping more and more from his mind. Then, thinking she was surprising Caleb for his graduation ceremony, she showed up, and instead got her own surprise—he was with another girl.

Walking in on them, Sadie's eyes went blank, her voice vanished, and what remained of her strength shattered. In slow motion, she turned and nearly stumbled while leaving. He should have chased after her. Instead, he watched, feeling ashamed, guilty, and angry, all at the same time. Thinking back, he doesn't even recall the other girl's name, or why he was with her in the first place. What he does remember, is how, afterwards, he lamely offered to drive Sadie to the airport.

The drive was gut-wrenching and he wishes he had acted differently there, too, and not been so foolish—driving without saying a single word, while Sadie, also, sat silent. When they arrived, she got out and he didn't even look at her. He abandoned Sadie when she needed him the most, and then ended it all, by dumping her off alone at the airport.

Afterward, it was a whirlwind of women. He went from one to the next, losing track of himself along the way. Even though he never admitted it, even to himself, in some way he'd compared all of them to Sadie, and none ever measured up. He's not sure why he's stumbled back into her life, but feels fortunate for the opportunity, even if it's only to finally apologize.

His mind replays their time together and the happiness they shared, but now, everything's different, including Sadie. The more he reminisces, the more he begins to realize that some of his fondest memories were with Sadie at his side. Caleb begins thinking fate reunited them for some purpose. "Maybe..." he starts to ponder, but before he can finish his thought, the door opens as Sadie returns. He spent the entire day either napping or thinking of nothing but her. As she sets down her gear, he notices she brought back his rifle and ammunition, which surprises him.

"That's mine. How'd ya...know?" He lifts his head to look at her.

"I didn't. When I found you, I went through all the Splitters' supplies...carried what I could, and stashed the rest. I thought you'd feel better havin' it."

She sets the rifle down near Caleb and helps him sit up. The underlying notion of him being left alone hangs in the air between them and he takes another moment before responding.

"The Splitters took it from me when they...captured us. It was the only gun we had."

As Sadie unpacks, Caleb gathers his thoughts. She's a mystery to him and he wants to know more. She begins making dinner and he can't help but feel fortunate. He was beat-down, broken, and nearly dead when she found him. She came along, saved his life, and now, is taking care of him. He doesn't deserve it and wonders how she feels about it.

Sadie disappears outside and comes back cleaned and refreshed. Her hair is wet and she's wearing a change of clothes. The soup she prepared is ready, and as she leans over to hand him a bowl, his nostrils fill with her scent. She smells just like he remembers and his face flushes with a particularly fond memory. Sadie pretends not to notice and after they finish eating, Caleb speaks first.

"I'm a little lost here…" he starts, then trails off not sure which direction he intends to pursue. "How'd I get here? How far are we from where you found me? And…exactly how long, have you been here?" Now that he's started, he can't stop, and the questions keep pouring out. "How do you keep gettin' water? Where are you goin'…how long will you be gone? And…do you have…to… leave?" His last question comes out awkwardly and it embarrasses him.

Sadie just looks at Caleb, which only makes him more uncomfortable. Caleb lowers his gaze and takes a deep breath. When he looks back up, Sadie is still watching him. She takes another moment and decides to start with how he got to her shelter. She shares all the details of dragging him, covering their tracks, and getting rid of the Splitters. The only thing she emits was her breakdown along the way and the damage her hands suffered. Caleb remains silent through her explanations and is shocked at what she's accomplished. He didn't realize how far they were from where she found him. Then, Sadie hesitates, not sure how to answer his remaining questions.

"Caleb, I've been alone since…the earthquakes. You're the first person I've…talked…with. I…ummm…" she swallows, switches directions, and tries again. "I need to know how the Splitters got here, and… if there are more. I need to know if we're safe or not. Findin' out I'm livin' on an island…baffles me…I need to see it with my own eyes. As for supplies and water…don't worry. There's more than enough for the two of us. You just heal so…we…can move together. Until then, I…" Sadie pauses, trying to estimate how long she'll be gone, but she's not sure.

In fact, she needs more info from Caleb. Unzipping one of her many bags, she grabs a journal and rips out the last page. She returns to his side, hands him the sheet of paper, and a pencil.

"I need a map…of what you saw," she says.

Caleb still hasn't digested everything she's told him and he can't fathom being alone since the earthquakes. He barely survived and that was with the help of so many others. And she did it solo—for all those years—and it mesmerizes him. He hesitantly takes the paper, unsure how to start.

"Sadie, when they dropped us off, we didn't get the chance to see much. The marine layer was too thick...it blocked most of the view." He stares at the blank page.

"Just draw what you did see and...the ground you covered," she says, scooting closer.

Caleb isn't sure where to start and gets distracted by her proximity. He takes the pencil, closes his eyes, and tries to remember.

"Okay, we flew in...from the northeast...followed the coast south...before flying inland. Right here," he marks the paper, "there are a few ridgelines and the clearing where we landed. I didn't see the entire island, but this side is sort of shaped...like this."

Caleb sketches a rough outline for the section of land he saw when airborne, and then adds more details from the time he spent on foot. He erases and re-draws several lines, until finally, he feels like he can add no more.

"This is the best I can do," he says, handing her the pencil.

Sadie uses it to draw in the details from her land. She's exact with the locations of each canyon, ridgeline, logging road remnant, and even the coastline to the west, as well as part of it to the south. She's also able to include some of the property surrounding her territory from all the years she's spent exploring and patrolling. Her section of the map could be the largest part, but she needs to check the unfamiliar areas to know for sure. Sadie outlines her tentative plan of covering the island, making sure Caleb knows where she intends to start, along with which way she'll travel. Caleb doesn't speak and isn't happy about any of it.

"I'm not sure how long it'll take, but...once I get here," she points to the east side of the island straight across from their current location, "I'll head back to check with ya. I think I can do it in seven...maybe... ten days. If I'm not back..."

Caleb cuts her off, "Not back! Not an option!" He nearly yells, letting his emotions get the better of him as a stab of pain jolts through his torso.

It catches Sadie off guard. For years, she's survived alone, not interacting or even communicating with another soul and she isn't prepared to have her decisions questioned, especially by him. She dragged his sorry ass all the way here, saved his life, took care of him, and now he's going to tell her about options? She starts to snap back but thinks better of it, after all, he's in a strange place, hurt, and obviously concerned.

"Caleb, I'll be all right. I know this land. I've been travelin' it for years. We should have a back-up plan, that's all. You've got enough food and water…for two months, maybe three…if you conserve."

He's still upset and not calming down. "I don't wanna hear 'bout being alone for a couple months!"

"Caleb, please. We have to be smart…and work together. If somethin' happens to me you need to know where to go…how to find… stuff, and," Sadie looks up, as their eyes meet, "how to help…me."

He grows quiet, and Sadie uses his silence as an opportunity to show him the route back to her main shelter and how to gain access. She copies their map and hands Caleb the one he started.

"Come on, get up. I wanna show you somethin' outside."

A feeling of discomfort washes over Caleb. He's going to be left alone, and there's nothing he can do about it. Sadie's right, she's the only one able to scout about and she is a local expert. Caleb doesn't like it, but some fresh air might help. He's been cooped up, and suddenly, he feels the need to get out. Once outside, they settle between the two big logs, while Caleb recovers from the effort. The pain, emanating from his ribs, serves as a reminder of his limitations.

It's just about dark, but there's just enough light to still see. Sadie points out the details of their surroundings while explaining what's located in each direction. Using the map, and indicating their location on it to review with Caleb, she can tell he isn't happy with the conversation, but he's listening and concentrating. Ducking back inside, Sadie returns with a water kit.

"You need to learn how to use these…just in case," she says.

Sadie explains how the collectors work and where it's best to use them. She also demonstrates how to collect rainwater at the cave, if, by chance, more appears. As she finishes returning all the materials to the kit and putting it away, Sadie steps back to find Caleb's head resting between his hands. He doesn't hear her return, and in that moment, Sadie sees how distraught he really is. She recloses the door, so it makes noise, and Caleb immediately looks up.

"Let's get you back inside," she says, returning to his side.

They lock eyes again, and she freezes with what his show her. In that moment, Sadie fights the urge to dismiss her plan and stay with Caleb.

She breaks eye contact first. "I have to go. I have to find out if we're alone, if there are more Splitters, and…if so…how many. I won't be able to sleep or relax until I know."

Caleb steps closer to Sadie. He hesitates and then takes her hand.

"I don't want you to go. We just…found each other," he says, lightly caressing the back of her hand as a rush of emotions surges through Sadie. "Please stay. When I get better, we'll go together."

Sadie jerks her hand away and stares at him. "Caleb, that's not fair! You can't ask that of me!" Upset, she nevertheless maintains her train of thought. "Broken ribs take at least six weeks to heal. I can't sit here that long knowin' they're out there. I have to find 'em, before they stumble upon us."

Sadie turns around and goes back into the cave so upset, she wants to scream. She didn't sleep well the night before, the nightmare's visions followed her all day, and now—when her gut is saying, "Go!"—Caleb wants her to stay. She's tired and letting him confuse her. Sadie looks around for something to take her mind off of things, but everything that needs to be done, is done. She's packed for the trip, the cave is clean and organized, and everything Caleb might need is available. Then, she has an idea. Sadie grabs a bucket, heats some water, and fills it part way. She goes back outside, trying to think logically.

"Caleb, I'm too tired to argue. I know I have to do this. Think it through. You'll see the logic and agree. Besides, you're not in a position to fight me." She goes to his side and sets the bucket down. "I brought you here to save your life. This is the only option…the only safe place to heal, and that's what you need to do. Here…" She hands him a small bar of soap. "Clean up, you'll feel better."

At first, his anger rises, but as she comes even closer, he softens. As Sadie undoes his bandages, Caleb carefully lifts his arms so she can unwind them from around his ribs. When she finishes, Sadie returns to the cave, giving him privacy. Caleb stands there for a few moments, and then washes the best he can, which does make him feel better. Finishing, he calls to Sadie. She appears almost instantly, carrying a few more items. Checking his cuts and stitches, she applies some ointment and fresh bandages and then begins to re-wrap his ribs. As she works around him, Caleb faintly detects the scent of her hair and enjoys the pleasure it brings. Sadie's focus, however, is entirely somewhere else.

"Your stitches will dissolve. But you have to keep 'em clean and limit your movement so these ribs heal. When they do…" Sadie pauses, not sure how she wants to continue, "then…you can move around and…be able to…travel."

Caleb remains silent as she helps him back inside. Sadie puts everything away, still feeling a little unsettled.

"I'm leavin' early in the morning, and…I need to sleep," Sadie says, lying down on her side of the cave. She's tired, but her mind stays on the map and exploring the island. She forces herself to focus solely on breathing and as she tries to relax, Caleb finally speaks.

"Sadie, please be careful. Make sure…you come back."

TWELVE

Sadie leaves the cave while it's still dark with plans to scout the areas she's familiar with first. To shorten the search, she decides to skip the entire western side of her property along the coast. Yesterday, she returned there and to the clearing where she found Caleb and since it appeared no one had been there, she feels comfortable heading out today and eliminating that section. Instead, she's weaving the long way back to her main shelter where she'll re-supply and then push south.

Along the way, she kills two mourning doves by slingshot, and by nightfall of the third day, arrives to where she calls home feeling rejuvenated to be back in her sanctuary. She roasts the birds and sits down to enjoy a hot meal. When finished, Sadie cleans up and gathers what's needed for the rest of her journey. With full intentions of being properly prepared, Sadie knows she'll be traveling heavier than usual, so she carefully scrutinizes each item.

The following morning, she's out again before sunrise. Even with a heavy pack, traveling goes fast, and within two days, Sadie's at the southwestern tip of her property, where her in-depth exploration will begin. Emerging from the woods, she walks to the edge of the cliff that juts out into the ocean. From her position, there are views north, along the west coast, and towards the east, along the southern edge of the island.

Sadie, taking in the sight, plans on walking along the entire southern coast and then up the island's east side. On several occasions, she's traveled parts of this coastline, but she's never gone more than a mile or two past her own land. She's been under the impression it remained connected with the rest of California and assumed so, because the land eventually curves south. This discrepancy is confusing for her and it's the reason she couldn't understand Caleb's explanation of her home being an island.

As always, the marine layer clouds most of the ocean view while she travels. Sadie continues east, following the coastline, and by the end of the day, she scouts for a place to camp. Never having over-nighted along this particular route, she normally would have returned inland, where she maintains a small emergency foxhole, dug into the side of a slope. It's nothing fancy, but it serves her well as a place to safely overnight. Sadie actually has several of them, strategically located in various sites and she contemplated using the one nearby, but instead, decided to save time by staying on course. Besides, from here forward, she'll be camping in new areas—without the safety and comfort of her go-to locations—so she figures she might as well get used to it.

Finding a suitable location, she sets about constructing a basic lean-to. A fallen redwood, lying against another tree's trunk, creates most of the structure, making its set-up an easy task. Finishing the shelter, she scouts for a second site and hides the rest of her supplies, in case she's forced to evacuate quickly. It's an emergency strategy Sadie implemented years ago, and she intends to use it every night, this way, if she needs to leave in a hurry, she'll be faster without the heavy load, and she can always return to retrieve it once it's safe. Using this precaution provides her some peace of mind, allowing Sadie to relax enough to sleep, as she settles in for the night with a knife in one hand and her crossbow at the other.

For the next two days, Sadie continues her journey without difficulties. She enjoys the scenery and feels apprehensive only at night, when she has to let her guard down to rest. As her journey continues, she catches herself reminiscing about the area as it once was and how much it's changed. When the tsunamis hit, entire communities, worldwide, were instantly submerged, and the flooding that continued forced survivors towards any remaining higher ground. The small mountain community, which once existed below the cliffs she's hiking along now, not only managed to avoid the rising waters but also provided a refuge to others. The small town's inhabitants, scratched out what existence they could and over the years, transformed the homes and nearby lands into a small cooperative of farmers, mountain folks, and newcomers.

It's barely visible, but Sadie reaches what remains of the road that once traveled down to town. She stands on a broken slab of concrete. To her right, the paved section of road used to descend into the community below. To her left is the overgrown dirt road that curves through the woods, eventually reaching her home. It was her family's private drive and the only accessible path to where they lived.

Turning towards the ocean, Sadie remembers the last time she drove on this road and the terrible ordeal that followed. Three of them—Sadie, Markus, and her dad—were on their regular trip down the mountain. The first of each month, they descended from their home to check in with everyone, as the community became an extended family who pulled together to survive. Together, they helped to transform the area's apple orchards and berry fields to grow additional crops to feed everyone. It wasn't much, but with her dad's ingenuity, they were even able to produce small amounts of biofuel to operate a few pieces of farming equipment and to keep a couple of vehicles operational.

Sadie's father, beloved by all, played a crucial role in everyone's survival. He spent years accumulating supplies, was incredibly adept with anything mechanical, and was a masterful self-educated engineer. There wasn't anything he couldn't fix, build, or design, and he rose to the occasion, time, and time again. When traveling into town, Sadie's dad would meet with several families, trade goods, and orchestrate any repairs or necessary changes.

Sitting down, now, on a giant stump, Sadie gazes below. Small waves crash against the rocks, and with each one, she grows sadder. She used to love the ocean, but now, looking at it reminds her of what's lost. She thinks about that fateful day coming down the mountain and discovering how much humanity changed as she got her introduction to the Splitter Nation.

Sadie and Markus, along with her father, had driven to the settlement unaware of an invasion that arrived a couple of days earlier. Sadie's dad stopped the truck when he noticed smoke, and then, in the distance, they heard gunshots. Before going any further, and into view, they parked behind a patch of trees. Both her husband and her dad tried to convince Sadie to head back home and leave them to scout the situation, but she wouldn't, and refused to leave their sides. As the men grabbed their hunting rifles, Sadie shouldered her crossbow.

They left the truck and kept cover in the trees as they walked the last mile or so towards where the homes started. It was there they first witnessed Splitter brutality. The invading hoard had raided homes, shelters, and barns, killing and destroying as they went, and taking whatever they wanted. Most of the town's men had been quickly killed, but the women, hadn't been as fortunate. Sadie recalls the horrors of those sights, and then hearing the screams of a woman, coming from inside a nearby barn. On their approach, Sadie's dad went first and fired several quick rounds.

As Sadie entered, she saw the bodies of three dead Splitters sprawled upon the ground. Caught off guard, the brutes hadn't expected anyone, and were so engaged in abusing their victim that they didn't hear him enter. Sadie's eyes darted over the scene, but she couldn't reach her friend fast enough. The woman, naked and bleeding, rolled over, grabbed one of the Splitters guns, and put it in her mouth. All three of them, in unison, yelled for her to stop, but it was too late.

They watched in slow motion as her body went limp and fell to the ground. In utter disbelief, they stood in shock, feeling even worse by the sight of her two small children's bodies hanging from the rafters and her husband's limp body tied to a post, where he'd been beaten to death. Sadie fell to her knees, trembling, before Markus grabbed her by the shoulders and yanked her up, yelling to get Sadie's attention, as she moved trance-like while they exited the barn.

Outside, they ran to hide among the trees just as another group of Splitters arrived at the scene. The militants entered, but eventually came back out shouting orders, while the three of them, crept through the orchard. Nearing an old farmhouse, they heard more commotion and discovered the Splitters were using the home, so they headed in the opposite direction, but found they were unable to leave what safety the trees provided.

Crouching among the fallen apples, they could only wait for dark and hope not to be discovered. As the sun set, they looped towards the other side of town trying to find a better vantage point, knowing they couldn't just leave and abandon their friends. There might be survivors, and if so, they needed to help them. Along the way, they heard shots as a small pack of locals ran for cover. One by one, they saw each member of the frightened group gunned down, but from the corner of her eye, Sadie saw other survivors scrambling to hide, and carefully, Markus, Sadie, and her dad joined them. Once they found safety, all of them had turned to Robert, Sadie's dad, for guidance.

Reliving those moments, Sadie's no longer taking in her surroundings. All she sees is the terror across her friends' faces as she's transported back to that moment, vividly reliving every detail as it happened—including their conversations, and it's her father's voice, she hears first.

"We have to be strong." Robert says, to the scared and wide-eyed group. "Even if there's only one left, we have to find 'em...we have to be careful...and smart. This is a fight...for our lives." He looks at Sadie and motions as if he's writing.

Sadie, understanding his meaning, pulls out a small notepad from her pocket and together they create a list of the known dead and those still missing.

In hiding, they observe the Splitters, study their habits, and learn their routines. The militants are a curse on the land, like a plague or sickness, and tracking the invaders helps the group determine how many they're up against. At night, they break into groups of two or three to search for survivors and to cautiously gather anything missed by the Nation's searches. It's potentially a deadly game of cat-and-mouse, as they learn to dodge the invading force. Quickly, some of the missing, younger men are discovered as they are beaten and forced at gunpoint, to move equipment and supplies. At night they're locked in a storage shed and guarded, and knowing that the Splitters will eliminate their captives once they've served their purpose, Robert devises a rescue plan.

"I'm gonna need Ned," he blurts, surprising everyone.

The others stare in disbelief: they'd forgotten all about Ned, the local recluse living on the outskirts of town, who hasn't even been seen in years. Besides his brothers, Robert's the only person that's ever spoken to or interacted with the war veteran, who suffers from post-traumatic stress disorder after serving two tours of duty. Once home, his only refuge from the psychological trauma came from collecting military goods. His younger brothers supported his habit because it helped, but as Ned's impulses became excessive, they became unsure of how to handle his behavior. Instead of fighting it, they took on a different strategy and talked him into opening a surplus store. The brothers handled all the daily operations of the business, and Ned's responsibility was solely locating and ordering the stock they sold.

Sadie's dad became one of the store's regulars and spent a good bit of time among the aisles and shelves full of military-grade supplies. It was one of Robert's specialty requests that eventually brought Ned and him together, since the outcast usually refused to interact with customers. The day the two met was the beginning of a unique friendship and Ned found solace in Robert's questions and unusual orders.

Then, when the ocean levels first started to rise, it was Ned who acted. He began moving merchandise to his brothers' place. When he ran out of room in the shed and house, he bought a tractor, tore up the back of the property, and built a storage bunker hidden in the seclusion and privacy of his family's land. A feud followed, as the brothers tried stopping him, but Ned refused to back down. Gossip spread, as the townsfolk, who were denied access to the site, tried to guess what he was doing. Robert helped with the design and construction, but respected Ned's privacy, and never shared anything about the project with anyone else. When the Enders hit, and the floods approached, Ned's shop disappeared under water—along with most everything else—and then, his excessiveness and vast supplies of goods proved helpful.

Even though he was forgotten about, everyone agrees that Ned's probably still holed up in the back of his property. Robert, still keeping his friend's secrets, refuses to share much, and says he has to go there alone. The group trusts Robert but Sadie isn't satisfied. She argues until her father agrees she can come along and keep watch.

In the cover of darkness, the two of them head toward the outskirts of town where only two homes remain. Besides Ned, a young couple—who are still unaccounted for—live out this way. Sadie and Robert move carefully and at the first home, a body in the yard, comes into view, but they can't get close enough to determine more, because Splitters are milling around. Moving tactfully towards Ned's, the father-daughter team discovers that his home is nearly destroyed.

Obviously the site of a lengthy standoff, the house is torn apart, riddled with bullets, and both brothers lie deceased inside. Any remaining supplies are long gone, confiscated by the Nation. After seeing more than enough, Sadie finds a secure hiding place that offers a view with a clear line of sight to both Ned's and the neighbors' home.

"Sadie, if I'm not back by sunrise, head back to the others. If I'm not back by the following night, then…something's wrong," Robert warns his daughter.

"Dad…" she begins, but before she can say another word, he interrupts her.

"No! You stay safe! I've lost everyone else and I won't lose you! I'll be back." He looks fiercely at his daughter. "Promise." He grabs her by the shoulders. "Promise me! Whatever happens…please?"

"Okay dad…I promise," she says, obliging him after a long pause.

As he creeps away, a terrible feeling washes over Sadie. Something isn't right and for hours, she stays hidden, watching and listening as the sensation strengthens. The only action she sees is when one or two Splitters go inside the neighbors' home and then emerge a short time later. As night lengthens, the traffic at the house slows, and then stops. When the last man leaves and no one else appears, Sadie can no longer ignore her sense of unease.

Leaving her hiding place, she creeps toward the house and finds out whose body lies on the ground. Sadie gets close enough to confirm it's her friend's husband before moving to a window, but peeking in, it's too dark for her to make out any details. After checking several windows, she heads to the back door, finds it's open, hesitates, and then enters.

With a racing heart rate, she pauses just inside, allowing her eyes time to adjust. Sadie isn't sure what she's doing, but her gut commands her to continue. The Splitters are up to something, and finding out could help. Trying to be stealthy, she makes her way to the stairs, taking each step with care, and gets scared as one creaks. Paused, half-way up the flight, she hears the voices of two approaching men, who unknowingly, announce their arrival. There isn't a way for Sadie to get out before they see her, so she hustles up the remaining stairway and ducks into one of the two rooms.

She can hear the men's laughter as they stumble up the stairs. They're drunk, and the lantern they carry casts odd shadows on the walls where she's hiding. The extra room, set up as an office, has a sofa along one wall, a desk with all its drawers ripped out, and a small closet with its door left ajar. There aren't other options, so Sadie slips into the closet, and eases far enough over so she can't be seen. At the top of the stairs, the two Splitters argue.

"Oohh…you wen firrrs las time! Is my turn," slurs one of them.

"Tha don' madder. I'mmm…higher rank, sooooo I…go first. You wait yur turn."

One of the Splitters departs into the bedroom across the hall, while the other turns to where Sadie's hiding. He sets his lantern on the desk and plops onto the couch. Sadie catches herself holding her breath as she leans to look, before quickly retracting her head. The Splitter has positioned himself facing the closet and time stands still as she remains trapped, hearing the man's breathing, along with the tipping of a bottle each time he takes a drink. Muffled sounds come from the other room, and suddenly, Sadie realizes what's going on. It doesn't take long before the absent Splitter comes over.

"Yur turn buddy," he says, swiping the bottle from his friend's hand and taking a long swig. "I'll wait for yah, but make it quick," he chuckles and settles on the sofa.

Sadie waits for a moment and then peers out again. He's lain in the opposite direction with his back towards Sadie, and feeling her anger rise at an alarming rate, she finds an opportunity has presented itself. Slowly, she sneaks from the hiding place, and stepping on something, makes a crunching sound. She acts immediately and with knife drawn, Sadie closes the short distance. From behind, she slits the man's throat from ear to ear, before he even turns around.

She leaves the scene of her bloody killing and heads across the hall, where she pauses at the door to gather her courage before barging in. When she does, a horrendous excuse for a man is on top of her friend—Gabby—and Sadie reacts by stabbing repeatedly. As he rolls over, Sadie finishes the job by plunging her blade deep into his heart. There's blood splatter everywhere, but the muffled sobs from Gabby keep Sadie focused. She takes the gag from her friend's mouth and cuts the rope that ties her arms and legs to the bed.

Gabby tucks into a fetal position and weeps, while Sadie looks around, collecting the poor woman's clothes. Thinking, Sadie runs down the stairs to the back of the laundry room where she knows emergency supplies are hidden. The community continued to survive because all of its members decided to pull together and adhere to several survival tactics. Each home has a secret space, holding specific items, used only in emergencies, and Sadie hopes the Splitters didn't discover the one here.

The room's a mess, but uncovering the hidden spot, she finds everything is still there. As adrenaline continues coursing through her veins, Sadie carries two jugs of water in each hand, and runs up the stairs double-time. She sets the water in the bathroom and carries Gabby there.

"Gabby, we have to be fast...more could be comin'," Sadie says, lightly pouring some water over the defeated woman.

With the water, Gabby finally reacts, and her hands and body shake uncontrollably as she fiercely scrubs her body with a small piece of soap. Sadie goes back to the Splitters' bodies and takes their weapons. She finds matches and cigarettes on the body in the office and it gives her an idea. She grabs the half empty bottle of alcohol, douses the dead Splitter, as well as the window's curtains, and then strikes a match just before her and Gabby exit.

The growing fire will definitely attract others, and since Sadie doesn't see any sign of her father, she decides to get the two of them to safety while she can. Gabby, who is frantic and weak, can barely function. When they finally return to the group, who are shocked at the women's sudden appearance, the only details a blood-stained Sadie shares are about the fire, while Gabby just continues to weep.

THIRTEEN

Sadie runs a hand through her hair, remembering those days with Gabby. Her dear friend endured such cruelty and injustice and the mere thought of it sickens Sadie. Gabby was a mess, and kept to herself, sharing an unspoken knowledge and bond with Sadie that the others simply didn't question, including Markus. The experience transformed Sadie. She'd seen the bodies of dead friends, witnessed Gabby's rape, and brutally slayed two men. To make matters even worse, her dad hadn't return as scheduled. Still reliving those horrors, Sadie can't let go of the terrible visions. They continue to overrun her mind, transporting her back to all those years ago, and once again, it's her father voice, she hears when he finally came back and joined them.

"I'm sorry. It's okay, I'm here," he says, embracing his daughter, realizing something terrible has happened. Knowing they'll talk privately later, he turns to quickly address the group and to relieve their anxiety. "Ned's alive...he'll help. Tomorrow, at midnight...we meet him."

The group, overwhelmed emotionally, slowly disburses to settle in for the night. Robert looks from Sadie to Gabby, and then back to Sadie. He understands much in those few quick glances and breaking eye contact with his daughter, he focuses on Gabby, who's nearly delirious.

"You're safe." Robert takes a step closer as tears fall from her eyes. "I promise."

At his words, Gabby falls completely limp and Robert moves to catch her. Her tears turn to sobs and then she begins to wail.

"Sshhh...ssshhh...Gabby, we have to keep quiet."

Sadie, exhausted, turns to Markus. "I'll stay with her again," she says, watching her dad trying to console her friend.

The Splitters arrival has changed everything, especially his wife, and Markus worries excessively about Sadie. Since Gabby's return, he hasn't gotten the chance to be alone with Sadie and he knows killing those two men has traumatized her. When she returned—covered in their blood—she could only stare blankly ahead, as he wiped the gore from her face while she sat on her hands, trying to keep them from trembling. He mentally chastises himself, knowing he should have gone with Robert, or at least stayed with Sadie. He shouldn't have left her alone and he'll make sure, it'll never happen again. Moving to hold his wife, Markus knows she isn't okay. Sadie's being strong for the others and especially for Gabby, but she needs time to heal, too.

He wraps an arm around Sadie and silently, they stand entwined, overwhelmed with fatigue. They haven't slept much, death surrounds them, and more killing is inevitable. Eventually, Robert walks over with Gabby, who's barely able to stand, and speaks directly to his daughter and son-in-law.

"We're leavin'…grab your stuff," Robert commands.

Sadie unwraps her arms from around Markus and looks at her father. Robert and Sadie never utter a word, but it seems an entire conversation takes place. They share a bond and connection that Markus doesn't fully understand. He respects it, and loves them both, but at times, he feels completely left out. Not exactly sure what's going on, Markus grabs his gear and follows, as Robert leads the way towards Ned's. Nearing the area where her husband was murdered affects Gabby tremendously and she grows worse with each step as the smell of sooty remains permeates the air.

Entering Ned's property, Robert pauses and warns them to follow his every precise move. As they wander deeper into the parcel of land, he takes them to an old, dry-rotted outhouse. It's overgrown with ivy and barely standing. At its back, Robert taps the handle of a knife several times on a small metal pipe. He pauses and then repeats the same series. After several attempts, they hear a faint rumble from within, then Robert slides open a loose board and crawls inside.

"One at a time," he instructs, while pushing aside another board to expand the opening.

One-by-one, they climb down a ladder into what feels like a well. At the bottom, there's just enough room for the four of them to stand in a tight circle. Gabby starts to panic and in the darkness, her terror peaks. Sadie does what she can to comfort her as Robert slides his hands along the wall, adjusts two metal pieces, and twists. A faint light appears in a small crevice and he continues manipulating the levers, until the opening is big enough for all of them to squeeze through. Entering a small chamber, Robert closes the door and removes an already lit lantern that sits waiting for them. They move down the short corridor and stop at another door. This time, it's left open, but before going in, they stop.

"Ned...I'm bringin' company. We're comin' in," Robert warns, then he nods to the others and enters first, as they follow.

Inside, the structure is large enough to hold at least thirty people and three adjoining rooms are visible. Sadie looks around the bunker, noticing similarities, but before she can say anything, her eyes met Ned's. He's standing to the side, positioned to watch, but out of their initial sight. Without pause, she walks over, reaches out, and shakes his hand.

"Thank you, sir," she says, looking him straight in the eyes. "I'm..."

"Sadie," Ned says, completing her sentence. Then, he looks over her shoulder, nods at Robert, and continues. "I've been hearin' 'bout you for years."

Ned greets Robert then looks past him to the others.

"Markus, Gabby," Ned says, abruptly nodding in their direction.

"How...do you...?" Markus begins.

"Ned's an intelligence expert...recon is his specialty," Robert says, cutting Markus's question off. "We're fortunate to have him and lucky to be here. We've got lots to discuss, but it's late...everyone should rest first."

They enter one of the adjacent rooms that's set up with cots. A small alcove is situated off to one side and it gets curtained off from the rest of the room so Gabby and Sadie, the only surviving women, can settle into it. Markus sets his cot nearby, desperately wanting to curl up with his wife, but he knows Gabby needs Sadie more. Hours later, an unsettling dream wakes Sadie, and since Gabby finally found sleep, she makes sure not to disturb her as she goes to Markus. He's snoring lightly and it's the first time in days, he's slept soundly. Sadie, understanding his need for rest, lets him be, and leaves to join her father and Ned who are deep in discussion. Before they even realize it, she's at their side.

They stop talking and look up, but Sadie ignores their stares. Instead, she absorbs the details from the table they stand around. On its surface sits a precisely drawn diagram of the town and the surrounding area. It depicts every structure, the places the Splitters occupy, and where the prisoners are being held. It contains notations about the enemy's numbers, the type of equipment they brought, and what they've commandeered. Even Gabby's burnt home is clearly labeled. After looking over the details, Sadie knows this isn't something Ned and her father recently created. Obviously, Ned gets out—a lot.

Sadie points at the map. "The wood pile's much smaller now. There's...twenty yards of space between it and the shed. But...it'll still give plenty of cover for two...maybe three people."

Ned's surprised by Sadie's observation and her comprehension of the strategies depicted before them. For hours, the three of them discuss plans and talk through sequences of events. Throughout the process, Sadie's impressed with Ned's intellect and begins to see why her father trusts, and even enjoys the man's company. Their conversation provides a much-needed distraction, and as it grows later, Sadie finally feels ready for bed.

Back at her husband's cot, Sadie watches as Markus rolls over, opens his eyes, and spreads both of his arms out wide. She accepts the invitation, curls up on his chest, and falls into a deep slumber, but at some time in the early morning, Sadie's arm starts tingling, and the sensation wakes her. As she starts to move, a ghastly shriek scares them both. It's Gabby and her night terrors have returned, so Sadie pulls the curtain back and joins her. Markus, now wide-awake, gets up and explores the bunker. He was impressed by its design when they first entered and wants to take a closer look at it. No one else is around and he wonders where Ned and Robert could be. As if reading Markus's thoughts, Ned appears from a hidden passage.

"Where's Robert?" Markus asks.

Ned takes so long to respond that Markus thinks he isn't going to answer.

"He's out." Ned says, turning to leave, before anything else can be asked.

Not sure what to think, Markus decides to let it go. He spends time examining the details of the shelter, the items it holds, and the giant map lying on the table. Eventually, he grows bored and returns to check on Gabby and Sadie who are whispering together. Since his presence goes ignored, he lies back down and rests further. When Sadie finally emerges, he's grateful for the company.

"Hey baby," she says, nestling up with him.

"Your dad's been gone all day. What's goin' on?" he asks, wrapping his arms around her.

"Sorry. I've been distracted…with Gabby. He went back to get the others. He'll return just before midnight…then we'll meet." She rests her head and closes her eyes.

"Robert and Ned have a plan?" he asks, moving a strand of hair away from Sadie's face.

"Yep, I stayed up with 'em last night. Did you see the diagram?" Sadie moves, trying to get comfortable, but unable to, she gets up instead. "Come on, I'll show ya."

Together, they head over to the table and Sadie gives him a quick overview. Markus is astonished with how relaxed his wife is while explaining the symbols and information. Talking about it has a calming effect on her, but with each detail she shares, he grows more anxious. Markus knows the risks and he isn't sure what part they'll play, but he's sure Sadie knows. At the moment, though, he really doesn't care. For now, he's had enough, and just wants Sadie. He grabs her with astonishing force and kisses her passionately.

"Ahh…hum…" A throaty interruption stops them.

Sadie and Markus look up to see Robert, and behind him, stand the others.

"Dad, why are you back early?"

"After you went to bed last night, Ned and I went out. We decided I'd come back sooner if…it was safe. And…it was."

Robert helps settle everyone in and requests the groups' presence in an hour. When they gather, Ned's standing next to Robert and the quiet outcast nods to each person as they join them around the table. Everyone is present except Sadie and Gabby and when they appear, a collective gasp escapes. The women altered their appearances, and Markus can only stare in disbelief.

"I know…it'll grow back," Sadie responds, running a hand over the stubble that remains on her head. Then, she turns to address everyone else, "For however long this takes…and whenever Splitters are around, call me…Zaid."

Gabby takes a small step forward, clears her throat, and for the first time, lifts her eyes from the ground. "And me…Gabe."

The men hate seeing the women this way, but they understand their choices. Every time they see Gabby, they're unsure of what to do, or say. Now, she looks like a badly beaten-up adolescent boy.

Robert speaks, looking at Gabby. "We thought...you'd be...more comfortable stayin' here."

"No. You need more people. Sadie and I talked...I can help. Please...I need...to do this." Gabby may look horrible, but for the first time since her return, it's not fear in her eyes.

No one argues, and Robert begins by outlining the plan. The next two days are a flurry of action, and preparations fill the hours. It's during this time that Ned shares some of his secrets. They learn he's nocturnal, as his nightly outings continue, and besides the bunker's obvious areas, there are hidden rooms, stockpiles, and tunnels, but it's his weapons arsenal that shocks them the most.

He outfits the entire group, complete with assault rifles, ammunition, and grenades. Each item comes with instruction and drilling, until Ned feels confident in their abilities. They hold one final meeting, with plans to strike later in the night, and people walk away fighting their fears and uncertainties. Before they exit, Ned calls to both Sadie and Gabby.

"Here," he says, handing them camo flak jackets. "Your hair and clothes help with...your disguises...but..." he pauses, looks down at their chests, back to their faces, and then continues, "You're still shaped like women. Besides stopping bullets," he wraps his knuckles on the surface of one of the jackets, "these will...flatten...yur...curves."

The women take them, nod in gratitude, and leave for bed, but— before getting to the curtain—Gabby stops.

"Sadie, I'll sleep out here. You and Markus should be together. I..." she starts to cry and does her best to fight it. "I don't know how... things will work out, but...you two deserve time together. I know what you've sacrificed for me, and...I'll never be able to thank you... for...everything...for...what you did." Gabby wraps her arms around Sadie and then quickly lets go of her.

Dragging the cots away from the curtained area, Gabby makes sure to give the couple a little more privacy. Markus takes his wife's hand, thanks Gabby, and crawls into bed with Sadie. At first, they talk. They share all the details lost between them during the past few days. Sadie tells him everything and he listens intently. The horrors she's faced scare him and he pulls Sadie tight, feeling unable to get her close enough.

They don't have to say it, but both know this could be their last night together. Even the best of plans can go wrong. Markus kisses Sadie's forehead and then her eyelids. He moves to her ear, nuzzles down her neck and back up the other side. When he gets to her mouth, Sadie's breathing heavily and arching her body to his. She pulls at his clothes, helps remove them, and they make love in near silence. The intensity of it brings tears to Sadie's eyes, and afterwards, they fall asleep entwined in each other's limbs.

"Sadie...Markus."

The two awaken, hearing their names called from behind the curtain.

"Dad?"

"It's almost time," he says, respecting their privacy.

"Okay," Sadie responds. Hearing her father leave, she rolls onto Markus. "I guess we've got to get up."

Sadie feels doubt creeping in, and begins thinking they could just stay here, or go into hiding back on their property. The desire to spend her days with Markus is tempting, and looking at him, she senses the same. As long as they have each other, things will be all right, but neither says anything out loud. They both know that abandoning the others isn't an option. The community must be reclaimed and the Splitters eliminated, or their cruelty will only spread to the next set of victims. Mischievously, she looks down at her husband, kisses him, and using her lips, lightly tugs on Markus's bottom lip.

"Quickie?" She asks, begging with both her eyes and body.

He responds without words, instantly switching positions, and is more than happy to oblige. His reaction is so immediate that it catches Sadie off-guard and her desires explode. They don't have much time, but they make the most of their last few moments alone. Finished, they lie still just a moment longer, allowing their heart rates to slow. Neither wants to leave, but they dress quickly, and do so anyways.

FOURTEEN

Pausing at the height of an inhalation, Sadie continues controlling her breathing using the simple technique to control her nerves. Slowing each exhale, she stretches it to last three times as long as the inhalations. With each gradual release of air, she relaxes her muscles while scanning the area from left to right and then back again.

Markus breaks the silence, "Ready?"

Looking one more time, Sadie nods and in a crouch leaves first, as Markus watches while providing cover. Safely arriving at the wood stack, she disappears into the darkness of its shadow. The cover of night works in their favor and Markus quickly joins her. The moonlight does brighten some areas, but in their position, they're undetectable. Keeping their backs against the wood, they wait and listen to the approaching footsteps. When the steps once again fade away, Sadie takes a better position.

She detects the distinct rhythm of the returning man's strides long before his shadowy view appears. As the guard nears, Sadie aims, exhales, and shoots. Her target falls instantly and Markus responds with haste. He drags the dead Splitter into the darkness, hiding the evidence, as Sadie sights another arrow on the second guard. Every night, two militants get assigned to the prisoners, but tonight, Sadie and Markus got lucky, as one fell asleep. He's leaning back in a chair against the shed, oblivious to his surroundings and missed everything that just happened.

Their movements and faint sounds weren't enough to wake the man, and Sadie makes sure he doesn't. She fires and the body slumps over and slowly slides off the chair as Markus hustles to catch it and drag it away. Returning first to the wood stack, then to the cover of the trees, the husband-wife duo takes their next position with their weapons drawn.

It's their turn to supply cover, as Ned and Robert move to the woodpile. Safely there, Ned goes to the shed and uses a pair of bolt cutters to open the door so Robert can step into the building. He emerges, helping direct the captives to freedom and as he leads them away, Markus and Ned drag the two dead guards into the shed. Ned re-chains the latch and places a new lock on it, while Markus brushes away the drag marks they left behind.

So far, everything is going as planned and there's still hours of darkness left. It's the next phase of the operation, though, that holds uncertainties. Its success depends largely on the roles of their recently freed friends. The rescued townspeople must be updated, armed, quickly instructed, and most importantly, be able to function after what they've endured. They reconvene at the fallback position and all of the rescued captives are eager to help, giving the entire operation a boost. They work efficiently, and within an hour the group—split into two—is on the move, creeping to their designated places with synchronized movements.

In different locations, men cautiously saturate the perimeters of two homes with gas siphoned from the Splitters vehicles. All the doors get chained, locked, or barred and, with the completion of these tasks, final stations are manned. A small window of time—allocated for any discrepancies in their plan—passes, and even though their targets are almost a half-mile apart, the timing is crucial. The gas-soaked homes house the invading forces and the mission's success hinges on hitting them simultaneously. With each fire lit, flames quickly engulf the buildings, as the groups sight weapons along each door and window. The anticipation climaxes and at first, it seems the fire might do all the work.

Sadie sits alert in a position providing the largest sector of coverage. She's designated as first-response. Her accuracy with the crossbow and its deadly stealth capabilities, has already laid the foundation for their mission. Now, her skills may be able to extend their advantage. She watches the front and one side of the house, responsible for any targets trying to leave. Fire engulfs the sides of the home and as it reaches the second story, yells can be heard over the flames. As bodies approach the window, Sadie fires and reloads. The yelling from inside intensifies, and then, gunshots are heard in the distance. Since the silence of Sadie's bow is no longer needed, she picks up her recently-issued assault rifle.

An upstairs window opens in Sadie's target range and at the same time, a chair is thrown out of a bottom window. The heads of two Splitter men appear, but they're instantly bombarded with shells. Anytime one of the invaders comes remotely close to a window or door, they're met with a hailstorm of bullets. The Splitters can't escape the punishment the town has elected to enforce. The Nation's representatives can either burn for their crimes or be executed by gunfire. One militant comes close to escaping, but he's shot as he stumbles along the ground, injured from diving out of a window. As the fires rage through the homes, the Splitters grow desperate. Several try to avoid a fiery death by leaping from windows, but their burning bodies fall to the ground in futile attempts.

As night turns to morning, the only sound coming from Sadie's area is the roar of fire and the crackling of burning wood. Gunshots can still be heard from the other home and Sadie begins to fear something's wrong. She sees her dad running between positions while issuing new orders. When he reaches Sadie, her fears are validated. Some of the Splitters weren't in the homes and they're fighting back.

"You and Markus stay together...head south. Take position on the hill...keep watch. Not sure how many are left...but I think we've got 'em cornered," he tells his daughter.

Robert leaves, just as quickly as he appeared and Sadie doesn't like it. Her gut insists she follow, but when Sadie looks over, she sees Markus running towards her. She joins her husband, and they settle into their newly assigned position. The hill provides just enough elevation for them to see both burning homes and where the remaining Splitters have holed up. Sadie knows her dad sent her here for two reasons. First, it offers a clear view of anyone coming towards them, giving Sadie and Markus a huge advantage, and second, it's further from the gunfight and therefore, a much safer place.

Watching from their high ground, Sadie and Markus see Ned making his way towards the Splitters. He moves, from cover to cover, until he settles into an attack position. He tosses two grenades, waits for the explosions, and then tosses two more. After they go off, he charges into the area while releasing non-stop bullets. Close behind follows Robert. Sadie, knowing her dad is risking too much, starts after him.

"Sadie! Sadie! God damn it!" Markus can't get her attention and runs after her. He catches up and tackles Sadie to the ground.

"What are ya doing?!" she screams at her husband.

"Your dad said stay put...and hold this spot! Wha d'yah think you're doing!?"

"Look," she points to her father, "he needs cover!"

"No! Stay here." God, he's so mad, but the look in his wife's eyes isn't one that can be stopped. She's so damn stubborn. Unhappily, he agrees, and changes tactics. "Fine…lets go."

Together they run down the hill, pausing first behind a small group of trees and then behind an old car. They're close enough to see Ned running from Splitter to Splitter still shooting. He's on a rampage, and continuing to fire bullets even into the obviously dead bodies. Behind him, yelling for Ned to stop is Robert.

"Ned! Ned!" Robert's calls have no effect.

When Ned runs out of ammo, he pulls out his hunting knife and starts towards another body. Two Splitters are lying crumpled together and as he approaches, Robert finally catches up.

"We got 'em. Ned! We did it!" Robert continues yelling, trying to get his friends attention.

Instead of stopping, Ned turns with his knife raised, making Robert take a step back.

"Ned, it's me…Robert. It's okay. Look…we got 'em all."

Ned stills as recognition slowly settles in, but as he lowers his knife, a final bullet fires. The sequences of events that follow occur in a dreamlike trance. Markus and Sadie burst from their position, as Robert takes three steps backwards and drops his gun. Ned turns and leaps onto the Splitter trying to get out from beneath his dead companion. As the two fight, Markus runs towards them with gun held ready, while Sadie goes to her father's side.

"Dad!" she yells, getting his attention.

"It's okay, Sadie. I'm alright," he instinctively responds.

"No…it's not."

Sadie and Roberts's eyes meet and then, together, they look down. Robert touches the tips of his fingers to his stomach and then stares at the blood on them. He sits down and Sadie, alarmingly, examines the damage. There's an entry and exit wound, but the bullet has pierced his abdomen and they both know it's serious.

*   *   *

The tears, filling Sadie's eyes, suddenly snap her back to the present moment and to her perch above the ocean. Realizing she's stopped way too long, she hops over to another section of broken pavement, as thoughts of her father linger and she wishes her dad could be here now. Missing his company and help, she lifts her face towards the sky.

"I miss you Dad," she says, aloud.

Suddenly, the sky lightens and grows brighter. The marine layer thins and the sun appears. Sadie keeps her face tilted upward and closes her eyes. The sun's rays provide encouragement and the rarity of the moment isn't lost on her as she feels the connection with her father and absorbs its positive influence. The entire coastline clears as the fog burns off, giving Sadie the chance to examine it completely. For the first time, she can clearly see where the land ends. A section of the island juts out, far into the ocean, making the land appear to continue south. The clear skies above reveal the true nature of the area, and now Sadie understands her original confusion. The observation gets her back on track, as she returns to her current reality.

Sadie, fueled by curiosity and no longer distracted, hikes along, allowing the sunshine to lift her spirits. It's such a rare occurrence and she makes sure to appreciate every second of it. She can see the edge of the marine layer, hanging offshore, and she wonders how long it'll last. As she continues heading east, the terrain grows steeper, causing Sadie to focus on her footing.

As she nears the section of land that turns south, it becomes harder to climb, but Sadie works upward and slowly makes it to the top. The slope levels and she's able to walk south, attempting to see how far she can go. The vector of land she travels is narrow and in several places, Sadie's able to see the Pacific on both sides of the landmass. To her left, out in the ocean, are giant, mesmerizing sea stacks, and all that remains of the land to the east. The giant masses of land protrude from the water's surface, some only barren, rocky outcroppings, while others support small clumps of redwoods and ferns.

Then, abruptly, she stops, unable to continue. There's a gap, and the land further south is, actually, another small island. At one point it was all connected, but now the space between prevents Sadie from continuing. She contemplates tossing her backpack across and jumping over, but standing there, Sadie suddenly grows cold, as the fog rolls back in. It comes in fast and thick, causing Sadie to pull on another layer of clothes, before she decides to head back and play it safe. The thick marine layer makes navigating a challenge and she nearly stumbles over an edge when her footing gives way.

She alarmingly falls sideways, grabbing a tree root for security. Even though it wasn't a bad fall, it's enough to scare her. Sadie settles between the trunks of two redwood trees and regains control of her breathing. "How stupid would it be, to fall off a cliff?" she thinks, especially with everything she's endured over the years, only to have it all end in a hiking accident. "Ridiculous," she remarks, taking it as a sign to slow down.

The fog is too thick for Sadie to safely travel back to the where the peninsula starts, it's too narrow to allow her to hide off to a side, and it's a dead-end. She's trapped herself, and Sadie grows upset at such a stupid mistake and it doesn't help, that soon, it'll be dark. Getting caught up in the curiosity of exploring, she failed to think ahead. Her frustrations aren't helping, so, taking another deep breath, she tries being logical.

First, she reminds herself, there haven't been any signs of anyone this entire journey. Second, with dark approaching, if any Splitters were around they'd be setting up camp for the night. And lastly, if, for some reason, they were out and about, the fog would also be limiting their movements and visibility. These thoughts ease Sadie's frustrations just enough to get her back on track. She scouts a little further ahead and settles on what's available.

She tucks her pack beneath a cluster of giant ferns and settles herself in a larger patch only twenty yards away. She rips off handfuls of fronds from the bottoms of several ferns to clear just enough space so they won't poke her while lying down, then, she crawls into her sleeping bag and tries to rest. The night is silent and eerily still, but just as Sadie starts to drift off, a faint rustling draws her attention. She isolates the noises location and determines it's coming from near her pack. From the sound of it, something's chewing on her stuff. She slowly sits up, and her movement causes the rustling to stop.

Sitting in the darkness, Sadie begins to think she scared off whatever it was. Then, it starts again. She feels around on the ground and picks up a couple of small stones. She tosses one in her pack's direction and once again the noises stop. A pattern develops. Sadie sits and waits in the quiet and when she hears it, another rock gets tossed. Only two things change: she's able to pinpoint the location better in the dark and she's running out of things to throw. Her last attempt must be close, as she hears something small scurry away.

"Finally," she whispers, trying to get comfortable enough to sleep.

As Sadie begins to drift off, the rustling returns. Pissed, tired, and done with the whole ordeal, Sadie stands and heads toward her pack. She hears the animal run off, grabs her bag, and takes it back with her. "So much for that strategy," Sadie thinks, realizing keeping her gear separate from her won't do much good if an animal tears through it. In the darkness, and without using a light, she runs her hands over all the compartments, trying to detect any damage. Without finding any, Sadie places the backpack next to her and settles in, to at last, get some much-needed rest.

FIFTEEN

Sadie rolls over, striking a leg on her backpack. She lies still before getting up, and then, she checks the area. It's still foggy, but it's not nearly as thick as it was the evening before. She returns to her makeshift bed to gather her things and now that she can see, she closely inspects the damage to her pack. The chew marks suggest a small rodent and whatever it was, it left a tiny hole in the bag's side compartment to get at crumbs remaining in an old food pouch, she shoved in there out of convenience and forgot to dispose of.

Usually, Sadie's ultra-efficient when it comes to these types of things. She painstakingly re-purposes items until they literally fall apart and are no longer useful, and then, she's careful with their disposal. When things wear out or can no longer be used, she shreds and buries the garbage, allowing it to decompose over time. She does so now with most of the remaining wrapper and thoroughly checks the rest of her pack. The hole isn't ideal, but it's not bad so she slings her pack over a shoulder, adjusts the straps, and gets moving.

Still leery from her poor decisions the evening before, as well as itchy from a few bug bites, she moves with the utmost of caution. She finds relief in leaving the narrow peninsula and mentally notes the sensation it elicits before dismissing it just as quickly as it arrived. Making it back to the main section of the island, Sadie's not sure of the best route to take. She stands atop the remnants of what was once the tallest ridgeline in an expansive series and thinks it might follow the entire eastern coast but, further along, it could become impossible to descend. If so, she'd have to backtrack all the way to where she climbed up the day before.

Continuing along it, she decides the advantage outweighs the risk, especially since the ridgeline provides views both inland and along the coast. It's densely forested, providing excellent cover, and she can chart the unfamiliar land below. Throughout the day, Sadie stops regularly to add new details to her evolving map of the island and she hopes the sun will again appear and open up the views, but she knows yesterday's sunshine was a rarity. As late afternoon nears, the ridgeline veers inland, matching the coastline, and then it begins to descend.

The ocean, still a steep drop beneath her, is astonishing. Massive sea stacks dot the view and Sadie's amazed at how much the landscape has changed since the earthquakes. Halfway down the slope—and of great concern—she detects the smell of smoke. Checking the wind direction, she decides it's coming from the canyon below. She scans the area with her binoculars, but is unable to locate its source. The slope she's descending dips into a box canyon, and from the looks of it, the entire area is bordered by extremely steep terrain.

Sadie knows the source of the fire must be found and more importantly, the people who lit it, but she's hesitant, concerned with staying undetected. She needs to find a safe location to better observe from, so, instead of descending further, she stays parallel to her current elevation and continues hiking around the south, and then the west side of the canyon. As she travels, Sadie also scouts possible areas to shelter for the night.

When she locates a grove of old growth, she quickly goes to work. Out of all of her gear options, Sadie chose the pack she carries specifically for this journey. Its larger, providing far more room for supplies, and it's incredibly versatile, offering several attachments called vectors, for what best fits her needs. For this journey she chose the day vector and is thankful to have it now. When removed, it's actually another self-contained backpack, only smaller, and perfectly sized for day hikes. Sadie keeps it supplied and ready, so when needed, the transition to it is fast.

Detaching it and strapping on her sleeping bag, Sadie hides the main pack in a group of trees sprouted around an old hollow stump that has an opening in its side just big enough for the pack to slide in and sit to one side, so it can't be seen. Sadie continues looking around the area and returns to the stump carrying two large flat stones. One of the stones she places inside, next to her pack, and the other, outside, behind a small gap in the decaying wood. Carefully, she lifts an edge of each stone and balances them on two sticks notched to angle together. From her pocket, she pulls out the small remaining corner of the food wrapper she saved, including bits of the crumbs that didn't get eaten the night before. She sprinkles them onto, and around, each angled stick, and then leaves.

Sadie scouts every possible location that might offer a better view of the canyon below, but she's unable to find the fire's location.

When the wind shifts, she loses the smoke's scent, and several areas, too steep to climb, force her to go further around. It's getting late and soon, she'll need a place to keep watch for the night. Resting with her back propped against a tree, she's made it nearly halfway around the canyon and decides the bit of view she has will have to suffice.

For hours, Sadie sits scouting with the binoculars until it's just too dark to see. Beginning to tire, she looks up one last time and immediately straightens, trying to focus her vision. Keeping her eyes glued to the spot, she lifts the binoculars, peering intently. A soft orange glow is barely detectable and Sadie marks its direction with a stick, then, she carefully moves through the dark. Slowly, she works, setting three more markers—each twenty to thirty yards apart—before returning to her original position.

She sleeps intermittently and each time Sadie wakes, relocating the fire takes precedence. After her second catnap, the fire's soft glow disappears entirely, and she never finds it again. With the approach of morning, Sadie closely rescans the area where the glow came from, but still failing to detect its source, she quickly heads back to where she hid the rest of her gear. When she arrives, she finds both stones have been knocked over. She checks her main pack, removes some food, and slides the bag back in its hiding place. Adjusting the angle and notches of the sticks, she resets the stones and heads back to the markers she placed the evening before.

Arriving at each marking stick, and in hopes of pinpointing where the fire might have come from, Sadie uses the directions of their placement to align her sight with what visual indicators the terrain offers. By the last stick, she at least has an idea of where to search and continues to circumvent the canyon. Traveling along the north slope, she reaches an area that opens up to a much better view. She rests to eat and notices a small puff of smoke.

Scanning the area below her, Sadie locates what she thinks could be the corner of a roof. She's amazed at the discovery and looks for a better position to spy from. From a closer location, Sadie's able to see most of the cabin and the area surrounding it. The home's construction is unique as three sides are built with giant redwood logs, while the back of it butts directly against the slope of earth behind the structure. The cabin's roof extends out from the slope it sits against and is covered in ferns, moss, and other small plants that succeed in blending it into the area. Although extremely old, it appears well maintained. Along with the dwelling, there are small outbuildings, many well-manicured paths leading in several directions, and what appears to be an extensive garden system.

The smoke, Sadie first noticed, is coming from an outside fire ring. Above it hangs a large cast iron pot and piles of wood are neatly stacked nearby under a covered structure also made from redwood logs. Sadie finds herself appreciating the craftsmanship of the home, shed, and other hand-hewn buildings, along with the usefulness of everything's layout. She gets the sense it's a peaceful place and holds to that notion, hoping Splitters won't appear, as the door to the cabin opens. An old woman emerges and goes to the fire, where she stokes the coals and adds a few items to the cauldron hanging above the flames. The woman moves with ease and wanders down a trail, carrying a basket.

Sadie wonders if there's anyone else around and keeps watch for the rest of the day. She only ever sees the elderly woman who continues going about her business. As night approaches, Sadie decides to get a closer look and make contact. She leaves her lookout spot and hikes the rest of the way into the canyon, trying not to make any noise. Sadie heads into the garden area before curving around a tiny greenhouse and as she nears the cabin, the woman suddenly opens the door and looks straight at Sadie, but instead of instinctually raising her crossbow, Sadie greets her.

"Good evening. Sorry to trespass, I saw your fire and hiked down. My name's Sadie...Sadie Mae Larkin," she says, standing there.

As the lack of response lengthens, the old woman smiles and finally speaks, "I know...I heard you comin' down the mountain before you veered into the garden." Stepping away from the doorway, she continues, "I figured you might be lost and not sure if it was safe. My name's Clara Jones. Join me for dinner. I got hot stew."

Sadie, feeling relieved and immediately at ease, sets her pack on the porch and follows the old woman, who takes the pot off of the outdoor fire and carries it to the cabin. Sadie, invited to enter, observes all of the home's quaint details, but it's the stonework along the back wall that draws her attention first. The craftsmanship is outstanding and Sadie walks its length, admiring it.

Clara smiles at the sight and enjoys the chance to share it. "It was a labor of love. My husband and I gathered every stone. It took us three years."

Sadie's impressed, "It's absolutely beautiful."

"Thank you," replies Clara, bustling about.

The stones at the base of the cabin's back wall are huge and sit between two boulders that were cut to make a solid wall face. There are arched passageways along the far right and left side, each with double wooden doors, hand-carved, and absolutely exquisite. An arched fire-place sits in the middle with equally impressive, intricate metal work that serves both in function and decoration. Two beveled glass doors encase the fireplace's opening and where they meet, an iron redwood takes shape. The art piece, outlined with incredible detail, sits brilliantly silhouetted by the glow and soft orange of the fire.

Clara is in the kitchen area on the right, where a hand pump is set in another stone masterpiece. The stone sink and counter tops sit underneath two large windows overlooking the garden area. In the corner there's an antique, large wood-burning stove that also heats the cabin but serves mainly for cooking. The floor beneath it and where the two walls behind it form a corner is also constructed of stone. The kitchen area is separated from the rest of the cabin by a large wood-slab island, serving both as a counter and table, and is surrounded by four handmade wooden stools. Hanging above all of it is an assort-ment of pots, pans, baskets of produce, and bunches of dried herbs.

Clara disappears into the passageway off the kitchen and returns with two wooden bowls and spoons, half a loaf of bread, and a couple of cloth napkins. She fills two mason jars from the pump and sets the table. Clara isn't sure why, but immediately she feels a connection with Sadie, sensing her like a long-lost family member. She's grateful for the company and for having someone to share a meal with and eagerly looks forward to some conversation.

Gesturing towards the sink, Clara speaks, "Please, feel free to wash up…then, let's eat. I'm hungry."

Sadie washes her hands and rinses her face before sitting down across from Clara, who ladles out two large portions of stew and then pauses briefly to give thanks. The food smells incredible and tastes even better. There are chunks of meat and plenty of fresh vegetables.

Clara watches Sadie enjoying the food, "It's the last of my venison. I got a dear last season. I smoked most of the meat and made jerky, but it rehydrates nicely in stews."

Sadie swallows a mouthful. "It's really good. Thank you for sharing."

"My pleasure," the old woman responds, before eating another spoonful.

For the rest of the meal, the two ladies eat in near silence. Both women observe each other without being intrusive, knowing soon they'll talk. As Sadie enjoys the comforts of the hot food, she tries to determine Clara's age. The woman's wrinkled and gray, her hands show a lifetime of hard work, but Clara sits with perfect posture and moves with ease and comfort. The wrinkles around her eyes deepen with every smile and her eyes twinkle with an ageless softness. Clara breaks off a piece of bread and hands the loaf to Sadie.

"It's a day old, but still pretty good. Tomorrow, I'm thinking of baking more…it's so good straight out of the oven, and…it makes the house smell so nice and inviting."

"It already feels that way," Sadie says, smiling while wiping the excess stew from her bowl with a chunk of bread.

Clara's smile widens as she watches her guest. "You can rest here tonight and…tomorrow, I'll give you the grand tour."

Sadie accepts the generous invitation. Clara washes the dishes and then swings a hanging teakettle over the hot coals of the fireplace. When the water boils, she disappears into the pantry.

"Mint or chamomile?" the old woman asks, returning with a cup in each hand.

"Chamomile, please."

They settle into rocking chairs near the fireplace, each with their hands wrapped around a steaming mug.

"Who's first?" Clara asks, looking into Sadie's eyes.

The smile on Sadie's face turns into a light chuckle and Clara's does the same. Since her host asked, Sadie answers.

"It's your home, so…the honor's all yours."

"Yes, but you're my guest." The old woman slides a small stool under her feet, leans back into her rocker, and sips her tea. Looking content, she finds joy in an evening of sharing tales with the woman across from her. Clara tries to remember the last time she enjoyed another's company, and really, she isn't quite sure how long it's been. In that moment, she realizes she's been alone for a really, really, long time.

Sadie, too, leans back in her rocker, contemplating where to begin. She wants to know and ask so much.

"Well, then...I guess," Sadie starts, "I'd like to know everything... everything 'bout you, this beautiful cabin, your canyon, what you grow...and make, how long you've been here, and...if there are...any others here, or...in the area."

SIXTEEN

The firelight twinkles in Clara's eyes while she shares her life story with Sadie. She's unusually comfortable sharing the details of her personal life with a total stranger and it amuses her to be this relaxed and at ease. Sadie enjoys watching the old woman and asks only a brief question here or there, seeking a clearer picture of what Clara describes. The old woman explains how she, and her husband, found the canyon, and were fortunate enough to make it their home. Their plan was to live off-grid, be self-sufficient, and then raise a family. Clara gets up and goes to the fireplace.

"We were blessed in every way…except with children. I guess… it wasn't meant for us." Clara refills their teas and sits back down. "As the years passed, we put our energies into the property, creating a beautiful existence for ourselves. We learned to produce everything we needed…and with each passing year, we left the canyon less and less. Eventually, we got to the point where we didn't leave at all. We were so happy…" Clara trails off growing quiet.

Sadie senses deep emotions lingering with Clara as they watch the flames flicker and engulf the burning wood.

After a while Clara continues, "One morning, my husband woke up with what we thought was a cold…he just couldn't shake it. After three weeks, we talked about leaving to see a doctor, but…we decided to wait. He was out in the garden…tryin' to help, but struggling. I came over to his side and he gave me the sweetest, most tender kiss, and told me he loved me." Clara takes a sip, then continues, "He said he was going to lie down for a while. When I came in later…to check…on… him," her voice catches, "he looked so peaceful napping in our bed. I made soup and bread…the smell of baking bread always called to him."

Clara leans back, closing her eyes while rocking her chair. "I should've known something was wrong when he didn't stir as the aroma filled the house. Normally, he couldn't keep his hands off it… half of it'd be gone by the time we'd sit down to eat." She chuckles with the memory.

"When everything was ready, I brought it to him in bed but…he… didn't…wake. Even though I knew he was gone…I still put my head on his chest to listen. I crawled in next to him and wrapped my arms around him for the last time." A tear escapes from the corner of Clara's eye and glistens slowly down her wrinkly check.

Sadie's heart aches. She knows how it feels to lose a husband. This time, Sadie gets up to pour more tea. When she hands Clara her cup, their eyes meet and in that brief moment, they share more than words ever can. Sadie sits back down and Clara picks up where she left off.

"The next morning, I dressed him in his best clothes and said my goodbyes. I buried him near our favorite redwood grove. After that...I...struggled."

Sadie understands all too well. When Markus died, she was a mess and came close to death herself. It took a long time to recover, and still, there are difficult times.

"How long has your husband been gone?" Sadie asks.

"Well, over the years we sorta lost track of time. We never kept the hour of the day, or the days of the week, but...we tracked seasons. The arrival of spring was our measure...that's when we moved out here...it's our favorite...everything looks so fresh and vibrant, new fronds uncurling on the ferns, the moss thickens, and the native flowers, oh...they're so lovely...especially the Queen's Cup and Trillium. Everywhere you look, things are brilliant and alive. This upcoming spring will be..." she pauses, attempting to calculate the math, "twenty-seven...twenty-seven springs without him."

"You've been here for twenty-seven years? Alone?" Sadie asks, shocked.

Clara's a little surprised, too. It's been a long time, but it went so quickly, the elder really hadn't thought much about it. A rush of thoughts, insights, and concerns hit Sadie all at once. It's like sitting across from an older version of herself—it could've been her future. She's been living alone for years—not quite as long as Clara, but still, for a substantial length of time. How long would she have continued living that way? Going day-in and day-out without sharing any thoughts or words with another soul. Sadie could easily have survived for decades just like Clara—that is—if Caleb hadn't appeared and changed everything.

The thought of Caleb reminds her about the Splitters and she wonders whether Clara knows anything about them. Her isolation could mean she's unaware they've returned and even worse, Clara might not know about them at all and what they're capable of doing. More than likely, Clara also doesn't know their home's an island or what's happened to the rest of world. Sadie's thoughts continue to avalanche and she realizes that, as much as Caleb disrupted her world, it was nowhere near how much Sadie could ravish Clara's.

If this kind old woman is unaware of the world's ugliness, Sadie can either let her continue living without that knowledge or be the one to share the grisly truth. Clara seems at peace in her home and what Sadie has to share could change it. She's at a loss and doesn't want to be responsible for bringing fear into Clara's life or somehow diminishing her happiness. Sadie, realizing she's getting ahead of herself, knows there's a possibility the old woman already knows and simply chooses to live carefree and unafraid.

"Twenty-seven years. Alone? That's...a long time. Do you have any family or friends that visit?" Sadie asks gingerly.

"Honey...I haven't got another person in the world. It's been me and the trees for just about as long as I can remember."

Sadie finds humor in the old woman's response and body language. Clara's a strong, proud, and resourceful lady who obviously doesn't shy away from hard work. Sadie thinks for a moment and decides on taking a different approach.

"I lost my husband too...and...been alone for years. You and I are...neighbors. I live several ridgelines over...and spend most of my days hiking around my property...but...this time I decided to explore a little further. It's the sanctuary of the forest...and wandering among the giant redwoods, that I love so much." Sadie sips her tea thinking carefully about her next words. "It was the smell of smoke that drew my attention and brought me here. I didn't know anyone lived around here and was surprised to find your cabin."

Clara knew from the start that her and Sadie were brought together and connected in some way. She feels strongly about it now, and not only understands Sadie's love of the woods, but also cherishes finding another woman who appreciates its splendor.

The old one shares more. "Lately, I haven't hiked much. I used to climb all over these slopes. My husband and I enjoyed findin' places with views of our canyon, but...after he died...it wasn't the same... and then...well...it's sure easier moving around down here. And there's always something to do...this place takes a lot of work."

Sadie doesn't doubt Clara's abilities for a second. The elder sitting across from her, looks more than capable of hiking everywhere and anywhere she pleases, and Sadie believes her intimate knowledge of the landscape and its features is still sharp.

"I hiked most of this area the last two days," Sadie starts. "There are lots of steep slopes and a few really treacherous spots. I came in from the southeast corner...headed west...wrapped around until I saw your place, and then...came down near the garden."

"Child..." Clara grins slightly, shaking her head from side-to-side, "you took the hardest possible route. You should have continued north from that corner. The slope becomes gentler and nearly levels before turning west and coming here. You went around the backside. The best way in and out of here is towards the northeast corner. That's how we used to bring in our supplies...back in the early days. The road was barely passable then...now...who knows?"

"No one uses the road?" Sadie asks, continuing her inquires.

Clara nods no. "We were the only ones. No one else lives anywhere close enough. But...I haven't been that way since the earthquakes. Too many trees fell. It's a disaster...needs a whole crew to clear it out. It took me years to clean up around here. I still feel like I'm recovering from that awful day. Besides...I'm not going anywhere and I don't expect any visitors."

"That...awful...day," the words echo across Sadie's mind. The mention of earthquakes ignites her subconscious and the image of Markus's twitching leg flashes, but she forces it to pass.

"Sadie," Clara begins, sensing her guest's hardships, "there's much the two of us...will...share, but it's late and I'm tired. Let's continue tomorrow, when it's my turn to hear your story and ask questions." She gets up, sets their cups in the sink, and adds more wood to the fire. She pulls out extra blankets and starts making a bed on the only couch. "Please, make yourself at home. What's mine is yours. We'll chat again over breakfast."

Sadie gets up to help. "Thank you, Clara...for everything. I left some belongings on one of the ridges, so it was easier to hike. I'm planning on gettin' up early to retrieve them, but then I'll return. Is it okay to postpone our chat until later?"

Clara pauses in front of Sadie, looking her straight in the eyes. "Do whatever you need dear...but please, come back. I have a feelin' we have much to discuss." She leans over Sadie, who's climbing under the covers and kisses her lightly on the forehead. "Goodnight child."

Sadie can't believe how comfortable and natural it is having Clara tuck her in and she wishes her host the same. Clara leaves the main living space and walks into her bedroom. She kneels at the edge of her bed and silently prays for the young woman in the next room. Crawling into bed, she feels blessed for the companionship and offers another heartfelt round of gratitude. This time, she gives thanks, believing a daughter, after all this time, has finally arrived.

SEVENTEEN

Sadie wakes to a stoked fire and a steaming cup of tea within reach. Clara's already up and bustling around the cabin. Sadie can't believe she didn't wake sooner, since it's rare for her to stay asleep whenever there's movement around. She sips the cup and watches the old woman.

Clara smiles, noticing Sadie. "Good mornin', child."

"Good mornin'. Thanks for the tea." Sadie takes another sip.

"I thought it'd be nice to have something hot before your hike. I've got fresh melon, a little bit of toast, and some honey. You hungry?"

"Sounds perfect," Sadie says, folding the blankets.

It's still early and Sadie's amazed that Clara's so full of energy, and asks if this is her normal routine.

The old woman responds through a giant grin, "Every day, my husband and I got up to watch the sunrise before startin' the day's chores. Sometimes…after…we'd go back to bed, calling it our mornin' nap. Now, it just depends. I sleep in more, but…today seems like a good day to be up before dawn."

They eat breakfast together and Sadie washes the few dishes they used. She inspects the sink's design as Clara comes to her side.

"My husband was genius. He hated how society wasted resources…he wanted to build a place to prove how simple living could be. Nothing here is ever wasted. Even our dirty water is collected, recycled, and re-used," Clara beams with pride.

"I can't wait to see everything," Sadie says, curious about the rest.

Clara's smile widens, "And I can't wait to show you."

Sadie grabs her daypack and picks up her crossbow. "I should be quick. I'll bring back some lunch," she says, lightly patting her weapon.

Clara, looking proudly at Sadie, responds, "I'm sure you will. Just be careful, dear."

With Clara's words, Sadie walks out the door with plans to hunt first and then retrieve her things. Slowly creeping through the forest and carefully listening to the surroundings, she hopes for quail, but knows they won't be on the wooded slopes. There's likely to be plenty of animals coming into the canyon, especially with the lure of such a delicious garden, and Sadie wonders where Clara found that deer.

As Sadie nears a dry creek bed, she stops, straining to detect a faint noise. Crouching behind a boulder, Sadie watches as a raccoon slowly walks down a fallen tree, jumps off, and starts digging in the dirt. It uncovers a couple of tubers and sits on its hind legs, eating. Sadie sites her target and shoots. The raccoon looks up then drops to the ground.

"Thank you...for your sacrifice," she says, before removing the arrow.

With hunting done, Sadie changes course and heads straight to her hidden belongings. She finds the area relatively quickly and checks both stone traps, finding both knocked over. The stone behind the stump reveals nothing, but to her surprise, a squirrel lies dead beneath the other. She can't believe her luck.

Never before has she caught a squirrel with a deadfall trap. Usually, it's a mouse or a rat, and occasionally a useless banana slug, which is an odd creature, huge and bright yellow, living only in the redwoods. Smashing one of them leaves a slimy mess that's nearly impossible to clean off. She heard ages ago their slime could be licked and eaten as a source of protein, but she's never needed to try it and she hopes to never have to.

Sadie removes her pack, checks it over, and heads out, carrying two animals. She can't remember smiling so much and finds herself getting more and more excited as Clara's cabin nears. She's grateful for the food shared with her and is looking forward to being able to repay the favor. Still unsure of what to tell Clara about all the changes she's learned of, Sadie doesn't worry, knowing instinctively it'll work itself out as her gut feeling is nothing but reassuring while approaching Clara's place.

The old woman, busy working in the garden, looks up as she hears Sadie return, "That was fast. I see you didn't come back empty-handed."

Sadie holds up the squirrel. "Lunch," raising the other arm with the raccoon, "and dinner." She sets the animals down and helps Clara. "I got the raccoon by the creek bed. The squirrel...a complete surprise...it was in one of the traps I set near my pack. I don't normally set many traps...I worry the animals could suffer...especially if it doesn't work perfectly. But something chewed on my pack recently, and...I didn't want to risk it. I found a couple nice, flat stones...and thought they were large enough to kill any size rodent, but...I guess they were big enough to also handle a squirrel."

Clara sets her basket down and picks up the raccoon. "It's perfect. I'm almost out of oil for the lanterns, and there's plenty of fat to render from this guy." She checks the fur pelt and turns to Sadie. "Well...I guess your tour will start with this."

Clara walks over to the garden's shed and Sadie follows. A small lean-to, attached to one of the shed's sides, serves as a separate work-station. The area's large enough to house a giant counter top and several cabinets. The space contains all the tools, apparatuses, and supplies that Clara, or anyone else, could need to butcher animals, carve bones, dry and stretch skins, and do leather work.

She hands Sadie a small metal basin, "There's a hand pump just below the kitchen window. Would you please fill this, 'bout... half-way?"

Sadie takes the container and returns quickly. Every item Clara needs has been laid out and is ready. The old woman disappears into the shed and returns carrying a small sage bundle.

"I grow it in the garden," she says, lighting one end and setting it in a stone bowl.

A dance of smoke drifts away as the patterns gently entwine before disappearing entirely.

"First...we cleanse," Clara says, as she moves her hands through the smoke in a washing motion, and then, brings handfuls of it to her face.

When she stops, Clara gestures to Sadie, who follows without hesitation. When Sadie's done, Clara takes the smudge bundle and lifts each animal to encircle it in smoke. Each tool is cleansed, in the same fashion, then, the smoking bundle is returned to its bowl. Before the first cut is made, Clara finishes the last preparation, with closed eyes.

"Thank you for the life you give us," she says, and after a pause, the old timer goes to work.

Sadie watches and listens feeling connected to Clara at so many levels. The old woman starts by expertly removing the pelts. Her hands are swift and sure of their movements, with a precision that comes from years of experience. She continues working, explaining the various steps, as well as how she'll use all the different parts so nothing will be wasted. When both animals are soaking, separately, in their own brine solutions, Clara washes her tools. She finishes by cleaning the area with water from the shed's rain barrels. As the last of the sage turns to ashes, she purposefully pours the dirty water between a couple of plants.

Leaving the shed, they head to the outdoor fire pit where a small fire is already burning, and the coals are ready for cooking. Clara rubs a mixture of fresh herbs into the squirrel meat and stuffs the carcass with more. She uses a piece of sinew to secure it before slow roasting it on a spit. She skewers the organ meat and fresh vegetables and also places them over the fire.

As the two ladies sit on the porch eating another meal together, Sadie lets the morning's wisdom soak in. The woman next to her is a master of resourcefulness and is skilled in a myriad of ways. Her garden is spectacular, well-tended, and a model of sustainability. It's perfectly designed and obviously the result of years of trial and error.

Clara possesses a true passion for the art, and the simple—yet utterly brilliant—watering system and the homespun version of aquaponics, complete with tiny steelhead swimming about, is incredible. The descendants of spawning trout that Clara rescued decades ago from the nearby stream produce waste, which supplies nutrients to the plants, while they, in turn, purify the water. It's still a battle keeping the fish safe from hungry raccoons, but—Clara's right—her husband was genius. The old woman beamed with pride explaining its design, capabilities, and natural flow while picking ingredients for their meal. Sadie could see the love Clara still feels all these years later, and without a doubt, in that way, her husband's still here, in the canyon with her.

They continue nibbling away at a truly delicious lunch while washing it down with fresh squeezed lemonade, sweetened with honey—Clara's honey, since she also keeps bees and produces a few products from them. It'll take Sadie years to gain Clara's skills and to learn all she has to teach and the young woman looks forward to it. Sadie can't help but wonder how different things could have been if they'd met sooner. Sadie doesn't always understand why things happen, but she's beginning to sense there's indeed a higher purpose and for whatever the reason, now's the time their paths were meant to cross.

With lunch finished, Clara speaks first. "I've been adding to my list of questions for you. But first, I thought I'd finish giving you the tour…then, over dinner, we'd get back to your story."

Sadie swallows the last of her drink. "Sounds wonderful."

For the next few hours, Clara bounces with excitement, getting the opportunity to share more with Sadie, who's just as excited. The old woman has the energy of a little girl, moving from location to location, explaining how things were developed, built, and used. Everything has a story and she shares most of them.

Clara estimates that her homestead is currently seventy-percent operational, as compared with its height of efficiency and production. Losing her husband, and his helping hands, made it difficult, and not just emotionally, but physically, as well. What efforts used to be split by two were left only to her. And then, the earthquakes took their toll. They destroyed quite a bit, requiring several years worth of work by Clara, and a few things never recovered.

As the day continues, Sadie's impression of Clara only strengthens. Sadie's so engaged in absorbing everything that Clara says, she doesn't get the chance to put a lot of thought into what she should tell her tonight. It's nearing dinnertime, and soon it will be her turn to share and answer questions. Sadie has no hesitations in regards to telling Clara the most intimate details of her personal life. In fact, she looks forward to sharing them. What she struggles with is whether or not to share the news of the changed world with Clara, knowing it could disrupt the woman's entire outlook on life.

The two women work side-by-side throughout the kitchen and pantry preparing dinner, and one would think they'd been at it for years. The table is set and they're enjoying homemade persimmon wine while putting the finishing touches on their meal. It looks like a holiday and for Sadie and Clara, it is one—they're celebrating life and the discovery of each other.

They start with fresh greens and sprouted seeds, topped with sun-dried tomatoes and a light herb dressing, accompanied with hot bread and honey. The main course is slow roasted raccoon with carrots, potatoes, onions, and lots of garlic. The meat falls from the bone and is seasoned to perfection. Clara jokes that it's extra tasty because, more than likely, it's the same coon that's recently eaten a few of the larger steelhead from her fishponds, leaving behind only the little ones.

Throughout the entire meal, Sadie catches herself making sounds of pure delight while enjoying the gourmet meal. Clara, finding it both amusing and charming, only smiles and nods in agreement. They decide, with their first bite, to save talking for afterwards. The meal is too spectacular and deserves their full attention and gratitude. For dessert, they enjoy persimmons that drip juice down their chins. When they finish, and everything's cleaned, they settle into their rocking chairs, holding tea and silently contemplating the day.

About halfway through their first cup, Sadie begins. She explains her growing up in the woods with her family and the childhood she spent learning all about the forest and how to live in the mountains. She shares stories about her father and all the lessons and skills he passed on. When she talks about the accident that took her brothers and mom, Clara's eyes water. Sadie shares the struggles faced in coming back home to help, and then returning years later, to live on the family's property with her husband.

When Sadie gets to the earthquakes and how Markus died, both women shed tears. Clara sensed Sadie's strength from the start, but now she's learning how strong Sadie truly is, and can't believe the amount of grief, and sorrow, the young woman has suffered. Clara understands the struggles Sadie faced after losing a husband and feels bonded by their suffering. When Sadie finally reaches the part of finding Clara, the old woman asks her first question.

"I've felt your joy...sorrow...and pain, in everything you've shared, and I thank you for that. It's very special for me to have you come into my life. I want you to know that you've got a home with me anytime you need...or want, and that...I already consider you family." She pauses. "So...with that said, there's something I'd like to know. Last night, and a couple times today, you seemed...preoccupied. You said you were hiking to explore, yet...you're prepared for much more and using extreme caution. Yesterday...some of the questions you asked, seemed to lead me...down a particular path...somethin' you're interested in, but don't want to ask." Clara turns to face Sadie, clasps her hand, and finally comes to her point. "What I want to know...is...what you haven't told me."

Sadie looks into Clara's eyes and sees the woman for who she is, kind-hearted and honest. A seeker of knowledge, wisdom, and—above all—truth, and Sadie isn't going to be the one to keep it from her.

EIGHTEEN

Sadie contemplates how to begin the daunting task that lies ahead. In order to update Clara, she'll need to know the extent of the old woman's knowledge. So, Sadie starts by asking more questions.

"Before, I tell you…everything…can I ask…a few more things? It'll help me figure out where to start."

Clara nods, giving Sadie the go ahead.

"Have you left your canyon since losing your husband…or had any visitors?" Sadie asks.

"I haven't gone anywhere, besides around here, but…about… three…or four years after my husband passed…I did meet…a couple out hiking. They were young…and in love. We enjoyed a day together…then camped. We had so much fun…I invited 'em here… and…it became a regular thing. Usually, around summertime, they'd return, bringing small gifts and fillin' me in on current events, but…as time passed, I saw them less. Eventually…they stopped."

"How long has it been since you've seen them?" Sadie asks, intrigued.

"O' jeeze, at least…sixteen, maybe seventeen years, but…could be longer."

Just as Sadie thought, Clara's lived isolated for almost two decades, without any knowledge of the outside world. Sadie takes a depth breath, organizing an outline of events, and starts by briefly explaining global warming: it's effect on climate, the melting ice caps, and ocean acidification. She accounts for years of extreme weather patterns, using terms such as super storms, arctic blasts, killer cells, polar vortexes, and weather whiplash. Sadie speaks of record-breaking hurricanes, tsunamis, fires, and droughts, while Clara sits silently, absorbing everything, until Sadie pauses.

Clara, barely audible, speaks while gazing upward. "You knew." She turns back to Sadie, who's confused by the comment. "All those years ago, my husband worried about the planet. He was convinced we were ruining things…what upset him even more…no one seemed to care, and obvious abuses went ignored. Living here was…his solution. He thought people could live simply, work with nature and…

escape the cycle of destruction humanity seemed set upon. Our canyon home was an ever-evolving experiment...and, eventually, his proof...of...a better way." Clara fades into a long silence.

Out of respect, Sadie waits until Clara looks ready, and then she continues with her personal account. "I'd just finished my graduate degree when the ocean's started rising. At first, it was gradual, measured in inches and feet...at beaches around the globe. The levels were reported and charted weekly. You could check 'em like the weather... or tides...but...from the start, it didn't feel right. Somethin' was wrong...it nagged at me and filled my dreams. A sense of...urgency just...kept gettin' stronger, until...I knew...I needed to go home and return to our mountains."

Clara shifts in her chair as Sadie continues. "Markus and I decided to move back to my family's property. He had a huntin' trip with my dad planned and...we figured he'd share the news then, and...when he got back...we'd start the move. While he was away...and in the middle of the night, my...trepidations...intensified...I couldn't ignore them, or sleep, and it forced me out of bed."

Sadie swallows, and then continues. "At first, I tried to placate my fears. I rationalized that...my feelings...were just gettin' the better of me, 'cause I was alone. But I knew I had to go...so...I packed a few bags, grabbed what I could, and started the drive home. I had a long night ahead of me, and all I kept thinkin'...was how they'd react with me suddenly showing up. I made great time and...just before sunrise an emergency announcement interrupted the radio. It warned of an eminent tsunami hitting the entire Pacific coast. The broadcast looped continuously, repeating the same information over and over...warning of the danger."

Sadie stops for a moment, letting the information settle before getting to the worst of it. "No one in the scientific community expected the severity of the phenomenon, especially on such a global scale. It wasn't just the Pacific that sent killer waves...but...mega-tsunamis, of unprecedented magnitudes, also traveled across the Indian, and the Atlantic. Three oceans, three tsunamis, and monstrous wave trains... accompanied by already higher water levels, made for something... the world...had never seen. They called it the Tri-nami...and the intensity of the catastrophe caught the world's population off guard and unprepared."

Clara, in near slow motion, shakes her head dumbfounded by the information, unable to visualize the extent of what she's hearing.

Sadie, returning to her testimony, tells about the events she experienced on that catastrophic day. "When a live news bulletin began, I got off the road…pulled into a parking lot and found video coverage on my phone."

"What? Phones with…videos?" Clara asks, confused.

Sadie shakes her head, realizing Clara has no idea about the technological advances the world had seen by that time. "They were called smart phones. Pocket-sized…everyone had one. They could send instant messages, to anyone…all over the planet…take pictures, keep notes, organize a calendar, and of course…access the Internet."

The more Clara hears, the more confused she grows. "Inter…net?"

"The internet was…a global communication system…linking the world. Everything you can imagine was on it…all at the push of a few buttons." Sadie realizes there's just too much Clara's missed and it's impossible to update the old woman in one night. "But…we'll catch you up on that another time."

Sadie gazes at the woman rocking across from her. Earlier, Clara filled the role of teacher sharing her knowledge and now it's Sadie's turn—it's just too bad her subject is the world's destruction.

Getting back to her story, Sadie continues. "I knew I needed to act, and fast. There was a grocery store where I parked so…I jumped out… ran inside…and grabbed a bunch of carts. I loaded 'em with obscene amounts of stuff…moving armloads at a time…non-perishables, bottled water…whatever I thought we could use. By the time I lined up at the register, all kinds of people started runnin' into the store. News spread quickly…people panicked. It was eerie…shelves were cleaned out by the second. By the time I got back to my van, more cars were pullin' in."

Sadie feels a spike in her heart rate. It's not as intense as it was during the actual ordeal, but still, it reminds her of how scary and surreal it was. "Everywhere I looked, people were scramblin' to get their hands on goods or…driving to higher ground. I saw desperation… and panic…like I'd never seen before. That's when I realized…it was happening…the world was changin' and…the only thing I could do… was…go home."

Clara places a blanket over her legs, chilled to the bone by what's she's hearing.

Sadie takes a deep breath, steadies her nerves, and goes on. "The images from that day...I could never have prepared for. If I hadn't left when I did...I would have died. When it hit our coast...San Diego, LA...San Francisco...all...disappeared...destroyed by the ocean...and our tsunami...although, a record-setting monster...was the weakest of the three."

Clara's hands tremble lightly as they rest crossed over her chest. The news is horrifying and hard for her to grasp. Thinking about the destruction, she turns her attention back to Sadie.

"You were smart to act so fast...it's a good thing you listened to your instincts. If not...we wouldn't be talkin' today." Clara leans over and squeezes Sadie's hand.

Sadie appreciates the validation, but it doesn't help to make the story any easier to tell. "When I got home...to the safety of higher elevations...my dad and Markus weren't there...I feared they might've left the area...or gotten trapped someplace...or...worse, but...thankfully, they hiked in...unaware of what was happening. For as long as we could, the three of us kept up with the news as it developed."

Sadie pauses as Clara sits—staring into the flames—slowly rocking her chair. When Sadie doesn't continue the old woman turns to her.

"Go on child...what else?" the elder encourages.

Sadie swallows, and reveals more. "All around the world...complete annihilation...the Tri-nami's wave's...nicknamed *Enders*, lived up to their names...instantly ending lives, cities...even entire countries. In the wake of the massive deaths, the water never retreated...in fact...it continued to rise, even faster. The planet...swallowed...us... and...humankind suffered."

Sadie feels drained from sharing such exhausting circumstances, but there's more Clara needs to know, so she continues. "Over a billion people lived in low-lying coastal regions...and...on initial impacts, the tsunamis instantly killed most of 'em...tides full of bodies...all over...washed ashore. It was the largest recorded death toll in history..." Sadie, feeling ill, hesitates, trying to regain her composure.

"Casualties were re-calculated daily and continued to rise... it seemed the world was truly at its end. People...fortunate enough to survive the worse-hit regions were forced to migrate inland and upward. Massive refugee camps sprung up, but...there wasn't enough space, food, water…or sanitation to keep up with the influx. By the time the water finally stopped rising, almost twenty-five percent of the world's population was gone. All the coastlines…shifted… the entire planet was…re-shaped."

Clara, hearing the fate of mankind and all she's missed, is in shock, and she struggles with formulating a question.

"So…the…world…as…I…know it…is no longer?"

Sadie can only nod. When Clara looks ready for more, Sadie continues.

"The Tri-nami created massive power outages but…for a short while, some news was available. The footage and stories were horrific and…the images of the disaster were repeatedly exploited…and burned into…our minds and souls. Massive, floating piles of debris and dead bodies…San Francisco, completely submerged. Entire states vanished under the water…the East Coast was…lost, along with most of the Midwest. Out here, we held up a little better, and parts of Northern Cal, Oregon, and Washington survived…" Sadie pauses, struggling with being the bearer of such ugly news.

Knowing Clara wants to hear it all, Sadie doesn't stop. "People were exposed to starvation, disease…and crime. As supplies diminished, brutality rose. The desperate…seeking anything to survive… destroyed homes and businesses. Martial law was attempted, but… there wasn't enough resources and corruption ran rampant. And…it only only got worse. The first winter set new extremes and killed off the majority of people livin' in camps. They were too weak, too sick, and too hungry to fight death." Sadie remembers feeling helpless, yet fortunate, during those times. She survived simply because their land was spared and her father was so prepared.

"When spring arrived, the county was in a complete state of turmoil. Valuable agricultural land was lost…most crops didn't get planted and…the ones that did…struggled, as a major drought set in. What food was grown didn't supply the masses…riots erupted, until…they were no longer riots, but…small wars in just about every surviving city."

Clara's hand moves over her heart and she closes her eyes. Sadie knows this is hard on the woman and that, sometimes, knowledge comes with a hefty price. When Clara opens her eyes, Sadie goes back to divulging more of the devastating truths.

"Not much remained of our government...but...a small faction... lead by a former, top-leading official...spilt-off and created a new regime. The first thing they did was expose a huge underground facility in Colorado where...remaining government agents had secretly relocated. They stockpiled enough supplies for tens of thousands of people, but...kept it to themselves. Only the elite members of our government and society...along with their families...and a small force of armed soldiers protecting them, had access. Our surviving troops served as their private protection and the group...that split-off... exposed their corruption and brutalities."

"The faction...or Splitters, as they were called...raided the facility, took over...and put themselves in power, calling for a new Nation. At first, people thought they'd help, but...they were even worse."

As it gets later, Sadie wonders how much more the poor woman can handle. "Do you want to stop for tonight?" she asks, checking on Clara.

Clara looks straight at Sadie. "No, I think I need to know what else you have to share."

Sadie takes a deep breath and shares her first experience with the Splitter Nation's militants. She tells the entire horrific story, leaving out none of the brutal details. It's a struggle sharing the events of those few days and Sadie's forced to pause several times. When she gets to the part of her dad getting shot and then dying, Sadie can barely control her breathing.

Clara slowly gets up, goes into the pantry and returns with two glasses and a bottle. She pours each of them a small amount and hands one to Sadie. "I need a drink...and...it looks like you do, too. It's scotch, aged for...decades."

The drink soothes and warms Sadie's throat, giving her enough of an edge to continue.

"After my dad passed...Markus and I stayed home. We were in mourning, and...the experience with the Splitters...changed us. Then...shortly after, San Andreas dealt the last blow...the quakes... took him...and...left me...alone."

Sadie downs the rest of her scotch and to Clara's surprise, pours them another, before telling the old woman all the grim details about her husband's death. Then—when she's able—Sadie continues with finding Caleb, the Splitters he killed, and the news he's shared.

"We're...on...an...island?" Clara says, shocked by the revelation Sadie shares.

"Yeah, surprised me too. I'm checkin' it out for myself...that's why I'm travelin' now. When I smelled the smoke from your fire, I thought it might be more Splitters."

Sadie gets up and retrieves something from her pack. She returns with her map and spreads it out on the small table between them.

"This is what I've got so far." Sadie points with the end of a pencil, "Here's my property," she moves her pointer, "and where I found Caleb." Then, slowly tracing her route, she continues, "I traveled along the south coast, then up your canyon...I'm planning to finish this side...then explore the entire northern territory." Sadie taps a light rhythm with the eraser end of her pencil. "The Splitters must be up there."

"May I?" Clara asks, motioning to Sadie's pencil.

Sadie nods, passes it to her, and Clara fills in the details of her canyon and that of the ridges to the west and north. The east coast, Clara isn't sure about and she leaves that area blank.

Pointing in that direction, she looks back up at Sadie. "Tomorrow...after breakfast, I'm hiking out there. Care to join me?"

"I'd love too," Sadie replies.

"Then, let's turn in for the night...we can get back to it in the morning."

They stare at the map for another few moments before getting up, and then Sadie and Clara embrace in silence, comforting one another from the emotions of the evening. They're both tired and emotionally drained. Saying their goodnights, they leave each other's company and go to bed. This time, Sadie kneels before her bed saying a small prayer for Clara, knowing the old woman will struggle finding sleep.

NINETEEN

Clara's up extremely early, feeling it was more of a short nap than a goodnight's sleep, but she's anxious to start the day. Both women eat a small breakfast, preparing for the day's journey. With their travel bags packed, they head out with Clara in the lead, and Sadie's surprised at the pace the old woman keeps. The elder hikes in a pair of homemade moccasins, accompanied by a twisted and gnarled walking stick worn smooth from years of use. She carries her water, food, and supplies in a leather satchel and rarely pauses.

They travel towards the northeast corner, where the route is the easiest to traverse. As they near it, the slope on each side grows steep and the canyon narrows. The women make their way among tangled masses of fallen trees that cover their path, and as the mess grows thicker, Sadie stops to offer Clara a hand while they maneuver through the branches of a monstrous fallen madrone. The old woman looks at Sadie with a glimmer in her eyes.

"Honey…you don't need to worry 'bout me. I've been doin' this my whole life, and…I don't plan on stoppin' any time soon," Clara says, while working her way through the tangle.

Sadie laughs, hoping to be as agile in her old age, and once beyond the downed tree, they find the former road is barely detectable. Along its side parallels a dry streambed full of boulders and decaying logs. As they hike, Clara shares details of the area, pointing out key features, the places she and her husband hiked, hunted, or just spent time enjoying a picnic. They make their way farther out of the canyon and Clara stops at a spot that offers a view.

"Over there," she points with her walking stick, "is where you hiked in and the route you took to my cabin." While talking, Clara traces the path Sadie described, "If you would've continued just a little further north, you would've descended here and been able to follow the route we're takin' now."

"Clara, from that ridgeline," Sadie points, "before, I hiked down… I was able to see the coast."

The old woman nods. "I thought we might be gettin' close."

Deep in thought, they walk the rest of the way in silence. Recently, both women's lives have changed in ways they never imagined. The knowledge they've gained has altered their existence forever and it's still evolving in ways yet to be known. The road they're attempting to follow deteriorates to the point where they can no longer use it, forcing them to continue in the creek bed. As the lighting ahead grows brighter and the trees open, both women anticipate the view.

"Oh…my…lord," Clara gasps, taking in the sight.

The creek bed ends abruptly, dropping over fifty feet to the ocean below. In the sea, directly across from them, a giant, forested sea stack juts out of the ocean. Even through the marine layer, they detect more stacks to the north and south. Clara clutches her heart and bows her head. When she looks up again, she turns to Sadie.

"Child, I knew you spoke the truth…you told me what to expect, but…I had to see it with my own eyes. Now that I have…it's…it's…" Clara trails of, at a loss for words, and Sadie sympathizes with the poor woman.

They stand in silence, until eventually, Clara breaks it. "I've lived here happy…for a long time…in my canyon…away from everyone. I never missed the rest of the world. But…now that…it's gone…I feel like…I took it for granted. I'll never get that back. I always expected it to be there…and now…it's too late."

Clara, distraught with her own insights, sits down on a giant stone and gazes below. Sadie sits next to her but says nothing. What can she say? There isn't any comfort to offer and it's something Clara will have to come to terms with on her own. Sadie watches as her companion picks up a rock and tosses it over the ledge. It falls to the water, leaving a small ripple on the smooth surface below, and they watch the rings glide across the water, until disappearing altogether.

"Get out your map, let's take a look." Clara suddenly says.

Sadie, caught slightly off guard by Clara's change of demeanor, does so quickly. The two women hover over it, studying the detailed area and what still remains unknown.

Clara puts her finger on their current location and moves it while speaking, "It's too steep to climb here, but…if we back track, we can head up the dry ravine and get a better view from above. Depending on what we find…we can decide how much farther to explore and record. Then…we can follow this ridgeline to where another ravine descends into my canyon."

Sadie agrees and instantly they're up, retracing their steps. Their ascent is cautious and they help one another up the rocks and boulders in the mountain's wash. At one point, it served as a major drainage artery and Clara talks of the days when it ran thick with water during the winter months. Now it's dry, sandy, and full of decay. By the time they reach the top, it's early afternoon and neither wants to stop long. They eat quickly before continuing along the ridgeline and mapping the coast until the terrain changes and a decision needs to be made.

"Wha d'yah think?" Sadie asks, curious to what Clara's thoughts are. " Follow the coast, or…head back along the ridgeline?"

Clara stares long and hard at the view ahead. She scans the coastline, looks towards her canyon and then below, to where the land continues north and west. She points towards the next few ridgelines. "Let's continue, then…find a place to camp…so we can explore more tomorrow."

Sadie's glad to hear these words from the old woman. She wanted to continue but knew, if Clara had been set on returning home, she would have accompanied her, instead she nods, and they move on. As evening approaches, the women find a place to spend the night, and Clara begins building a fire as Sadie argues strongly against it.

"Come on child, look at the wind direction. It'll carry any smoke directly out into the ocean, where there's no one. On top of that, there hasn't been a single sign of anyone in the area…and that's since I've lived here. Plus, the only Splitters were on the other side of the island and…they're dead. If others traveled this far, and…by some chance… are nearby, they would've set up camp and built a fire long before we did, and…we would've detected it."

Clara pauses, letting Sadie absorb the information. She knows her logic and charm are winning the debate. "Besides, I'm an old woman. I hiked all day and plan to do so again tomorrow. I wanna rest and warm my old bones."

Sadie chuckles while shaking her head. "Clara's good," she thinks. The woman's points, remarks, and grandmotherly way would make it difficult for anyone to disagree. At this point, Clara is all smiles. She knows she's getting her way and without pause, returns to starting a fire. With a warm blaze to sit by and food in their stomachs, Clara unfurls her bedroll next to Sadie's and settles in.

"I tend to fall asleep quickly out in the fresh air, but wake me if you need to. Goodnight dear." Clara says, rolling over.

Sadie stays awake, scanning the area and keeping watch. She adds more wood to the fire, even though she still feels uncomfortable taking the risk. The warmth and gentle crackling is soothing, though. She looks at Clara and smiles. The old woman is sound asleep, peacefully resting in the soft glow of the fire and her old bones do look warmed.

Sadie decides to lie near Clara and makes herself comfortable. She too falls deep asleep and is surprised when she wakes just before morning. She slept through the entire night and is well rested. As the darkness fades to light, both women pack up their belongings and cover the evidence of their presence. When Sadie is satisfied with the efforts, they head out with Clara once again leading.

The exertion from the day before doesn't slow Clara down a bit and Sadie's amazed at the old woman's stamina and energy. She's fit, and even pushes the pace, allowing them to explore as much as possible. The morning passes peacefully and again, they rarely pause. By mid-day, they need to change course in order to head back to Clara's canyon. Before they set out to return, both women stop and look at one another. They stand in silence sharing similar thoughts and concerns. As the silence lengthens, Clara knows it'll have to be her decision.

"It's okay." Clara says. "I'll head back…you should continue. I'll see you at my place…lets say…tomorrow, before dark."

Sadie disagrees. "Clara, I'm not going…"

Before she can finish, Clara holds up her hand and shuts her eyes. Opening them, she speaks softly. "Sadie Mae Larkin…"

Sadie feels about eight years old at the mention of her full name. How does Clara do it? This woman, whom she just met, is able to simply melt her, using a few words and subtle looks. Sadie can only acquiesce and listen to what Clara has to say.

"We both know you can cover a lot more ground alone and…"

Sadie interrupts, trying again, "Clara, we've been keepin' a great pace and …"

"Sadie, let me finish," Clara warns.

"Yes ma'am."

"I know you can run these ridgelines…doubling our coverage… and fill in a lot more of the map. We need to know what the rest of this area has to offer…and…if the Splitters made it to this side. This is your chance to cover a new section…without having to backtrack and return later. Finish it up…then come back to my place. You can fill me in, rest overnight, and then…return to Caleb."

"Clara, we both know it's safer to stay together," Sadie says, knowing Clara can't argue with the age-old wisdom of her statement.

"True, but think how absurd that is? It doesn't apply to us. We've been at this…alone…long enough, to know our limits. We know what we can handle…and this…we can handle…easily. I'll be home by nightfall, and…if for some reason, it takes longer, I'll camp and return first thing in the morning."

Sadie remains quiet. She wants, and needs to continue, yet she feels responsible for Clara and could never forgive herself if something happened to the elder.

Clara steps closer to Sadie and wraps her in a giant hug. She holds her tight for a moment, and then speaks softly, "Ooh, child, your concern touches my heart. You've brought me such joy, but please…don't worry. It's okay. Now…stop wastin' time and get this done," she says, as they break from their embrace.

Sadie straightens her shoulders, looks Clara in the eyes, then turns and jogs off. Clara watches her move with an upwelling of pride. After a moment, she, too, turns around and heads out, only her pace isn't anywhere near a jog.

TWENTY

Clara stretches, reaching down with her leg for the next step while clutching a piece of a twisted and gnarled root ball. Releasing one hand, she braces it against another boulder for support. She's making excellent time and should be home by evening. It's the thought of home, a hot meal, and a nice cup of tea, sitting fireside, that fills her thoughts. She and Sadie covered a lot of ground, and the old woman looks forward to relaxing. She isn't getting any younger, and her body's feeling it.

Before she secures her footing, the root snaps. In that split second, her focus shifts back to where it should have been in the first place, but it's too late. Her foot slips, she instinctively reaches out, and goes down—really hard. Her leg twists and sinks to mid-thigh between two large stones. Immediately, Clara knows it's bad, as pain shoots through her body. She drops her chin, closes her eyes, and stays silent curled with pain, trying to gather her senses. Breathing carefully, Clara reminds herself to stay calm. She dismisses any feelings of panic, gets an idea of what could be wrong, and stays still.

Slowing her breathing, she mentally scans her body before attempting to move. With a better sense of the situation, Clara opens her eyes, while slowly inhaling. The throbbing pain in her leg is her greatest concern, but her hands and forehead also hurt. Making sure not to do anything to worsen her injuries, she gazes down, inspecting the affected leg. It's wedged between the rocks, but not stuck. Before removing it, and with her hand, Clara touches her forehead, feeling a small sensitive bump. She didn't think it struck that hard, but to her astonishment, there's blood. Checking again, she realizes that both hands are bleeding from a patchwork of small scratches on her palms and fingers, so she wipes them on her pants, and re-examines the bump.

"Thank god," Clara murmurs, her forehead isn't bleeding, and the blood is from her scratched hands. She re-examines her palms and fingers, determines their injuries are minor, and then turns her focus back to the painful leg. She cautiously removes the limb from between the rocks and recovers to a seated position to evaluate the damage. There's a large tear in her pants where blood is darkening the material and dripping down her leg, but she's able to move both it and her foot. Clara feels along her femur, even though she knows it's not broken. Then, she checks her knee. It's a little tender, but nothing seeming serious. Even with the pain, she continues feeling along the lower bones. It's the gash, continuing to bleed, where it hurts the worst. Nothing below the knee seems broken, and Clara gives a moment of thanks for the blessing.

Suddenly slipping, and then twisting between two stones, is a brutal combination for any fall. The shear force could have snapped both the tibia and fibula, leaving her stranded, alone, and in dire condition. She rolls up her pants' leg to better gauge the extent of her injury. The blood makes everything look worse, but the gash is rather severe. It's deep, running along the fleshy area of her leg, just below, and to the left, of the knee. From there, it curves towards her shin and then, it runs straight down, exposing the bone for a few inches.

Clara opens her satchel, finds what she needs, and begins cleaning the wound. The more she cleans, the more grateful she becomes. The realization of how scary this situation could have been humbles the old woman. Along with the humility comes a fluttering in her stomach and heart, reminding her that she should've been more focused. With most of the blood wiped away, Clara's able to get a better look at the tear, and she grimaces. It hurts like heck, and it throbs while she picks at the skin collected at the bottom, where it scraped along the rock. It's scrunched together where the last of the tissue remains attached. As she works around the area, Clara thinks it looks like old paint, scraped clean off.

When she finishes cleaning and bandaging her wound, Clara returns everything back to her bag and examines her options. There's no chance of getting home before dark, especially since the journey back will be slower. She needs to figure out what to do for the night and shifts her attention back to the surroundings. Clare sees where the root snapped and her leg slipped. Slowly, rising to a standing position, she's relieved to find her leg can bear weight.

There's dampness where she slipped, and Clara examines it carefully, following its path while uncovering debris, until it ends in a small muddy puddle. Grabbing a flat rock lying nearby, she uses its edge to dig away some dirt, creating a small ditch. She works at removing loose soil until striking a larger rock stops her progress.

She deepens the tiny trough and as it widens, she wipes the partially uncovered stone's surface clean. Once satisfied with the work, she sits back and watches. A small drip runs from a crack in the rock, and drops into the dirt below, followed by another, and another. It's slow, but steady.

Clara removes a small wooden bowl from her gear and sets it below the drip. Looking around, she climbs down the ravine another ten yards, and stops atop a humongous boulder. It's flat and butts against another massive rock at its rear. Clara cleans off the surface and gathers fire-building materials that she can easily carry.

With a fire crackling, Clara sets about making a sleeping area. She collects a large pile of duff and carefully dangles it above the fire, balancing the material on a forked branch. When it smokes long enough, she covers an area of the stone with it and uncurls her bedroll over the padding. She removes a few hand-sewn leather pouches from her bag and stretches them as wide as they'll allow, before setting them near the fire.

She returns to her bowl, brings back the small amount of collected water, and heats it over the fire in a metal mug before tossing in a pinch of chamomile. It isn't exactly the fireside cup of tea she thought about earlier, but at least it offers some warmth and comfort. Using two sturdy sticks, Clara plucks single rocks from her fire and sets one into each of the pouches. When all of them contain a heated stone, they get placed near her body as the old woman settles in for the night.

Even though Clara knows she's going to be okay, the elder can't shake the realization that it was pure luck that saved her. Her leg should be broken, and it's a miracle that it's not. Intending to be more careful from now on, she knows the consequences of old age will require more consideration. Her body isn't as durable as it once was, even if her mind thinks otherwise.

Early the next morning, Clara wakes stiff and sore. She makes another cup of tea over the fire's remaining embers and packs her belongings. It wasn't the most comfortable night perched on a giant rock, but she did manage to sleep. As she prepares for the final leg of her journey, Clara scratches at two bites, one along her waistband and another in the crease at the back of her knee.

"Not as bad as it could be," she mumbles to herself.

At least the smoke evacuated most of the bugs from her makeshift mattress. Using a fingernail, Clara puts an X through both spots, and starts towards home. This time, she takes it slowly and more cautiously. Every step and handhold gets her full attention, as Clara refuses to let her mind wander, while descending what remains of the drainage artery. By late morning, her route joins the streambed that drops and runs through her canyon. She's anxious to get home and feels a little discombobulated with the pain and her error that caused it.

Some of the uneasiness lifts when the site of her home comes into view. The last of her travels end safely, and Clara heads directly into her cabin. At the door, she drops her bag, kicks off her shoes, and quickly starts a fire. She's ultra-efficient with every move, wasting neither time nor energy, heating water to bathe and getting dinner prepped.

She doesn't stop moving until settling into the washbasin where she pours hot water over her body, and relishes its warmth. Out of the tub and dressed in warm clothes, Clara checks the food. Its smell is wonderful, and the aroma fills the air as she lifts the lid to stir the pot. It's almost ready and while she waits, Clara cleans up her bath and repurposes the dirty water. As it gets closer to dark, Clara begins to feel uneasy again. The days are much shorter now, and maybe, she shouldn't have talked Sadie into venturing too far on her own. Clara, becoming extremely worried—which is something of an oddity for her—realizes it's been a long time since she's felt concern for another.

As the sky darkens, Clara moves from inside to out. She wraps a blanket around her body and sits on the porch's corner bench. Sadie should've been home by now and in her absence, Clara mentally runs through potential scenarios. The girl could have gotten hurt or lost. She could have traveled farther than anticipated and needed more time to get back. Or—something terrible—what if she ran into more Splitters? Clara's negative thoughts aren't helping, and she tries clearing her mind by getting up to make another pot of tea.

Blowing lightly on a steaming cup, Clara swings open the cabin door. Her head jerks up, followed immediately by the sound of shattering, as her cup strikes the ground, but the old woman steps right over the mess, and wraps her arms around Sadie. They stay embraced, even though Sadie's still breathing heavily, and her clothes are all sweaty. When they separate, both women notice the other's injuries.

"Clara what happened to your head?" Sadie steps closer, examining the bump. "And your hands?" she adds, noticing them.

"Me? What's wrong with your leg?" Clara asks, concerned.

Sadie glances at her ankle and looks back at Clara. "It's fine. I overdid it. I ran too hard, too far, and then, when I could barely see...I kept going. I almost waited until mornin'... but...I knew if I pushed, I'd make it...so...I did. I just took a bad step...that's all." Sadie, without pause, turns the focus back to Clara. "And...you?"

"A root I was holding snapped and...I slipped."

Stepping inside, Sadie removes her shoes and outer layers, while Clara gets her a drink of water, which gets downed immediately. Sadie eats and when finished, Clara has a hot bath ready for her. While soaking, Sadie realizes how sore she is, as the muscles in her legs ache, both feet throb, and her ankle is a bit swollen. The sprain is minor, but some of the scrapes surrounding it are stilling oozing a little blood. The injury occurred because what she thought was solid earth was actually layers of forest debris, and her foot broke through, snapping a couple sticks that jabbed into her flesh. One tore through the bottom of her pants, causing the most damage, but it's nothing that won't heal quickly.

With her wound and body clean, Sadie gets out of the tub and wraps up in an old, soft blanket, Clara set out for her. While Sadie dresses, the old woman bustles about, putting everything away for the night. Sadie comes over to Clara in the kitchen, puts an arm around her shoulders, and then starts helping with the dishes.

"I'll finish the last of these," Clara says, "and then...we'll sit by the fire. Go...go on, child...rest your feet. I'll be right there."

Sadie leaves the old woman's side and swings the teakettle over the fire. She finishes picking up her discarded things next to the door and stretches. Her body's abused, and Sadie knows she needs to start treating it with more care. Lately, she's been pushing too hard and her ankle serves as a reminder to be smarter about things. Clara settles into her rocking chair as Sadie pours each of them a hot mug, but instead of sitting down, Sadie drops to a knee.

"Alright, lady. Let me see that leg you think you've been hiding." Sadie says.

Clara slowly sets down the tea mug and pulls the blanket off her leg. Without speaking, Sadie checks it.

"Jeeze o' Petes, this girl is thorough," Clara thinks, as Sadie examines the knee, ankle, and leg, before uncovering the actual wound.

With it exposed, Sadie shakes her head lightly while looking for signs of infection. When she finishes, Sadie gets up, goes to her bag, and returns, carrying a small soft case. She opens its contents, inspects the items she removes, and then talks calmly, but with authority.

"You did more than just slip. From the looks of that shin you're lucky nothin' broke. I'm concerned about infection...especially, in the bone. If that happens, there's nothing we can do. But, we're not gonna risk it. You need to stay off it...at least a week...so it can heal. I mean it. This could have been bad. Also...I'm giving you these."

Clara's quizzical look says it all.

"They're antibiotics. Here, take these two now." Sadie hands them to Clara, followed immediately by the old woman's tea. "You need to take two more at the same time tomorrow, and then, one a day for the next three days."

Clara continues holding the meds in her hand and still hasn't spoken.

Sadie goes on, "It's important to finish the whole dosage. Each evening take 'em after you eat." Sadie looks at Clara, who is still holding the pills, and then, she raises her eyebrows just a fraction.

"Oh...you're good," Clara says, feeling like a child caught in a mother's gaze. She knows Sadie won't have it any other way, so she pops them into her mouth and swallows carefully. Holding the cup in two hands, Clara takes a second, and then a third sip from it.

"Good," Sadie says, finally sitting down, "Now, tell me 'bout your accident."

Clara folds her hands underneath the blanket that's draped over her lap, finds a rhythm in the rocking chair, and settles in for an evening chat. The old woman starts with sharing details of her return trip and accident, making sure to note the spring she literally stumbled upon. With Sadie's map out, Clara sees the freshly drawn areas as Sadie takes her turn explaining where's she traveled and Clara's astonishment grows. The girl covered an enormous section of land and Clara doesn't think she was ever capable of such a feat, even at the height of her youth and fitness.

Finished chatting, and before the two settle in for another much-needed night of sleep, they duplicate the map, so Clara has a copy. The elder woman plans to fill in some minor details missing from her area, and also intends to explore, at length, the potential of the newly discovered spring. These thoughts give Clara something to look forward to while waiting for her leg to heal. After saying goodnight, the women rest their tired and sore bodies. Both know there's much ahead to face, and as they close their eyes, they're filled with curiosity about what their futures hold.

TWENTY-ONE

Caleb wakes in a fog, unsure of his surroundings. Fumbling about, he tries to shake his uncertainties and as pain grips him, he's reminded of being in the cave waiting for Sadie. Scratching his itchy face, he isn't sure how long she's been gone. Everything's jumbled, and days are disappearing. Since her leaving, Caleb's divided time between sleeping and shooting morphine. Sometimes it's light and sometimes it's dark, when he wakes from slumber or from a drug-induced delusion.

Caleb, beginning to think more clearly, realizes he should keep better track of the passing time. With his realization comes another: he needs to use the bathroom, which entails having to move. Rolling onto his stomach, he makes it to his hands and knees, and painfully stands, only to discover that his bucket needs emptying. Pausing from an initial dizzy spell, he moves slowly, feeling feeble and absolutely terrible.

Attempting to lift the bucket, Caleb immediately sets it back down. The throbbing from his ribs feels as if he's still being repeatedly kicked. Keeping his torso upright, he bends from the knees and tries again. Getting the receptacle to the door is the easy part. His next challenge is moving it under the first log. Returning to hands and knees and trying to push the bucket becomes a mission in itself. By the time he reaches the latrine, Caleb's sweating and exhausted. After regaining his composure, he empties the waste container, uses the pit, and covers it all with a thin layer of dirt.

The smell from the dirty task, in conjunction with the painful exertion, makes Caleb nauseous, and he desperately tries fighting the urge to vomit, but failing, he finds each purge, intensifies his pain. Wiping his mouth, Caleb moves to the far side, away from the mess and smell. Taking a few cautious breaths of fresh air, he returns to trying to figure out how long Sadie's been gone. He really isn't sure, and the more he thinks about it, the more it doesn't even matter. She'll return when she's ready, and he's completely at her mercy.

Leaning against one of the logs, Caleb scans the surroundings. Everything looks peaceful, and normal, and he anxiously waits for the day when he'll be capable of walking about and exploring, or, at least, moving in a pain-free manner. Feeling thirsty and hungry,

Caleb wishes he brought food and water outside. Instead, he'll have to make his way back inside. He's eaten little and knows that part of his weakness is from lack of sustenance. Back inside, he drinks, emptying the canteen, and then, to refill it, Caleb realizes he'll need to boil more rainwater from the hanging collection bags. Using the spigot, he drains enough water to fill a pot and carefully sets it down, feeling faint. When the sensation passes, he grabs the hand generator, and taking a controlled, deep breath, Caleb prepares for what he knows is going to hurt.

Through clenched teeth, he pulls the cord multiple times, trying his best to limit twisting his torso. Sweat drips from his forehead as his body revolts against the movement. After several series of pulls, and profanities, Caleb plugs in the burner, sets the pot on it, and rests. The headache that started when he'd first gotten up is in full throttle now, and Caleb can't take any more of the pain. He goes back to his sleeping area to prepare another needle, but there's only a half-filled vial left.

Caleb, contemplating what to do, rolls the glass container across his hands. He really wants it, but he fights the urge and sets it down. He'll wait until after he finishes purifying the water and cooking. It'll be his reward. As the water boils, Caleb finishes prepping what he needs. Pouring half the water into another container to cool, he puts what's left back on the burner and re-charges the hand generator. This time, the effort nearly knocks him over. Placing his hand along the shelf, he catches his balance and rests his head against the wall. The pain won't subside, and he tries slowly breathing through the worst of it.

Trying to avert his attention away from the morphine, Caleb focuses on his hunger. When the food finishes cooking, he brings it to his bedding and lets it cool; then, he fills the canteen, and places it nearby, as well. Getting back into a seated position takes too much effort, and he nearly gives in to taking the awaiting dose. Instead, he focuses on the importance of eating. If he wants to regain his strength, and heal, he has to stay fueled. Taking his time, Caleb finishes the rice and beans, drinks a warm glass of re-hydrated milk, and then reaches for what he desperately needs. The morphine has an immediate effect, and he slumps over as it courses through his veins.

*   *   *

Caleb's body jerks as each round jolts his shoulder backwards. Gripping the rifle tighter, he fires while sprinting towards the cabin. He yanks open the door, partially ripping it from its hinges. Inside, his terror grows. There's blood everywhere and it leads to what he fears most. All three of them are dead. Dropping to his knees, he lifts her limp torso, pressing it to his. Suddenly, he's outside, running uncontrollably and shooting. Shots fire back, hitting nearby as he runs.

BANG! BAANNG! BAAA...NNNG! BAAAAAAANNNNNNNG! The firing's sounds stretch in length until they merge into a constant assault of monotonal noise. Momentarily conscience of everything, Caleb's find he's out in the open, and there's no cover. Panic stricken, and fearing for his life, he zigzags, but the terrain cracks as he pushes harder and faster. Suddenly, his arms are empty as he sprints weaponless. With each stride, chasms appear, and the ground begins to drop away. The earth shakes and he struggles to stay upright. A bone-shattering tremor erupts and he's swallowed in complete darkness, falling to a certain death.

Caleb's eyes open abruptly. He's not quite awake, and is completely confused. Blinking, he attempts to gather his senses, and turning his head, he sees Sadie re-charging the hand generator, but the image doesn't really register. Remaining disoriented, his eyes close briefly, and Caleb passes right back out.

*   *   *

This time, it's dark and cold, and Caleb's covered with blood. He crawls on his belly trying to get to safety, and the effort is just too great. The harder he tries, the slower he seems to go. As he stops to catch his breath, a nearby disturbance catches his eye. Suddenly, a man appears, and Caleb's terror heightens. It's a Splitter, with a knife raised, crashing towards him. Fluttering his eyes, Caleb breathes deeply, causing his pain to shatter the dream. All that remains is a series of fleeting images, as he succumbs to the fact that once again, he's awake and in pain.

The morphine's effect makes for uneasy sleeping, leaving him feeling weary. Lying perfectly still, he takes slow, controlled breaths and begins what he's decided is his healing therapy. It's his fourth or fifth attempt at it and so far, he hasn't done too well with it. Caleb starts by visualizing the fractures in his ribs and the remodeling taking place by his bone cells. He focuses on the healing, along the entire length of one rib, before moving to the next. Every time he loses focus, the image disappears, and he has to restart. It's a slow and tedious process, but each attempt provides a much-needed distraction, while, simultaneously, making him feel like at least he's doing something productive and, hopefully, helpful.

Working along another rib, Caleb loses his concentration, and struggles with regaining his focus. Something smells good, and he's amazed it didn't draw his attention earlier. He takes a cautious, long, but slow inhalation, relishing the scents and then, it clicks. Sadie's back! With his realization appears the image of her charging the hand generator. He looks over and sees her smiling.

"It's about time," she jokingly teases, moving to him with all kinds of goodies.

He smiles before rolling over onto his stomach and taking his all fours position. As he turns around to sit, Sadie helps. She hands him a steaming plate that looks and smells incredible. Caleb stares from it to her face, and Sadie giggles again. There's something different about her, and Caleb can't figure it out. He's struggling with comprehension and realizes that he's yet to speak.

"Wel...cum...back," he finally squeaks out, as random thoughts and questions try to take shape all at once. He looks back to his plate, jabs his fork into the freshly sautéed vegetables, and fills his mouth.

"Mmmmmm...fresshhh...bedgies," he mumbles, barely audible, through his full mouth. "Warmmmmmm...ffread...am honmey!" This time, crumbs drop from his mouth as he dabs another spoonful on his half-eaten slice.

Sadie, saying nothing, smiles, watching him. She's enjoying her meal, too, and feels better seeing Caleb eat so much. Halfway through his plateful, numerous questions have finally formed in his brain.

"Where'd you get these?" he asks, pointing with his fork toward the fresh greens and vegetables. "Is this...raccoon? Mmmm...and fresh bread," he says, biting into another piece while talkin, "How... mmmm...how...mmmmmmmm. How long..." he chews a few more times, then swallows, "have you been gone?"

Not pausing to wait for any response, he pops a piece of meat into his mouth relishing its tenderness and flavor. It's seasoned to perfection with rosemary and other fresh herbs. Sadie says something, but he can't hear it through all his chewing and noises of delight. With each bite, he's moaning, hungry for more. Sadie can tell, he hasn't heard anything, and changes her tactic.

She waits for him to swallow, then speaks, "Let's talk after we finish eating."

Caleb nods, while filling his mouth again. Sadie takes it as confirmation and returns to her meal. Sitting contentedly, Caleb tosses the last morsel of bread into his mouth, sucks a bit of honey off of his finger, closes his eyes, and leans back against the wall.

"That was amazing," he says, lightly rubbing his belly.

"I thought you'd like it," Sadie says, while cleaning up.

"Where'd the fresh produce…and honey, come from?" he inquires, this time, clearly audible.

Sadie doesn't stop what's she's doing and looks at him with another big grin. Then, it hits him. He realizes what's different. She's completely relaxed and happy, even peaceful-looking.

"Well…" she stalls, bringing two mugs of hot tea over, "I've been waitin' to tell you."

She takes a seat next to him and settles in to begin her story, sharing every detail of her experience with Clara. She talks rapidly, with enthusiasm, and simply listening and watching Sadie's facial expressions and gestures captivates Caleb. She doesn't even pause to sip her tea and when she does finally stop, Caleb is just as amazed. He shifts slightly, and pain tears through his body. Sadie, silently debating with herself, finally gets up, and then returns with something from her pack.

"I brought more morphine back," she says, getting Caleb's full attention. "But, first, let's get you cleaned up."

Caleb would prefer the pain meds now, but he's thankful there are more, as she helps him outside. Sadie leaves Caleb for a moment and returns with hot water and a fresh bar of handmade soap.

"Here, smell," she puts it under his nose and Caleb takes a gentle whiff of the fragrant soap, "Clara made it. When you get better, you've been invited to her place. She wants to meet you." Sadie helps remove his shirt and begins unwrapping Caleb's bandages.

Her closeness has an immediate effect on him, but he tries to remain nonchalant.

"I can't wait...she sounds...amaz-ing," Caleb says, grimacing with a bolt of pain.

Sadie waits for it to pass and when it does, she hands him an old beach towel. "Wrap it around your waist so you can...remove...the rest of your clothes."

Before he can respond, she's turned her back, but Caleb struggles and can't get his pants over his ankles. Frustrated, he checks, making sure he's properly covered before speaking.

"Can you...ummmmmm...help?" he embarrassingly asks.

Sadie turns and sees the problem. She drops to a knee, removes his pants, and stands, without ever looking him in the face, and then, she helps him further.

"Lean your head back." As he does, Sadie pours water over his head and his upper torso. "Lather up, then I'll help you rinse," she says, turning her back once again, giving him privacy.

The silence grows awkward as Caleb fumbles about washing himself. Trying to think of something to fill the void, he asks, "So exactly... how long...have you been gone? I...sorta...lost track."

His question only emphasizes what Sadie already knows—he's been staying drugged up. She was shocked upon arrival, finding him passed out with the needle still stuck in his arm. She couldn't believe Caleb was so messed up he hadn't removed it. The needle, along with the track marks along his veins, made him look like a junky, and it worries Sadie.

"I'm ready," Caleb says, interrupting her thoughts.

She turns back around and carefully pours most of the remaining water over him. She leaves a small amount so he can manage what's left on his own and finish in private.

"Let me know when you're done." Sadie disappears before he can respond.

Although he struggles, Caleb works quickly. Feeling clean but cold, he yells out to Sadie who returns with fresh bandages and a change of clothes. She re-wraps his ribs, puts a clean shirt over his head, and helps get his arms through the holes. The additional movement sends shock waves of pain through his torso. As the pain subsides, Caleb opens his eyes and looks at Sadie, who's staring at his arms. When she notices him watching, she stops, and looks him straight in the eyes.

There's a long awkward pause before Sadie finally breaks the silence, "You went through the morphine too fast. There's only a little left...you need to wean yourself off." Caleb feels his checks blush with embarrassment as Sadie continues, "I've been gone almost two weeks...there should've been enough for much longer."

She's nothing but serious, now. Her happy and light demeanor from earlier has disappeared.

"Aahhhhhhhhhh...I...aaaaaaaahh," Caleb stammers not sure how to respond. "Two weeks?" Is all he eventually gets out.

"Yeah, and I'm not sure how long I'll be this time," she responds as Caleb grimaces with the news.

He knows she'll leave again, but hearing it makes him feel even worse. Caleb needs to use the latrine, and Sadie gives him privacy before helping him back inside. She can tell his pain is bad, even though he's trying to tough it out. He's a little sweaty from the effort, his ribs are throbbing, there's a fuzziness in his head, and all he can think about is another shot, but Caleb doesn't want to say anything about it to Sadie.

He settles onto his back, the position he's been basically living in since she found him, and tries calming down his body. Beginning to feel cold and shivery, his hands tremble as a wave of nausea hits him. He's worried about throwing up his meal, when Sadie comes over to his side and puts her hand on his forehead.

"You feel a little clammy," she says, while picking up the vial of morphine, trying to decide whether supplying him with more is a good thing. "Caleb, tomorrow, after breakfast, I'm headin' back out to explore the north side of the island and find out where those Splitters came from. I'm not sure how long I'll be, but...it could be several weeks."

Caleb tries to focus on Sadie's words, but his attention keeps drifting to the vial she's tapping against her leg while talking.

She notices, stops, and holds it up, "This is it...the last of it. You're gonna have to ration...reduce each dosage, until it's gone."

Caleb, growing paler and impatient, desperately wants the pain meds. He doesn't say anything to discourage Sadie and simply nods while she goes on.

"Okay, so here's the plan. Take one dose...at night, before bed to help you sleep...and then another, mid-day after lunch. After four days, only before bed..." Sadie pauses looking at him.

He stares back, until realizing she's looking for some type of response. When Caleb slowly nods yes, she inserts the needle into the vial and pulls some of the drug into the syringe.

"Lets start with...this much," she shows him the amount, holding it near his face.

He fights the urge to take it from her.

"This way, it'll last...just over a week and a half. After that...you're on your own."

He doesn't say anything and Sadie isn't sure he's following.

"Caleb. Caleb...Caleb!"

"Sorry." His focus drifts back to the morphine. "Okay," he replies.

"Okay? Okay what?" Sadie asks, getting frustrated.

"Two doses a day...before bed and...at lunch. Then...just one."

Sadie flicks the shaft of the needle, then tying up his arm, runs a finger along its inside, trying to find a good vein. Before inserting the tip, Sadie pauses again. "What else?"

At this point Caleb wants to scream but knows Sadie won't react well to that tactic. He tries to calm himself, and answers. "Reduce the dosage," he clenches his teeth, "until it's all gone."

Sadie injects the needle, and slowly, gives him his reward. As the morphine enters his bloodstream, his eyes close, and his head leans to one side. Immediately, he feels better.

"Thank you, Sadie," he lightly whispers, with a grin on his face.

TWENTY-TWO

Knocked to his knees, the youngster is kicked from behind.

"Boy, we warned you! You ungrateful," a kick strikes his side, "little," another kick, "maggot!"

With two boney and bruised arms, the boy continues protecting his head while staying balled-up.

"It wasn't me!" he yells at the top of his lungs.

"Shut up! We've heard ah nuff of ur ungrateful...mom-meees, little boy, bullshit."

This time, a kick lands directly upside his head knocking him unconscious. His entire body goes limp as it takes another nasty blow.

"This little piece ah shit is gettin' lippy." The man lands one last kick before pausing to catch his breath.

"Yeah, but he sure iz ah handy little fucker, I ain't never seen nobody fix nutin' like he can." The other man adds.

"Shut up! I'm tired of yer shit too. If he's so god damn good, then why ain't the radio...or boat fixed. Huh? Tell me dat." Disgusted, he pushes aside and stomps off to the house.

His partner glances down at the kid before following.

"When that little bastard wakes up, I wanna find where he's hidin' stuff." The first man says, as he looks around the root cellar. "Son of ah bitch! He got da rice!" He slams the cellar door and plops into a chair, putting his feet on the table.

Hours later, the boy somehow finds his way back to the boat, curls into a fetal position, and falls back into the darkness. He shouldn't be sleeping. It's dangerous, especially with a head injury, but there's no one looking out for him and it's been that way for years. Life hasn't been fair for the poor kid, and existence, for him, is dirty, lonely, and abusive.

He fades in and out of consciousness for two days, and luckily, is nonresponsive when they come and begin tearing apart the boat looking for their missing items. When he does wake, it takes another two days of nursing his wounds before he can get up. The boy's weak, and he barely moves about, yet he understands the need to venture out, or he'll die for sure. Problem is, running into them—they won't help, especially since they think he's been stealing food and more than likely, they'll just beat him again, possibly to death this time.

Barely managing getting out of the boat and back on solid ground, he heads into the woods to a place he discovered when they first arrived. Uncovering his old toolbox, he rummages through it, and takes inventory. Not much left, a few unlabeled cans of mystery food, a couple handfuls of beans, and a small bag of flour. He learned years ago to always have backup and an emergency stash. Unfortunately for him, it's been survival the hard way.

Removing the last item, he cradles it in his hands for what feels like an eternity. When the courage arrives, he carefully unwraps the old worn cloth, exposing the gun. It's his secret treasure, and it plays a major part, in his ever-evolving escape plot. He daydreams endlessly of freedom and a life away from the Nation. He's invented rescue scenarios, planned routes for running away—even ways to get rid of his capturers.

Not sure in which direction events are headed, the boy feels it's time to keep it loaded and with him. He was fortunate to survive this last beating and next time, he might not be so lucky. Besides, the odds are better, since the other two Splitters have yet to return. He swallows with difficulty loading the ammunition. Tucking the loaded gun into the back of his pants, he randomly picks a can, and holding it to his ear while shaking it, the boy tries guessing at its contents.

After a meal of cold canned beans, he hides the toolbox and heads off into the woods where he's decided to stay while contemplating any further actions. Only a few steps away, the screams of a woman are clearly audible, stopping him dead in his tracks. His heart races, and he strains listening. The second time a scream pierces the silence; he changes course and heads back.

"Oooo…looky looky. Wha'd we got here?" The man's hand gropes her backside and his fingers trace down her crack until they're deep between her legs.

The foulness of the action sends shivers along her spine, as her deepest fear is upon her. She jerks away, only to be held tighter. Fighting back, she yanks one arm free while kicking, only to get punched in the jaw.

She falls, screaming, as both men hover above, laughing. One side of her jaw is dislocated, and unable to focus her eyes, all she sees is pulsating lights. Their laughing starts in slow motion, then slowly, it returns to correct speed. She has to get up and doesn't want to be on the ground. While trying to get to her feet, one of the men knocks her back down. As he steps closer, she quickly sits, bringing her knees closer to her chest. Every time he gets close, she kicks fiercely, backing him up. She's strong, and fairly quick, for already being so hurt.

"Quit dickin' around already! Get her!" Yells his Splitter comrade.

She lands a kick to the side of his knee, causing a good deal of pain.

"Son of a BITCH!" he yells, looking even more fearsome.

"Come on. You gonna need help? Wha's the matter...can't handle dis little one?" His buddy laughs at his own joke, pissing off his partner further.

"Shut da fuck up! There's gonna be," he strikes at her head and she's unable to deflect the blow, "no problem here." Before she can recover, he's upon her again.

As she tries to kick, he catches her legs, and she thrashes at his face with her hands.

"Git 'er arms, already!" he yells frustrated.

His partner, eager to help, leaps into action, ready to join the fun. Within moments, both her arms are held together overhead and a gun is pressed into her temple.

"Now...we're gonna have a little fun and...yer gonna play nice. Got it?" he murmurs, taping the gun against her temple.

Fright fills her entire being, and tears stream down her cheeks. "Pppp wease...wompt," she tries to plead, unable to move her jaw.

Suddenly, the boy appears at their side.

"Hey boy, guess you weren't lyin' after all. Musta been this nice-lookin' piece of ass." He tears open her shirt, exposing her breasts.

She screams again and gets backhanded across the mouth. It splits her lip open and sends another shock wave of pain through her jaw.

The boy, unable to take watching it anymore, screams. "STOP!"

"Oh, is mom-mees' little boy not okay?" He starts yanking off her pants. "Wha's da madder, you don't like pussy, boy."

The other Splitter laughs, while watching and pressing his gun into her forehead. His accomplice starts undoing his pants.

"I said STOP!" The kid fires a bullet into the air, shocking them all.

There's a brief silence, then both Splitters start laughing.

"Really? You think you can shoot us? You think you got wha' it takes?

The youngster's hand shakes as he points the gun directly at the man posed ready to take his victim. The boy's close enough that he can't miss, and they both know it, what's uncertain is whether he's capable of pulling the trigger. The silence lasts only momentarily.

"That's what I thought." The Splitter turns back to the woman, finishes undoing his pants, grabs her hips, and thrusts.

Before he can complete his move, an arrow pierces his head, and a single shot fires. Two things occur. The man with an arrow through his head falls in perfectly timed slow motion, and blood pools around the woman's head. The boy stares in shock, unsure of what has just happened. Realizing she's dead, the kid's gaze turns from the victim up to her killer. They stare at each other, then, the man slowly raises his gun, and the boy follows suit.

They stand only a few feet apart from one another, locked in a dual of uncertainties; both trying to decide if the other will fire. Seconds pass, then, suddenly, movement is detected in the nearby brush. As it gets louder—and closer—a young girl bursts from the woods firing a rifle while running towards them.

"Mama! Mama! Ma-ma!!" She aims, fires, and is upon them, as the man falls, holding both hands against his bloody abdomen.

The boy rolls over onto his side, sits up, and puts his hands in the air. The girl, confused and disorientated at the site of her mother exposed and shot point blank in the head, is inconsolable. She drops to her knees, and her hands tremble uncontrollably. They hover above the body darting from area to area, unsure of what to do, and where to touch. She fumbles, trying to cover her mother's body.

Managing to almost cover her mother's torso, she's unable to function further. She sobs in massive waves of sorrow, as bubbles form around her mouth, and her eyes swell shut. Mucus builds and collects, creating a web of wetness between her nose, mouth, and hands, as she balls her fists and bites them. In her terror, she forgets everything; her surroundings, her situation, herself. When the girl's eyes finally reopen, her mother's bare lower body fills her with rage. Suddenly, remembering she's not alone, she grabs for the rifle lying next to her and winging it around, points it at the boy.

His eyes are swollen, too, but she doesn't notice. He stares blankly, overwhelmed with emotion. He put the gun down long ago, but it's a detail the girl's missed. He raises his empty hands, but doesn't speak. Suddenly, he realizes that if he doesn't, he's dead. She'll pull the trigger. Actually, he's surprised she hasn't yet, and reacts quickly, before it's too late.

"Please! Please! PLEASE!! I tried...I tried to help!" He pleads.

None of his words register with the girl. Thinking fast, he tries another tactic.

"Look my gun's over there," he says, nodding towards the weapon sitting closer to her than to him.

She looks down, only to see her murdered mother, as pain and terror erupt within her again. She turns, prepared to kill, when the rifle is abruptly ripped from her hands. Neither of them noticed Sadie, who now, stands over them holding the girl's rifle, the boy's gun, and a crossbow. Both kids stare blankly. The girl falters, and then breaks down, sobbing; she can't take any more.

"They killed her! They killed her!" She continues screaming.

Suddenly, she realizes that her mother is still exposed and tries covering her with the pants still caught on one of her ankles. The struggling girl can't pull them up, or off, and stuck, the pants don't reach far enough to cover anything. Getting frantic, she tugs at the material. Sadie kneels down and gently removes the clothing from around the ankle to help the girl. She turns to the boy.

"Get something...to cover her," she demands.

He stares back at Sadie.

"Go!" Sadie yells, staying next to the girl.

"Those men...they-they...they..." she can't finish her sentence, but Sadie knows what the girls is trying to say.

"No," Sadie looks directly into her eyes, "they didn't." She states it so matter-of-factly that the young girl only stares back, hoping it's so. Holding her crossbow, Sadie kicks the Splitter who'd been shot through the head. "Your mom fought hard. I saw, and I stopped him before he could." Sadie's voice fades into a whisper, "They didn't rape her."

Hearing the words, the girl trembles and collapses into Sadie, who catches the poor thing in her arms.

Holding tight, Sadie gently speaks, "They didn't get her. Sshh... ssssshhhhh...I'm sorry...I couldn't save her."

Still hugging the girl, Sadie watches the boy return with a blanket. She releases one arm from holding the distraught girl, to accept it and communicate with him. He places the blanket in Sadie's hand, backs away, and sits where directed.

Sadie whispers again. "Let's cover her."

Sadie releases her grip to show the young girl the blanket. Without speaking, the two of them open it and carefully place it over the woman's body. They finish smoothing out the wrinkles, and Sadie takes a small step back. The girl falls to her knees and places her head on her mother's stomach, sobbing in full mourning.

Giving her more space, Sadie steps further away and signals to the boy. The two of them drag away the men's bodies. The man shot in the gut is alive and moans in pain. Setting his body down, Sadie looks at his wound. There's no way to save him and if there was, Sadie isn't sure she'd even try. He's a terrible man, dying a painful death. As he begins fluttering his eyes and opening them briefly to look at Sadie, she responds by leaning in closer so only he can hear what she says.

"You've done horrible things and…your time has come. The pain you feel now serves as a reminder of what you've inflicted…" she pauses then finishes, "you should pray for forgiveness…if there's any to be had."

With these words, Sadie leaves his side, makes eye contact with the boy, asks him one question, and returns to the girl. She's cried herself quiet and is nestled up with the body. Sadie puts her arms around the child and lightly helps her sit up. She gives the girl a moment and then takes her hands.

"Can you get your mom's room ready?" Sadie speaks calmly. "Let's rest her there. Then, later, when you're ready, we can bury her. Okay?"

The girl nods a slow motion yes, carefully stands, and walks back to her home.

Sadie motions to the boy. "Help me wrap the body. When she's ready," Sadie nods in the girl's direction, "I'm gonna need your help."

He doesn't speak, but nods in agreement. They finish their task in silence and with it completed; Sadie locks eyes with the youngster, who swallows nervously.

"Now…we talk," she says, with authority.

TWENTY-THREE

Checking on the boy, Sadie takes a shovel to continue helping with the dig. The abuse he's suffered is clearly evident, and she's surprised the boy's even functional. He looks nearly starved to death and badly beaten. Surprisingly though, his spirit is quite jovial, and Sadie's been enjoying his company during the past day and a half.

Sadie digs out the last rock and tosses it in the pile. When the remaining loose dirt gets shoveled out, she climbs from the grave. They're almost done with this task, and both look forward to getting rid of the two dead Splitters. Their bodies lie nearby, wrapped in old worn tarps. The man Sadie shot with an arrow died immediately. The other ignorant militant wasn't so lucky. His was a slow, painful death that met him sometime during the night.

"Jose, help me," she says, looking to the boy. "Let's roll 'em in."

They get the first body to the edge of the hole, pause for a moment, and then push it in. They do the same with the second.

"Dang it." Sadie murmurs.

One of bodies doesn't land perfectly, and it needs to be adjusted. Jose climbs in, and Sadie helps from her knees. Once they get it settled, both grab shovels and begin filling dirt back in. It goes rather quickly between the two of them and when the dirt is gone, they finish by piling on the rocks they dug up. As they place the last stone, there's a long pause while they stare at the mound.

Sadie breaks the silence. "I didn't know 'em," she starts, not really sure what to say, or if they even deserve any parting words, "and the only thing I saw from them, was…cruelty." She feels her anger rising and tries to control it. Turning to the grave, she says, "I hope, for both of your sakes, it wasn't always that way. May God have mercy on your souls." She turns to Jose. "You knew 'em for years. Is there anything you want…or…need to say?"

He stares blankly at Sadie then back at the grave. What can he say? These two made him suffer. They'd beaten, tormented, and humiliated him every chance they could. They took advantage of his youth and weakness and never looked out for his well-being or even offered to help along the way. His mind replays horror after horror, all at their hands, and Jose can't find a single good memory. While taking a deep breath, the sadness of their existence hits him.

"I…forgive you," he says, barely above a whisper.

Sadie is surprised, then overwhelmingly touched. Already, at such a young age, he's able to be the better man. She puts an arm over his shoulder and pulls him closer. They stay, standing together in silence, for a couple more minutes, and then Sadie speaks.

"Come on." She smiles, looking at Jose, "it's time for my tour. I wanna see your boat."

The words, "your boat," do something for Jose that he isn't yet able to conceptualize.

"Okay!" he says, enthusiastically turning about and leading the way.

Ten minutes down a well-worn trail, the scenery completely shifts. The forest thins, and a small, rocky cove appears, with deep and glassy smooth water. At its mouth, a sea stack blocks the view out into the ocean and it's entirely outlined by steep cliffs.

Sadie, even more surprised, gasps, "Oooh…I…I didn't realize it… was…so…big. I pictured something…smaller."

Jose smiles ear-to-ear.

"I can't believe it fit in here," she adds, looking over the vessel.

The boat, anchored only feet from shore, is nestled along the shortest cliff edge. From the mast platform, a cargo net runs to the cliff, where's it's secured to a nearby tree. On the ground lies an old wooden plank that Jose picks up.

"Here, at high tide, this works better." He sets the board across the span between the boat and the shore, creating a bridge to the plat-form. Jose pauses at the edge of the plank, turns to Sadie, and finds amusement in her astonishment.

Sadie still can't believe what she's seeing.

"If it wasn't for the high tide, the boat would never have made it," the boy says, proudly.

"I think more than tides were on your side," Sadie replies, while carefully walking across the makeshift bridge.

From her vantage point, she detects a faded emblem, along with a partial registration number, on the forward half of the boat's bow. Once onboard, Jose's manner changes—he's a kid again, probably for the first time in years. While storing the plank walkway, he rattles off information and the vessels specs.

"Welcome to the Intrepid II," he begins proudly. "She was the Coast Guard's primary heavy-weather boat...designed to weather hurricane force winds and heavy seas. If she capsizes...she'll self-right in less than thirty seconds...with all equipment functional, and...she has a forty-passenger capacity. The intrepid II was out deep to sea during the tsunami and survived. After...she ran rescue missions longer than any other vessel." He pats the boat's side. "I think, she's the last of 'er kind."

They make their way down from the platform and to the bridge where Jose's focus shifts to the controls.

"We employ a fly-by-wire system that can be operated from four different locations. Two out here and two from inside." He points to the enclosed bridge as they enter.

His excitement and fondness for the watercraft is refreshing. The boy's knowledgeable and appears fully capable of operating the vessel and repairing a great deal of it, too. Sadie finds comfort in seeing him light up with each description, detail, and story. It's such a drastic change from their previous chats about his injuries, how he ended up with the Splitters, and the terror he's lived with.

As he continues giving his tour, Sadie notices the damages inflicted by the two Splitters. They tore his possessions into shreds, and the few books he owns are ripped to pieces. He's neatly recollected them, and what remains is organized into piles. From each pile, he's apparently attempting to piece together the pages. Some are finished, while others lie in varying stages of organization.

Sadie bends down, lifting the cover of one book torn in half. It's worn, and the spine is cracked, but the title is clearable legible. It's "A Christmas Carol," by Charles Dickens. Still undetected in her snooping, she peeks at the others. There's a bible, a children's storybook in Spanish, and an old beaten-up copy of National Geographic. Checking the last pile, she can tell it's a technical manual and upon closer inspection, she discovers it's the lifeboat's operators' handbook. Those idiots didn't even realize they'd ruined reference materials necessary for the very boat they wanted fixed. Shaking her head at the mere stupidity of it, Sadie shifts her attention back to Jose, better understanding how he knows all the precise specs of the vessel.

Listening to him talk about the forward compartment and the seventeen vertical bulkheads composing the frame, Sadie finds it hard to believe several things: first, that he's survived this long, and second, how gifted Jose is. It's hard to grasp the fact that he's only fourteen, has never attended school—at least, in the traditional way Sadie did all those years ago—and has an obviously budding intellect. They head back to the main deck as the boy wraps up the tour. It gives Sadie an opportunity to ask another question, but before doing so, she compliments the boy—after all, she's very impressed.

"Jose you've done an excellent job." She ruffles the hair on the top of his head with one hand. "Everything looks really good."

His grin widens, and Sadie moves on to what she's curious about.

"What caused the boat to break down?" she asks.

He looks a little surprised, scared, and proud, all at the same moment. Combined, they make for one strange look, but he's very candid with Sadie and tells the truth.

"Well...it didn't exactly...break down. I...temporally stalled the engine and...let it drift."

Sadie raises her eyebrows.

Jose, shrugging his shoulders, explains more, "The wind direction, timing, and tides were perfect. It was my chance...my chance to stop 'em. Or at least...slow 'em down." Jose drops his shoulders and lowers his head. "It was luck...the currents kept us from crashing on the rocks. Somehow, we safely drifted by the sea stack and right into this cove. We dropped anchor and...with the corresponding tides... manipulated it...until we could maneuver closer to land." He sounds disappointed with their success. "I didn't think we'd make it ashore. But, as you can see...they figured that out, too."

He remembers being forced, dangerously along, making sure to secure their access, so they could cross ready to plunder and murder.

"Seeing what they do...I mean did...to people is...eerrr...ahhhh... was..." he pauses. Words, can't convey how witnessing and hearing all the abuse, affected him. He'd been helpless, and all he could do was pray for their victims. He recovers his voice, "I never stopped 'em. So many people got hurt. I thought...that...if we were stranded... at least others wouldn't suffer." Jose grows quiet.

Sadie, surprised yet again, is taken by his unselfishness, courage, and actions. They should have crashed upon the rocky shore and died. This young boy was willing to sacrifice his own life for the safety of others he'd never even met. He isn't simply, a better man—he's a better person. Putting her arm back around him for the second time this afternoon, Sadie finds herself believing their paths were meant to cross. She doesn't know why life brought him here, but she's glad he survived. Tilting her head to lean against his, Sadie squeezes his arm, reinforcing the excellence of his actions.

"Ya did good, kid. Ya...did...good. They're gone now, and Anna's safe," she reminds him.

At the mention of the girl's name, Jose feels another wash of sorrow. Seeing her mourn is heartbreaking, and it will bother him for a long time, but Sadie's right: she's safe now. Those men would have— he stops, not wanting to finish the thought. Sadie, too, is reminded of the poor girl and knows it's time to return and check on her; but first, one more detail needs attending.

"Alright, kiddo, show me the radio thing."

Jose's smile reappears while he's explaining and demonstrating to Sadie how he makes the radio work, and how he made it appear to be completely broken. Proud of his ingenuity and cleverness, Sadie doesn't hesitate with her decision.

"Alright," with one word, Jose senses her seriousness, "we're gonna radio your headquarters.

"It's not my headquarters!" Jose abruptly states.

Sadie, understanding her mistake, fixes it. "Sorry, your right, it's not. We need to contact 'em...and make sure they don't come lookin'. They need to think the island's inaccessible and doesn't offer anything for possible survival. Let 'em know the radio's been malfunctioning, making contact sooner impossible. We'll give 'em a different location...far from here...making 'em believe the crew's still continuing their search. This place can't be on the Nation's radar."

Jose, understanding her logic, agrees to do it. Together, they hash out a short radio dialogue and practice various scenarios, before putting out the call. It takes longer to make contact than they expected, and they're ready to give up, when a static-sounding reply lifts their spirits. Jose, although nervous, plays his role well. He operates the radio perfectly, faking interference sounds to cue their planned dialogue. He finishes the charade by losing the radio signal. Everything is eerily silent, and he looks to Sadie as she speaks.

"That was good...I think they fell for it. Over the next couple of days...we'll finish the task." Sadie winks at Jose, who wonders what else she's planned.

Before he can ask, Sadie shifts the direction of their conversation.

"Anna's been alone too long. I need to head back." Sadie gets up to leave and takes a few things out of her bag first. She keeps talking while opening various compartments, "Stay out here again tonight. Tomorrow mornin'...we'll finish preparations and bury Anna's mom." Sadie hands Jose a bag of beans and another full of rice. She adds a handful of jerky and digs through another pocket. At the very bottom, she retrieves an item.

"Here...." she hands Jose a small book, "it's to start your new library."

Jose looks at her, and then stares at the cover. It's an old, worn military field guide. His hand slides down the intact spine and he opens the pages.

"They're all here...every one!" He looks up, then quickly back down at the gift. His giant smile touches Sadie's heart.

"I've carried it around for years and...it's come in pretty handy... but, now...I think it's time to pass it along."

Still carrying the book, he follows Sadie as she leaves the Intrepid II. Standing on shore, she turns for a last goodbye, but before she can speak, Jose does.

His giddy excitement turns to shy sincerity, "Thank you...thank you for...everything."

Sadie nods her head, "Goodnight, kiddo. I'll see ya in the morning."

"Goodnight, Sadie," he says, happy to have someone he can wish that to.

TWENTY-FOUR

Anna lies on her bed, exhausted, but unable to sleep. Adding to her difficulties is a severe headache from crying so intensely. At thirteen, she's orphaned, and carries the burden of killing one of her parents' murderers. It's a lot to handle for anyone, let alone for such a young child. Curled into a fetal position, she fails to hear Sadie come in and stand by the door. Sadie's at a loss and not sure what's best for the girl. Entering the room, she sits down on the bed next to Anna. The girl barely moves her head, stealing a quick glance, before closing her eyes again.

Sadie, not sure what to say, decides it's best to be straightforward, "Anna, you've been through a lot. I'm not gonna tell you...it'll get better. It won't...at least, not for a long time. For the rest of your life... you'll miss your parents and...the next few months...are going to be rough..." Sadie pauses momentarily then decides to share her own losses. "I lost my family, too."

Anna opens her eyes.

Sadie continues, "Then, my husband died, and...it nearly...killed me. I was left all alone...for about, as long...as...you've been alive. I couldn't do anything, and...to be honest...I didn't really want to."

Anna senses Sadie's sincerity and can't image being left alone.

Noticing she has the girl's attention, Sadie continues, "I stopped doing everything...even eating. Then...I realized that...by allowing myself to slip away...I was lettin' my family down." Sadie slides a little closer to the girl. "I decided to try...for them. By living, I keep their memories alive...it's all that's left of 'em." Sadie pauses, letting her words take hold.

Anna shifts to a seated position, and Sadie joins her. They sit shoulder-to-shoulder, leaning against the bedroom wall. It's a natural feeling for both women, as if they've always hung out this way. They sit in silence as Sadie finds faults in how she planned, and doubt about her choice of direction takes over. She should have gone north first. If she had arrived sooner, Anna's mom might have been saved.

Looking back, it's obvious to Sadie. The signs were all there: Caleb's account of being captured, where he was found, along with the two dead Splitters, and the trail they left with the quad. Sadie's disappointed

148

with herself and the costly mistake. Finding the old logging roads leading to Anna's home, she was astounded by how easy it was to travel on this side of the island. She could have been here days ago, and even a few minutes sooner would have made a huge difference.

Making her analysis even more difficult is seeing the sadness and confusion Anna bears. Sadie forces herself to stop. Hindsight always paints a clearer picture, and right now, she needs to stay positive and figure out what's best for the two kids. Slowly, Sadie gets up from the bed and stands next to the girl.

"Anna, I'm gonna make us some dinner. Can we eat together... and then talk later?"

The girl stares at Sadie without responding.

Sadie sits back down on the edge of the bed and chooses her words carefully, "You're all that's left of your family. You have to do it...for them. Okay?"

Fresh tears appear in Anna's eyes. She doesn't speak, but nods yes, as Sadie's heart aches for the youngster. Overwhelmed with emotion, she leans over and lightly kisses Anna on the top of her head. Anna's tears turn to sobs and she collapses into Sadie's arms. They hold on to one another, embracing in sadness.

When Anna's crying finally stops, Sadie speaks, "Come on...help me with dinner. It'll be a good distraction...and...I don't know where anything's at."

Anna looks at Sadie. The girl's eyes are bloodshot and swollen, and at first, she still isn't able to respond.

"Oohh...kay," she finally manages to whisper.

The two women leave the bedroom and head into the kitchen. While preparing their meal, Sadie shares more with the traumatized young girl.

"When, I lost my mom...and brothers...the people around me... didn't know what to do or say. Everyone acted...different...being careful not to mention 'em...or anything that might bring up sad memories. I hated it. I wanted to talk about my family...I wanted to share their stories."

Anna, grateful to learn more about Sadie, sets the table.

"Then, before the earthquakes...my dad died. A Splitter shot him...during an attack where...I also lost a lot of friends." Sadie stops what she's doing, saddened by the memory.

"When Markus died...I was all alone." She grows quiet and sits down.

Anna joins her at the table curious for more. "Markus...was... your...husband?"

Sadie answers by nodding yes.

"How did he...die?" Anna asks.

Sadie looks at the girl, sees her concern, and sadly answers. "During the earthquakes...a tree fell...smashing...him." His twitching leg appears in her mind.

Sadie, pushing the image aside, tells Anna the entire story, making sure to include her personal struggles, nearly starving to death, and the fear she developed of going outside. Anna hangs on every word, and can't believe, that the woman sitting across from her had once been feeble and scared. It gives the girl a glimmer of hope. As Sadie finishes her story, she gets up, checks on the food, and serves them both. They begin their meal in silence, and Sadie's pleased to see Anna eating. Feeling a little better about Anna's situation, she distracts the girl with more stories. Sadie speaks of her life, about living in the woods, the safety patrols she makes, and staying on the lookout for Splitters. At the mention of Splitters, a visible shudder runs through Anna. Sadie hesitates, and then decides it's best to be straightforward.

"The Splitters that came here captured two men. One...they murdered. The other managed to escape and kill 'em both. His name's Caleb...and I found him...out in the woods, nearly dead, and took him to safety. He's recoverin' from broken ribs back in...my...hideout."

Anna catches Sadie's last word, as she hoped. "Hideout?" the girl questions.

Sadie, with the hint of a smile, gives Anna the fully-detailed story of the cave, including her childhood exploits there.

Anna's eyes clear, and there's even a faint hint of excitement, as she takes a turn talking. "I've got a hideout, too! Well...it's more of a campsite. My parents surprised me with it for my tenth birthday."

Sadie, quick to encourage the girl, replies, "I'd love to see it, maybe...tomorrow?"

Sadie's mention of tomorrow reminds Anna that it's the day they plan to bury her mother. She grows quiet again as the light goes out of her eyes. Sadie makes the connection, feels a pang of sorrow, but still decides to discuss a couple of things.

"Anna, I know we've only just met, but…there are a few things I need to check with you about."

Curious as to what Sadie wants, Anna looks up again.

"Tomorrow needs to be a day of honoring and celebrating your parents. Can you tell me more about 'em so I can prepare something to say? I think it would proper…and nice."

Anna's heart nearly explodes at the request. For the next couple of hours, the girl shares memories that make her both laugh and cry. Sadie listens intently, knowing it's good therapy for Anna. Eventually, she stops talking, and Sadie uses the break to breach another topic.

"Thank you…for sharing the memories of your parents with me. You were lucky to have such a wonderful mom and dad. Now they live in you…" Sadie pauses and then transitions to a topic she needs to address. "Anna…Jose is the name of the boy that came here with the Splitters."

The mention of him, conjures his image, and Anna realizes she'd completely forgotten all about the boy.

"He's been stayin' on the boat. The Splitters killed his parents… then, he was forced to…be their servant. But…he stood up against 'em and tried to save your mother."

Anna, confused, keeps listening.

Sadie cautiously continues, "Is it okay…if he goes to your mom's burial? I need his help…and…he asked if it was all right."

The girl's slow to respond, "Why does he…want…to be there?"

Sadie picks up Anna's hands and holds them. "He wants to be there…for you, and…to pay his respect to someone he wanted so desperately to save."

Anna keeps staring at their hands and Sadie can see how tired the girl's become. She's not sure if Anna is going to respond, until finally, a soft whisper escapes the girl's lips. With Anna's approval, Sadie has her get ready for bed and then rejoins her back in the bedroom.

Sadie tucks her in and kisses her forehead. "Goodnight, little one."

Before Sadie blows out the candle, sitting on the nightstand, Anna speaks, "Will you stay…with me?"

Sadie's not sure if Anna means always, or just tonight, and doesn't want to ask.

"Sure, kiddo. Let me get my bag and change first. I'll be right back."

When Sadie returns, she slides in next to Anna, and the two settle in for the night, but the following morning, Anna wakes alone. She looks around, noticing Sadie's bag is gone, too. In a panic, she throws off the covers, but before her feet touch the ground, Sadie's back, standing in the doorway.

"Morning sleepy head. I was comin' to wake you," she says.

Anna pulls the blankets back over her legs, seeing what Sadie holds. It's the same tray her mom used whenever she was stuck, sick in bed. Sadie sets it down on the girl's lap. Staring at the tray and the food on it, Anna notices the two steaming mugs.

"There's chamomile or mint tea. Which would you like?" Sadie says, noticing the look of confusion on Anna's face.

Anna shrugs her shoulders, "I dunno. I've never had tea before."

Sadie's flabbergasted. "Well, try 'em both and pick the one you like best."

Anna tastes the first mug.

"Take another sip or two. Sometimes it takes a couple to really tastes the flavor," Sadie suggests.

Anna does so and chooses the mint. Sadie takes the other and sips on it while Anna slowly eats her oatmeal. The girl eats silently, and Sadie uses the opportunity to talk.

"I got up early this morning, went huntin'…hiked around a bit… and checked on Jose. I'm usually up early, to scout everything…I like to make sure it's safe. But…for me to keep doin' so, I'm gonna need your help."

Finishing the last spoonful, Anna looks at Sadie. "My…help?"

It's the perfect question, and Sadie's thankful. She pulls out her map, sets it open on the tray, and points with her finger. "This is my property and where I live. This section is Clara's…I'll tell you all about her later… she's amazing." Pointing to the incomplete section, she continues, "This is your place…I'd like you to show me around and help finish my map."

Anna picks up the map and traces her finger along the nearly completed outline of the island. Under her breath, she makes an incoherent comment. Locked on the map, her finger keeps retracing its shape, and then, she stops.

"We live…on…an…island?" Anna's question is barely audible.

Sadie, not sure about Anna's knowledge, knows the girl's not old enough to remember the earthquakes.

"Yes…our island. Me…Clara…and you."

Anna keeps looking from the map to Sadie. Her look of wonder changes to excitement. "Dad was right. Dad was right!" She pushes aside the tray and stands up on the bed. "DAD WAS RIGHT!"

She starts jumping up and down, still chanting. Sadie giggles, watching the girl. Eventually, her chants slow, along with the jumping, as her emotions swing.

"He…wa-wa-was…right," she says one last time—only now, through tears—and falls to her knees sobbing.

Sadie lightly rubs the girls back until she calms, then Anna tries to speak before she's gained full control of her emotions.

She finally manages getting something out, "My-my…my da-da-dad…was right." She sits up and wipes her eyes. "He thought…we lived…on an island, and…my mom and I made fun of him for it. We always joked…and teased him…he tried to get us to go explorin' with him. For years…he talked about it."

Anna's demeanor changes again, but telling her story, Sadie can see the love this family shared. "We hiked a little…and…sometimes…dad treated us to the quads, but we never traveled too far…but here," she points to a blank area on the map, "I know. That's where my campsite is."

"Here, draw it in." Sadie says, pulling out a pencil.

Anna carefully draws the missing section of coast. She stops twice; erasing parts of the line she doesn't like and when finished, looks to Sadie.

"What else can you add?" Sadie asks. "I've labeled some of the old roads…comin' in here, but…I'm sure I'm missing others."

Anna studies the map, turns it a couple of times, and adds a few more details, talking and explaining as she does. When there's nothing more to add, she gives it and the pencil back. Although Sadie's impressed with what Anna's been able to share, she hopes to get more from the girl.

As Anna gets up from bed, Sadie praises the girl for helping, and talks with her about the surrounding property. Sadie, wanting to explore the area in depth, hopes Anna will join her.

"Anna, I'd like to take a short hike later this afternoon. Would you join me? Maybe show me around a little?"

The girl turns to reply. "Maybe, we can go to my campsite…it's not too far."

Sadie smiles ear-to-ear. "I'd love to!"

TWENTY-FIVE

Anna appears, transformed from a child dressed in tattered play clothes to a woman in mourning. Her long black hair is tied neatly in a bun and she wears a loose-fitting dark blouse and skirt and a pair of shoes that are a little too big. Sadie hands her a matching jacket and, together, they return to her parents' bedroom. Walking over to the dresser, Anna picks up a small wooden box and rests it on her lap, while sitting next to Sadie on the bed.

The girl remains motionless, takes a deep breath, and then slowly lifts the lid. Starring at her mother's jewelry, she begins to tear up. Trying to be strong, Anna removes a small string of pearls and Sadie helps her put them on, along with a matching bracelet. Wearing her mother's things makes Anna feel older, but also uncomfortable. Emotions continue to course through her as she stands in front of the mirror. Sadie rests her hands on the girl's shoulder as they look at their reflections.

"Anna, you look beautiful. Your parents would be proud."

Anna's eyes close briefly, threatening to overflow, and she blinks back the tears.

Sadie pauses, waiting for the moment to pass, before continuing. "This is all yours now."

Anna remains gazing into her own reflection. For the first time in her life, she's not sure who's staring back. Her world has shattered, and no longer does she feel like a child.

Sadie speaks, breaking the spell, "Anna…it's time…you ready?"

Anna nods, and both women leave the house, holding hands. They make their way up the slope as Jose joins them. He's self-conscious approaching them and nervous about meeting Anna as Sadie introduces them for the first time face-to-face.

"Anna…this is Jose…and Jose…this…is Anna."

The two kids barely acknowledge one another before turning immediately back to Sadie. Together, they continue up the hill stopping only when they're under a huge oak tree. Two large wooden crosses mark the spot. One's erected towering over a mound of stones and the other over a freshly dug grave. From their hilltop perch, they can see the entire homestead below, as well as a partial view of the ocean. Sadie agrees with Anna; it's the perfect place.

Anna's hands finger her mother's pearls while she stares at the empty grave. Her hands continue nervously caressing the necklace as her vision sweeps across to the mound where her father lies. Slowly, her eyes travel up the crosses and finish by darting over to Jose. She's only brave enough to sneak a quick glance at him, before returning her gaze to the gravesites.

As she suffers through the sorrows of her parents' death, knots and butterflies fill the girl's stomach. Mixed in with these emotions, and adding to her unease, are feelings of gratitude and appreciation. She's attending her parents' burial, standing in a spot they loved, with two people she's only just met, and one of them—on his own—happened to pick the absolutely perfect location. Making it even more incredible was he acted all alone while still under Splitter control.

Jose did more for Anna than just pick a beautiful place. He managed to get her father up here on his own, when he could have easily buried him some place easier to access. Instead, the boy acted honorably, taking the time and effort to do it properly. Now, Anna's mother will be joining her father's side, and she finds it comforting to think about them resting on this hillside together, forever. She's thankful for Jose's actions and steals another look at the boy, but catching him watching her causes both to quickly turn their gazes downward.

Anna turns her attention to Sadie, who nods. When Anna returns the gesture, Jose and Sadie lower the woman's body into the grave. When it settles, Sadie returns to Anna's side, leaving the boy standing alone across from them. Sadie pulls from her pocket a folded sheet of paper with her prepared eulogy. She checks her notes, looks up, and begins using words that penetrate Anna's heart, making her weep once again. They're beautiful, and Sadie's sentiments will stay with the young girl.

With Sadie's closing remarks, the three of them each throw a handful of dirt in the grave. After a long pause, Jose and Sadie grab the shovels. They work alongside one another, maintaining an even pace without stopping. They smooth the remaining dirt, cleaning up the area, and then start piling on the rocks as they carefully fit each stone, making sure the mound is solid, even, and done with care.

Anna, who is sitting nearby, on a giant stone, has been watching the process in a complete daze. For her, time's standing still, and the girl has no idea how long she's been up on the hill. Anna realizes she's been staring at the work without actually seeing anything. She doesn't even remember sitting down, or how she got the blanket that's draped over her shoulders.

Still watching, she notices they're nearly done. When there's one rock left, Anna walks over to pick it up. She puts it on the mound and places both of her hands on the grave's stones. Her head remains bowed and motionless for a very long time. When she finally moves, it's to do the same at her father's. This time, she stays even longer, and when finished saying her goodbyes, the poor girl feels completely drained. Backing away, she notices Jose, who's holding two wreaths made of fresh redwood cuttings and dried foliage.

Jose, embarrassed by Anna's staring, avoids her eyes and places a wreath over each cross, then returns quickly to his position. Sadie, watching them both, continues thinking about how much every-thing's changed. She's gone, from being completely alone, to saving Caleb, to discovering she has neighbors, and ultimately, adopting two orphaned kids. Dismissing the synchronicity of what it all means, she puts her arm around Anna and motions to Jose. He stands at her side, and Sadie wraps her other arm around him.

The three stand in silence, creating the perfect ending. Anna rests her head against Sadie and surprisingly, Jose does the same. She lightly kisses the top of their heads, overcome with the comfort and ease in which these two have taken to her. They've been through more than their fair share of tribulation and have been incredibly resilient. The kids stand a little longer until Sadie moves them back to the house.

Inside, it's eerily quiet and the atmosphere between them returns to being awkward. Sadie knows it will take time for the two youngsters to become comfortable with one another. For now, she fills the void by getting Jose to help her with lunch while Anna changes clothes. Sadie and Jose talk in detail, in an almost business-like manner, speaking in hushed voices, until Anna returns. With the girl back in the room, Sadie shifts the conversation to Jose and his boat. She gets him to talk about various things, allowing Anna to simply listen.

When they eat, Sadie takes over the conversation, talking about both Caleb and Clara, deciding that the more these two know, the easier their transition will become. She shares details, locations, and how she's traveled between them, along with her route here. As she speaks, both kids listen intently, especially as she reminisces about her childhood and building the cave. Talking about her brothers with the kids makes Sadie happy. It's been so long since she's spoken about them, and her words from earlier ring true—by living, she's keeping their memory alive.

Anna, sensing what Sadie's feeling, fondly remembers a camping trip, and speaks for the first time in Jose's presence. Initially, she's hesitant, but as the memories flow, so does her spirit. She tells stories from over the years about her parents and their secret site. Her tales are happy and fun, but as the memories shift to more recent times, she grows sullen again. The campsite is where they hid, in fear and uncertainty, when Anna and her mother fled the Splitters.

Sadie, reading the girls face, makes the connection, "Anna, is that where you and your mom went?"

Anna looks at Sadie and whispers a reply, confirming what Sadie thought.

"Where?" Jose asks, so curious he actually braves a direct question to Anna. "Where's your…campsite?" He asks again.

Anna is unsure how to answer and Jose takes the delay as a sign to elaborate.

"I've hiked around and…didn't see anything like that. Is it far?" he tries, hoping she'll say something.

This time, Anna's able to reply. "No, it's not too far," she answers, and for the first time, they're looking at each other without turning away. "It's sorta hard to…describe, but…" she hesitates, thinking about her next words, "it'd be easier to show you. When…I take Sadie. You could…come, too." Suddenly, she's embarrassed, doubts inviting him, and looks away.

Jose, almost too quickly, responds, "Yes, I…I'd like…that." He too, feels a little awkward and is grateful as Sadie joins the conversation.

"Anna, is there enough time to go now?"

"Uh-huh." Anna says, looking forward to the distraction, and hopping off her chair, more than ready.

She puts on her shoes and coat, Sadie grabs her daypack and bow, and Jose follows behind. At first, they head towards the boat, but then, they veer farther north towards the rockier section of the little cove. The trail becomes less apparent as they make their way among fallen trees. As they travel deeper into Anna's property, the terrain grows steeper, stones jut through the ground at odd angles, and the footing becomes difficult.

They continue following Anna as she navigates through the last of the fallen debris. The passage becomes narrow and crowded, and they're able to squeeze through, but before moving too much further, Anna stops and turns, smiling at them. They look at her, but she doesn't say a word. Anna's not giving away the hidden local, so they begin to look around, trying to figure out what they've missed.

"What, already?" Jose asks. He's got his hands on his hips, and it makes Anna laugh.

Laughing feels good, and she lets it continue until she's able to answer. "Sadie, it's like your cave…it's hidden."

Sadie looks past Anna, and then realizes the girl means behind them. They all turn and start back the way they've just come, with Anna returning to the lead. This time, when they climb through the debris, Anna pushes aside an armful of foliage along the cliff wall, and then disappears. Re-opening the passageway, she sticks her head back out smiling beautifully.

Jose and Sadie make it through, discovering the way. They squeeze around one boulder and then climb over another, finding a trail that heads up the cliff. There are handholds and steps cut along the way, helping them to navigate the more difficult sections. They continue to climb, until emerging atop the cliff on the northeastern point of the island, where the view is stunning.

The more they see, the more Sadie's impressed. It's the perfect place to scout from, offering incredible vantage points. On the side they hiked, there's an impressive view all the way to the cove where they can see part of the boat, the sea stack blocking the harbor's entrance, and other stacks dotting the coastline. Further along, in the opposite direction, offers a view down the coast towards the south.

Gazing in that direction, Anna speaks, "This is why my dad thought we were on an island. He'd stand here…all the time, trying to convince my mom…and me…that this view proved it. We'd argue, it only proved water was here, and…we still didn't know what was further south…or…on the opposite side."

Over the years, Anna grew tired of hearing her dad talk about whether or not they lived on an island every time they came up here. Standing there now, she misses hearing his argument, and realizes, she'll never hear it again. She closes her eyes, as his words echo through her mind, making Anna feel his presence. Returning her attention back to Sadie and Jose, Anna's emotions transition from sadness to excitement, as she wants to finish giving them the tour.

"Come on...let me show you camp." She turns inland, and they follow.

Quickly, the trees become thicker, offering better shelter, and they're walking on a well-worn trail. It curves around one last boulder, and then the campsite comes into view. It's gorgeous, complementing its surroundings like it's a national park. Sadie and Jose keep staring in awe, as there are many little features that add comfort and usefulness.

Anna, walking them around, shows off the small shelter house, a raised platform for tents, the fire pit, and a huge table with redwood plank benches. There's even an outhouse and past it, another small structure Anna calls the camp shed. When they get to it, they're shocked at what's inside.

"No way," says Jose, giggling a little.

Sadie looks beyond the shed and turning to Anna, inquires about the possibility of driving from here to the girl's house.

"Yeah, but it's the long, long way." Anna answers. "My dad worked for years puttin' in a trail, but it's really rough...we haven't used it in a while. This is our camp quad," she says, turning back to the shed. "It's for work around here...but...my dad only ran it occasionally." She taps one of the steel drums lining the back wall, while continuing, "Cuz...we're almost out of gas."

Jose, thinking back, finds that it all makes sense. When he first arrived on the island, there were two large, work quads near Anna's house with all kinds of extra parts and accessories, some of which didn't match. Now, he recognizes some of those parts, as he runs his hands over the small four-wheeler. He suddenly realizes Anna is talking directly to him and turns his attention back to her.

"I learned on this one. The other two at the house..." she remembers, one's gone, and looking at Jose, a question forms in her mind. "Why'd they only take one?" she asks him.

Sadie, still curious about the road, hears the question and looks straight to Jose. He removes his hands from the machine and stands up. A sly look sweeps across his face and Sadie recognizes it. He looks at Sadie, then back to Anna, before answering.

"Only one started." His mischievous grin reappears. "I got to 'em a few minutes ahead of those idiots. But...I didn't have enough time."

Anna, confused, turns to Sadie, who's smiling at Jose.

"Again...huh, kiddo," She says, tousling his hair.

His smile is gigantic and as Sadie's hand returns to her side, he finishes explaining.

"I made sure it wouldn't start and then convinced them it couldn't be fixed." He pauses, as his smile fades and he grows serious. "I didn't want 'em to...find anyone else. With the quads, they were able to travel further...spreading more of their...terrible ways..." he pauses, building courage, "Anna, I'm...I'm sorry. I'm sorry...they...your parents. I wish I could've...stopped 'em."

Sadie puts a hand on his back and an arm around Anna.

"We did," she says. "We did stop 'em." She lets go of each and gets them moving.

Closing the shed door, the three leave, and on their descent, Anna talks a little more, giving them small insights into her family and the area. Nearing the cove, she asks Jose about the boat. Sadie, seeing it as a good sign, jumps at the opportunity for them to interact alone.

"Jose, why don't you give Anna a quick tour?" She suggests.

Both kids stop to look at Sadie.

"Be fast, though...I'll go ahead...and start dinner."

They don't move and remain silent.

"It's almost dark, so hurry...be quick. Okay?" Sadie says.

Neither responds.

"Okay?" she repeats with a little more authority.

"O-kay," they finally reply in unison.

When they both answer, Sadie walks away feeling a tingle of pride.

TWENTY-SIX

Over the next week, things become routine. It helps Anna and sets a tone of normalcy among them. They eat every meal together, explore and map the area, and spend evenings either in the house, or on the boat. Sadie takes them hunting every morning and with each outing, she adds to their education. Both are fast learners and equally impressive in their own ways.

Besides providing ways to spend time together, Sadie makes sure to interact individually with both kids whenever possible. They speak at length on a variety of topics, until they've gotten the lesson being offered or until Sadie's satisfied with their progress. Both Jose and Anna have witnessed and experienced life in ways kids should never have to. Sadie can't imagine growing up the way Jose was forced to or witnessing her mother's brutal attack and murder like Anna. It's heartbreaking, and Sadie catches herself reflecting on her own youth and the privileges she took for granted. These two kids are growing up in the new world—one Sadie still has much to learn about.

They work well together and a welcomed transition is taking place. They're becoming a team and Sadie continues to nourish and encourage this development. It's not just their conversations, or even the sharing of words that the kids need, it's just all of them being together that matters. They're not alone, and for the youngsters, having this basic need fulfilled lays the foundation Sadie hopes will support their recovery and growth. Life has brought them together and with each day, their bond grows a little stronger. Sadie fuels their curiosity, gets to know them, and feeds them heartily. Both are undernourished, and she's just as concerned about their physical well-being as she is with their mental health. Continuing to think ahead, Sadie does what she can, and understands, that time is really what they need and she doesn't want to rush the kids.

Sadie never planned on staying this long, but finds herself in a unique position that is forcing her to take everything into consideration. She's become a teacher, leader, surrogate parent, and friend, all through an interesting web of connections. All three of them have lost, suffered, and survived, and Sadie plans to see they continue to heal and grow. The kids sense it, too. They look to her, follow her lead, and most importantly, feel safe with her around. They inherently know she'll take care of them.

Over dinner one night, Sadie outlines sections of her plan. Anna and Jose listen, taking everything in, while understanding the seriousness of it. She prepares the kids for their parts and confirms their comprehension. At the end of the meal, she takes out her map, so they can study its features and talk travel distances. The island's outline is complete, and most of the interior is mapped, as well. There're still unfamiliar spots, but Sadie plans on getting to those areas as soon as the chance arises.

For now, though, the focus shifts to tonight's preparations with Jose, as he and Sadie leave for the cove for their grand finale. They've been manipulating the radio, continuing their charade with the Nation, and tonight, it will end. Part of the Splitter fleet continued scouting south and believes their former asset—now, Jose's boat—is far from its current location, and running low on fuel. Jose and Sadie plan to radio the fleet, after the craft fails to arrive at its scheduled refueling location. By now, the boat is several hours late and the awaiting crew should be concerned and realize something's wrong.

In broken radio signals, Jose will inform the vessel waiting for him that his boat has gone adrift and, in the thick fog, has wrecked on a sea stack. While making the distress call, the fatal accident, which will be thought to have sunk what remains of the boat, will conclude when the radio cuts off for the final time. Hopefully, the Nation's followers will buy it, thinking all aboard have been lost. Splitters aren't known to shed many tears—for anyone, including their own—and Sadie hopes the militants won't waste the time or energy to come looking for a few that must be, by now, lost causes.

Sadie looks at Jose, "Ready?"

The boy takes a deep breath, mentally reviews his part, and takes the radio's controls. Their farce goes off perfectly and afterwards, Sadie finalizes a few things with Jose before returning to the house to do the same with Anna. They have two days of preparations to complete before they leave, and each of them is responsible for certain items. A whirlwind of activity takes place the next day and they come together only briefly to share food before heading back to their chores. At dinner, Sadie checks off the items each has completed and verifies what's still left to accomplish. They've done well, are nearly ready, and everything is on track.

On their last day, Sadie helps Anna and verifies all the remaining preparations the girl made are complete. When Sadie leaves the house to check with Jose, Anna heads up to her parents' graves for an important last detail. With each step, the girl's emotions strengthen and at their graves, she stumbles, falling to her knees, as grief erupts and runs its course. As it subsides, Anna's able to return to her feet, speaking to her mom and dad.

She fills them in, talking in depth about Jose and Sadie. When she gets to the part about leaving, she jokes with her dad about him being right. She's going to see the proof he always wanted, but choking up, the girl's unable to continue. She blubbers through tears in an incoherent jumble of words and afterwards, is exhausted, but feels better.

The following morning begins, as always, with Sadie's early morning patrol. When she returns, they eat a small breakfast before departing. There's apprehension and a little fear in Anna's eyes as she leaves the only home she's ever known. Her decision to fulfill the family's trek and explore the island is what pulls her forward. She wishes her parents were here now, since her family was supposed to do this together, but instead, she's making the journey in their honor. Anna wears her mother's old worn backpack and drinks from her dad's water bottle, in an attempt of keeping them with her as she travels.

Jose also feels a little unease. He's concerned one of the Splitter fleet's crews might find the hidden cove and search the island. Even though the odds of that happening are small, its possible discovery still worries him. At least there's no one there to harm, but on the other hand, there's also no one guarding the boat and house, and he doesn't want anything to happen to any of it—or to any of them. He vows to do whatever it takes to protect Sadie and Anna, and never again, will he let the Splitters harm others.

Along the way, uncertainty also creeps into Sadie's mind. Even though their charade went smoothly, the knowledge that Splitter crews have been scouting the surrounding waters concerns her. By now, they should be far from the island, but there's always the possibility they'll come back. She contemplates each detail, looking at things from different angles, and decides to stick with the wisdom of her plan.

Stopping, she looks back to watch the two kids trailing behind. Watching them move, Sadie notices subtle differences and smiles at them. They've done well and she's proud. It's a solid pace and they've kept up, without once complaining. Today's hike is easy, as much of it's on Anna's section of the island, and they're able to follow old logging roads and trails.

When they hike beyond the territory the kids already know, Sadie points out various landmarks, ensuring they'll learn it. She's especially focused on Jose's learning, as she explains alternative routes and ways to make the trek even faster, preparing him for his return, when he'll do it solo. Once they get to the cave, the girls will continue on Anna's journey, fulfilling her dad's wishes, but Jose will play a much different role. He'll move every few days, dividing his time between Caleb and Anna's homestead.

As evening approaches, they near their resting place for the night, which Sadie debated whether to use or not. Setting down her pack, she signals for Jose and Anna to do the same. Sadie contemplates where to begin and how to approach things with the kids. She takes a deep breath and decides on sharing the ugly truth about what occurred at this spot. As she talks, they look around as Sadie tells them how she'd like to transform the site. When she finishes, the kids remain silent.

"Well, what do you think? Will you help me?" Sadie says, after giving them a few more moments.

Both nod in agreement, feeling a sense of loss and responsibility, but they realize, turning such a horrible thing into something positive is empowering for them. Sadie retrieves a few things from her pack, sets the items aside, and goes about gathering materials to make a fire. They collect wood and rearrange the stones from the previous fire ring to create something new. Repeatedly striking her flint, Sadie gets the flames going while thinking about the next lesson she plans on teaching. She holds the sage bundle and explains what it is, how it's been used over the generations, and where she got it. Using some of Clara's words, Sadie describes the way the old woman uses the cleansing and purifying plant.

Jose and Anna comprehend all Sadie explains and feel a deep-seated righteousness about it all. Sadie lights the sage, and all three purify their hands and bodies with its smoke before encircling the campsite with the small bundles they carry. Jose and Anna walk in opposite directions until they finish their circle and are back together. Sadie uses hers to cleanse the area where she found Caleb's friend. She burns the last of it, saying a few words of closure, and then returns to setting up for the night.

Anna searches for the perfect branches and makes a cross, while Jose sets about creating another wreath. While the kids are busy, Sadie buries what remains of the Splitters' garbage, and as they finish, the three of them erect a memorial by mounding stones around the cross's base. With it completed, they stand in a moment of silence for the murdered man, and then settle down next to the fire. Even though such a terrible event occurred here, each feels they've helped right a wrong. From now on, this place will remain as a memorial to all of those who've suffered at the hands of the Nation and a place of honor for the few who have pledged to fight them.

At sunrise, the two kids are up hunting with Sadie and along the way, she uncovers the stash of items she confiscated from the dead Splitters. She decides to give the remaining rifle to Jose and talks with him about relocating the fuel cans and ammo boxes, also hidden there, back to Anna's. He'll carry something each time he makes the hike, hiding them along the way, until he finally manages getting them all the way there. Hiking further, Sadie shows them where she sent the quad the Splitters stole form Anna's family over the cliff, apologizing to the girl while doing so.

"I was coverin' the tracks and…worried more Splitters would come lookin'. I'm sorry…I destroyed it."

The girl carefully approaches the edge and peers down. There's no evidence of it below, only the crashing of waves. The ground is still unstable and she quickly retreats back to safety. The quad was her father's, and Anna remembers the times she rode with him. When she was littler, she sat tucked in front, with his hands over hers, while he taught her to drive and work the controls. He'd do donuts with it, making her laugh and forcing her to hang on even tighter. She misses him dearly and realizes those days are gone. Instead of crying, Anna shares the stories with Sadie and Jose.

Soon, they arrive at the clearing where Sadie first discovered the two dead Splitters. She shares the information with the kids, shows them the rock where she spent the night when she found Caleb, and what supplies she's stashed nearby for emergencies. She talks survival strategies, shelters, and water collection techniques, along the way. By mid-day they're nearing her cave, and Sadie's excited to show it to the kids. Their anticipation grows and they're ready to finally arrive at their destination.

When they near the water collection trees, Sadie removes from her pack a condensation bag she travels with and teaches Jose and Anna how to use it. She sets it up and then removes it, allowing each of them to practice the procedures. It's an effective way to learn and when she's satisfied with their level of mastery, the group continues forward. Instead of heading directly to the cave's entrance, Sadie takes them around the perimeter, explaining why she does it this way.

Once the perimeter check is complete, Sadie heads towards the cave, stopping only to have the kids wait nearby. They can see the fallen trees and are surprised to learn that Sadie's hideout could be among the mess. They watch her climb over one log and then disappear. She seems to be taking forever, and even though they don't talk about it, both kids grow a little worried.

Inside, Sadie finds Caleb awake and reading a book. He looks a little better than he did the last time she was here, and he's relieved to see her. He starts to get up and Sadie goes to his side to help. She's been gone a lot longer this time around and he's been worried about her safety. When he gets to his feet, he surprises Sadie by wrapping his arms around her. He continues holding on, until it becomes awkward, and embarrassingly lets go.

"We've got company," Sadie interjects, before he can say anything.

At first, the words scare him, but then he sees her relaxed body language and the smile on her face. Sadie gives him a quick update on all that's happened since she left and lets him know they'll talk in detail later. For now, she wants to introduce him. He looks around, feels a little embarrassed about how messy he's left things, and starts to clean up. Sadie joins him, rearranging items so there'll be more room to accommodate two more people.

The kids' initial excitement shifts to uncertainty as they crawl under the last log on their way to meeting a stranger. Inside, they feel shy and a little uncomfortable in the cramped space. They aren't sure where to stand or put their things. Sadie breaks the ice with introductions as Caleb greets them by shaking their hands while she places their belongings to the side and makes room for all of them to sit.

At first, the kids are quiet, but Sadie knows them well enough to ease their uncertainties and get them interacting. It's easy getting Jose to talk about his boat. With Anna, it's a little more difficult, but eventually, the girl shares information about her upcoming journey with Sadie. As the girl speaks, Caleb looks over to Sadie giving her a look conveying that, they do indeed, have a lot to talk about. As the two kids relax, they feel the soreness in their muscles and the hunger in their bellies.

Sadie starts charging the hand generator and both kids swivel around to see what she's up to. She lets them take turns pulling the cord and then gives them small tasks, keeping them occupied. Before they eat, and it gets too dark, Sadie asks Jose and Anna to do the short perimeter check, reminding them of the path and markers. The kids remember to leave quietly, pausing to listen to their surroundings, before emerging into the woods.

With the kids gone, Sadie and Caleb have a chance to talk privately. Sadie continues preparing food and while working, she talks, as Caleb finds himself frustrated that, once again, he'll be stuck in the cave, while she's out and about. At least, this time he'll have some company, even if it's a young kid, whom he's only just met. As they talk, Caleb agrees with Sadie's logic, and voices the same concerns she has about leaving Jose, at times, all alone, at Anna's. However, they agree that—really—there's no other way.

TWENTY-SEVEN

Sadie wakes before anyone else and steps outside. Her little hideout is full of bodies and all of them stayed up late—talking, laughing, and hanging out. It felt like old times with her family, except, now, she's the adult. Sitting in silence, she finds it enjoyable to think back to those fun-filled days of her youth. A subtle noise draws her attention, and listening, she hears when Jose finally emerges.

"Morning, kiddo," she says, noticing he's carrying the rifle she gave him yesterday.

He smiles back. "Can I join ya?"

"Of course." Sadie says, glad he wants to go.

Sadie hasn't said anything about it yet, but she's curious about Jose's level of experience with a rifle. After a quick perimeter check, and thinking Jose would enjoy it, she heads towards one of her father's favorite hunting grounds. It helps that the weather's cooperating and it's clear enough to make the spot a viable option.

They climb quietly, occasionally stopping whenever Sadie signals. Before they crest a ridge, she pauses, points, and whispers to Jose. They descend at an angle, almost halfway down a rather steep slope, hiking along a game trail, until an impressive oak tree comes into view. Sadie carefully scans the area before slowly approaching the unique oak. The trunk separates into four individual sections, making it appear to be a tight cluster of trees, and they climb a rope ladder up to a platform constructed between the separated trunks.

Sadie visits the area often, but it's been a long time since she's hunted here, as the weather hasn't been clear enough to see what unfolds below. It's a mystical place, carpeted in every shade of green. The mountain sorrel, which looks like giant clover, is thick and vibrant from the recent rains, and moss covers nearly everything. Ancient ferns grow thickly and some of the oldest redwoods in the mountains tower above the forest floor.

The unique contour of the land often traps the fog, which aids the landscape's ability to support such lush vegetation. The fog's moisture seeps into the canyon, keeping the forest floor damp, and there-fore, much greener than its surroundings. Today, however, it's clear enough, that, from their perch above, they have a wide view of the expanse below. All around, thick redwoods dominate, and their lone oak is the only one of its species in the canyon. It sits high up the slope, where there's just enough space—and open sky—for it to thrive.

After brushing debris off the platform, the two sit down. Sadie settles into a comfortable position with her crossbow and Jose does the same with his rifle. She scans the surroundings, seeing nothing of interest, and decides to use the opportunity to talk instead. Jose's got a big day ahead of him and it's important that he's ready, but first, she wants to check his rifle knowledge, as it's obvious he's never used one before. At times, he's a little clumsy, and noticeably unsure, so Sadie inquires about it in a low whisper, and once again, the kid surprises her.

"It's not loaded. I'm not ready for bullets...I don't want to waste 'em. I need to practice carryin' and handlin' it. But," he reaches into one of his pockets and shows Sadie the ammo, "I'm ready...just in case."

Sadie spends time teaching Jose everything she knows about the gun. They never see any animals, but it doesn't matter. For the time being, Jose's satisfied learning how to use his new tool, along with working on becoming a true marksman. He's an excellent student and Sadie has him practice loading and unloading the rifle, repeatedly, until he's more confident doing so.

With the bullets back in Jose's pocket, Sadie progresses the lesson to aiming and pulling the trigger. His first few reps are from a prone position, then, he transitions to kneeling, and finally, he practices while standing. Wrapping up the instruction, Sadie encourages him to keep training, and to work with Caleb, reminding him of the importance of actual target practice and getting the feel of shooting live rounds.

When they climb back down, Sadie leads him deeper into the carpeted canyon. Along the way, they come across a huge patch of nibbled vegetation. All the leaves are missing from the sorrel, leaving perfectly erect stems. Sadie excitedly points out this obvious deer sign to Jose and walking further, they approach a huge redwood log. One end is overgrown with ferns and Sadie pushes them aside to remove an old section of chicken wire hidden beneath the thick fronds. Setting the barrier aside, she uses branches, kept nearby, to hold back the ferns. The open gap reveals the hollowness of the log and a dark, damp, rich layer of soil and decay lining its bottom. Sadie stops at the opening, checking over her crop.

She's particular in her selection and while cutting, she's careful not to damage their fine root structures. Gently harvesting two different varieties, she shakes what spores she can from the caps, explaining to Jose why it's important to do so. She places the mushrooms in a small sack looped into the strap of her daypack and recovers the log's opening. On the way out, each of them picks sorrel greens, filling another small bag. Sadie's already said it once while gathering the mushrooms and before she can finish saying it again, Jose cuts her off.

"I know. Never go back empty handed...there's always somethin'...you just have to know how to look." His eyes roll slightly, accompanying his heart-felt grin.

Realizing her point's been made, Sadie smiles. "Alright, let me show you one more thing."

She returns to the opposite side of the log and squeezes between it and the slope behind, where several large stones hold back most of the earth. Hidden beneath another canopy of ferns is an arrangement of rocks that's obviously not naturally formed. At the bottom of these, a small pipe sticks out several inches, and a piece of black irrigation line runs angling down the remaining slope.

As the water line descends, it disappears behind more rocks. Sadie removes several stones from the top of the stack and slides off a section of old plastic roofing material, exposing two five-gallon buckets tucked neatly into the stone cache. They're connected to one another by a short section of tubing, have tightly sealed lids, and at the buckets' bottoms, there are small valves. There's just enough room underneath the spigots to place a water bottle, which Sadie fills now. When she finishes, Jose does the same with his.

She shows Jose how the overflow runs out another line, when the buckets are full, dripping water directly into the log's bottom. The small spring produces enough water to keep the mushrooms growing, and Sadie hydrated, anytime she's in the area. It's rather simple, but incredibly impressive at the same time. Jose takes his time checking all the connections, making sure he grasps all aspects of the set-up and then together, Sadie and Jose return the lid and stones and head towards the cave. When they return, it's only for a quick check-in, before leaving again. This time, Anna joins them, and Jose leads, since Sadie wants to make sure he's able to find his way when alone. The ladies plan to accompany him all the way to the Memorial Campground, and then, in the morning, he's solo.

They make good time traveling together and at camp, they quickly set up, eat, and settle in for the evening. Sadie starts on watch, and the night passes smoothly and uneventfully. Early the next day, they say good-bye to Jose, as the girls go their separate direction, each occupied with their own thoughts, doubts, and concerns. Jose will only be away a single night, but since it's the trial run, and such a major component of their plan, each of them wrestles with a touch of anxiety.

The plan's success hinges on Jose's being able to trek solo and his comfort with spending time alone at Anna's. For his first attempt, he's returning only briefly, and then leaving early the next morning so they can reunite the following evening. Once alone, Jose picks up his pace and pushes forward, determined to be successful and achieve the goals he's set for himself. First off, the boy wants to finds ways to travel the route faster. He figures, with each attempt, he'll improve, until getting it down to the shortest possible time. Walking at a brisk pace, Jose mentally takes note of the various markers along the way. As he nears Anna's place, he veers around to check the perimeter before heading into the home. Once there, he drops everything but his rifle, and heads up to the lookout camp before inspecting the boat.

Early the next morning, Jose re-checks the surrounding area, gathers a couple of items Sadie asked for, and leaves. He's confident with his task and works on developing a rhythm to help keep a fast pace, finding enjoyment moving through the quiet and beauty of the woods. When he slows to drink, he controls his breathing, then, he takes off again at a trot, even as his muscles start to scream and fatigue begins to set in. His desire to improve motivates him, along with the mindset of not disappointing the girls, especially Anna, whom he'll never let down again.

Nearing the campsite, Jose forces himself to slow and approach with caution. He walks around the perimeter, carefully scanning the surroundings. As he draws closer, he sees Anna working nearby and pauses. She's using a small cutting tool to saw redwood branches into similar lengths. Once cut, they get stacked nearby, and the left-over pieces she tosses into a pile near the fire ring. He knows she's struggling with the death of her parents, but at the moment, an air of ease and peacefulness is about her.

Jose, absorbed by watching Anna, is caught off guard by hearing his name from directly behind him. Even though the voice is recognizable, it still makes him jump. He was completely unaware of another's presence and realizes his mistake. Sadie reads the boy's disappointment in his body language and eyes, knows he understands the potential danger of such an error, and doesn't make him feel any worse by lingering on it. Besides, she wholeheartedly believes he'll never let it happen again, so instead, Sadie switches tactics.

"I didn't expect you for a few more hours. That was fast," she says, with praise.

Jose, caught off guard again—this time by her compliment—struggles with finding a response. He expected corrections, and instead, finds relief she's not berating him for his obvious oversight.

He hesitates a little longer before shyly replying, "Next time...I'll do it even faster."

His eyes, still a little downcast, peek up, as Sadie pats him on the shoulder.

"Don't be so hard on yourself...I have no doubt you'll keep gettin' better."

Jose looks at Sadie, and together, they enter camp. As they near, Anna turns, also surprised.

"Jose!" Anna's excitement at seeing him suddenly embarrasses her. She quickly regains her composure and walks over to him. Shyly, she speaks. "We didn't think you'd get here until later."

Jose, feeling better after Anna's initial reaction, smiles and quickly changes the subject. "What'cha doin' with the branches?" he asks, looking at her pile.

Anna's eyes follow his, and her excitement returns. "I'm helping Sadie...she's teachin' me how to build a shelter. Wanna help?"

Sadie smiles watching the two interact. She knows Jose's exhausted, sore, and probably hungry, but he's not letting it interfere. Instead, he's cutting branches as Anna stands nearby, helping. Sadie leaves them, for work of her own, and by dusk, the three gather at the fire ring to sit down for a dinner of roasted squirrel, mushrooms, and sorrel greens before crawling into their newly constructed sleeping quarters.

The shelter's design keeps them elevated off the ground, and there's just enough room for four people to lie down comfortably. It's by far the largest shelter Sadie's built, but it's also the first time she's needed to construct something bigger than for just herself. The thought spreads another smile across her face and Sadie doesn't fail to recognize how good it makes her feel.

When they awake in the morning, Sadie takes them nearby to the other sites she's prepared. Near the base of an old redwood stump sits a small boulder, where two ferns, squeezed between them, serve as camouflage. It's obvious the ground's been disturbed, but time will quickly erase the signs of the fresh work, making the cache hidden below the perfect stash location. Sadie shows them the items she's already placed in it, and talks about what other supplies will get added. Moving on, they curl around the camp's perimeter and head up a nearby slope to a tightly-packed group of redwoods, thick with branches and surrounded by bushy tree shoots protruding from around all the trunks. They maneuver around the branches, squeeze through the younger growth, and then circle a large stump until Sadie has them climb up on it. Standing atop it, the two kids look curiously down at Sadie.

"Keep looking," she responds, to their unasked questions.

The two turn circles, gazing about at the trees surrounding them, and then look up. Jose gently pushes aside a few branches and discovers what Sadie wants them to find. Camouflaged by the branches, there's a couple of foot and hand-holds, recently cut into the neighboring tree's burls, allowing them to climb higher, where Sadie's begun constructing another hideout.

Most of the structure is simply an enormous chandelier arm, protruding several feet out from the redwood's trunk before turning back skyward at a ninety-degree angle. At some point, long ago, the tree suffered trauma, which resulted in the unique feature. The trees surrounding it grew so close together they created a natural barrier, almost completely enclosing the arm on one side and partially on the other. Varying gaps of space between the trees provide lookouts and defendable openings, if needed. It's at the perfect vantage point, allowing views back towards camp, to the south, and the north, while keeping them completely hidden from below.

The kids, impressed with Sadie's discovery, make room for her to join them. It's a little crowded with all three, but they sit down, and Sadie discusses the rest of the preparations she wishes for the spot. Feeling blessed with the location, since it offers a safer place to overnight, Sadie's more comfortable with Jose eventually being out here alone. After they finish talking, the three of them depart, with the boy once again in lead position as he navigates them back to Caleb. Sadie, watching him closely as she follows, has a growing confidence in his abilities and is put a little more at ease with her plan.

TWENTY-EIGHT

Sadie's worried. Anna hasn't spoken or eaten much, and her pace continues to grow sluggish, even though they've been taking it easy and stopping often for breaks. Sadie hoped to prevent the girl from fatiguing on this first leg of the journey and acclimate her to back-to-back, all-day hiking, while building stamina for what lies ahead. Pausing again to drink water, she's patient while waiting for Anna.

"We'll go only a little farther today," Sadie encourages.

Anna simply nods and trudges on. Initially, the drive to complete her father's quest and the excitement of traveling helped the poor girl, but the distraction didn't last. Thinking about ways to keep Anna functioning, Sadie begins talking of her home and how close they're getting. She tells Anna about what awaits their arrival, but the struggling youngster shows no signs of interest, until Sadie talks about taking a hot bath.

"You have...a bathtub?" Anna looks up, and for the first time, joins the conversation.

"Yep...and right now there's plenty of water," Sadie chimes in, not wasting an opportunity to create something for the girl to look forward to. "You wanna go first when we get there?"

Anna gazes at her for a long time before replying in an almost trance-like fashion, "I'd...like...that..." then trails off, back in a haze.

Sadie lets her be; knowing they'll arrive tomorrow and hopefully, the girl will recover some motivation. The following morning, they break camp early and head off. Sadie walks even slower, trying not to push Anna too hard, but it's a struggle for the avid hiker. She's never taken so long to travel from the cave to her home, and nearing her main shelter, Sadie points out the route they'll take for a perimeter check. It's a safety procedure Sadie lives by and wants to instill in Anna. Even though both women are anxious to be done, it's too important to skip. When everything checks out, Sadie takes Anna through the hidden tunnel. At first, the girl isn't impressed, especially, as they navigate the dark and narrow entrance.

"Welcome to my home," Sadie happily says, unlocking the door.

It's rather dark, with only a single lantern casting light, but Anna can sense the spacious living quarters. Sadie takes off her pack, has Anna do the same, and then disappears momentarily. Suddenly, the entire place lights up and Anna gasps. Sadie, returning to the child, has a huge smile on her face and is almost giddy.

"You're my very first guest and…that's special." Sadie takes Anna's hands in hers, "I'm glad I can share this with you. Come on…I'll show ya around."

Sadie's contagious excitement, along with all the new things, is enthralling for Anna. There's a plethora of items, rooms, and equipment to distract the young girl. The two of them could spend days, weeks, even months, and still not get through everything. It's a lot to take in, but they make a pretty quick run of it. Before Anna gets too overloaded, Sadie changes things up.

"Why don't you keep lookin' around…I'll start dinner and heat your bath."

Anna stops looking at the items on a shelf and turns to face Sadie. The girl's eyes tear up, but she's able to control her emotions enough to speak. "Thank you…for…everything. You've been so good to me… and…and…" she loses what composure she has and breaks down crying.

Sadie steps closer, wrapping her in a hug, "It's okay Anna, it's my pleasure, really…I should be thankin' you…for…travelin' here, with me. I know it hasn't been easy, but…I'm proud of you."

They remain embraced until Anna gets herself back under control, and when she does, Sadie kisses the top of her head and lets go.

"Alright kiddo…I'll get things started…make yourself at home," Sadie says, leaving the girl.

While Sadie works in the kitchen, Anna thumbs through several of the books that line nearly an entire wall of one of the rooms. It's Sadie's personal library, and Anna's amazed. She's never seen so many books, and she can't wait to tell Jose. He'll love them. Flipping through the pages of one, she reads the captions underneath the pictures. Even though she doesn't understand several of the bigger words, or fully comprehend it all, Anna's interested because it's about gardening, and there's a large section dedicated to the subject.

Anna's parents taught her to read with extremely limited resources. Her home schooling was minimal as helping run the homestead kept her busy. It took a lot of effort for the family to survive, but in the evenings, when work was done, her parents would take turns teaching Anna, or sharing stories about how it was before the Global Flood drowned the planet.

Both her mom and dad worked in the agricultural industry, starting early in their childhoods. They toiled alongside their parents in the berry fields, eventually working upwards in the system. Working hard, they earned enough to buy land and build their own place, where they raised their daughter. Gardening was what her family did together, and as Anna closes her eyes, she realizes she took it all for granted. The finality of it is gut-wrenching and tears run down her checks. When she opens her eyes, she sees Sadie standing nearby.

"Come on kiddo...dinner's ready."

Anna returns the book to its place, wipes her cheeks dry, and turns around, as Sadie drapes an arm around her shoulders while they walk out of the room.

"In honor of your arrival, I made us a few treats. Let's enjoy 'em first...then you can soak in a nice hot tub. Okay?"

"Okay," the child responds, leaning her head against Sadie's torso.

Suddenly, Anna's senses are overwhelmed with all the enticing aromas. Her stomach growls in response as she greedily inhales another nose full. Anna didn't realize how hungry she was and can't wait to see what smells so good. The dining area is set with the finest china owned and the décor is festive.

Anna looks from the table to Sadie. "You were busy!"

Sadie pulls out a chair for the girl to sit and lifts a miniature bottle of champagne.

"I've had this forever...couldn't imagine when I'd ever drink it. But...thinkin' about tonight's meal...it popped into my head." She laughs at the joke as the bottle pops. "It's not as cold as it should be... and honestly, you're still a little young, but...this is a special occasion." She fills both their flukes, raises her glass, and nods to Anna to do the same. "I've been on my own a very, very long time...and I'm glad fate brought us together. May we enjoy each other's company... learn from one another...and, one day, discover the reason we've been brought together."

They clink glasses, and Sadie sips hers first. Anna follows Sadie's lead and takes a drink.

The girl scrunches up her nose. "It's bubbly and tickles my nose!"

Sadie laughs. "It's champagne, enjoyed on special occasions." She clinks the girl's glass again. "Cheers."

Both ladies empty their glasses, and Sadie pours what remains from the miniature bottle. This time, Anna raises her glass first.

"Thank you…for sharing…all this with me." Anna says, gesturing to everything around before they sip their second glass.

Anna, feeling pretty good, is ready to eat. Her face is warm and a touch tingly, she's smiling and incredibly hungry. She's never had alcohol before and it's making her a little giggly. Sadie serves them each a small bowl of soup, accompanied with hot bread sticks. Anna digs in, eating loudly. Everything tastes so good. She wipes her mouth, watching Sadie serve up the main course. The rising steam sends another delectable aroma through the air, and Anna's, never seen this type of food before and asks about it.

"It's lasagna. Layers of noodles, cheese, and vegetables all smothered in tomato sauce. But what makes it really incredible are the fresh herbs and garlic. For that, we have to thank Clara." Sadie answers, cutting the food into squares.

A smile spreads across Anna's face. She's looking forward to meeting the old woman. She's already heard so much about her from Sadie. She takes the first forkful and the taste overwhelms her.

"Mmmm…dis iz sooo…good!" Anna says, talking with her mouth full and already taking another bite.

As soon as Anna finishes, Sadie serves her another portion. It makes her feel good to see the young girl eating so heartily. As the two finish their meal, Sadie takes the plates away and returns with yet another item. Its smell is completely different and Anna's not sure how much more she can eat, but it smells so good.

"Hope you saved room for dessert," Sadie says, while cutting a piece.

Anna, stares at the dark brown item Sadie just set on the little plate in front of her. Once again, she has no idea what it is and looks to Sadie. Seeing the amusement in Sadie's eyes, Anna doesn't ask this time; instead, she just takes a huge bite. An explosion of sweetness erupts and Anna can't believe how incredible it is. She takes another bite, and then another, before she remembers Sadie's watching.

Sadie bursts out laughing. It's so contagious that Anna joins her. The two are laughing hysterically, and Anna has no idea why. When she asks, it only starts Sadie up again, which in turn, gets Anna going. They laugh so hard that Sadie has to wipe the corners of her eyes. When finally able to talk, Sadie first takes a bite of her dessert and makes the girl wait another moment.

She swallows. "They're chocolate brownies. From the expressions on your face...I gather...you've never eaten one before?"

Anna shakes her head no. "It's delicious. My parents told me about chocolate, but tastin' it is so much better." The girl uses her fingers to pick up the last crumbs on her plate.

"Watchin' you eat it...may have been even more pleasurable." Sadie laughs one more time and begins to clean up.

Anna gets up to help, but Sadie stops her.

"No, but thank you. You're my guest...I can't have you doin' anything but enjoying yourself. Besides...you have a bath that should be ready, but...first...how 'bout some music? Wha d'yah feel like?"

Anna shrugs her shoulders. She's never heard anything but an occasional song from her parents. "I've never heard any. So...pick somethin' for me."

"Ohhh, kiddo...no music...we'll fix that. Tomorrow, while I do my chores...and get us ready, you're gettin' the full music experience. In the meantime...I'll pick somethin' to start ya off." Sadie scans her collection and turns the sound system on. She scrolls through her digital collection, finding what she wants. "Something, like this." She hits "play," and the music immediately spreads throughout the entire compound.

Anna finds pure enjoyment in the sound and finds her head keeping beat.

Sadie, smiling and lightly dancing, sings along, *"Don' worry... 'bout a thing. Cuz, every little thing...gonna be all right,"* she takes Anna's hand and circles her around, *"Woke up this mornin', smiled at the risin' sun,"* she leads her away and into the bathroom area, *"Three little birds...besides my doorstep. Singing sweet songs..."* She trails off from singing to show Anna the process for bathing. "Take as long as you want."

She leaves the girl to her privacy and, right as Sadie begins to think she's taking too long, Anna reappears. It's obvious she's been crying again, but at the moment, the youngster seems okay. Sadie motions for her to sit down, and slowly, she starts to brush the girl's long beautiful hair. Anna remains quiet the entire time and only the light music drifts between them.

"There, that should do it," Sadie says, setting down the brush and getting up to bring a box over to Anna. "I pulled out a few things I thought you might like. Some of the clothes might be a little big, but... you'll grow into 'em. Go through it...try things on...keep whatever you want. I'm gonna rinse off...then, I'll join you for a late-night snack before bed."

Anna, trying her best to fight back the emotions battling within, can only nod a reply. When Sadie returns, she brings them each a hot cup of tea and another brownie. Noticing the empty box and the pile of items neatly stacked near the girl, Sadie smiles. The girls probably never owned anything new, and Sadie's got more supplies than she'll ever use. It makes her feel good to help Anna, but it's more than that. For the first time, Sadie begins to realize, she's a part of something much bigger than herself.

As the two finish their treat, Sadie turns off the music and gets Anna, who's already nodding off, some bedding. "Are you okay sleepin' here?"

"Yeah," Anna says, looking forward to lying down.

The girl stands up, thinking she'll help Sadie with the blankets, but instead, Sadie hands her the entire pile and opens up the futon.

"It turns into a bed!"

Sadie chuckles at the girl's surprise. "Kiddo, there's lot of things I'm gonna show ya. Remember, the world wasn't always the way you've known it. But...for now...let's get you to bed." Kissing the top of the girl's head, she wishes her goodnight.

Early the next day, Sadie's up and working on a rather long to-do list that needs to be done before they continue their journey. As soon as Anna wakes, the music is back on. It starts with some swing, from the roaring twenties, and progresses through the decades. Sadie finds something representative of each era and gives Anna little tidbits of information along the way.

Most of the work, Sadie does alone, but she assigns small tasks, keeping Anna occupied and her interests piqued. Every time the girl finishes an assignment, she checks back with Sadie to get the next one. They continue this way throughout most of the day, taking small breaks only to change the music or to eat. As the day nears evening, Sadie heads out for a quick patrol and leaves Anna behind.

Musically, they're wrapping up the fifties with a compilation CD, followed by two more from the sixties. The girl, now fully capable of using the stereo, sits nearby, flipping through a book Sadie left out for her. When the next song starts, Anna freezes. When it plays all the way through, she repeats it, again, and again, and again. She turns up the sound and doesn't hear Sadie return. Anna, singing along as loud as she can, is surprised when Sadie enters the room.

Frozen mid-lyric, Anna turns the music back down. "Sorry," she says, embarrassed, thinking Sadie will be upset. Instead, she's surprised when Sadie turns it up and also starts singing along. The two sound terrible, but they don't care.

"You ain't nothin' but a hound dog, barking all the time…No, you never caught a rabbit and you ain't no friend of mind."

"How do you know this song?" Sadie asks, when it finishes.

"My mom used to sing it to my dad. Whenever he did something that bothered her…she'd call him a hound dog and…would start singing. I didn't know it was a real song…" she pauses, deep in thought. "There were others. Maybe you have them, too!" Anna, excited about the possibility, turns to Sadie.

Realizing how important this is for Anna, Sadie grabs a notebook and pen. "Here, think about the songs they sang and write down what you can remember. Then, I'll see if I have 'em."

Anna takes the paper and stares at it. "I can't think 'bout other songs with the music on. Is it okay to…turn it off?"

Sadie does so immediately. "No problem kiddo. I've got a few more things to finish up…you work on those songs…we'll eat some dinner…and, then, see what we can find."

As Sadie sets the table for dinner, Anna appears with notebook in hand. Sadie reads through the girl's writing. It's full of misspellings and the penmanship is terrible. Most of it is in English, but there's some Spanish, as well as a mix of both languages. Making corrections and labeling what she recognizes, Sadie hands it back to Anna.

"While I finish our food, I'd like you re-write these." She points out various lyrics, gives the girl more direction, and leaves her to the task.

After they eat, Sadie re-checks the girl's writing. "This looks much better. Nice job!"

She makes a single correction, telling Anna why. "I know for sure I have some of these songs. The Spanish ones...I'm not too sure. I'm not as familiar with that part of my collection, but...we'll check."

She clears the table, this time letting Anna help and when they finish, Sadie reminds her they need to pack, suggesting they do so next to the sound system, so they can also look for Anna's songs. They gather their backpacks and a pile of supplies they've been adding to all day. Dropping everything in front of the music collection, Sadie knows they're in for some heavy travel.

There's no way Anna can handle too large of a load, which means, Sadie will have to carry the bulk of it. While Anna organizes her things, Sadie heads off and returns with two different packs. She tosses one over to Anna and as the girl turns it over, Sadie speaks.

"We've got a lot to carry and we're going to need more room. So... it's yours...take care of it, and it'll last a long time."

Anna's already seen, tasted, learned, and received more new things than ever before in her life. There's no way she can ever repay the kindness or fully explain how much it means.

"Thank you. I can't say it enough." Anna feels her eyes beginning to water and wipes away an escaping tear.

Sadie teaches Anna a few techniques for properly fitting and packing her new bag. For the remaining part of the evening, they listen to songs while finishing their preparations. They manage getting everything to fit, briefly talk about the route they'll take, and estimate how many days it'll take to get to Clara's. Anna's curious to see the south coast and looks forward to meeting the old woman. Before closing her eyes for the night, Anna thinks about her parents and how much they'd love Sadie. She falls asleep, once again, on a tear-soaked pillow.

TWENTY-NINE

Jose and Caleb set a routine, and so far, it's working wonderfully for both. The boy travels between the cave and Anna's homestead, spending three days at the house and a day and a half at the cave. He patrols, manages the homestead, moves supplies, and gains confidence with each trip. He doesn't mind being alone, and it's peaceful knowing he's no longer in the forced company of the Splitter Nation. He's grateful for the change and for the first time, feels hope.

At the homestead, he brainstorms ways to guard the cove and house, keeping a small notebook with drawings and notations as his ideas mature. He monitors the property, keeps it maintained, and of course, there's the boat he takes pride in keeping clean, functional, and organized. With the Splitters gone, he runs it more efficiently, and starting at the bridge, Jose systematically goes through every compartment and area, inventorying and relocating items. He keeps a list of additional supplies and equipment that should be onboard and designs better ways to load and unload the vessel in a more secure and safe fashion.

Staying at Anna's is a full-time job, keeping him busy from sunrise to sunset. Even after dark, he works by candlelight or reads for a few more hours before bed. Hiking between the two places provides Jose with time away from his continuous chores, allowing some of the best thinking and design breakthroughs to happen. With each trip, he attempts to make it faster, but carrying various loads slows him, as he transports items Sadie requested for the campground cache, as well as for the completion of the lookout, hidden up in the trees.

When overnighting at the Memorial Campground, Jose finds comfort sleeping up in the tree surrounded by the forest's canopy. Its elevation provides a more secure feeling than the shelter below, and it's enjoyable making the place more hospitable. Jose takes pride in his role and the assigned responsibilities, committing to finishing each task while striving to do them at the best of his abilities. Sadie's and Anna's trust means more than they know, and the seriousness of his responsibilities is a huge step towards his manhood. Even with an overachiever mentality and strict focus, Jose always looks forward to relaxing when visiting Caleb and finds the time spent at the cave just as valuable.

Caleb looks forward to the boy's arrival, too. The company distracts him from the pain, loneliness, and the fact he's still rather helpless and stuck. Caleb's limitations keep them near the cave, but both men look forward to moving about and hunting together as soon as it's possible. In the meantime, Caleb continues Jose's shooting lessons.

The boy's an avid learner, wanting to live up to the personal vow he made to protect Anna and her place. In order to do that, Jose wants to become a skilled marksman and hunter, while striving to one day become completely self-sufficient. As he improves, Caleb believes the youngster is ready for live ammo, but Jose still doesn't want to waste it on practicing. He does, however, feel confident enough to keep the rifle loaded when out patrolling and hunting, but nothing worth shooting ever appears. So far, the only thing that does provide for them are his snares, which catch mostly small rodents and an occasional squirrel, allowing Jose to bring fresh meat when visiting Caleb.

When Caleb and Jose are together, the boy asks a myriad of never-ending questions. His quest for knowledge is insatiable and nonstop. He doesn't speak much about himself or his past, but when Caleb makes an inquiry, Jose does answer. His responses are often short with minimal detail and the boy's talented in steering things back to gaining information from Caleb. When they're not talking together or working around the cave, Jose buries his nose in a book. The few kept on the cave shelves are a valuable resource, and he plans to read every word. As Jose reads now, Caleb interrupts, asking for help charging the hand crank.

"Thanks kid. That thing hurts like hell when I do it," Caleb lamely offers.

They heat water and begin preparations for an evening meal. Tomorrow, Jose leaves again, and Caleb always feels like their time together goes too fast. He never looks forward to his days alone and if he was able-bodied, it'd be different, but until then, it's dreadful. Caleb's confined by his limitations and it's driving him crazy.

"So, what's new with the boat?" Caleb asks, knowing it's a topic that'll get Jose excited.

He smiles as the boy goes into detail about his latest rearrangements and the additional supplies he hopes to store. As Jose continues to list items, Caleb interrupts.

"How long of a list ya got?" he asks.

Jose, taking the question to heart, pulls out his notebook, flips to the correct page, and hands it over to Caleb, who whistles softly. He looks from the list to Jose and sees the seriousness in the boy's eyes.

"It's extensive," Caleb comments, handing it back.

"I'm sure there's a few more things I haven't thought of, but...I think I got most of it," Jose replies, scanning the items. His body language shifts and his shoulders slump. "I'm not sure if I'll ever get my hands on all of it." He looks unusually defeated and grows quiets.

Caleb, hoping to return the boy's good cheer, ruffles Jose's hair and jokes, "Come on, kid...who has their own ship? And...at your age? One of these days, when I'm able...you're gonna take me out on it."

Caleb's comments do the trick, and the boy's excitement returns. Jose speaks about what it'll take and how they'll have to manipulate the tides just to maneuver the boat out to open water. Caleb smiles, knowing it's what the kid needs. Sitting beside the boy, he can't fathom growing up the way Jose has. From the little bit Caleb's gathered, along with what Sadie's mentioned, he knows Jose's life hasn't been pleasant.

Early the following day, Jose leaves for a morning patrol and a quick hunt before beginning the journey back to Anna's homestead. He keeps trying Sadie's deer stand, but once again, there's no luck. Climbing down, he heads to the mushroom patch where he can at least gather some food and refill his water. Since learning about this place, Jose always returns to the cave with one to two gallons, making sure they don't deplete the water stored there.

Crouching on one knee while filling his second container, he's alerted by a sudden thrashing noise that causes his heart to jump. It's coming straight toward him—and fast. Jose gets to a defendable position, tracking the growing commotion and taking aim. A small doe bursts into view, bounding down the hillside, and leaps almost directly over Jose's head, startling him. It's running too fast and just as he aims, prepared to shoot, another blur of movement distracts him.

Flinching, he fires, causing a mountain lion to bolt off in the opposite direction, scaring them both. Jose's adrenaline is pumping, and he can't believe what's just happened. He reloads and holds his position until all the noise completely fades away. After waiting longer than necessary, he allows his pulse to fully recover, and then returns to filling the containers. Even though common sense dictates that both animals are long gone, he keeps checking around anyways.

Over and over, Jose reviews the sequence of events, contemplating his every mistake. He simply didn't pay attention to the details and missed every sign. The deer's panicked route and total disregard for its own safety should have been enough to warn him. Then, clearly evident, was the fear in the poor animal's eyes. Even worse, he failed to realize something was in pursuit because the first target, which was completely missed and a waste of a bullet, held his full focus. Thinking positively, he realizes that, at least, he succeeded in firing the rifle, getting a true feeling for the weapon, and he scared off a mountain lion.

Caleb, back at the cave, slowly moves about the tiny space wondering how much later it'll be before Jose returns. Feeling that he can manage the pain, and needing fresh air, Caleb goes out. Leaving is a slow process, but standing in the morning air leaves him feeling invigorated and even a little cheerful. He's been actively focusing on his body's healing process, and each time Caleb makes it outside, he walks parallel with and between the logs, retracing the short distance over and over. It's the only exercise possible for him and he views it as rehab, yearning for the day he'll be able to leave the confines for real walks.

Several minutes into his workout, he hears a loud and clearly audible gun shot. Straining to listen and hearing no more shots, Caleb crawls back into the cave, retrieves his rifle, and returns outside, pissed at himself for not bringing it in the first place. Back on his feet and gasping from the effort, Caleb's pain worsens. He curses, trying to control his breathing and the throbbing pain. After a few focused inhalations and exhalations, Caleb checks the rifle and realizes he left the rest of the ammo inside.

"Damn it!" he exclaims.

He debates going back to get extra rounds, but really, Caleb doesn't want to go through the entire crawling ordeal again, and logic indicates, the shot had to be made by Jose. The kid must have finally fired his first round, and hopefully, he found success on his hunt. However, instead of smiling with the good thought, Caleb worries. An irrational amount of fear sets in, gaining momentum with each passing minute. "What if Jose wasn't the shooter, but the target?" he thinks. "He could be hurt… or…dead. What if…it's more Splitters? What if they've captured him?"

Beginning to sweat, Caleb's anxiety builds. Not knowing is brutally worrisome, and his arms grow heavy from continually holding the rifle aimed above the log. A faint noise draws his attention and when he hears something again, it's closer and definitely coming from the opposite direction of the shot he heard. Clenching his teeth, Caleb fights back his fearful thoughts.

Suddenly, Jose appears, scrambling over the first log and is surprised to find Caleb holding the rifle. Shaking slightly, Caleb quickly lowers his gun, relaxes, and takes a deep breath. For the first time, he gets a sense of the concern parents feel over their children. He's so relieved; he can't refrain from hugging the kid. Jose, realizing the cause of Caleb's reaction, doesn't hesitate and goes right into telling his story. The boy shares every detail, talking excitedly and leaving nothing out. As the boy wraps up his tale, Caleb wants more.

"How come…you returned from that way?" Caleb nods towards the direction Jose arrived from.

Jose's a little confused. He expected some type of excitement or at least questions about the mountain lion, the deer, or the shot he finally fired.

Answering quickly, Jose responds, "I looped around…to complete the patrol."

"So, even with the importance of communicating back to me… you still hiked the long way around?" Caleb asks, trying to figure out the kid's thought process.

Jose, unsure of where the line of questioning is going, simply responds honestly.

"Yeah."

"Why?" Caleb tries to control his anger, but there's a slight edge to his question.

Jose isn't sure if he's being tested or if he's done something wrong. Trying not to hesitate or anger Caleb any further, he continues, "I had to make sure the perimeter was clear. I didn't want to jeopardize our safety…or the cave's location…by heading straight here without checking. It'd be a huge mistake and…I've made enough of those today."

The boy's logic is sound; Caleb realizes its wisdom and is slightly ashamed of his emotional reaction. There's an awkward silence before Caleb attempts some type of explanation.

"The shot…I thought…I'm sorry…I was worried…I thought some-thin' happened to you…and…I had no way of findin' out…or…helpin'."

Jose understands his friend's concern and appreciates the sincerity of Caleb's words. It's been a long time since someone's worried over him. It touches the youngster, and a memory of his mother surfaces. He struggles finding the image of her face and just as it begins to take form, it fades and quickly disappears. Caleb realizes that Jose made sure to take the time to do his job correctly, even with his adrenaline pumping and all the excitement. He acted methodically and with a sense of duty, then, hurried to update Caleb. The kid's actions give an indication of how he'll handle future emergency situations.

"Ya did good…real good." Caleb says. "You were correct to finish the patrol. Come on…let's grab some food and get you moving."

The two men make their way back inside and this time, Caleb asks all the right questions. Jose answers with enthusiasm and in detail. It was the first time he'd ever seen a mountain lion, and he couldn't believe it was chasing the deer he tried to kill. When they talk about Jose's first shot, the two men review it at length, discussing every aspect imaginable. Finishing up, Caleb reveals he has something he'd like the boy to help with. He wants Jose to design and build some type of portable ladder or stepstool. Something simple, lightweight, and easy for Caleb to use so he can get over the massive log that he's still unable to climb over on his own.

With some type of steps, Caleb could get over it and begin taking short hikes, or be ready to help in an emergency. They sketch a couple of ideas, talk about materials that could work, and plan on getting something started when Jose visits next. Afterward, and a little later than originally intended, Jose rearranges his pack to accommodate the next batch of supplies and heads out. Hiking away, he contem-plates the day's events and the fondness he has for Caleb.

Jose wants to help with the step idea, but isn't sure if Caleb should be hiking yet. His injured friend can barely get up and down on his own, and when he does move, painful grimaces always follow. Even more important is Sadie's approval. The boy's not sure she'll be okay with their system, or with Caleb hiking about, and Jose doesn't want to do anything that would upset her in any way.

THIRTY

"Almost there, kiddo," Sadie encourages Anna.

Their trip's been brutal and even Sadie feels it. The extra weight not only slowed her, but it's been havoc on her shoulders and low back. They've taken extra days of rest along the way, providing recovery both physically and emotionally, since Anna's a wreck and grew worse as they approached the opposite side of the island and traveled the southern border. Going on her family's quest to discover the truth about the land's shape has brought a deep sadness because she's constantly thinking about them. The journey itself, even though strenuous and at times tedious, is the motivation that drives the girl's every step. She's doing this for them, in their honor, and at this point, that's the only thing keeping Anna going.

When they near the bottom of their final descent, Sadie removes her pack and lowers it the last couple of feet, letting it drop onto the dry creek bed. Anna does the same, and—one at a time—they hop down. Suddenly, Sadie straightens an arm across Anna's chest, forcing the girl to stop. With Sadie signaling silence, they lower into a crouch. Anna's scared and hears nothing but her own breathing as they tuck behind a twisted root burl while Sadie draws her crossbow. Nothing happens until a low whistle floats toward them. Sadie lowers her bow and softly replies in her own way, then leaves Anna, who remains hidden.

"Ooooohh, child. I'm so glad to see you!" Clara cries, wrapping Sadie in a hug. "I thought it was you I heard comin' down."

"And what if it wasn't?" Sadie puts her hands on her hips. "You gave your location away. You have to be more careful."

"But…it was you," Clara replies, dismissing Sadie's concern. "And you brought company!"

Sadie turns to see Anna timidly standing just within eyesight. "Clara, this is Anna…and Anna…this is Clara."

Anna takes a hesitant step forward as Clara closes the gap, wrapping both arms tightly around the girl.

"Welcome, child…welcome," Clara says, gently rocking Anna as she does.

For the girl, it's strangely comforting and the embrace offers a sense of security. For the old woman, it's pure joy—like the happiness gained by hugging a grandchild—but she senses the despair lurking deep within Anna. When the old woman looks to Sadie, whose eyes confirm what she's sensing, it obvious they have much to catch up on.

"So, Anna," Clara begins, looking back at the girl, "what has Sadie told you about me?"

The question's designed to get the girl talking, and it works. Anna goes on and on about everything Sadie's said—especially, about Clara's garden and cabin. As they speak, the ladies continue walking along the creek bed until it abruptly ends at the cliff's edge, causing Anna to gasp.

"That was my first reaction, too," Clara says, leaning close to the girl.

They stand in silence, looking at the ocean below, until Sadie speaks. "Anna's home is on the north side..." she pauses, looks to Anna for confirmation, and then continues, "She's recently lost both her parents."

This time, Clara gasps. She looks at the girl and wraps her in another hug. "You're not alone. I was...for a long time...so was Sadie." She releases Anna to make eye contact. "But now...we've got each other."

Clara's words and demeanor touch Sadie. The old woman has such a way with people it's hard to imagine she's lived without others for so long.

"Come on, you two...let's get home. You can clean up...we'll eat and chat around the fire. I want to hear everything." With Clara's words, they turn and leave.

Retracing their steps to where the packs were left, they once again sling them on. Anna's tired of carrying a load and is really sick of hiking. In truth, she doesn't really enjoy it, can't wait to get to Clara's place, and feels like sleeping for a week. Entering the cozy cabin, she finds everything's beautifully crafted as she slowly walks around the furniture and stonework, taking in the astonishing details. When finished, the young girl joins the others, who've been talking softly in the kitchen.

Clara looks up and addresses Anna, "Water's just about ready. Why don't you wash first," she turns to Sadie, "then you. By the time you're done, dinner will be ready."

Sadie shows Anna the bathing procedures, and then gives her privacy, returning to Clara's side, anxious to share more with her. They have lots to discuss, and it's important to show Anna unity in their decisions. When Sadie takes her turn washing up, she returns to find the girl listening to Clara and hanging on the old woman's every word. It already seems a natural fit between these two, and it warms Sadie's heart. They sit down, Clara has them hold hands while offering thanks, and as they eat, Anna asks questions, mostly directed towards the fresh produce, herbs, and seasonal varieties the garden produces.

Between the two of them, an entire gardening seminar seems to be taking place. Sadie simply smiles, thinking these two were meant for one another. As the thought takes shape, Clara pats the top of Sadie's hand, then squeezes it briefly, seemingly in agreement. With dinner done, the women sit near the fire, holding mugs of hot tea. Talking starts with updates on Caleb's health and then turns to Jose, as Sadie fills in the latest information for Clara. Then, everything is directed back to Anna and the family quest she's undertaking in honor of her parents. Clara, aiding in the girl's efforts, suggests a vantage point that offers a view up the coast. Upon hearing this, Sadie looks at Clara sideways.

"You've been hiking? How much?" she asks the elder.

"Ooohh...not too much," Clara replies, winking at Anna, who giggles.

"Let me see." Sadie says, shaking her head and kneeling in front of Clara.

Clara rolls her eyes while removing the blanket draped over her legs. It's another attempt at getting a giggle from Anna, and it works. While Sadie examines Clara's injury, the old woman continues where she left off.

"I think the view may reach to your property. When you're ready, I'll take you there," Clara offers.

At the mention of "her property" Anna feels odd, as it's a little overwhelming being acknowledged as its owner.

"Clara, there's still swelling." Sadie interjects. "You shouldn't be hiking yet. Let it heal...all the way...no long explorations...not for another week, at least."

The old woman knows Sadie's right and agrees.

Satisfied, Sadie sits back down. "Alright, then...show me what you've discovered."

Distracted by her thoughts, Anna doesn't notice Sadie and Clara pulling out their maps of the island. They share a look, and then get the girl's attention.

"Anna, scoot over here," Clara encourages.

The youngster slides near the old woman to get a better view, and Clara points out the route she's talking about, while also showing Sadie a few other additions.

"No wonder there's still swelling," Sadie says, giving Clara another look.

Clara smiles, while shrugging her shoulders.

Sadie copies the details, shares her own updates, and then points to a section of the map. "This is Anna's place, here...we mapped a majority of it." Sadie glances up to make sure Anna's paying attention. "I looked for a possible route straight here, but...it's gonna take a lot more time to find one. This area..." she moves her finger between Clara's and Anna's property lines, "is difficult to hike...it's super steep and rugged."

Sadie asks Anna to get her notebook and make a copy of the map. Besides the lyrics to songs, Sadie finds something nearly every day for the girl to write or calculate. When she returns, Clara and Sadie are deep in discussion, debating possible routes to Anna's and how long it could take. As Anna draws, she listens intently.

"It's steep, which means...lots of backtracking." Sadie shakes her head side-to-side, glances at the girl, and continues, "We should be able to find a way through." This time she speaks directly to Anna. "But...if we don't...we'll have to hike back around the way we came."

None of it sounds inviting to the young girl; she doesn't want to do any more hiking than necessary, and going forward to simply return the way they started sounds exhausting. Honestly, she doesn't even want to think about the trek. Along this journey, Anna's discovered, in regards to hiking, she takes more after her mother than her father and she'd like nothing more than to rest for a really, really long time. Sadie, sensing the girl's hesitancy and weariness, looks to Clara.

The old woman nods, taking over, "Anna...Sadie and I have been talking...there's another possibility." She takes Anna's hands. "I know we've just met, but...I feel like we're meant for each other. I could use some company and you...need...a place...to heal."

Anna's eyes open wider, she looks to Sadie, then back to Clara.

"Why don't you stay with me for a while? Rest, recover, help me with the garden, and then…when you're ready…return to your home," Clara cautiously offers.

"We also need to check in with Jose and Caleb," Sadie interjects. "We took longer than planned to get here…they're expecting us back. I don't want 'em worrying, or worse, for Jose to leave his post and come looking. To make up time…it's gonna be a push…meaning, heading out tomorrow, and…you really should rest."

Shockingly, it's not surprise Anna feels. Without the girl realizing it, Sadie's been preparing her along the way, and Anna, understanding it's for her own good, still finds it upsetting that they didn't talk about it before now.

"How come you didn't tell me 'bout this?" Anna snaps so abruptly it surprises even her.

Sadie, recognizing the pain behind the question, takes a deep breath before replying. "I'm sorry, kiddo. Please believe I'm doin' my best to make sure you're okay. I thought about whether to tell you or not so many times." She glances at the old woman. "But first, I thought it proper to talk with Clara…it is her home."

Clara smiles lovingly at them both.

"Second, I worried you'd think I was tryin' to get rid of ya. You needed to meet Clara…see her home…and understand how healing this place can be. And, more importantly…I thought you needed the journey with your own thoughts…I didn't want it to get muddled with somethin' new. The time was for you…and your parents."

At Sadie's last words, Anna's eyes tear and she doesn't even try holding them back.

"Sss-sss-sorry," she barely squeaks out after a while.

"Oh, child, there's nothin' to be sorry 'bout," Clara soothes her, while wiping dry the girl's cheeks.

Anna, looking miserable, needs rest, and seeing she's done for the night, they make a bed and let her sleep, knowing they'll finish their discussion and figure out what's best in the morning.

Early the following day, Sadie and Clara sit in the kitchen talking intently while waiting for Anna to wake. They let her sleep longer, before Sadie goes to check on her. Anna, curled up in bed, and barely awake, stirs as Sadie nears. Standing up and feeling sore, Anna helps fold the extra bedding before joining Clara, who wishes the girl a cheery good morning while handing her a small basket.

"Come on...follow me." Clara takes Anna's hand and turns to Sadie. "We'll be back."

Anna, still a little groggy, follows her through the garden and up a short path. Clara talks the entire way, filling the girl's head with interesting tidbits. Anna's legs ache with each step, especially as the trail grows steeper, but once they reach a gate and enter a small orchard surrounded by overgrown berry brambles, Anna is once again amazed. Of the many trees, she recognizes apple, avocado, and lemon. The others, she isn't sure about. Clara continues to talk about each, the care they need, and when they're in season. She moves swiftly and leads them directly to the last two trees, which are filled with a waxy-looking orange fruit. Anna doesn't recognize it and looks quizzically at Clara, who picks a piece and hands it to her.

"Not sure, are ya?" Clara asks. "They're persimmons...and they're just coming into season. I thought they'd be nice with breakfast."

She teaches Anna how to tell when they're ripe, and the two of them fill the basket. When they return, Sadie has the rest of breakfast ready and is excited to see the bounty. They sit down, starting with the fresh fruit, and although the flavor is new, Anna is surprised by how much she likes them. After eating several bites, she wipes away some of the juice from her chin and smiles.

"They're so good!" Anna says, sounding once again like a little girl.

Sadie, smiling back, agrees, while eating another and hoping not to jeopardize the enjoyment by changing the topic. "Anna," she begins, "we should finish our conversation from last night."

The girl, knowing what's coming, feels better prepared. Anna's thought a lot about it, and the conversation starts with the difficulties both Clara and Sadie faced after losing their husbands, along with the healing they needed. All agree, Anna needs time and it's just a matter of where it would be best for her.

Thinking about home, Anna knows she's not ready to run the homestead, nor is she able to handle all the memories the place holds. Staying with Sadie would mean joining her as she patrols back and forth among all of their places, and Anna definitely doesn't want that. If she stayed at Sadie's place, she'd be alone most of the time, and staying in the cave with Caleb doesn't sound good either.

Really, the best option is staying right here with Clara. The more they discuss it, the more logical a solution it seems. It's a safe place with someone who cares, where Anna can learn much, and when ready, she can finish her quest. Maybe, by that time, they'll discover a shorter route that leads directly to her home. All three ladies feel good about the plan, and as Clara gets up to make more tea, Sadie leans close to Anna.

"So...for sure, you're okay stayin' here...without me?" Sadie whispers, asking the girl.

Anna, grateful Sadie's checking with her privately, replies positively. Sadie, reassured, leaves the kitchen, telling them to wait and grabs her backpack. Returning with the behemoth bag, Sadie rummages through it while talking.

"I've got a few things for both of you...and I'm looking forward to getting 'em out of this pack." She removes several packages, and as the pile grows, both Clara and Anna look at each other in shock and with excitement. "Okay...that should do it," she says, removing a smaller item from yet another compartment.

"Is there anything left?" Clara asks, looking into Sadie's backpack.

All three women laugh, and it's a joyous sound. Sadie takes back her bag, lifts it up and down, happy with its lighter weight, and smiles. Then, she begins sorting the pile of goods and hands each of them a package wrapped in brown paper.

"Open 'em," Sadie instructs.

They do as asked and find themselves holding an item they're not sure what to do with. Sadie laughs at the looks on their faces and Clara and Anna enjoy seeing Sadie so lighthearted. When Sadie stops chuckling, she leans over and pushes a button on each of their devices.

"They're tablets. I charged 'em before we left my place so they'd be ready," she says, as both screens flick on.

They stare while Sadie demonstrates their new gift's basic functions and what's been downloaded onto them. She's filled the tablets with books, games, and music. Moving through Anna's screens, she shows the girl how to access the playlist.

"It's got some of your parents' music...here..." she shows Anna, "plus, all kinds more."

Anna hugs Sadie, quickly selects a song, and plays it. Moving closer to Clara, Sadie shows the old woman how to open a variety of magazines and newspapers it stores.

"It'll give you information...and...coverage on everything... until...just after the Tri-nami...by the time the quakes shook, access to any updates were gone, but most of the years you missed are there. Remember...a lot...isn't good..." Sadie hesitates, not sure what else to say.

"It's okay...I want to know," Clara says.

Sadie demonstrates how to charge the tablets using one of her hand-operated generators that she's also leaving them. Now that both women understand their gifts, the full excitement of what Sadie's given them ignites. Even more exciting is the still rather large pile from her pack, and they take turns opening and looking at all the items. Sadie provides Anna with notebooks, art materials, and plenty of other supplies to encourage an educational and creative side. There's plenty of notepads and journals for Clara, too, and Sadie requests the old woman start recording specifics about her practices so the wisdom and knowledge she's developed over her lifetime can be shared.

What remains is a large supply of dry goods, a couple of clothing items, and a small case of personal hygiene products—complete with new toothbrushes and dental floss. The best of it all, Sadie saved for last. Watching her carefully open two wooden boxes wrapped in cloth, both Clara and Anna's eyes fly open, then look up at the same time.

"Seeds!" they exclaim in unison.

The boxes contain airtight packages of clearly labeled seeds. The two read out loud what each contains, and Sadie smiles at their joy. Their happiness is as much a gift for her as it is for them. Finishing their examination, Sadie's anxious to start her trek, and telling the ladies what her plans are and when she'll return, Sadie shoulders her pack.

"Before you go, I've got a couple things for you, too." Clara turns and whispers to Anna, who giggles, and then runs off with the basket.

Clara disappears into the pantry and comes back with an armload of food. Just as she sets everything on the table, Anna runs in, breathing heavily.

"These are for you," the girl says, handing the heavy load of persimmons to Sadie and feeling good to be the one giving something.

Sadie's grateful for all the fresh food and carefully packs the supplies. As she re-straps on her pack, heavy once again, they say their goodbyes. Sadie asks Anna to learn all she can from the old woman and reminds the child about preparing to one day run her family's homestead. While wrapping her in a hug, Sadie kisses the top of Anna's head.

"Take care of Clara too…okay?" she whispers.

The girl holds back tears, saying she will. Sadie, turning to Clara, embraces her, and while holding onto one another, Sadie reminds Clara to take it easy on her leg. All of them walk a short distance together until Sadie hikes off alone.

THIRTY-ONE

It's later than usual and Caleb worries about Jose, but pacing while waiting proves helpful for him. He can manage only a couple of steps before running out of space and having to turn around, but the little bit of movement feels good. All the lying around and sitting has his back in knots, his legs cramped, and his neck tight. Physically, Caleb needs to move, and psychologically, he needs the boy to arrive soon. Keeping a steady rhythm, he counts each step, and, as the number grows, the counting becomes Caleb's mantra, alleviating his anxiety while working as a walking meditation. Finished, he heads back inside, and when a light tapping on the cave's door begins, Caleb hurriedly opens it. Realizing his error, Caleb finds a rifle pointing in his face as Jose frowns and then lowers his gun.

"Sorry, kid, I forgot."

Jose closes the door, sets down his pack, and takes a seat.

"Come on...I'm sorry. I'll do it next time," Caleb says, reassuring the boy.

Jose, not really too upset, has much to share and struggles holding back what he really wants to discuss. "Okay, just...make sure you follow protocol."

Caleb, shaking his head at Jose's seriousness, nods, and offers him leftovers, knowing the kid's hungry from his long hike. They're cold, but Jose devours the food, washing it down with the last of his water.

"Thanks," he meekly replies, realizing Caleb's been watching him scarf down the meal.

"How come you're so late?" Caleb asks.

Jose wipes his mouth on the sleeve of his jacket and regains his urge to explode with the information he carries. Caleb hasn't failed to notice the twinkle in Jose's eyes or the excitement he's bursting with, but before the kid can speak, a faint knocking interrupts them. Both men excitedly turn to the door, but before Caleb opens it, Jose stops him, and together they respond appropriately. Hearing the signal that it's safe to enter, Sadie opens the door, and seeing she's alone, Jose grows alarmed.

"Where's Anna?!" the kid blurts before they've even said hello.

"Don't worry, she's okay." Sadie replies, relieving Jose's concern as she provides a brief overview of her travels with Anna, the difficulties the girl had while hiking, and the decision for her to stay with Clara.

Jose, feeling a little better, is still disappointed.

"Come on, kiddo." Sadie wraps Jose in a hug, properly greeting him.

Caleb, a little jealous of their affection, simply gets a polite nod.

"So...what's with the stuff outside?" Sadie asks.

"Oh, yeah!" Jose, distracted by her entrance, and then by Anna's absence, returns to his feelings of excitement. He turns to Caleb, "I brought you somethin'." He ducks outside and returns with an old collapsible stepstool. While opening it, he explains further. "Obviously, it needed repairs...and...I had ta make a couple modifications, but...it works great!"

Two of the three steps have been replaced with small sections of wood, almost the entire length of one side is reinforced with random pieces of metal, two rope attachments have been added, and it's painted in camouflage. The boy demonstrates how the ropes work, explaining to Caleb he'll be able to lift it from atop the log without bending over.

"It's perfect! Thanks!" Caleb says, also excited.

While Caleb looks over the stepstool, Jose glances at Sadie. She doesn't look upset, but the boy doesn't take any risks. He quickly informs her of the discussions the two of them have been having about Caleb's ability to get out. After listening to everything the boy shares, Caleb chimes in, explaining his frustrations with being trapped in the cave. He updates Sadie on his recovery, explaining the minor amount of walking he's already been doing and how he increases it each time.

"Please, Sadie. I need this. Can I keep it...here?" Caleb asks humbly, seeing she's not immediately accepting of the idea.

Sadie's overwhelmed by the look in Caleb's eyes and has to break contact with him. Looking at the boy, she senses the same from him.

"Alright, you two...let's see how it works," she finally says.

Both men smile and high-five. It makes Sadie smile, even though she's not overly fond of the idea. They make their way outside, as Sadie closely observes Caleb. She's trying to gauge his pain, and he's trying his best to not show any. Both realize what the other is doing, but neither says anything. Jose picks up a small sack—also left outside—realizing he didn't finish telling Caleb why he was so late returning to the cave.

"This is one of my other surprises," he says, holding open the bag for Caleb and Sadie. They look in and glance back to Jose, who's smiling from ear to ear. Sadie removes the raccoon, finding it's been shot in the head, while Caleb proudly pats Jose on the back.

"I spotted it...caught in one of my snares. It was close to escaping...so...I took aim, but missed. So...I tried again." A little bit of his excitement falters. "I know...I had an unfair advantage..."

"But...it's a good clean shot," Sadie says, cutting him off.

"There's something else, too. I've made a huge discovery!" Jose can barely contain himself. "And...it's the biggest surprise yet!" Jose nearly yells, "I found fuel! And lots of it!"

Jose's words stun both Sadie and Caleb. Quickly, Sadie's sense of curiosity takes over and her questions begin. She asks so many, so fast, that Jose can only laugh. Sadie, realizing the error of her eagerness, allows the boy to divulge all the details without interruption.

Excitedly, Jose begins his story. "I thought it odd that Anna's family has a huge semi truck on the property. So...I climbed in the cab... to inspect it. Sitting in the driver's seat gave me a different perspective. I kept lookin' over the truck, the tractor next to it, and the hillside everythin' butts against. The hill's shape is perfectly symmetrically... it's not like any of the others and...that too seemed odd."

Jose takes a deep breath and then jumps right back into his tale. "I got out...walked around it, and did the same with the tractor before climbing the hill. I wasn't exactly sure what I was looking for...but something 'bout it...was...puzzling." He turns to Sadie. "You know where that old shed sits? Up against the same hillside?"

She nods, and he goes on.

"Well...one side and its back are built into the hill...just the roof sits above ground. It's full of broken furniture, rusted garden tools, and a bunch of random junk." Jose turns to Caleb. "That's where I found your stepladder and the materials to repair it." He turns back to Sadie, "there's also a couple gas barrels...almost empty, and...when I moved 'em, it cleared enough space to see a huge section of the back wall. That's when I really noticed the shed's unique construction. From outside...it looks old and fallin' apart, but...inside, it's solid. The wall against the side slope is all cinder block...the opposite side and the front are wood, but the backside…is outlined with concrete blocks with wood in the middle…" He briefly pauses, making sure they're following.

Sadie squints, while thinking out loud, "It should all be blocks…otherwise…"

"Right!" Jose interjects, not letting her finish, "otherwise it'd rot…'cause it butts against a dirt slope! It appeared solid, but…when I pounded…it sounded hollow. I didn't see or feel any ways to open it, but I knew there was somethin'…then, I noticed a small gap at the bottom. There was just enough room to squeeze my fingertips into the space. I tried lifting…then pushing, but it wouldn't move…until I pulled it towards me…and the entire section swung open! There's a hidden compartment!"

Jose, breathing rapidly, sips his water to re-moisten his mouth. "I know why they had the truck…to haul an entire tanker of fuel! There are hose connections that smell of gas and…I think it's pretty full! At least it sounded that way…when I banged on it."

Finally sharing his discovery, Jose feels a surge of pride and accomplishment. Realizing the experience wasn't the same without being able to tell the others, Jose's grateful for his new friends and appreciates belonging to a team. Making sure to finish the remaining details and report the rest of his findings, Jose's tone shifts to a more controlled manner.

"I examined the tanker and its set-up," he continues, "only the first few feet of the trailer are visible…the rest is buried. The only operational gas-powered items on the homestead are the quads and a couple chainsaws. All the other things…are in disrepair, but…maybe, with some time…I might be able to get 'em working." He chooses his next words thoughtfully. "But…I think, Anna's family used gas…sparingly…at most. From the looks of the tanker…and how much growth is on the hillside over it…I think it's been buried a long time."

He hesitates, swallows, and adds his last thoughts, "I think it's been hidden all of Anna's life. I…don't think she even knows it's there." Suddenly, he feels uncomfortable, and looking at Sadie and Caleb's quizzical expressions doesn't help. He sheepishly goes on. "I just think…that…if Anna knew about it…she would've told us."

"I don't think she knows, either." Sadie says, before telling him what a great job he's been doing.

Caleb does the same and both adults are proud and pleased with Jose, but more importantly, they're gaining confidence in his abilities.

"Okay," Sadie begins, "we've been here long enough. Let's see how this thing works," she says, pointing at the stepstool. "And then…let's move."

Sadie hands Caleb the stepladder, wanting to see how well he does. Carefully setting it up and climbing to the top, he presses his palms into the log and slowly crawls before attempting to move the apparatus. Caleb braces his body, lifts on the ropes, and painstakingly slow, raises the ladder towards him. As it nears the top, it folds flat, making it easier to manipulate. Caleb lowers the ladder, and when it reaches the other side of the log, he dips his legs over until both feet rest on the top step.

Cautiously, he stands on it and descends the last two steps backwards. The ladder wobbles and shifts slightly, nearly making him fall. The pain from the unexpected movement jolts Caleb, but he tries hiding it. Instantly, Sadie and Jose are at his side securing him and the stepstool. Standing on the ground, Caleb turns to smile at Sadie, but it fades quickly when he sees her concern and growing doubt. Jose, using his foot, kicks at the dirt to level the ground for the ladder's placement.

"There…next time it won't be wobbly," he says, looking directly at Sadie.

It feels like they're being tested, and the two men aren't sure how they're doing. Sadie scouts around and finds an easy place to conceal the ladder. She's adamant regarding it being hidden after it's used, and Caleb, winking at Jose, takes Sadie's directions as a good sign—both quickly agree to it.

Sadie takes the lead, moving slowly to ensure Caleb doesn't overdo it. She's not going far and appreciates how both boys have handled everything. They remain silent while hiking and, knowing they're waiting for her official approval, Sadie still doesn't give it. Besides the concern of keeping the cave's location safe, she worries Caleb's movements will make his injuries worse and slow his recovery. She didn't fail to notice the pain he endured to get out, but she's impressed with how he's handling it.

Eventually, the conversation turns to Jose's hunting, and Sadie gets to hear all about his deer and mountain lion experience. She asks questions about both animals and Jose finds he isn't able to answer them all. Her line of inquiry educates the kid, and he realizes how many additional details were missed and what else he should have observed. Getting to where she intended, Sadie sends Jose off to find fire-starting materials and gather wood. When he disappears, she turns all of her attention to Caleb, who's leaning against a tree. She walks over as he straightens up.

"Alright...I know it hurts...bad...and probably more than ya thought it would," Sadie starts.

Caleb doesn't like the way she's sounding.

"When we return, we'll help you over, but you've moved too much." She's serious, and annoyingly, Caleb finds it charming. Sadie, keeping her focus, isn't letting up. "I mean it...and you know it...you shouldn't be moving this much...not yet. We both know you need more time."

He knows she's right, but being outside, and away from the cave, is giving him just the lift in spirit he needs. Caleb, without talking, keeps staring at Sadie. It's unnerving, but she maintains her composure.

"I get it...you need to get out...I'd be going crazy if it was me." Sadie says. "But...after today...all the movin'...and pain...almost fallin'...you need to wait at least another week or two before you attempt it again. And...make sure Jose's there to help."

Between the penetrating look of his eyes and the sly smile on Caleb's face, Sadie's tone softens.

"Just...be smart...and careful. Please," she adds the nicety, almost as an afterthought.

Caleb still has the same look on his face, but nods in agreement, stepping towards her. Standing extremely close, he hesitantly lifts his arms and wraps them around Sadie. He's wanted to do this for some time, and getting out today gives him the courage to act.

Pulling her closer, Caleb leans to whisper near her ear. "Thank you, Sadie. I'm sorry...for...everything. I should've been there for you."

Caleb's words and lingering presence stirs up memories from their past. The thoughts and feelings they produce vary and rapidly change for Sadie. She breaks from his embrace just as Jose returns, glad for the boy's presence and the chance to change the topic. Caleb, on the other hand, hoped for a little more time, but feels, at least he's finally apologized, and it feels good. He never thought it possible, but being with her again is all he thinks about.

Sadie distracts herself with Jose. They start a fire, and then together, clean the raccoon. She instructs him along the way, lets the boy do most of the work, and talks about caring for the pelt so it cures properly. The three of them eat their fill before putting out the fire's remaining coals, and hiding the evidence of their presence. Full, and ready to head home, they set off at a slow pace. This time, Jose leads, trying to give Sadie and Caleb a little more privacy. He's sensed a change between them and notices the way Caleb keeps watching Sadie.

Back at the cave, Caleb is absolutely exhausted, and his ribs ache. Sadie reiterates what she's told him, making sure both men clearly understand. Caleb's to recover from today, for at least a week, and then, Jose must be around to help until Caleb can easily use the ladder without pain. With her instructions accepted, they settle in for the night, and Sadie continues talking with Jose. She plans to accompany him back to Anna's so she can see the gas tanker, check his work, and start scouting a route from there to Clara's. Jose's excited, finding out he'll have company, and he can't wait to show Sadie everything. Caleb's reactions are exactly the opposite—he's disappointed she's leaving, and that once again, he'll be left alone. Lying still, he wonders if she ever thinks about staying with him.

THIRTY-TWO

Before he knows it, Caleb's alone—again. Making it worse, Jose won't be returning as usual. Instead, he'll stay at the homestead—helping Sadie for weeks—while all Caleb will be doing is lying flat on his back, since, once again, pain immobilizes him. His ribs are definitely worse, and spasms continue twitching across his muscles, but even with the setback, he's still happy about getting out. Walking did wonders for his morale, making recovery seem within reach, and it provided him an opportunity to apologize to Sadie. Even though there wasn't any response from her, he hopes she's forgiven him.

As Caleb drifts into his third nap of the day, Sadie and Jose are working away at the Memorial Camp's overlook up in the trees. Having an extra set of hands to maneuver materials or simply hold things in place is something both of them greatly appreciate. As a duo, they're getting an incredible amount accomplished, working efficiently as a team, and Sadie assigns Jose additional tasks, adding to his responsibilities. The young man's maturing in front of her eyes and Sadie finds comfort in his dependability.

With the work done for the evening, the two eat a small meal and turn in early. Before falling asleep, Sadie makes sure to praise all Jose's efforts. There were only a few minor changes required in the hideout, and a couple of his modifications were pleasantly surprising. Jose's ingenuity is quite remarkable, and Sadie looks forward to arriving at the homestead to see what else he's accomplished.

By mid-day, they return to Anna's, make a quick patrol, and then immediately head to the decrepit shed so Sadie can see the fuel tanker. Outside, Jose points out the symmetry of the hillside and the sheds external features. Opening the door, they enter, and Sadie gets the complete picture of what Jose's explained. From inside, the structure's appearance is very different from the exterior. It's sturdy and well designed, but its hard to notice because it's crammed so full of junk.

Jose removes a couple of items and the barrels, showing Sadie how they block access to the rear wall, then, he opens the hidden compartment and steps aside. Scanning the visible portion confirms what

Jose believes—an entire fuel tanker has been buried. Sadie knocks on the end of the metallic tube and closely examines the edges where the shed's structure butts against it. Thick white sheets of plastic appear to cover the entire trailer. Sadie hasn't spoken since they entered the shed and rubbing the material between her thumb and first two fingers, she turns to the boy.

"You're definitely right. This…" she nods at the plastic, "probably covers the entire thing. I think," she examines it again, "it's…the same material they used on the berry fields. It was used as ground cover for strawberries…and, for the plastic canopies over the raspberry and blackberry crops."

Sadie clearly sees the images from long ago but knows Jose doesn't have any concept of what's being described. Berry fields and apple orchards once surrounded these mountains, but now they're submerged under the ocean and when she makes eye contact again, it signals Jose and his questions begin. Answering him, she explains the different types of berries, their tastes, and even the annual strawberry festival she loved as a kid. When she talks about strawberry shortcake, Jose's eyes widen, and he can't fathom whipped cream—it sounds purely imaginary.

Eventually, his questions slow, then, finally stop, and they exit the shed. Standing outside, Sadie climbs the hillside covering the tanker and examining the area, she believes only a few feet of dirt cover it. They walk towards the shed's roofline, checking its exterior edges where it sits just above the ground. From the roof, Sadie walks the length of the hill taking large, exaggerated steps while counting as she goes. Reaching a depression in the mound, she stops.

"About forty-eight feet." She whistles, "That's a lotta gas!"

Climbing down at the low spot peaks Sadie's curiosity. It stretches several feet before recovering to its original height into a second, much smaller mound that blends into the slope encompassing this section of the property. Wondering what caused the depression, Sadie thinks of possibilities, but is interrupted by hearing Jose's stomach grumble, making her realize she's hungry too.

"Alright, kiddo, let's head in and make some lunch," she suggests.

While eating, Sadie reviews what needs to be done, but her mind keeps returning to the gas tanker and the depression in the hillside. When they finish, she tells Jose to grab a couple of shovels and they spend the next few hours digging into the side of the slope. It's hard manual labor and exhausting. As their hole grows, Sadie keeps them digging deeper and deeper into the depression's area. Jose's tired and begins to think Sadie's theory is wrong, when suddenly, his shovel unearths pieces of plastic.

The material matches what they found inside and the two of them drop to their knees, using their hands, until discovering a long length of metal underneath it. When a large enough section is exposed, they're able to pull away the plastic, revealing an old rusted hitch that appears to continue into the second mound. Jose looks at Sadie. He's filthy, sweaty, and breathing hard.

"I think your right!" he says, high fiving Sadie.

The celebratory atmosphere changes when Sadie points out how much dirt they'll have to move in order to access the second buried trailer. There's not enough daylight left to complete the task and neither has enough energy to continue. Before wrapping up for the evening, Sadie scrambles up the slope of their dig site and sits. Wondering about easier access designs, she climbs to where the steeper slope starts and rests on a rock. Scuffing her feet side-to-side, she clears away some of the forest debris that's accumulated over the years. While leveling the area with one last foot sweep, her shoe catches on a metal edge. The more dirt she kicks away, the longer the exposed metal piece becomes.

"Jose, climb up here…and bring the shovels."

The boy, curious as to what she's found, grabs the tools, but he's not overly happy about needing them again. He lifts a shovel to Sadie, and she works from one knee. Standing at her side, Jose sees the out-line of what Sadie's uncovering and joins in the effort. At least it's a minimal amount of earth that needs moved and the two get it done easily. Brushing away the remaining dirt and looking for ways to open the metal latch they've just unearthed, they find a small notch big enough to squeeze a single finger into it. Sadie sends Jose to retrieve a crowbar, and he scurries down, jogs to get it, and returns quickly. Wedging in the tool's metal tip, Sadie pries up the lid, uncovering a concrete block shaft that has a ladder descending into its depths.

"Sorry…but…we're also gonna need a light," she says, turning to Jose.

"I thought so," he says, reaching into a pocket for the small flash-light he also thought to retrieve.

Sadie smiles in response, shines the light downward, and goes first. Once she reaches the bottom, she calls for him to follow. There's barely enough room for the two of them to stand there, but Jose holds the light so Sadie's hands are free to inspect a small opening where a nozzle and hose protrude from the second tanker. Only a partial section of the smaller tank is visible, but when Sadie knocks on it, it also sounds full. It'll be a little more difficult to carry the fuel out from this location, but both are excited by the find. Halfway back up the ladder, Sadie stops and returns below. Using the light to scan the entire length of the shaft, she finds an opening near the bottom. Getting down on all fours, she peers into the hole and discovers it's a tunnel containing another length of hose.

Using the connector at its end, Sadie attaches the two hoses and climbs up. Staying on the top rung, she tells Jose what she's discovered, and sends him down the slope with a shovel. Directing him from her position, in line with the shaft, she has Jose dig around the base of the mound. Uncovering what's below doesn't require much effort, and almost immediately he uncovers a single cinder block. Removing it exposes the opening of the tunnel and the hose's other end.

"Well...that's handy," Sadie says. "And easy...too bad we didn't figure it out sooner," she says, looking back at the all the earth they moved which, now, needs to be returned.

Even though it's getting late and she's tired, Sadie starts shoveling dirt. She'd rather get it done tonight then start the day with it tomorrow. Jose's not thrilled, but he joins her. Seeing how exhausted the kid is, Sadie takes his shovel.

"Jose...I'll finish. You head inside and shower...there should be plenty of water."

He's grateful to hear her words and even more thankful for the gravity-fed spring that supplies the house. Without regular use, the amount of stored water on the homestead has increased dramatically, and he can't wait to use some. He knows he stinks and as the boy begins to leave, Sadie calls to him.

"After you shower, make us food. I'll eat when I get in," she says, barely pausing in her work.

Sadie works efficiently, tossing dirt to rebuild the mound. She finishes just as it gets too dark to see, and heading back to the house, she finds Jose passed out on the couch. She wanted to review tomorrow's agenda with him, but he looks too peaceful to disturb, so instead, she lets him sleep, eats what he prepared, then showers and goes to bed. When they awake, it's to the start of a routine that continues for days.

They're busy from sunup to sundown and each day finishes with them looking forward to sleep and feeling like they've accomplished a great deal. Mornings always begin with a patrol and hunt that takes them towards Clara's. They've yet to find passage to her property, but both Sadie and Jose are determined. They eat on the return and then spend a few hours working at the cove, constructing two small bunkers on each side of the inlets mouth to protect the tiny harbor.

From the bunkers, they head to the boat, where they battle with trying to move empty steel drums out of the hold and onto shore. Jose's system for off-loading materials, although greatly improved, still needs work, and the two struggle getting the empty containers onto land. Developing a better method for loading supplies on and off the watercraft is a prominent feature in their conversations and a growing priority. When Sadie gets the chance to speak with Anna about the gas they've discovered, she wants everything in place for refueling the boat, so it can be kept fully operational, ready to evacuate, rescue, or search, at any moment's notice.

In the remaining part of the afternoons, they work around the buried tanker. Sadie organizes the shed, finding out what resources it contains and tries to figure out a way to filter gas. It's been stored for a long time, and she's concerned about sediment ruining the homestead's gas-powered equipment along with the boat's engine. While she works on her task, Jose dives into his with enjoyment. He's attempting to get the tractor running and finishes each day with grease up to elbows, smudges covering his features, and a huge grin on his face.

A week and a half into their regimen, both are making considerable progress. The shed is cleaned and organized, yet arranged in a way that will easily disguise the entrance to the hidden tanker, and Sadie's ready to test her third and hopefully, final filtering technique. Finding success, she carefully transfers the fuel into a large gas can and gives it to Jose. When he manages to pry the gas lid off the tractor, he pours the fuel in and tries firing up the engine. When it doesn't start, he makes adjustments and systematically rechecks everything. He tries over, and over, and over again. Jose, sitting on the tractor's seat, is hesitant to turn the ignition key. If it doesn't work this time, he's out of options. He takes a deep breath and tries it.

"Come on…come on…come on!" the boy encourages.

It starts and between the noise of the running engine and the shouts of joy from the boy, Sadie comes running. It's an exuberant feeling to hear it working, and Sadie hurries to congratulate him.

"Nice job, kiddo! Let's see if it'll move," she squeals, equally excited.

Between Sadie and Jose, they figure out how to raise and lower the bucket, then, feeling a bit more confident, they decide to drive it. It lurches forward, grinding gears, and they quickly run out of room and have to stop. Figuring out reverse is a little more challenging, but they manage to do so, and get the tractor clear of everything. Turning off the engine and then immediately starting it again, Jose smiles.

"I just wanted to make sure," he says, answering Sadie's questioning look.

With the tractor parked, the two head inside, declaring their work done for the day. Over dinner, Sadie suggests celebrating by taking the next day off. Instead of toiling away, they can practice driving and maneuvering the tractor. Jose immediately agrees, excited for the change. When they finish their meal, Sadie and Jose talk at length about what they can do with the newly functional equipment. Sadie has several ideas but lets Jose talk first. He'd like to cut a road to the boat and dig out a section of the cliff for easier access. Sketching a few ideas, he diagrams a plan.

Sadie, on the other hand, suggests re-doing the old logging road, since it's already a part of the homestead and is in dire need of maintenance. Along its route, they can gather the downed redwoods for future use and make the roadway easily drivable for the quad.

Jose's eyes light up. "I could drive supplies! I wouldn't have to carry 'em!"

"Exactly," Sadie grins with her reply, "we'll start practicing there. It's level and safer. If we make mistakes, we won't ruin anything."

The talk continues and the two become giddy, creating more and more outrageous feats for the tractor and uses for all the wood they'll gather. As their energy settles back down, Sadie switches topics, asking Jose about his growing list of supplies for the Intrepid II. She looks it over, makes a copy for herself while doing so, and let's Jose know which items she can contribute. The next morning, Sadie and Jose, both carrying daypacks and hunting gear, meet on the trail between the house and the boat.

"I knew you wouldn't sleep in," he says, looking at Sadie and shaking his head.

"Well...I was comin' to check with you. How 'bout...we mess with the tractor later this afternoon?" Sadie asks.

He knows there's more coming, and waits.

"I was thinkin'...after a patrol, I'd hike a little further. Maybe... half a day...or so."

Jose, still shaking his head, figured as much, but asks anyways. "Like...maybe towards Clara's?"

"Yep." Sadie responds casually.

"Alright...I'll join ya." The boy says, slinging his rifle over a shoulder.

The patrol goes as always, uneventfully, with everything in order. Afterwards, they set a course and Sadie leads. On every trip, she's studied the landscape, recorded its details, and there's only a couple of options left to explore. Jose and Sadie hike steep terrain, and at times, it's dangerous. They've gotten stuck on prior hikes and been forced to backtrack several times, but Sadie believes if they can descend the slope they're on, and climb over the next, they'll be able to make it the rest of the way. It's the closest they've been and after another back-track; Jose points below to an area where a rockslide left debris piled up. They head toward it and cautiously climb down.

Excited to be this far, the two scout for a way to climb the next ridge. They travel along a dry creek bed at the bottom of a small can-yon with walls that grow steeper on both sides. If they don't turn around and head back soon, they risk running out of daylight.

"Let's keep followin' this," Sadie suggests. "It'll either drain to the ocean...or curve toward Clara's. Worse case...if forced, we can always camp for the night."

"Let's go for it!" Jose says, excited to be so close this time.

They move quickly and surprisingly, reach the ocean in a short amount of time. The view and drop to the water is similar to that at Clara's property, and Sadie notes both its similarities and differ-ences. Briefly taking in the sight, the two turn around, return the way they came, and reaching the landslide where they climbed down,

Sadie calculates how much additional time they can squeeze in before returning.

Instead of climbing back up, they head in the opposite direction, and after encountering a few bends in the terrain, they discover a drainage artery coming down from the ridge above. Looking at each other, they nod yes and start the climb. Sweating and breathing heavily, they reach the top and Sadie pauses to examine her map. She's confident that, by following the ridgeline, they'll make their final descent where Clara fell and discovered the spring.

Sadie points it all out, and Jose, realizing they could be at Clara's by nightfall, is thrilled. He can't wait to meet Clara and see her place, especially after all he's heard. Jose's also anxious to see Anna, but finds himself getting nervous, not sure if she'll be as excited to see him. Along the way, he mentally practices things to talk about and ways to say them. Jose wants to impress Anna and let her know he's taking care of everything—for her.

THIRTY-THREE

Today's not a good day, but at least it's not as bad as others. Anna, somewhat functional, is slowly going about her task. She hasn't spoken more than a few grumbles, but she's moving about, and Clara's happy for that. Some days the poor girl simply lies about, alternating between sleep and bouts of crying. The old woman's heart goes out to her, knowing the tragedy of losing a loved one, and she lets Anna mourn, while doing what she can to help.

Besides taking care of and comforting her, Clara finds ways to hold Anna's interest, assigning small chores, even if they're as simple as making tea. Typically, they're basic skills, teaching Anna how to manage when alone, although, thank God, none of them are anymore. Anna's also encouraged to keep a journal and write daily in an effort to cope with the emotions and pain, but as much as anything, Clara's kindly manner and genuine love nurtures the girl's recovery.

Sometimes, Anna has good days, especially ones spent in the garden. She loves all aspects of growing, planting, and harvesting. It was her family's livelihood and it's amazing how much there is to learn from Clara. The old woman's a master and it'll take years for Anna to absorb it all. Today, the young girl works alongside Clara, cleaning out the old hen house and coop. It's been neglected since the earthquakes, and seeing it in disrepair always bothers the old woman. She misses the chickens, but more than anything, she misses her morning eggs. As they work, Clara talks away, but Anna's barely present.

"Anna..." there's a long pause, "Anna..." then a longer one. "Anna...did you hear my question dear?" On the third attempt, Clara finally gets the girl's attention.

Anna, totally lost, didn't catch a thing. Looking at Clara, she shakes her head no, and the old woman tries again.

"I asked if you've ever had eggs."

While nodding yes, tears slowly fall down Anna's cheeks. She attempts to speak, but it takes a great deal of effort. "We-we...ha-ha-had chick-ens." She wipes away the tears, as anger emanates from her eyes.

The change sends a chill down Clara's spine.

"Those men! Those...Splitters! They killed 'em...and ate 'em. All of 'em! They're all gone!" The tears return, this time uncontrollably, as Anna slouches to the ground.

Heartbroken, Clara's at her side, swaying the limp and weeping girl back and forth. They sit for some time until Anna's voice returns. She tells Clara all about her chickens, their names, and the number of eggs she collected each day. Upset they're gone, Anna knows—she'll never have them again.

As the women stand, Clara hears movement. Her reactions, recently changed, have her grabbing a shotgun leaning nearby and standing between Anna and the sound's direction. Moving them behind the hen house, the old woman scans the area, attempting to pinpoint the disturbance. Anna's nerves aren't handling the suspense, and she's trembling in near panic.

Clara glances at the girl and whispers, trying to ease her anxiety, "Anna...it's okay. It's probably just a deer."

Before Clara can tell for sure, they hear a faint whistle. When it occurs again, both ladies strain to listen, making sure they heard correctly. Anna responds in kind and seeing her react accordingly, reassures Clara. Lowering the gun, she's proud of Anna regaining her senses, and she squeezes the girl's shoulder. Together, they step out from cover, greeting their unexpected guests, excited by the surprise. It's even more of a surprise when they see Jose following Sadie. Clara and Anna walk towards them as Sadie and Jose make their final descent into the canyon. When they reach each other, Clara wraps herself around Sadie, kissing both of the woman's cheeks.

"It's so nice to see you, dear. And," pulling away, she looks to Jose, "you've brought more company!"

Jose reaches out a hand to introduce himself, but Clara grabs him.

"Around here, we say hello with hugs," she says, in her grandmotherly fashion.

Jose, caught off guard by the old woman's actions, simply relaxes into it and responds politely, "Yes, ma'am."

Clara steps back with a loving smile. "Oh...a good looker, and polite as well."

Jose, embarrassed by the compliments, blushes, losing his nerve to say hello to Anna. She's standing next to Sadie, who has an arm around the girl. The kids remain quiet while the adults chatter away.

Noticing the youngsters have grown shy, and wanting to talk a little more privately, Clara finds a way to send them off. She asks Anna to show Jose the orchard and pick another basket of fruit. When they depart, Sadie inquires about the shotgun since it's the first time she's seen the old woman carry it.

"The girl's changin' me," Clara shrugs, explaining, "I've grown protective and…in all the years I lived alone…I've never experienced fear. But now…I just want to make sure she's safe."

Sadie understands; it's not just Clara, she's been changing, too. As they move towards the house, the old woman updates Sadie on how Anna's doing, the progress she's made, and what struggles still exist. Sadie absorbs all the details, asking a few questions. Meanwhile, walking up the orchard trail, the kids have yet to speak. Each considers things to say, but neither can find a way to begin. Reaching the orchard, Anna leads them to the correct trees and picks a piece of fruit, offering it to Jose.

"You ever had a persimmon?" she asks, softly.

Jose motions no, looks over the strange orange fruit, and takes a bite. The skin is a little tough, but the meat inside is delicious. He's surprised by how tasty it is and takes a few more bites. He stops, noticing Anna smiling.

Jose swallows, wipes his mouth, and finally speaks, "Mmmm 's good." It's all he manages to say, feeling like an idiot. Anna's giggles relax Jose, allowing him to make another attempt. "You know… they sent us here…so they could talk…in private…probably 'bout us," he says, before taking the last bite.

"Yeah…I figured as much." Anna responds, while picking more persimmons.

She shows Jose how to tell which pieces are ripe, and together they fill the basket. Jose, not too confident, attempts to tell Anna more. He flusters and stumbles like a fool, but recovers, and gradually shares with Anna all the work he's done at her place and on the boat. While talking, Anna begins to see Jose in an entirely new light.

He doesn't share everything he's been thinking or practiced to say. Partly, it's because he's not sure, and some things, Sadie asked him to wait on, especially information concerning the fuel. She wants to discuss it with Anna first and he agreed. Occasionally, Anna asks a question, but mainly she just listens and when he runs out of updates, the silence returns.

Heading back to the house, Jose asks Anna what's she's been up to. His attempt is successful, and the girl begins talking at length about the garden and all the things Clara's place has to offer. Sitting on the porch, the two women look up from their conversation, and Clara, taking the basket, brags about how helpful Anna's been. A second set of hands has really made a difference, and they've accomplished much. The warmth on Anna's cheeks spreads, especially since Jose's watching. Noticing the girl's embarrassment and knowing Sadie and Jose will leave early in the morning, Clara shifts the conversation.

"Alright," the old woman says, matter-of-factly, "Jose, you come with me." She drapes an arm over his shoulder. It's comforting and oddly familiar for the boy, as she leads him towards the door. Looking over a shoulder, Clara addresses the girls. "You two stay out here and catch up. I'll call ya when dinner's ready."

Inside, Jose's blown away! He examines everything and asks detailed and thorough questions. Clara never tires answering all he asks while busily preparing a meal. Outside, the mood isn't as joyful. Sadie and Anna's discussion started rather simply, but quickly turned serious. Sadie knows the girl's been struggling and talking about her parents isn't helping. Anna, shocked by Jose's fuel discovery, is confused, angry, and upset at finding out this way. She can't believe she wasn't told and even worse, feels foolish for failing to notice its existence. The more Anna thinks about it, the more sense it makes. The quads always had gas, and she recalls her dad leaving the shed once with a full can. She hadn't said anything at the time, and never thought about asking why it was there.

"Why? Why...didn't they tell me?" Anna asks, as tears fall.

Sadie's thought about possible reasons and shares what she honestly believes. "I think they meant to protect you."

Anna stares, not knowing what to think.

"Anna...having gas...is rare and...dangerous. People fight...and kill for it. Especially..." she pauses, before continuing, "the Nation. I think your parents hid it so no one would know it was there...or be able to find it. Not telling you, and barely usin' it, was a way to keep the family safe." Sadie hopes her words ease the girl's worries.

Anna understands, but still, it hurts. It's another thing she'll never know for sure or ever be able to ask. She misses her mom and dad, and knowing she'll never see them again, her tears reappear. Sadie needs to discuss a lot more with the girl, but she's not sure Anna's ready. The youngster looks at Sadie, sensing her hesitation, gains control, wipes her face dry, and asks Sadie what else she should know. Sadie, encouraged by the girl's sense of duty, decides to share what she's planning.

It starts with the good news about the tractor and all the different ways it can be used around the homestead. Sadie talks about creating easier routes of travel between their places making checking in and moving supplies a lot easier, especially, with the quads. Also, there's hope of making the ship safer to board and the need to keep the harbor protected. If they ever need to evacuate, a well-supplied and fueled boat is their only option.

As Sadie speaks, Anna listens intently, nodding the entire time. The girl's amazed at how prepared and well thought out everything is with Sadie. It reminds Anna of how little she's actually capable of and how many things she's failed to put thought into. Embarrassed by her naivety and realizing if it wasn't for Sadie and Clara, she'd be completely lost, or—dead, or—worse—a chill runs through Anna.

"Sadie," she interjects mid-sentence, "you know better than I do, you're smart...you know how to keep us safe, and...I trust you...completely." Anna doesn't wait for any type of response, but continues speaking her train of thought. "Whatever you think...do it. Use the tractor however you think best, build whatever the boat and harbor needs, and...take all the gas. I don't need it."

"Thank you," Sadie lays a hand on Anna's knee, "thank you for your trust. It means a lot." She gently lifts the girl's chin, making eye contact, ensuring Anna understands the sincerity of her next words. "The work around your home will help keep us safe...and connected, but...it will always be...*your* home. Remember that. It's not always gonna be this way."

Anna, understanding, nods her head.

Sadie goes on, "As for the gas...thank you, but...a day may come when you'll find a need. Don't be so quick to think you'll never use it...always plan ahead. You never know what tomorrow brings..." she pauses, smiling at the girl, "in the meantime...we'll use only what's absolutely required."

Anna hugs Sadie as Clara opens the door. Smiling at them, she announces dinner, giving them another few moments alone. Sadie briefly updates Anna on Jose's work and brags about what he's contributing. Anna's already heard most of it and tells Sadie so. The woman smiles—glad the youngsters have talked—and shifts the focus to the Intrepid II and Jose's list of missing materials. Sadie tells Anna how important it is to get what's needed in order to keep it ready and supplied, then, she pulls out the list, leans a little closer, and talks softly.

"The first item…" she pauses, keeping Anna curious, "and the most important thing…is fuel. Jose didn't think it was possible…and then…he found your tankers!" Sadie pauses again, quiets back down, and barely speaks above a whisper. "But…he won't use it."

Anna's face scrunches up.

"He won't use it…unless…you say it's okay," Sadie clarifies.

The girl's face brightens up.

"Before we leave, it would…mean…a lot…if you told him." Sadie lets the words sink in and then continues, "He didn't say anything earlier because I asked him not to. He's waiting for me, but…I won't tell him. I'll let you…okay?"

Anna attentively nods yes. It's exciting being able to say thanks with a gift, but it's unsettling having the responsibility of communicating it directly to Jose. She found herself unusually nervous speaking with him earlier, and Anna's not sure how to go about it. However, the more she thinks about all he's done, the more she knows it's the right thing to do. Giving fuel for the boat, which one day could help them all, seems like such a simple thing. After all, he's been taking care of her home and making sure it's ready when she returns.

As the two girls enter, Anna thinks about different ways to tell Jose. Deciding to wait until after dinner, she takes a seat. It's the first time the four of them will share a meal together, and Clara prepared a small feast. Before beginning, they grasp hands, bow heads, and give thanks. The entire time, Anna can only think about Jose. She finds herself thankful they're sitting across from one another; otherwise, they'd be holding hands, and the thought brings a blush to her cheeks.

Everything is delicious, as always, and the kids eat heartily, barely speak, and listen while the adults talk. Anna gets up first, puts on tea water, and starts clearing the table. Sadie and Clara sneak a glance between them, each thankful to see Anna pitching in and maturing. Before Anna can take Jose's plate, he's up and handing it to her. She takes it, thanks him, and distracts herself by washing the dishes. He stands nearby a little longer, unsure of what to do, before returning to his chair.

At the table, both women have their maps out examining the route Sadie and Jose used to travel to Clara's. When Anna rejoins them, she updates her copy, while listening to Sadie talk about the details of the hike. It's not an easy route to travel, and several sections need trail work, but they made it. Anna, glad to learn of the faster route home, doesn't consider using it now or any time soon. Instead, she finds herself wanting to stay with Clara in the canyon. Clearly, she's not ready to return, let alone, live on her own. Putting the map away, Anna gets up, asking everyone what type of tea they'd like. Jose, in turn, asks what kind they have, and the young girl playfully rolls her eyes.

"More than I bet you've ever seen," she replies, smiling.

Anna begins listing the types, most of which he's never heard of, and she has to check the pantry to see which ones she's forgotten. She disappears momentarily, pokes her head back out, and lists a couple more. Sadie, seeing the boy's uncertainty as an opportune moment, tells him to go look. When Jose joins Anna, both feel a little uncomfortable, but Anna tries covering it by showing Jose all the different jars of tea, and he, by asking something about each one.

When they've run out of containers, he's still unsure and asks Anna to select one. The girl's jitters build while she decides to talk about more than tea. It's the perfect time, since there're alone, and he's leaving soon. Setting down a jar, Anna gathers courage and makes a couple attempts. Trying different approaches, she falters, and Jose, uncomfortable seeing her flustered, grows nervous with anticipation.

She takes a deep breath apologizing, "I'm sorry…I've…been… struggling." Anna sits on a small footstool tucked in the corner, gathers her thoughts, and staring at the floor, continues, "I just…want to… thank you." She looks up, almost losing focus, but finds the strength to continue. "Thank you for taking care of my home."

"No…An-na" there's a lump in Jose's throat, it catches, making his voice break." He clears his throat, knowing it's his chance to say what he's practiced. "No, Anna…*thank you.*"

Confused, she stares.

"Thank you…for…your trust. Thank you…for letting me be a part of your place. Thank you…for giving me a chance…to…change my… circumstances and…have a better life." Growing confident, he says more. "I'll take care...of your place for...as long as you need. I'd do... anything for you." Embarrassed, Jose grows quiet.

Anna stands up, making the boy even more nervous, and takes a step closer. Touched by Jose's sentiment, she hugs him. It's quick and breaking from their embrace, neither speaks. Anna, almost forgetting what else she intended to say, regains her composure and nearly explodes.

"Oh! And...use the gas! For the boat! Take as much as you need! After all, you discovered it...I wouldn't even of know 'bout it if it weren't for you. Please. It's the least I can do."

Jose's not sure which feels better, getting hugged by Anna or learning he can refuel the Intrepid II.

THIRTY-FOUR

Gabby's gag tears deeper into her flesh and the coagulated mess at the corners of her mouth breaks open. Bound to the bed her body bounces in response to a furious rhythm. Sadie's arm rises, and the knife plunges over and over and over. Suddenly, Sadie's at a bathroom sink, frantically trying to clean blood off her hands and arms. Even with rubbing them vigorously and rinsing them under water, the man's blood won't wash away. The harder she scrubs, the worse it becomes, until she's completely covered by the gore and everything turns to shades of red.

Looking at her reflection, a blood-spattered face stares back. Sadie's hair shortens before her eyes, leaving dirty stubbles she can't stop rubbing both hands over. Compulsively absorbed in its texture, she initially fails to notice the ashes raining down as red fades to black. Brushing them off a shoulder, Sadie discovers she's wearing an oversized flak jacket. It weighs her down, growing constantly heavier, until she's unable to move.

Closing her eyes, she wills her body to respond. Opening them, Sadie finds herself outside the barn, holding a huge chainsaw and pulling the cord over and over, but it won't start. Panic sets in, and things turn frantic. She can't get him out, and looking at his twitching leg, she attempts again, and again, and again.

Both eyes fill with sweat and tears as Sadie's vision blurs. Wiping them with a sleeve, she catches a glimpse of several Splitters running through the woods. They're chasing something. No, they're chasing someone. It's a girl. It's Anna! Sadie takes off at a sprint, trying to catch them. They gain on Anna, but Sadie isn't making much progress. Her body continues to slow, no matter how hard she tries. Frustrated, scared, and unable to catch up, Sadie's fear grows as Anna gets knocked to the ground. Dropping to a knee, Sadie draws her crossbow, but reaching over her shoulder, she can't grab an arrow. After several attempts, she tears the quiver off her back, only to find it empty. Then, Anna screams.

Feverish and unsure of her surroundings, Sadie wakes drenched in sweat accompanied by a pounding heartbeat. Unable to shake the haunting images or fall back to sleep, she feels about, searching for the light, knocking things over on the nightstand. Fumbling about, she flips the switch back and forth without success. Disappointed by leaving it on, which drained the battery, Sadie sits up to re-charge the light.

The movement leaves her light-headed and placing a hand to her forehead, Sadie discovers what she already knows—she's burning up with a fever. Leaning back against the wall, she slowly peers around the room's surroundings. Even though she's been sleeping in Anna's bedroom, she hasn't taken the time to examine all its intimate details. Her feeble state matches her demeanor as Sadie scans everything over.

The furniture is depressive. It's infantile and grossly inadequate, even with the modifications made so it can be usable for an older child. A worn changing table, partnered with an upended log round for a seat, is set up as a desk. The dresser's been repainted and raised to add a makeshift third drawer, and hints of the original baby pattern exist around each of the tiny knobs serving as handles. They're pink, daisy shaped, and match nothing else in the room.

The vanity mirror, sitting on top of the dresser is cracked, reflecting only a partial image of Sadie from her chin down, but she stares anyway. The ache behind her eyes, accompanied with a need to quench an extreme thirst, finally snaps Sadie out of her daze. She mechanically turns toward the nightstand, made of stacked milk crates, looking for her water bottle. It's been knocked to the floor, and it's a strain to see it, let alone reach it. Leaning over the beds edge, Sadie grabs the bottle, while pushing aside a large handkerchief that's used as a tablecloth. The material dangles well beyond the top crate's edges and partially covers the container's opening, faced forward, which doubles as a storage shelf.

From inside the space, Sadie removes a small, thin photo album with a cover that frames the first picture. It's Anna as a toddler, sitting in a tub full of bubbles, with her mother kneeling alongside. A fluffy white patch covers Anna's nose and both she and her mom are frozen in the perpetual happiness of laughter. Her mother's sleeves are rolled to the elbows, and suds drip from her forearms.

Clambering back to a seated position, Sadie carefully turns each page, finding all the pictures are of Anna as a baby or toddler with her parents. Setting it aside, she drinks the last mouthful of water and needing more, she swings her feet to the floor. Steadying herself while standing, Sadie shuffles into the kitchen, refills the bottle, and collapses on the couch, where Jose finds her hours later.

She stirs hearing him and attempts getting up, but Jose tells Sadie to stay and rest. He'll cover the morning patrol and continue their work. The two of them have been toiling away since returning from Clara's and they've made staggering progress with the tractor. Sadie relinquishes quickly and curls back up on the couch. All the demands she's placed on her body have finally caught up. Aching with fever pains, she struggles finding a comfortable position and pulling the blanket tight, shivers run through her body. When Sadie next opens her eyes, she finds Jose setting a bowl of oatmeal nearby.

"Sorry to wake you. Here's some food…and more water."

"Thanks," she barely squeaks, struggling to sit up.

Sadie takes a drink, and eats slowly, as each bite takes too much effort to swallow. Halfway through, she sets it down, rolls over, and goes back to sleep.

*   *   *

Sadie's being chased through an orchard. The footsteps behind her are getting closer, when an old barn comes into view. She dashes in, shuts the door, and scrambles to barricade the entrance. Spinning around for something more, Sadie smacks into a dangling pair of legs. Falling backwards, she's horrified to see whom they belong to. As the body sways back and forth, she scuttles in reverse along the ground, using her hands for support.

In a panic and failing to pay attention, Sadie falls through an opened door and tumbles hard into the dirt. It's dark, but burning bodies, dropping from the windows of a building that appears above her, illuminate the area. Each lands with a stomach-wrenching thud. One hits nearby, and she's horrified watching it wither in agony. Melting flesh drips off in lumps, leaving sections of bare bones exposed as the flaming piles bubble and sizzle. Another falling body spreads flaming chucks everywhere and pieces land on Sadie, searing into her neck and chest.

Bolting upright, she rips away the blanket bunched near her face and repeatedly swipes both hands over the area before coming to her senses. Sadie's emotions are running rampant and the fear and horror that chased her about still linger. Her anxiety filled dreams serve as a reminder of her psyche's delicate state. She's trying to do too much and all the physical demands, accompanied by layers of psychological trauma endured over the years, have simply worn her down.

Sadie's felt a growing unease ever since finding the dead Splitters Caleb managed to kill, and the return of these terrible men is something she's feared and hoped to avoid. Their presence stirs up disturbing images, thoughts, and memories that Sadie's struggled with for years, and it's all on the forefront of her mind; only difference, is now, there's more than just her safety at risk.

Drenched from the fever-induced sweat, Sadie gets up, strips away her damp clothing, wipes her body down, and changes into clean clothes. Feeling slightly better, she returns to the couch only to grab the water and what's left of the oatmeal. She finishes them both and takes the dirty bowl into the kitchen. Still feeling fatigued and tired from the little bit of movement, she lies back down.

The next morning, Sadie wakes thirsty, and is surprised to find she slept through the entire night. Even Jose coming in for the evening didn't wake her, and the bowl of food sitting nearby is the only indication of his presence. Amazed, Sadie realizes how deep her slumber was, and then, how hungry she feels. Eating the cold beans and rice and happy her appetite's returning, Sadie hears the boy enter.

Seeing her eating, he smiles. "You look better."

Sadie swallows the last mouthful before responding. "I think my fever broke."

She finishes the water and still feeling weak, gets up carefully. Heading into the kitchen, they sit together at the table. Jose's already completed the morning patrol and excitedly fills her in on the progress with the tractor. Yesterday, his roadwork reached the helicopter clearing and he hopes to complete what's left to do within the next couple of days. When it's done, they'll have drivable routes to both it and the Memorial Camp.

After a short discussion, Jose leaves, fuels the quad, and loads it with the materials Sadie requested. When it's ready, he drives back to the house to get her, and together, they head out. Jose's done a nice job, and Sadie praises his work. They park in a newly cleared section under several redwoods and walk the circumference of the space that's been carefully worked just as Sadie directed. Two stacks of scavenged logs are neatly piled and several mounds of stones sit equally spaced apart from one another.

The freshly prepped soil, log piles, and stones are all hidden under the cover of the giant trees so none of it is visible from above. The original meadow wasn't expanded, but with the fallen trees dragged aside, it feels bigger. Walking its perimeter, Sadie points out various locales, explains the plans for each and what projects should be started first. Several times, they stop to sketch various designs, verifying each other's comprehension of what's intended.

Even though they're planning a few structures, what's more important is figuring out how to defend the area. This particular location is a major stressor for Sadie. She's been trying to manage her constant worry ever since learning of their vulnerability from the air. When Caleb and his buddy arrived, they came in completely undetected, making Sadie realize, that anyone, at any time, could land on the island. She pushes away the horrible thoughts of an aerial invasion and returns to focusing on the positive progress they've made.

Sadie has a timeline, but a lot depends on when, and if, the helicopter returns, as planned, for Caleb. Thinking of him, reminds her once again of the Splitter's cruelty, and an image of the tortured body she found surfaces. She works to dismiss the mental picture as they head towards the small field. Reaching the relocated logs, they shift their focus to what supplies Sadie wants brought up here first and where they'll be stored or hidden.

As they continue planning, the two walk around again. This time, they circle deeper through the woods, spiraling out in a larger and larger search pattern. Sadie wants to examine as much ground as possible, but grows weary, still weak from being sick. After another hour of exploring, they turn back to the clearing, start the quad, and begin the drive back to the homestead.

Early the next day, both are up handling their share of the responsibilities and preparing for what lies ahead. By mid-morning they're in the clearing and working hard. Sadie still doesn't feel one hundred percent, but knowing it'll make things go faster, she works through it. Afterwards they head out and, by the time they arrive at the Memorial Camp, she's exhausted.

It's a turbulent night, as once again, Sadie's haunted by her dreams. The last nightmare leaves her in a state of unease that lasts throughout the rest of the day while they hike. Nearing the cave, Sadie suddenly drops to a crouch and draws her bow. At first, Jose's unsure of what she's heard, but then, the distinct sound of crunching reaches his ears. Whatever it is, it's loud and moving toward them. Sadie signals, they sneak behind an old burnt-out redwood stump and wait. Forcing patience, she shifts to a better position and sites an arrow. Jose, peering from around the opposite side, also takes aim as his heart races.

He'll follow Sadie's lead and only shoot if instructed or she misses. He takes several deep breaths, controlling his fear. The approaching noise is nearly upon them when he gets a glimpse of a figure. This time, his heart skips a beat; it's not an animal. As he begins lining up his rifle's site trying to get a better view, Sadie stops him, and with a lowered bow, she signals silence. When the figure looms close enough to hear breathing, Sadie steps from behind their cover.

"Hello, Caleb," Sadie says, without a hint of emotion.

"Wha d'yah doin' here!?" Jose says, flabbergasted and overcome with joy.

Sadie, not quite echoing the boy's excitement, repeats the question. "Yeah...what are ya doin' here?"

Caleb looks from Jose's to Sadie's eyes when finally answering, "You were gone too long...I thought somethin' might have happened." Embarrassed, he looks back to Jose. "I expected you two back...a while ago...or at least...a few days ago..." he trails off, swallows, and then continues, "I just started patrolling...I'm...building my stamina. If another week passed, I planned to come lookin'...and...I needed to make sure my body was ready...just in case...I had to hike that far." Looking pathetic, he adds one last thing, "I...had to."

Sadie doesn't respond. Instead, she takes a long drink while Jose and Caleb wait in anticipation of what she'll say. They never expected what follows.

"Alright...you two finish the patrol. I'm heading in." Sadie hikes off towards the cave before the boys get a chance to respond.

They watch in disbelief as she disappears.

Jose speaks first. "She's been sick."

Caleb inquires about it and the two men talk nonstop, filling each other in since they were last together, but as they near the cave and enter, they grow quiet, since Sadie's already in bed. In the morning, Sadie wakes to find both men up and already eating, with their packs set near the door. Sadie finishes packing hers and puts it in line with the others. Taking the cup of tea that's offered, Sadie sits down and grabs a bowl of oatmeal. It's early and cold, but with each swallow, the hot tea and food warms her. Finishing breakfast, Sadie inquiries about the morning patrol, and Jose answers.

"I thought I'd do it...before we left." He sneaks a quick glance at Caleb and then continues, "Sooo...I'll go...and...you two...can...talk." Jose gets up and grabs his gear. "I'll be back in a bit," he says, leaving without waiting for any response.

As the boy disappears, Caleb speaks. "When you and Jose leave...for...your place...I'd like to come along."

Sadie eyes shift from the loaded packs back to the man sitting across from her. Finding themselves alone, both sit uneasily, not sure what to say or how to even begin. There's too much history between them and the level of intimacy they'll need to share—to really clear the air—is more than Sadie wants to contemplate. She's tired and doesn't want to spend the morning wasting any energy arguing, whether about the past or what lies ahead.

She pours another cup of tea, leans back, and stretches out. Looking at Caleb, her mood softens a little further. He's been beaten, forced to watch the torture of his friend, almost died, and since, been confined to the cave. He looks downright miserable and when his eyes meet hers, she fights to ignore their effect.

"Okay," she begins, "so...what...exactly...are you thinking?"

He's a bit surprised by Sadie's sincerity, and her warm demeanor distracts him from what he's been preparing, but he gathers his thoughts and answers her nonetheless. "My ribs didn't re-injure as bad as we thought. They still hurt...all kinds, but...they're healing...and...I can move better. Besides less pain, I'm able to walk...much further." He swallows and speaks with brutal honesty. "Sadie, I gotta get out of here...at least for a few days...I need...the distraction." His eyes can't hide the torment he feels. "I don't...I'm not..." he pauses taking a deep breath, "between my dreams and thoughts...I'm...a mess."

He runs both hands through his hair and determined to make the journey to Sadie's, he continues, "Walking...makes me feel better. The fresh air and exercise helps. I know my endurance isn't too great, but I know I can make it. And...I should know the route...for safety. If anything ever happens, I should have experience gettin' from here to there."

Sadie hasn't said anything, but putting herself in his shoes, she understands. She gets up and looks long and hard at Caleb, which makes him feel uneasy.

"Okay," she simply says.

Caleb, shocked, sits stunned as she cleans up from breakfast. He expected more of a fight with mention of his injuries, or even having to hear a bunch of reasons why it wouldn't be wise. Instead, she simply agreed. When Jose returns, all their packs are still at the door and he takes it as a good sign. Before the boy even shuts the door, Sadie's at his side, slinging her pack over a shoulder.

"Let's get moving," she says, exiting the cave.

Caleb winks at Jose as the two move to follow and not get left behind. Sadie isn't too far ahead, but they hurry, excited to finally get the chance to see her place.

THIRTY-FIVE

Sadie, Jose, and Caleb hike without speaking. It's late into the second day of their journey, and they're nearing Sadie's home. An extremely slow pace has been set, and Jose can't figure out whether it's for Caleb's sake or if Sadie's still not feeling well. He's never seen her move so slowly, but he's grateful, since Jose knows his friend's in a considerable amount of pain. Every incline they climb is a struggle for Caleb, and the exertion, accompanied by the heavy breathing it induces, is taking its toll and he's fallen behind.

Waiting for him and then pointing out several identifying features, Sadie directs their attention along each accessible route to her place. It's the most she's said all day and the boys make sure to take in every detail. When she finishes talking, they head out, anxious to arrive. After another hour, Sadie stops to make an initial visual inspection of her home, but the boys struggle detecting it. Approaching the area, it becomes clearer why.

"This…is where you live?" Jose asks, astonished and obviously dismayed.

Sadie, amused by his expression and relieved to finally be home, lets a small smile emerge. "No, not anymore. It's where I grew up."

Two large redwood trees crisscross over what remains of the cabin's roof that protrudes from underneath layers of old tarps, covered thickly with years of forest debris that block much of the cabin underneath. Only one side of the structure isn't covered, but all the windows are boarded up. Walking past the dilapidated home, Caleb inquires how long it's been this way.

"Since…the earthquakes." Sadie's smile disappears.

They hike away from the home and up a gradual slope until reaching another structure in even worse shape. It too, was crushed by a fallen tree, and it doesn't look safe enough to enter. Sadie pushes aside a loose section of boards, climbs through, and waits for the boys to follow. Inside, it's a disaster, and they're careful not to bump anything in fear of the entire thing crashing down. It's dark and dingy, and as their eyes adjust, random pieces of lumber, supporting the shed from complete collapse, become evident.

Sadie maneuvers toward the back, stops, and turns around. "When the Enders hit our coast...my husband and I came here to stay with my dad. We moved into the cabin down below and...my dad stayed out here."

The boys, not impressed with the surroundings, and wondering why they're there in the first place, begin to lose interest. Sadie ignores them, while uncovering a hidden lever. Using it, she opens a secret entrance, snapping Jose and Caleb's curiosity back, and they stand, staring with mouths wide open. Stepping inside, Sadie switches on a small light so the boys can see as they follow. She closes the door and shows them how to secure it before heading on to the next, at the opposite end of a short tunnel dug directly into the earth behind the shed. Opening this entrance, Sadie once again goes first, secures the lock once they're inside, and then moves about checking a series of batteries and flipping switches. Suddenly, the entire place lights up. The men, even more impressed, slowly turn, taking in the bunker's sights. Sadie gives them a moment to digest what they're witnessing and then starts with the pertinent information.

"My dad built this place with safety in mind...and...of course... to be self-sustainable. His design, technologies, and...craftsmanship are...unique. He could do anything," Sadie says with pride.

Jose attempts to interrupt her, but Sadie halts him. He's bursting with curiosity and questions, and at the moment, she doesn't have the energy or heart for answering them. She just wants to be in bed, but they need to be taught how to use things, so Sadie musters the strength.

"Alright...I'm sure you've got lots of questions, but we'll talk later. So," Sadie makes direct eye contact with Jose, making sure he understands, "not now, first...let me show you a couple things."

Sadie moves around the bunker's small studio apartment while describing, teaching, and demonstrating how the place functions. She covers generating electricity, recharging the batteries, cooking, water usage, food storage, supplies they're welcomed to use, the escape tunnel, and lastly, the composting toilet.

"Jose, you use this," she says, opening a spare cot, "and Caleb... take the bed."

Jose and Caleb, both attempting to respond at the same time, interrupt one another.

It's Caleb who gets the right of way. "No, Sadie...you take the bed."

"I'll sleep on the floor," Jose chimes in, "so Caleb can use the cot."

Sadie doesn't respond. Instead, slinging her pack over a shoulder, she slides a wall panel aside uncovering another hidden door. Both men are surprised yet again and shocked to learn there's another area, as Sadie's nearly gone.

They blurt out the same question. "Where are you going!?"

"To bed," Sadie replies, without pausing.

The door shuts behind her and the panel automatically returns to its proper place, hiding the entrance. Caleb and Jose shift their stares from where she disappeared to one another. Shrugging his shoulders, Caleb moves to the bed and carefully attempts bending over to remove his shoes. Jose takes over for him and helps, as they exchange a concerned glance. Caleb's tired, sore, and a little worse for wear, but he's proud to have made it.

As he rests, Jose checks the food supplies and prepares a simple dinner. He opens and closes every cabinet, drawer, and container, partly in search of what he needs and partly because he can't help himself. He's talking excessively while inventorying, examining, and admiring absolutely everything. His brain is on super absorption as he observes at full throttle. The only time he pauses is to make a quick sketch in his journal.

Jose stops talking, realizing Caleb's sleeping. He's not exactly sure when the man fell asleep, but thinking back, he hasn't spoken since first lying down. Trying to be quiet, Jose continues his exploration of the bunker while the food cooks. He wanders about the apartment in the same sequence Sadie used, which helps him recall each thing she shared.

It's hunger that finally pulls Jose away from his powerful sense of curiosity. With dinner ready, he stops looking about and gently wakes Caleb. At first, he thinks about letting his friend sleep, but Caleb needs to replenish his energy and food will help. They move to the kitchen area and sit down for a hot meal. Jose rattles off a good deal of the information he gathered while Caleb slept. Several times, the boy leaves the table to show and point out what he's talking about. Caleb says little in return, appreciates the boy's effort, but is too worn out to absorb much.

After dinner, Caleb returns to bed while Jose examines things further. Making more drawings and taking notes, the boy fills several pages before turning in for the night. The following morning, he's at it again, intrigued by the impressive feats of engineering the bunker offers. Jose has never seen or even imagined most of its features, but upon inspection, he finds they make sense. Anything that doesn't reveal an obvious answer, Jose notes it, along with additional questions it conjures.

By the time Caleb wakes, Jose's already eaten and is preparing to re-charge the house battery system. He brings a bowl of oatmeal and a mug of tea to his friend before hopping on the bike. He pedals away, talking the entire time, and after twenty minutes, the boy begins to sweat, but keeps up the effort. Posted on the wall next to him is the laminated protocol, complete with charts for energy conversion. He stands, leans his forearms on the handlebars, and pedals faster as the stationary bike whirls with activity.

While he's riding, the wall panel slides open and Sadie emerges. She sees Jose at the recharging station and walks over, checking each connection and then the timer. He's done everything correctly and Sadie appreciates the great job the kid does every time he's given a task. Jose smiles, and when he reaches the required energy production, dismounts.

He picks up an empty bowl and pours another mug for Sadie. Checking the pot, Sadie takes the last of the steel-cut oats and sits in the kitchen, where the boy joins her. Caleb, moving gingerly and careful to guard against the pain, stands and slowly moves across the studio. Joining the others, it's obvious to them he needs at least a day or two of rest. Caleb's been watching Sadie since she entered, but they've made eye contact only briefly. He inquires about her health, thinking she looks a little pale and maybe even a bit feeble. Sadie takes a deep breath, not exactly sure how to respond.

"I'm…not feeling so good," she says, stating the obvious.

Caleb hesitates, leans closer, and brushes aside a piece of Sadie's hair so he can press the back of his hand against her forehead. At first, she stiffens, but closing her eyes, she relaxes. Her fever has returned, and Sadie knows she should be in bed.

"You need to rest," he says.

"I know, but…there's a few things…"

"Sadie." Caleb interrupts her mid-sentence.

Her eyes widen.

"You've done enough. Rest."

Before Sadie gets a chance to finish what she tried to say, Jose joins them. She turns to him as he approaches. "Alright, kiddo, you ready?"

His smile widens. "Always!"

"Here…" she says, handing a small key over, "open the desk."

Jose excitedly gets up to find out what's locked inside. Caleb—feeling left out—pouts silently. Sadie ignores his looks, gives the boy more information, tells him which items to bring over, and then takes the notebooks from Jose. Grabbing a pencil, she tears an empty page out of a blank journal and begins drawing her property. While outlining the route they used getting here, she also adds the patrol she wants the boy to make. Sadie reminds Jose of the features she pointed out yesterday and provides estimations of time for traveling each section.

When she's finished, Jose reiterates the information, asking only a couple of questions. Sadie's a little apprehensive about not joining him, but feels reassured by his memory, willingness, and excitement at the chance to explore the area. So far, he's been able to handle everything asked of him and this is a fairly simple task. Sadie looks at Caleb. His face has softened and he too absorbed the information. When Jose finishes restating the directions one last time, Sadie's satisfied, and moves to the next item. She grabs the top notebook, opens the cover and silently reads the opening introduction, hearing her father's voice while doing so.

"These," she says, fanning the pages and piquing the boys' interest, "were my dad's."

She tries containing the emotions her father's desk and notebooks provoke. She can't look at them without seeing her dad sitting there carefully working. He was meticulous, diligently recording every detail, often spending hours at a time carefully writing. The notebooks are precious and represent a collection of work never before shared, but Sadie understands their importance and knows how valuable the information will be.

"These are final versions." Sadie gently caresses her hand across the stack before continuing. "My dad carefully transcribed each of these from his notes…experiments…and test designs." Feeling protective, she hesitates.

Sadie's recently thought quite a bit about how to best spread the wisdom they contain. Her dad's planning, preparations, and quest for sustainability play a vital role in her survival, and now, she's in a position to offer help, and sharing this knowledge may be only the beginning. For years, she worried her father was on the brink of insanity. After the accident that took her brothers and mom, his compulsions were scary, and at one point, Sadie considered getting her dad professional help. Then, the world suddenly changed, and his excessiveness became their savior. He stored away a lifetime of goods, along with a bountiful supply of survival gear. Because of him, she has everything she could ever want or need, with more than enough to help others. Continued thoughts of her father, accompanied by a weakened state, strain Sadie's emotional control.

"Jose...these will answer lots of your questions...and explain in detail how this place works." She looks at Caleb and speaks softly, "You'll find useful information, too."

Sadie takes a deep breath. "Please be careful with 'em...they're the only...copies I have."

Sliding a notebook over to each, Sadie invites both boys to learn from them. Jose carefully turns the pages, interested in all it contains, while Caleb does the same with the one in front of him.

"I think it's time...to share my father's work." Sadie slowly lifts her eyes from the stack of notebooks. "Will you help...me?"

Caleb and Jose, touched by her sincerity and vulnerability, feel it's the least they can do and nod slowly.

"Alright then," Sadie stands and gathers her sense of control. "Jose...go patrol and...when you return, pick one that interests you the most and start copying it. Caleb...start with whichever one you think would help the colony the most. If Gus makes it back for you, I wanna be prepared." She heads over to the hidden entrance. "I'll be back for dinner." Sadie disappears, leaving the boys alone.

Caleb looks through the collection of notebooks, while Jose prepares to leave. As the boy heads out, Caleb believes Sadie's correct: her dad's journals can definitely help. As dinner approaches, Caleb anticipates Sadie's arrival. He's spent the day copying a notebook, taking breaks only when forced to do so by the cramps in his hand. Jose, too, has been writing away and hopes to get the chance to read each journal. Both men have been particularly interested in the system used to generate electricity in the bunker, along with the research on alternative and biofuels. While they work, Sadie enters and takes a seat, looking over the journal Jose is copying.

"Good choice, kiddo," she says.

He smiles, finishes the section, and then gets up to check the food.

Caleb closes his and looks at Sadie. "You feelin' any better?"

Sadie leans to one side, shrugging her shoulders, and answers without speaking. She's still pale, and Caleb fights the urge to re-check her forehead. Instead, he gets up, sets the table, and brings her a bowl of soup. While they eat, Sadie outlines what she's been thinking.

"The cave needs restocking...and preparations for Gus's arrival require lots of work...we also need to keep watch at Anna's. I know it's a minimal risk, but...if the Nation finds the cove...or the helicopter clearing..." She shakes her head not wanting to think about those possibilities.

Just mentioning Splitters brings up too many painful memories and images for all three of them. Both men nod in comprehension, understanding her concerns and wanting to do their part. Sadie's responsible for saving them both and they'll do anything for her.

"I've got most of the cave supplies ready." Sadie turns to Caleb, "But...I'm not exactly sure what...or...how much to get ready for Gus's arrival. I need to know more about the colony...the people livin' there, what would help them, and all about the copter...especially, how much stuff can fit in it."

Caleb, not exactly sure how much more Sadie has to share, doesn't interrupt.

She turns to Jose. "I'm still counting on you to guard Anna's place. Tomorrow, I'd like you to take supplies to the cave. Then, hike back here for another load before returning to the homestead to finish your work."

Jose, as always, nods in affirmation while receiving his directives.

She turns back to Caleb. "While he's gone, we'll talk...I wanna be prepared for Gus. In another day...or...two, I'm hoping you're able to start helpin' with some of the lighter work. By then...I should be better, too. I also have to check in with the ladies...I told 'em I would. So...as soon as possible, I'll head there."

Caleb likes hearing he'll be staying with Sadie and is anxious to hear what she's thinking, but her health still concerns him. Obviously, she's been able to take care of herself all these years, but he can't help but worry.

"Sadie, you should just rest...at least a few days...especially, if you're plannin' on hiking to Clara's. We'll help with whatever you need. But please...you do too much. Rest. You've got...us...now." His last words are just above a whisper.

Sadie's touched by Caleb's sentiment and concerned look. Besides feeling ill, her nightmares have returned, and they're continuing to play havoc with her well-being. Unfortunately, it's typically for this time of year and Sadie knows she needs to handle it better. Besides being near the anniversaries of losing both her father and husband, it's nearing the holidays, which always make Sadie miss her family.

"Don't worry...I'm plannin' to rest. I'm stayin' here...for a bit. And," her eyes smile lightly, "I know I've got...both of you."

There's a brief silence, then Sadie stands and heads to the entrance of her place. The boys aren't ready to see her leave and make attempts to stall her departure. They're incredibly curious about where she disappears, but respecting her privacy, they don't ask. Instead, the two of them inquire about some of the bunker's features. After explaining a few things and staying longer, Sadie grows weary, says goodnight, and doesn't return until early the next day.

After a quick breakfast, she sends both of them out on patrol with a two-way radio and instructions to check in at regular intervals. She's never fully explored the handhelds' ranges and for years they've sat idle. With their help, communication capabilities can begin to be tested. When they return, Sadie has all the necessary cave supplies and instructions ready. Sadie checks over Jose's load, once he gets it packed, explains how often she wants radio contact, and sends him on his way. When the door closes, she sits across from Caleb, opens a notebook, and looks intently into his eyes. He swallows, almost afraid to break eye contact.

"Okay," she says, with pen held ready, "let's get started."

THIRTY-SIX

Caleb's exhausted, although it's not from physical exertion, and he looks forward to getting out on perimeter patrols. They're a welcomed break from the relentless inquiries Sadie's leading, as her questions never end. Their days are divided into segments with specific times devoted to different subjects. They always eat breakfast separately and when Caleb returns from the morning patrol, the questions begin. It lasts through lunch, when they eat together, and then, Sadie retreats to her place, leaving Caleb alone to continue copying from the journals.

They meet for the second time before Caleb's evening patrol. While he's gone, Sadie prepares dinner, and afterward, the third and final session of the day takes place. Each evening, Sadie stays later, gathering information. Even though he's tired of talking all the time, Caleb appreciates every chance to be with her. He just wishes it wasn't always business and hopes soon she'll be satisfied.

Tonight, as they wind down, Caleb decides to try and find some quality time with her instead of the grilling he faces three times a day. Sadie's always serious, leaves when finished, and hasn't shared anything about herself—although, he hasn't asked. While she glances over the evening's notes, Caleb takes advantage of her pause.

"So…how much more you gonna need?" Caleb doesn't let her answer, "I mean, how much longer will…my…interrogation last?" he says, smiling trying to lighten the mood.

Sadie sees the softness in his eyes and the weariness in his expression. "Sorry. I've been…on…a mission." Not exactly wanting to say more or sure about what she's willing to share, Sadie quiets.

"A mission?" he laughs, "don't I know it! You always have a plan," Caleb waves his arm signaling the expanse of the bunker, "and the means to do it…and comfortably, I might add. I mean…look at this place…it's incredible! Fully stocked…electricity…and water! Sadie, your dad was…genius. His work…this place…." he trails off, absorbed in a thought.

Caleb remembers all those years ago when Sadie was forced to leave college and he grows solemn, reminded about his selfishness.

When she needed him the most, he wasn't there, and even worse, he added to her torment and heartbreak. Sadie, on the other hand, in his greatest hour of need, was there, and still, she's providing for him.

Sadie, noticing the changes sweeping across Caleb's face, grows worried. She's been avoiding any personal topics with him since they've been alone and limiting their time together, making sure there's isn't any opportunities. It's too unsettling of a coincidence being reunited, and Sadie's not sure how to make sense of it. Whenever the subject breeches her mind, she quickly dismisses it, putting her energy back into all the preparations she deems necessary.

Sadie's life has become full of new things, entwined with others, and now there's the chance to help even more. It's a new focus and a well-needed change to the emptiness of her solo existence. Her dad ensured she'd always be better off than just okay, and Sadie's beginning to believe it means more than just her own survival. His legacy could be saving lots of folks and Gus's arrival could be the beginning of helping many.

Getting back on track, and cutting off Caleb as he's about to speak, Sadie finally replies, "If you can manage…I've got another question." She takes his eye contact as affirmation and immediately asks, "When Gus returns, will others be with him?"

Understanding her concern about more people arriving, Caleb shrugs in a doubtful fashion. "I don't know. I'm not sure what's been goin' on since I left, but…the plan was to scout 'til spring, then he'd return, and fly us back to the colony. But…there's always a chance things changed."

"What's the back-up plan?" she asks, straight-faced.

"There isn't one. If Gus doesn't return, it's…survive or die here."

Sadie's eyes narrow, staring directly into Caleb's, making him squirm. "So…you're plannin' on…living…here?" Her eyebrows raise a mere fraction.

Realizing his assumption and taking staying here for granted, he realizes he's given Sadie the wrong impression and quickly scrambles to correct it. "I mean…somewhere on the island, not…living…with… you, but…somewhere." His words only embarrass him further and Sadie's eyeing him doesn't help. "If Gus doesn't return, I'm stuck. So…I hope it's okay…for me…to stay."

His eyes plead, but Sadie remains silent. She hasn't put thought into his long-term living arrangements and only planned where to station him to help keep watch and move supplies. Caleb, who sits pathetically waiting, would much rather live on the island with Sadie then go back to the colony. Sadie doesn't respond, instead, she gets up and begins gathering her things in preparation for leaving. Caleb, not sure what to do, watches, hoping for some positive indication.

"Sadie," Caleb begins, gathering courage and lightly touching her arm, "please...stay."

His sincerity scares Sadie and an uncomfortable sensation builds in her abdomen.

"Please. Sit back down...at least for a little longer," he pleads.

Debating her options, Sadie finds she's not sure what to do. It's easier to retreat home, but at some point she's going to need to face the fact that, for whatever reason, Caleb's back in her life.

"Alright. I'll put some tea on," she finally says.

Caleb's happily surprised. He didn't expect it, but now that she's staying, he grows uncertain and starts with small talk. He specifically asks about how much water the structure collects, knowing already the entire unit acts as a giant cistern, collecting and filtering ground water that seeps down the mountain. His question gets her talking and opening up, as Sadie shares more about her dad. Caleb sees the love and admiration emanating from her eyes and wishes he'd taken the opportunity to meet the man. When she finishes her last tale, they laugh together, and then there's a long silence.

"I regret...never meeting him." Caleb eventually says. "I regret... lots more than that."

Their light mood completely disappears as he speaks what he's wanted to tell Sadie for a long time.

"I'm sorry...for everything. I'm sorry for not being there when you lost your family...for not making you my priority...for...abandoning you when you needed me the most...and for being...such an idiot. You didn't deserve it...I'm truly sorry."

Uneasiness stirs in Sadie's stomach as Caleb continues getting more off his chest.

"I've thought lots about us...being...together again." Seeing Sadie's scared and uncertain look, Caleb quickly recovers, "I mean... our paths crossing again after all these years. I'm just...grateful for the chance to finally apologize." He pauses before adding one last thing, "Can you ever forgive me?"

Sadie knew, at some point, their past would come up and now that is has, she's even more uncomfortable than she anticipated. She unconsciously spins the wedding band still worn around her ring finger, while Caleb stares unsure what to do or say. Nervously, he waits for a response, growing tenser with each passing moment, wishing she'd say something.

After what seems like an eternity, Sadie speaks. "Caleb, I forgave you...a long...time ago."

Even though her words are truthful, Sadie doesn't feel any better about sharing them. She wipes out her teacup and after saying a quick goodbye, retreats to her hidden side of the bunker. Once inside—and after several deep breaths—the uneasiness gripping her insides eases. Frustrated by her reaction and sudden anger, Sadie turns to the evening's tasks and moves on. Grabbing a clipboard hanging from its hook, she checks the food storage's inventory and starts moving meal buckets.

Continuing to add to the pile, Sadie's memories surface, transporting her to a long-ago day when she visited with her father and found a food catalogue mixed in with his mail. While flipping through the pages, Sadie joked about some of the items, only for him to open the pantry and come out holding an armful of pouches and cans. She didn't understand why he needed freeze-dried foods and MREs, but explaining it, he said that he simply wanted to try them.

Sadie's always preferred fresh food and living off the land when possible, but over the years, she's consumed many of these packaged meals. Even so, there's barely a dent in the supply and food buckets are stacked floor to ceiling, filling the storage area. The bunker's design holds a lifetime of food and this is only one of the many rooms scattered throughout the underground compound.

Finished and heading to bed for the evening, Sadie thinks about the Tri-nami first hitting and her move back to the family cabin, which was also stocked. All its cabinets, shelves, closets, and pantry were full. At the time, she thought the supplies would be enough to help through the hardest parts of the recovery, but it wasn't long after they realized the world would take generations to heal.

Between what they hunted, gathered, and harvested from the crops planted in town, they did better than survive. It wasn't until the

Splitters arrived that things turned worse and she can't help but think about her dad's death. He was so adamant about returning home after being shot. It was his dying wish and the journey back was slow and painful. Once home, he held on for several days, living on pure will, making sure Sadie was left knowing more details of his preparations.

He demanded to go to his apartment and not the cabin, and once there, he revealed the entire bunker. It was the first time Sadie learned the extent of his planning and how much he managed to hide. He handed over blue prints, revealed all the entrances, exits, hidden passageways, and vast stores of goods. Sadie couldn't believe the size of the compound, the amount of items he squirreled away, and how long he kept it secret, making the entire ordeal surreal and clouded in sadness.

He delayed his own death only to ensure her safety. In his final moments, her dad made Sadie and Markus promise to move into the security of the bunker, where the Splitter Nation couldn't reach them. As he lay struggling with his last breaths, Sadie held his hand. His last words still echo in Sadie's ears. "You must…survive…promise me…you'll live…find the strength…no matter…what happens." They both knew it was his final moment, and each word he managed to speak was a small victory. Sadie promised, and he fought to say more, but nothing coherent followed.

With the memory, a small tear escapes and falls down Sadie's cheek while she climbs into bed. Never a day goes by that she doesn't miss her dad, family, and heart-wrenchingly, her husband. As they often do when she's in bed, Sadie's thoughts turn to Markus. After her dad died, Sadie was distraught, but it didn't compare to the mourning she experienced after her husband's death. It's sad thoughts such as these that ignite Sadie's nightmares, and she attempts to dismiss them before sleeping.

Sadie snaps awake, unable to return to slumber, and gets up to start her day extra early. Working displaces the images from her dreams and after completing several chores and making additions to the growing pile, she makes breakfast and carries it next-door to share with Caleb. Sadie, entering earlier than normal, surprises him, and he's caught with only a towel around his waist, still damp from a quick rinse. Sadie's surprised too and a little embarrassed. Feeling her face blush, she averts her eyes, noticing he's gained some weight back and looks—stronger.

"Ahhhh…sorry. I wanted to join ya…for a…pa-trol," she stammers.

Caleb quickly dresses and it's momentarily awkward when he joins her, but it changes with a view of breakfast.

"That looks great and smells even better!" he excitedly says.

His comment puts them at ease and together, they sit to enjoy the meal. Sadie made more than they can eat, but knows leftovers will be appreciated. Caleb recovered his appetite a while ago and it makes her feel good to see him eat so heartily. He eyes what remains, looks at Sadie, and asks if she'd like any more. When she declines, Caleb grabs a pancake and slathers it with another serving of rehydrated eggs and cheese. Wrapping it like a taco, he wolfs it down, then, tops it off with a few more mouthfuls of orange drink. Setting his glass down, he notices the amusement twinkling in Sadie's eyes.

"What?" he asks.

"Still hungry? Here," she teases, pushing what's left of the food closer to him.

He sees she's joking and laughs, patting his stomach. "No, I think I'm done. But…"

Caleb grabs one last cake and tears it into pieces, "I'd hate to waste the syrup."

He wipes his plate clean, leans back, and states that now he's full. Not wanting to disrupt their casual interaction, Sadie keeps it light, but gets them moving. They check the charges on their radios in anticipation of Jose's scheduled return and head out for the day. Sadie starts the patrol in a completely different direction and Caleb follows her lead. At regular intervals throughout the morning, they receive and try returning radio contact. It starts as static, transitions to beeping, and later, a few broken words are relayed.

Nearing mid-day, Sadie turns toward an area she often neglects. As they hike, her thoughts turn dark, and she fails to notice Caleb talking. They step from beneath the canopies of several redwoods and an area opens before them. Caleb halts at the sight. It's not the impressive jumble of fallen trees that gets his awe. It's what lies hidden beneath the largest camouflage netting he's ever seen. Obviously, it's military-grade and hides a massive structure.

Forced to walk by the giant tree that smashed her husband, Sadie's mind materializes the image of Markus's twitching leg. An all too familiar internal pain develops, her pulse quickens, and her chest tightens. Still oblivious to anything Caleb's saying, she pushes forward and makes it to the barn door. Her arms remember the desperation they felt holding onto the frame for dear life and the bruises that covered them afterwards. Fumbling with the lock, she steadies herself with a deep breath and enters.

The huge expanse is full of machinery, a couple of vehicles, tools, and equipment, but everything's protected under tarps, covers, and old blankets. While Sadie hunts for what she came for, Caleb looks around and helps when needed. A pile builds on one of the many workbenches and as it reaches completion, Sadie switches to showing Caleb where to find various items, explaining the barn's organization. Satisfied, Sadie packs what she can fit into her bag and leaves what remains for later.

Caleb and Sadie return to the studio and begin cooking when Jose enters. He drops his pack, hugs Sadie, and reaches for the cold leftover pancakes. After his snack, Sadie gets out her map, and they update the ranges of their radio signals. With each trip Jose takes, they're attempting to pinpoint exact distances and locations where the walkie-talkies work best. Eventually, Sadie hopes to establish a communication network across the island, but the steep mountain terrain challenges her goal. She reaches for a radio and taps out a series of sounds, making sure the guys are paying attention. Intrigued with what she's up to, they ask.

"Listen again." Using the radio, she makes the same series of sounds, only slowly, while verbalizing each letter as she does: "S – A – D – I – E."

She does it twice more, writing out the dots and dashes, impressing Caleb with her knowledge of Morse code. She teaches them the basics, along with emergency signals, and then informs them she'll be taking a set of radios to Clara's. After dinner, Sadie presents Jose with the items she collected from the barn and explains Caleb will show him the rest another time. It's all for Jose's boat, but before he can say thanks; Sadie begins giving them the next set of instructions. First thing in the morning, they'll patrol before she leaves for Clara's. She provides an estimated timeline for her absence, along with an outline of what needs to be done at the Memorial Camp, the helicopter clearing, and at Anna's.

Stressing the importance of healing, Sadie reminds Caleb to take it easy. Once the supplies have been moved, she wants him to divide time between the cave and Anna's. Neither of the boys are happy to learn she's leaving so soon, but they agree to what's asked and wonder just how much they'll be moving. When they return from patrolling the following morning and enter the studio, they get their answer in piles organized by intended location. Sadie smiles when the men gasp in shock.

"You want us to move...all...this?" Jose says, surprised.

"Yep," Sadie glances from Jose to the piles, "these should help." She holds up two interesting-looking apparatuses. "These are for moving heavy loads. They're modeled after old bricklayer packs and can easily support over a hundred pounds. But...don't carry that much... no more than fifty, at most...and, Caleb...you way less."

Sadie suggests strategies to make the task easier, but she doesn't spend much time before heading out with a large, heavy pack strapped to her back. She tightens the hip belt, sets a comfortable pace, and looks forward to spending some time with the girls.

THIRTY-SEVEN

"SADIE!" Anna yells, setting down a basket and running to greet her.

Sadie has just enough time to set her pack down before the girl leaps into her arms. Good thing, because Anna nearly knocks her over. Wrapping the girl in an even tighter hug, Sadie relishes these precious moments. When they release from their embrace, Anna explodes with information and Sadie hears all about what the girl's been doing. The youngster talks about the plentiful harvest of persimmons, how she picked them all by herself, used the ladder, and almost fell. The girl's a whirlwind of chatter, making Sadie smile.

Clara stepped out of the cabin when she first heard Anna yell and, watching the two young women interact while walking towards her, she feels a heartfelt surge of emotion. The elder takes a moment to count her blessings, then gives Sadie the warmest welcome home hug the woman can remember.

"It's good to see you," Clara says, as they break from their embrace.

Once inside the quaint confines of Clara's home, Sadie's senses are overwhelmed with the incredible smells. While Anna puts away her basket of fruit, Sadie and Clara dare a quick dialogue while the girl's distracted.

"How's she doing?" Sadie discreetly whispers.

Clara raises a hand, tilting it side-to-side in a quick gesture. It's enough of a communication for Sadie to understand it's still touch and go with Anna. Later, she'll get a detailed explanation, but as Anna rejoins them, Sadie doesn't want to dampen the girl's currently cheery mood. Instead, she asks about the heavenly smells and the girl jumps, checks the oven, and returns carrying a small bowl.

"I'm making dinner. All by myself," Anna says, beaming with almost as much pride as Clara, sitting nearby. "And these," she hands the bowl to Sadie, "are a surprise...for you."

Looking into the container, Sadie picks up a piece of the dried fruit. She's never eaten dehydrated persimmons before and with her first bite, she's impressed. They're good, really good. She pops another piece into her mouth and then another. The women laugh at Sadie's enjoyment and after a few more giggles, Anna goes to the oven and returns with a hot, fresh loaf.

Carefully placing it on the cutting board, Anna retrieves three bowls and spoons and carries a pot of stew to the table. She serves the steamy vittles and cuts a piece of bread for each. Before sitting down, Anna fills the water pitcher and grabs glasses. They give thanks and dig in to a belly-warming, tasty meal. Then, for dessert, they finish the last of the bread smeared with persimmon jam.

When Anna gets up to clean, Clara leans closer to Sadie, places a wrinkled hand over hers, and asks Sadie how she's really been. Looking into the concerned eyes of the old woman, Sadie already knows Clara can sense her distress and the recent sickness she's been battling. No longer hiding it, Sadie provides a couple of quick insights into her state of health. The old woman has such a way and warmth about her that Sadie can't help but share more.

Retreating to the fireplace to settle in for a night of chatting and sipping tea, the women gather, as Sadie opens her pack to hand out all the items she packed. Both Clara and Anna find amazement at all she presents. From simple things Sadie views as basic essentials to items she deems essential for the safety of all of them. Handing out the gifts reminds Sadie how fortunate she's been.

Sadie teaches them a few radio calls, has them practice, and they laugh, keeping things light. She explains wanting to establish communication lines among all of them and thinks the radios will work best between Clara's and Anna's places, since it's a shorter distance and some of the areas at higher elevations should easily put them in range. They enjoy each other's company late into the night and when Anna falls asleep, the two older women quiet their voices and talk privately.

Clara speaks in depth, updating Sadie on all things concerning Anna. Even though the girl continues to mourn, she displays a willingness to learn and is incredibly helpful. Clara proudly brags and although she loves talking about Anna, she wants to hear more from Sadie, particularly about her physical and mental health. Sadie describes her fatigue and fever, but hesitates before mentioning the nightmares. Talking about her dreams isn't something Sadie's accustomed to doing and Clara senses it. She describes the images haunting her and their lingering effects as Clara nods her head and listens without interrupting. After talking at length, Sadie's exhausted, but feels a burden's been lifted. Clara's caring, soft words and loving ways are the medicine Sadie truly needed.

They stay up much later, sleep in, and when Sadie wakes, she's refreshed and energized. It's been a while since she's awakened in this state and it feels good. Heading into the kitchen, she finds Anna already has breakfast done, the oven is loaded with trays of dehydrating persimmons, and she's prepping the next batch. Sadie walks over, looks at the fruit being cut, and picks out a tasty piece. She pops it into her mouth, relishes in its sweetness, and grabs a knife to help.

Clara joins them and kisses each of her girls' cheeks. When Anna picks up the empty basket, Sadie moves to join her, winking at Clara in a quick sideways glance. They head off to the orchard and the old woman finds joy, knowing Sadie plans to stay for a few days.

Talking the entire time, Sadie and Anna fill their basket quickly and return to the cabin, where Clara waits to begin the day's chores. Besides adding wonderful company, having Sadie around the canyon shortens each job and by lunch, they've finished what would have taken Clara two to three days on her own. Finishing for the day, they eat well before joining one another for evening tea as this time of night, gathering around Clara's giant hearth, has become special. Sadie's brought an entire tray of dried goodness with her and picks out the fatter rings for an after dinner treat while Clara and Anna share a giggle, breaking Sadie's attention away from the fruit. Looking at their smiling faces, she gingerly shrugs her shoulders and bites off a chunk from the piece she's holding.

Clara turns to Anna. "You're right," the old woman says. "We're gonna need more." They laugh, then turn back to Sadie as she finishes her persimmon. "We're hopin' there's enough for the boys...that's...if you don't eat 'em all."

Sadie finishes her chewy mouthful and takes a sip of tea before responding. "They'd love 'em for Christmas. You know...it's only a couple weeks away." She pauses, testing their reaction before continuing. "We should all be together."

Clara loves the idea, Anna's excited, and a conversation ignites as they talk logistics and bounce ideas around. Sadie naturally assumed it'd be easier for Clara to host everyone, but the old woman suggests differently. She wants to get out of the canyon, stretch her legs on a long trek, and see Sadie's place. Thinking she should do it while capable, Clara's honest with herself enough to consider the fact that soon, she won't be, as there's no escaping old age.

Continuing their discussion, Sadie's place seems a logical choice, since there's plenty of space, its location is centralized, and it'll be easier for the boys. It'll also give Clara an opportunity to learn the route for emergency purposes. Sadie doesn't disagree, in fact, the more she considers the notion, the more she likes it. She's got plenty of resources, it'll save carrying gifts, and it aids in the execution of her timeline.

As the conversation dwindles, the women grow weary and turn in for the night. They've put in a good day's work and tomorrow there'll be more of the same. Tonight, as their eyes close, Clara and Sadie drift off with thoughts of gifts and holiday cheer. It's the first time in years, they'll each spend it with others and not alone. As for Anna, she grows upset as the excitement of gathering at Sadie's wanes, and is replaced with sadness. The girl misses her parents and isn't sure the holiday will feel the same without them.

Getting up once again refreshed, Sadie wonders at the effects of being at Clara's. It's a warm comfortable feeling that lasts throughout each visit. It's amazing, the three of them being brought together, and Sadie knows there's some greater purpose. All day they work side-by-side, tackling jobs with gusto, laughing and joking the entire time. The older women make it a point to keep Anna happy as they take turns sharing funny holiday memories and getting her to laugh. It turns almost game-like, competing for the girl's giggles and smiles.

Sadie still has an important agenda to discuss with them, but she keeps pushing it aside. Gus's scheduled return, the possibility of her leaving to visit the colony, and preparations for allowing other survivors to relocate to their island, are all major concerns. It'll take numerous discussions to resolve everything and at the moment, it doesn't seem appropriate, so Sadie decides to put it off until after the Christmas celebration. Pushing the thoughts of what still needs to be done out of her mind, Sadie returns her focus to Clara as she describes one of her favorite holiday treats. Anna has no concept of fudge and the women do their best to describe the sweet.

With the day's chores nearly complete, Clara leaves them, giving Sadie the chance to interact alone with Anna. Wrapping up their task, the two decide there's just enough light left to climb to the orchard and pick more persimmons. Along the way, Anna shares some of her holiday memories and talks about how her father always went turkey-hunting leading into the holiday. There was only one year when she remembers him not getting a bird, and instead, they dined on stuffed quail. Her family celebrated by adorning the house with fragrant red-wood cuttings and hanging the few decorations they have. Each season, Anna and her mother would unpack the Christmas relics, taking care not to damage the irreplaceable family heirlooms.

Each item was accompanied with a story that her mother would tell year after year. Some of the decorations and stories dated back to her grandma's childhood and even though Anna knows each tale by heart, she always looked forward to hearing them. They'd decorate the house while her dad hunted and he'd bring home clusters of redwood cones and other interesting forest debris, until finally, getting a turkey. His arrival with a bird signaled Christmas Eve and the next day they'd feast and celebrate. They'd exchange homemade gifts and talk about goals and expectations for the upcoming new year.

Sadie mostly listens, but when able, she asks questions, attempting to create a better understanding of the girl's holiday traditions and beliefs. Anna's at an age at which she may, or may not, still believe in Santa. The girl hasn't mentioned anything, making Sadie think there's a good possibility she's never been exposed to that particular Christmas folklore. It makes Sadie wonder what else will disappear as the Global Flood generation leaves their mark.

Retiring to the fire's side after dinner, it's only for a single cup of tea and limited chatter. Instead of talking much, they simply enjoy one another's company, silently watching the flickering lights of the flames. Sadie says good night first, packs her things, and slips quickly into slumber. Clara and Anna use the time to plan breakfast and decide what to make for Jose, since Sadie can bring it to him, along with a few other things Anna asks to include. Clara likes hearing the girl's thinking about how to take care of the boy and offers a couple suggestions of her own. When Sadie makes her way to the kitchen early the next morning, both Clara and Anna are bustling about. Besides breakfast there's a pile of goods set aside.

Sadie approaches the mound and turns, making a face. "All this, huh?" she asks, even though, she knows it is.

"We're tryin' to keep it small." Clara looks at Sadie, scans the pile, and shrugging her shoulders, adds another item.

The old woman's casual comment and carefree body language make Sadie giggle and soon, all of them are laughing. When it subsides, Sadie drags her pack over and sits at the table, rearranging things to accommodate all the additions. She knew they'd have a few things, but she didn't envision carrying another large load. Jokingly, Sadie tells them there's a little more room.

Anna doesn't catch the sarcasm and gets excited. "Oh good! Cuz... you don't have any persimmons...and Jose likes 'em too!"

She brings over an armload and Sadie fills the last remaining spaces in her bag. Now that her pack is stuffed—and extra heavy— they sit to eat as Sadie asks Anna if there's anything from her home she'd like brought to her. The girl shakes her head no and resumes eating.

"You sure? What about...Christmas...stuff? There's nothin' you'd...like...to have...or...need?" Sadie carefully inquires again.

Sadie's intentions are well meant, but Anna grows quiet and the adults aren't sure if that's a good or bad thing. Clara gets up to move closer to the girl and sits back down with an arm around the young child. She pulls Anna in closer, talking in her sweet grandmotherly way.

"When you think about Christmas," Clara kisses the top of the girl's head, "what immediately comes to mind? Maybe an item that honors your parents' memory?" She hugs her tighter. "Their spirit lives with you...and always will, but...it'd be nice to have them represented, too."

Anna continuously nods her head up and down while tears silently streak down her face. Clara lets her cry and then uses a cloth napkin to dry the girl's face.

Anna regains control, recovering from her sadness. "Christmas socks...the holiday starts when we hang 'em." She turns, facing Sadie. "They marked the beginning of turkey season for my dad. That's when...he'd go hunting...returning with stuff for decorations." Her head returns to its downcast position, but she manages to hold back the tears that threaten to reappear. "He'd place what he gathered in our socks, or...above, on the mantel for my mother and I. The house would fill with their scent. It made...it...smell...like Christmas. When he left the socks empty, we'd get excited, knowing he caught Christmas dinner." Growing quiet, Anna lets the tears spill over.

Clara thanks her for sharing such a beautiful and special family tradition and coaxes Anna into talking more about the stockings. The girl finishes their descriptions, explaining where they're kept boxed up, and becomes silent, signaling Sadie to get up. Wrapping each of them in a giant hug, she says her goodbyes, but with Anna, she takes another moment.

"So…you're okay with me gettin' out your Christmas stuff…and findin' the socks?" Anna nods in agreement, and reassured, Sadie feels better about it. "Oh good. It'll be so nice to see 'em hanging. It'll make it feel…Christmassy."

Anna, unable to talk, is touched by Sadie's words and all she can manage is one last hug.

THIRTY-EIGHT

Exhausted, Jose carefully removes his oversized pack and sits to rest. His shoulders, back, and legs ache, and even though it's difficult, the boy gets back up and resumes hiking. He's on a mission, finding ways to carry larger and heavier loads, attempting to reduce the number of trips needed to move all the supplies. Each time, it's more strenuous and on this particular journey, he's found the maximum he'll ever carry. The load challenges his balance and forces Jose to focus, especially along the steeper slopes.

Moving slowly, he creeps toward the homestead and heads straight into Anna's house. He unpacks the items that stay in the home and carries what remains to the boat. Once onboard, Jose makes himself a hot meal and fights the urge to lie down and rest. Instead, he grabs his rifle and patrols the area. Climbing the trail to Anna's family's campsite, Jose's grateful to be without the heavy pack as he ponders how many more trips are still needed. It's tough, but he doesn't think of it as work. Instead, he's appreciative, realizing how fortunate they are to have food, water, and safe places to live.

Reaching the campsite, Jose walks to the cliff's edge to peer out on the ocean. The overcast, grey weather doesn't offer much of a view, but he scans what's visible and wonders about the crews of Splitters heading south. He's grateful to be out of their company and in control of his own life. His thoughts shift to the trail of devastation the renegade fleet will leave in their wake, and fighting to block out a painful memory, Jose prays for any survivors they come across.

Before leaving, Jose decides to start the four-wheeler and do a quick maintenance inspection. It takes a little coaxing to start, but he promised Anna things would be taken care and wants to keep his word. As he backs the ATV out of the shed, Sadie surprises him. It catches the boy off guard, and he nearly jumps off the seat with a skyrocketing heart rate. Regaining composure and resettling his nerves, he's both excited and embarrassed. She's caught him off guard, again, and he's disappointed. He was so focused on his task that he failed to notice Sadie. Seeing the boy's reaction, Sadie feels a little guilty. She waited for the wheeler to start before approaching, knowing it'd be easy to sneak up on. It's still an important lesson, but she doesn't want him to feel too bad. Surprising him yet again, she hops onto the seat behind Jose.

"Come on. Let's go for a drive," she says.

Sadie directs him to the access road and they travel as far as they're able. When what remains of the road becomes impassable, Jose parks the quad, and they head out on foot. He carries his rifle and Sadie, as always, has both her bow and slingshot. Quietly hunting together, Sadie hopes to find evidence of turkeys. She preps Jose on hunting them for Christmas and they scout possible regions.

It's too late in the day to stay long and without any luck, they return to the quad and then back to camp. Along the way, she fills him in on the rest of the holiday plans and Jose looks forward to the celebration. It's been a long time since he's been with loved ones on Christmas, and it makes him think of his mother. Even though they had very little, his mom always found a way to make the holiday special. Thinking back to those days, Jose wishes he could share this place with her. She'd love the island, the safety it offers, and most of all, his new friends. Memories of his mother's homemade holiday magic linger as he contemplates how to create it for the people who now are an integral part of his life.

With the quad parked, the two silently make their way back to the homestead. It's been a long day for both, and Sadie's looking forward to unloading her pack, eating a hot meal, and curling up to sleep. They stop at the boat first and decide it'd be simpler to just eat there. As Sadie unpacks what Clara and Anna sent, they each snack on a persimmon while deciding on an easy dinner of leftovers she also brought along. Once heated, the stew is hearty, and the nearly fresh loaf accompanying it goes quickly. Using the last of the bread, they clean their bowls and then the pot, until only traces of breadcrumbs remain.

Feeling full and comfortable, Sadie decides to spend the night aboard the Intrepid II and makes sure Jose's okay with it. He swells with pride at being asked and makes every effort at being a gracious host. He boils water for tea and rearranges a sleeping bunk. It's cold and as Sadie curls up in her sleeping bag, she's glad to have brought its thicker liner. It keeps her plenty warm, but she wonders about the boys sleeping gear.

During breakfast, Jose gives a complete status report on the boat while taking Sadie on a quick tour. Even though he's been busy moving supplies and unable to spend much time aboard, Jose's managed a couple small improvements. Before heading out to patrol and hunt, they make a pit stop at Anna's house to drop off Sadie's pack and check the property. Once inside, she's tempted to retrieve the family's Christmas decorations, but knows it'll have to wait until later. There's lots of ground to cover if they hope to discover where the turkeys are roosting and Sadie has only one day before she'll need to return to Clara's.

All day, they look for turkey sign, but fail to find any. As time passes, they travel further, covering more area and narrowing their search. On the way back and nearing a small clearing, Sadie slows to a stop, signals to Jose, and they raise their slingshots. Her shot kills her target and his wings another. It's his first ever success with the sling and he feels a rush of adrenaline. The quail crashes to the ground and struggles trying to escape, but Jose quickly captures the injured bird and snaps its neck.

Back on the homestead, they cook their catch outside at the fire pit and talk more about the upcoming Christmas celebration. Sadie hopes to learn more about Jose's experiences and tries getting him talking, which is difficult because the young man doesn't like sharing much about his past, since it's too painful, but battling his anxiety, Jose shares some memories.

"Christmas was my favorite," he begins. "Mom would sing carols...she knew so many songs."

He closes his eyes, trying hard to hear her voice, but it's been too long. Staying quiet, Sadie encourages him to take his time. When he speaks again it's to tell Sadie about the last Christmas he spent with his mother.

"We were living in a shack...with nothing...along the shores of Lake Shasta. Our place was only one of the many. It was Christmas Eve...I woke up...and saw mom puttin' a gift under our tree." He pauses, remembering hiking in the woods with her and finding a small tree they took turns cutting down. As the image fades, the boy continues. "We made all the ornaments and...when she accidentally knocked one off, I pretended I was still sleeping...in the morning, I learned...Mom was Santa."

He grows quiet again fighting the terrible feeling growing in his stomach. It was only a few months later when the Splitter Nation arrived at the refugee camp and took over. After that, life was nothing but heartbreak, abuse and neglect, at least until now. Sadie, touched by the boy's openness, is genuinely appreciative of what he's shared, sees his struggle, and reinforces talking about it.

They hang-out a little longer, but both have work to do and as it grows dark, Sadie heads into the house. They'll meet again for breakfast to review the timeline and plan, before Sadie leaves for Clara's. In the meantime, she's focused on finding the box of decorations and searching by candlelight, Sadie realizes it would have been a lot easier to do this during daylight. The closet is packed full, and she carefully removes items, making sure not to disturb things too much.

With the closet nearly empty and still no luck, Sadie looks to the top shelf. She grabs a kitchen chair, returns to the bedroom, and takes down the few boxes and packages that rest there, finally finding success. Removing items from a large box, she carefully examines them. Many things are wrapped in old newspaper and deflated bubble wrap and she's curious to discover what's hidden inside. Each decoration has been carefully tended to and Sadie hopes to one day hear the stories that accompany them. The stockings are all rolled together and separating them, Sadie smiles.

As she places each item back on the shelf, the lid of a small box falls off—and before placing it back on—she peers into the container. Inside, there's a wrapped gift complete with red ribbon. The wrapping paper is old and worn and looks to have been reused several times. A homemade nametag, shaped like a Christmas tree, is attached and when Sadie checks, it has Anna's name on it. Utterly surprised, Sadie holds the gift, realizing it's the last present Anna will ever get from her parents and the thought brings tears. She sets it aside with the socks and puts everything back.

Finished, Sadie retreats to Anna's room, falls asleep quickly, and wakes ready to get back to the women waiting in the canyon. Jose heads out at the same time, only, he's hiking back to Sadie's for another supply run and to catch Caleb up on the holiday plans. Instead of taking the quickest route though, the boy meanders, trying to find where turkeys might be hiding. Along the way, he continues to contemplate what can be done for each of his friends and by the time he reaches the Memorial Campground, he's developed a few good ideas.

Jose climbs into the trees and spends the last of the daylight working on the hidden perch. He's spent several nights here and on each trip, it's made a little more comfortable. This time, his focus is on setting up a small A-frame, using some rope and a tarp to help keep in the warmth while he's sleeping. It's cold out and containing body heat while keeping the night's moisture off will help. He tries a couple of different strategies before choosing one and it doesn't take long for sleep to come, but almost immediately, Jose's eyes fly open. He sits up, brushing his head against the tarp as something scurries away. It's too dark to see, but he can hear whatever it is, and it's not far away. It's also not leaving.

"Go on! Get out of here!" He yells, to no effect, as it sounds like it's getting into his things.

Jose feels around for the rechargeable flashlight Sadie gave him and finding it lying nearby, the boy's never been happier to have light. As he shines it towards the noise, two beady eyes reflect back. It's a huge, mean-looking possum that hisses and ignores Jose as it returns to eating what remains of the persimmons.

Jose, unsure what to do and feeling trapped, notes the importance of keeping a weapon close. All he has are the underclothes on his back and the small flashlight. Even his shoes are out of reach. As the varmint finishes the last of the fruit, it begins to sniff around the boy's backpack, which worries Jose further. He yells again, trying to sound confident and aggressive. Transitioning to his knees, he crawls toward it—under the tarp—yelling the entire time, but the possum holds its ground, making him stop.

Reaching overhead, Jose tries to undo the tarp so at least he can stand. With his attention and light focused on the dirty critter, he fumbles with the rope. Struggling, he's only able to loosen a section, but it's just enough to pull aside and give him room.

"Get! Go on! GET!" he yells while standing, raising his arms, and taking an attentive step closer.

The possum looks up, bares jagged teeth, and hisses. Instead of backing down, Jose yells, louder and takes another step. His heart is pounding, but he braves another step. His shoes are nearly within reach, but he's hesitant about bending over to grab them, as momentarily, his face would be on the same level as the animal's. Jose shuffles both feet closer, drags one shoe back using his toes and sliding a foot partially inside, gets enough leverage to raise it and grab hold. He does the same with the other while keeping his eyes glued on the possum.

Jose yells, waving both shoes overhead. He throws one, it strikes with a thud, and another hiss follows, but the animal retreats several steps. Jose, encouraged, intensifies his yelling while waving the second shoe. This time the possum scuttles to the side, jumps to the stump below, and disappears into the woods. The boy takes a deep sigh of relief, but it takes a while for the adrenaline to wear off and even longer for him to fall back to sleep.

THIRTY-NINE

Anna wakes and heads straight for the Christmas stockings hanging in the living room. Sticking out of each are bunches of fragrant redwood cuttings. Most pieces of the dark green foliage end in tiny knobs of a much lighter shade, almost yellow, and gather to round the tips. Some of the bunches have a scattering of fully developed redwood cones and Anna's amazed trees so enormous begin their lives from such petite beginnings.

She slowly examines all the pieces and crushing a few needles between her fingers, releases even more of the heavenly scent. Anna inhales deeply and the olfactory response conjures images of making wreaths, garland, and bunches of holiday swag with her mother. Sadie's place is covered with decorations and she made most of them. Hearing noise in the kitchen, Anna heads over to find Sadie and Clara making breakfast and talking.

It's just the women this morning, since Caleb and Jose are away, finishing the last supply trips to Anna's and hunting in the ongoing search for a Christmas turkey. Sadie, too, has been hunting, but today she's spending time with the ladies first. Between hiking here and getting them settled, everything's been focused on holiday preparations, but Sadie finds a way to transition the conversation. She starts by discussing her preparations for Gus's return and the supplies already moved. Sadie shares some of what she's learned from Caleb about the colony and the struggles they face. Keeping it short, but introducing some possibilities, they listen and occasionally, Clara asks a question.

Sadie allows the information to settle, then returns the focus back to Christmas by offering two gifts. Clara looks through the box of items Sadie hands her as Anna does the same with hers. Smiling at what they contain, both the old and young woman know exactly how they'll spend their day. While Clara gets to work in the kitchen, Anna turns on a holiday playlist. The music reverberates through the entire compound and even though the young girl's never heard the songs before, they're enjoyable nonetheless. Clara, on the other hand, is delighted to hear the familiar tunes and moves about in a jolly good mood.

Carefully removing each bundle from the socks, Anna takes them over to a table set up for her crafts. There are just enough materials to complete the large wreath, laying half-finished on its surface, and nearing its completion, the bunker fills with delicious smells. Intrigued, the girl goes to check.

"Go on, get child. It's a surprise...you have to wait." Clara says, shooing her away.

Anna retreats to the living room, finishes the wreath and hangs it on the wall. Stepping back to inspect it, the girl smiles and begins emptying her gift box from Sadie. She has additional projects planned and Sadie's provided what she needs to complete them. Anna picks a couple of fabrics, and threading a needle, she carefully stitches the red cloth, making sure everyone will have their own stocking.

Overly focused on sewing, Anna fails to notice when Clara enters, bringing them lunch. The girl didn't realize how hungry she was and as they eat, Anna shares stories about learning to sew. Clara inspects the girl's work, praises it proudly, and comments on several of the patterns, but a timer goes off and the old woman hustles away. All day Anna sews, Clara bakes and Sadie hunts. By evening, Sadie returns, finding her place looking and smelling spirited. She hasn't felt such holiday magic since childhood and its return is astonishing.

When Caleb and Jose finally return, it's to the studio apartment and they're amazed at the decor. It's decked out in Christmas cheer as well and what's even more shocking—the passage to Sadie's has been left open. Not sure if it was by mistake, on purpose, or if something's wrong, they set down their belongings and head to the passage, where a short corridor leads to another door. Reaching it, they knock, pause, and then try the handle. It's locked and not sure what to do, they knock harder. After a pause, it clicks and slowly opens.

Sadie stands in the doorway as the boys suddenly grow self-conscience. When they see her smile, they relax and are ushered inside to the Merry Christmas's erupting from Clara and Anna. It's the old woman's and Caleb's first meeting, but in pure Clara fashion, she foregoes the handshake, wrapping him in a giant hug. Instantly, he melts, feeling like—it's—Christmas!

Like Sadie, Caleb hasn't celebrated since the floods and it's nice having some form of humanity return. Breaking from the embrace, Caleb genuinely wishes each a Merry Christmas with his attention lingering on Sadie, but Jose's excitement about the compound erupts in a deluge of questions and she doesn't have the heart to contain him. It's too joyous an occasion; so instead, it's diverted to Anna, who'll give both him and Caleb a tour.

As they wander off, Clara finishes cleaning from the day spent baking and makes sure all the goodies are tucked away before putting the final touches on dinner. Everything is ready just as Anna wraps up showing the boys around. They sit down, and never before have there been so many people at Sadie's. The place is alive with conversation as she plays host, answering inquiries about the bunker's design, capabilities, and features. Finished responding, she shares a few supplies, set specifically aside for each of them. Out of habit, she doesn't divulge all of her home's secrets and keeps hidden the extensiveness of what's stashed away.

Before they turn in for the evening, Sadie returns with the boys to the apartment. As soon as the door closes, Jose once again explodes with information he's been waiting to share. Both he and Caleb take turns filling Sadie in and she gets just as excited. They talk at great length and come up with a plan before saying good night. Early the next day, Sadie's up with the boys, moving about in preparation of their surprise. By the time the rest of the bunker wakes, they've gotten everything in place. On the way to the kitchen, Anna checks the socks, and, finding them empty, rushes to make sure it's not a mistake. Her eyes are huge and talking rapidly, she fails to notice all the meat spread across the counters. When she does, it stops her mid-sentence, giving Jose the chance to speak.

"We got a turkey yesterday morning! And then a deer!" He gleams with pride at being able to provide such an incredible bounty.

Even though the turkey's already plucked and the deer's cut into manageable sections, there's still lots of work to be done. Sadie and Clara prepare a brine solution full of fresh herbs to soak the bird while Jose and Caleb finish butchering the venison. They plan to slow-cook a roast for dinner, start a batch of stew to accompany tomorrows feast, and then, cut thin strips for jerky. Each strip is handed to Anna, who coats them with seasoning before filling the dehydrator trays. Random bits and pieces are thrown in a skillet and cooked with onions for a hearty breakfast. Even with all the messy work, the mood is cheery and when Anna turns the music back on, things become even more festive as Jose recognizes the first song and sings along as the adults join in.

When the boys head out to patrol, the women use the opportunity to finish their holiday surprises. They don't reunite until supper, where they dine on venison. Afterwards, Clara disappears momentarily and returns with a couple of trays. She thanks Sadie again for gifting her the ingredients to make it possible and then talks about her childhood traditions. Clara's family always gathered on the Eve of Christmas and after a huge meal, her mother would bring out her prized fudge. It was something everyone anxiously awaited and as the old woman talks, she cuts squares, giving each person two different types. Anna and Jose have never tried it before and the adults watch as the kids take their first bite.

Sadie's not sure which she enjoys more—watching the kids' reaction or letting the decadent treat melt in her mouth. While they eat, the discussion shifts to which type each one prefers: chocolate or peanut butter. The group gets a laugh when Jose says he can't decide and needs to try them again. With full bellies, this time it's Sadie who disappears. When she returns it's with an armload of gifts wrapped in brown packaging paper and decorated by hand.

"When I was a kid, we got one gift on Christmas Eve." She says, while passing out the parcels.

"Wait, you don't have anything," Caleb says, noticing everyone has something except Sadie.

"But I do," Sadie says, looking at him, then quickly turning to the others. "I have all of you."

Clara's eyes tear with the sentiment and she leans over to whisper with Anna. The girl jumps up, telling them to wait, and returns, handing Sadie a gift skillfully wrapped in cloth. Opening their presents, each of Sadie's visitors receive new dress clothes, as she explains they're for tomorrow's celebration. Sadie, staring at her gift, catches Anna's eye, then gets up for a hug. Sadie sets the gift—a small, handcrafted piece of artwork painted on deerskin stretched over a wooden frame—on a shelf so it's on permanent display. It depicts three women, obviously them, and a flower pattern, carefully seared into the material, borders it. Everyone compliments Anna, who reddens with the attention.

The next day, everyone is up early and full of excitement. They eat a simple breakfast and gather in the living room to find a small artificial tree lit up in the corner. It's another Sadie surprise and underneath it, sits more gifts. A few more are added before they begin opening the bulging socks, finding dried persimmons, packages of fudge, and an assortment of Christmas cookies baked by Clara. When the tree is void of gifts, the group takes their time unwrapping and savoring the experience. The mound surrounding Jose is overwhelming and he's never owned so many things. There's a stack of books he can't wait to read, two new blankets, a sleeping bag, new clothing, several jars of jam and vegetables, an electronic tablet, and one of Sadie's electric hand chargers.

Sitting next to him is Anna and she's just as stunned. Her pile is similar, but one gift stands out in its craftsmanship. An exact replica of the giant oak where her parents are buried, made from old copper wire, stripped and twisted to match the tree, is exquisite. The roots wrap around a stone base and Jose explains that all the materials used to make it were from her homestead.

"It's...beautiful. Thank you," Anna says, turning it in her hands.

Seeing Jose holding the tablet, Anna scoots closer and tells him it's the same as the one Sadie gave her. She explains its features and when shown its library, Jose gets even more excited. Caleb organizes his rather large pile that's full of things he never thought he'd have again. Sadie outdid herself and he feels a little guilty about how much she's given, especially, considering what she's already provided. Caleb's curious about how she's able to continually supply them with so many things—as her giving seems endless. Putting aside an electric trimmer set, complete with his own charger, and a shaving kit, he looks forward to a clean shave and a real haircut. He folds his new clothes, and stacking them, signals Jose before they excuse themselves with an air of intrigue. Even Sadie has no idea what they're up to. After a few moments, they return, wearing huge grins.

"Would you ladies...please join us?" Caleb asks.

Curious, the women follow. In the apartment, a square shaped item sits covered by one of Jose's new blankets. Jose looks to Caleb, Caleb gestures to Jose, and the boy clears his throat.

"I know this...isn't exactly...the same thing, but I thought you two would love 'em." Jose gestures for Anna and Clara to come closer and hands each of them an end of the blanket.

On the count of three they lift it, revealing the surprise below, and Anna immediately drops to a knee making cooing noises.

"Oh, child, this is truly wonderful!" Clara wraps Jose in a giant hug while Sadie shares a smile and a look with Caleb that makes his entire holiday.

Inside the portable coop are several quail nervously watching them.

"We thought you could raise 'em…in place of your chickens," says the boy.

Caleb brags about Jose, who designed the trap that captured them, constructed the travel coop, and then carried it here, but Jose hasn't taken his eyes off of Anna. She looks up, thanks him, and begins calculating how fast they can increase their covey of birds. They put the caged birds back out in the dilapidated shed before retreating to their duties and personal preparations.

Clara heads to the kitchen for another day full of cooking. The boys spend time recharging the house batteries before cleaning up and Anna sits making alterations to some of the clothes that were a little too big for her and Jose. Before long, Sadie comes over, carrying one last gift. Anna immediately recognizes the material it's wrapped in and looks at Sadie with uncertainty.

"I found it…while looking for the stockings. I thought…you should have it."

Anna tentatively takes the gift and holding it, stares for a long time at the package. Sadie sits, watching the various expressions across Anna's face.

"You don't have to open it." Sadie says, hoping to ease the girl's obvious dilemma.

The youngster nods in response, takes a deep breath, and slowly removes the small ribbon. It's been used over and over throughout her life, and twirling it through her fingers, Anna second-guesses the decision as tears appear. Wiping them away, she gains courage and finishes removing the wrapping paper, uncovering a small jewelry box.

"This was…my mom's." Anna slowly lifts the lid, revealing several pairs of earrings. Once again, her eyes overflow with tears, only this time, it takes longer before she's able to speak. "These…were also hers. I've wanted pierced ears for a long time, but my parents always said I wasn't old enough. I guess...they decided...to...surprise me."

She breaks down sobbing and leans into Sadie. She, too, is heartbroken for the girl, and they sit until Clara comes checking. Seeing them together, she's reminded how much of a struggle it is for the girl, as it's her first Christmas without parents. As Clara nears, Anna shows her the earrings and the three of them head to the kitchen, gathering the required items.

It's strange, but with each pulsating throb, Anna feels her parents' presence. The additional weight dangling from her newly pierced lobes feels odd, and realizing it's more than just the earnings and new dress, Anna feels adult-like for the first time. Everyone else is clean, manicured, and dressed beautifully, too, as the specialness of the occasion isn't missed. Sadie is the last to enter and Caleb's mouth hangs ajar as she appears. Sadie hasn't worn a dress, done her hair, or even put on make-up in years. It feels foreign to her, making her move differently as she carries a bottle across the kitchen. Placing it on the counter, she removes the cork and pours three glasses for the adults and a small taste for each kid. Without speaking, the wine gets passed around. Caleb's eyes have stayed on Sadie the entire time and she's very aware of it.

"I'd like to start with a toast." Sadie raises a glass and the others follow. "To the happiness we've found...the family we've become... and the future we'll share."

The group clinks glasses, wishing Merry Christmas's all around before sipping their wine. Both kids scrunch up their faces, making the adults laugh. Sadie giggles, retrieves a different bottle, and re-fills their glasses. This time they smile, liking the sparkling apple cider much better. They all sit and Clara has them hold hands while giving thanks, but Caleb doesn't even hear her words. His concentration lies solely on the hand he's holding and before they break, he lifts it to his lips and lightly kisses the back of it.

"You look...in-in-credible," his voice breaks, as Sadie blushes.

There's so much food on the table there's barely enough room. Plates get passed around and filled with mounds of delicious-looking and smelling food. When they finish, it takes the kids nearly an hour to do the dishes, and it's just enough time for the meal to settle enough for dessert. There's fudge, cookies, and a hot apple pie straight out of the oven that's been filling the air with tempting smells.

It's a new feeling being so full, and both Anna and Jose have never eaten so much in their lives. Sadie tells the kids to leave the dessert dishes. Grateful, they head to the living room. When she gets up to wash them, Caleb takes over instead. The adults chat while he works, and once done, they join the kids, only to find them both asleep. Anna is lying on the couch and Jose's passed out on the floor. Instead of waking them, they return to the kitchen where Clara, also feeling tired, pours what remains of the second bottle of wine into Sadie and Caleb's glasses before saying goodnight and leaving them alone.

Sadie catches the twinkle in the old woman's eye and watching Clara leave, she smiles. "That woman," she thinks, taking another sip. A warm tingling sensation fills her cheeks and lips. Caleb too, feels the effect of the alcohol and finds enjoyment in finally being alone with Sadie. He figures she'll go to bed as soon as her glass empties, so he finds ways of distracting her from drinking. Starting with a few simple questions, he gets her talking, and Caleb's mesmerized by simply watching Sadie. Fueled with wine and good spirit, she's more animated than usual and her answers are neither vague, nor short, and often leave them laughing.

As the glasses slowly empty, Caleb wishes the night wouldn't end. With the last sip, he takes the glasses to the sink and asks if she'd like tea. To his surprise, she answers yes. He puts the kettle on, but has no idea where to find anything else. Seeing him turning in circles, Sadie laughs. She brushes past him, as Caleb inhales her scent.

"Here," she opens a cabinet and picks from a wide selection of canisters. "How 'bout...kukicha?"

"Ku-ki...wha?" Caleb says, with a distorted facial expression.

Sadie smiles. "Kukicha. It's a decaffeinated, Japanese green tea." She opens the lid. "Here...look...it's made from roasted tea twigs."

Intrigued, he leans to look and suddenly, they're extremely close to one another and very aware of it. Caleb, feeling the moment is finally appropriate, carefully tilts his forehead to hers and slowly moves towards her lips. But, before they make contact, Jose walks in, rubbing his eyes, and Sadie, using it as an escape, steps aside.

"I'm thirsty," is all the boy manages to say in his groggy state.

"We're making tea. You want some?" Sadie offers.

The boy, already at the sink, doesn't answer; instead, he drinks straight from the faucet. Swallowing several huge gulps, he wipes his mouth with the back of his hand, then stumbles past, saying good-night, and heads into the apartment. As the door shuts, the teakettle whistles, and Sadie pours them each a mug. Her heart pounds excessively and briefly braving eye contact, Sadie tells Caleb she's going to get Anna to bed, and then also turn in. Standing on the opposite side of the kitchen, she doesn't give him the chance to get close again and says goodnight while quickly leaving. Unconsciously spinning her wedding band with her thumb, she makes it to the living room and takes a deep breath.

FORTY

Caleb can't believe how fast the time has gone and how soon he'll be separated from Sadie. There hasn't been another chance for him to be alone with her since that night in the kitchen and, strategically, she's made sure of it. Since Christmas, her focus has solely been on preparing for spring, when Gus is scheduled to return. Every day, Sadie gathers and moves additional supplies, and in the evenings, the women sit together planning, leaving Caleb curious about what they discuss.

After dinner each evening, the boys work on relocating the arranged materials to the apartment, leaving the women to their doings. Items are designated to three areas: the cave, Anna's, or the helicopter landing. Tomorrow, when the ladies depart for Clara's, the boys will begin the arduous task of carrying the cargo to its proper location. Jose is still the main workhorse, since Caleb has yet to fully recover, but they've got months of work ahead of them, and eventually, he'll be strong enough to do more.

On their last evening together, Clara casually reminds Sadie of what they've discussed. Sadie gets up to works alongside the boys, moving the last substantial pile, and when it's stacked with everything else in the studio, there isn't much room to maneuver around the apartment. Setting down the last box, she surprises the boys further with an invitation to come back over to join the women as they meet.

Shocked, Caleb jokingly comments to Jose, "You hear that, kiddo? Tonight...we get to join the...three sisters! We must be moving up in the ranks!"

Smiling, Jose doesn't respond. Instead, he turns around and heads right back to Sadie's. As Sadie follows, Caleb moves to quickly stop her—even if it's only for a moment. He lightly grabs her arm and unexpectedly, Sadie violently knocks his hand away while instinctively taking a defensive stance.

"Sorry," she replies, seeing the horrified expression travel across Caleb's face, "habit."

Taken aback and unsure how to proceed, Caleb hesitates long enough to give Sadie the chance to speak again. She knows he's aware of the distance she's kept between them and at some point, Sadie realizes their near kiss, needs to be addressed.

"Look, I'm not sure what...you...expect. I'm not even sure what I expect, but...right now...my focus is on gettin' ready for Gus and keepin' us safe." Not giving Caleb an opportunity to respond, Sadie quickly continues, "Splitters already made it here once...and they could do it again. If so...we gotta be ready."

Caleb sees the determination emanating from her eyes and, taking a breath before replying, he makes an attempt at softening her disposition.

"Sadie, there's more to livin'...than...preparing and plannin'...this place...this entire island...it's the safest location I've been...since...the Tri-nami." He takes an attentive step closer, carefully watching her. "It's okay...to sometimes let your guard down...especially...with me."

When she doesn't move, he takes another step, but this time Sadie stops him.

"Come on...we need to join the others...there's lots...to...discuss," she says, turning to leave.

Disappointed, he follows, wondering if Sadie will ever let something between them happen. His curiosity is aroused by the invite and it at least provides some form of encouragement. As Sadie and Caleb return to the kitchen, there's hot tea, alongside the remnants of holiday fudge and cookies. Jose, already seated, is dipping chunks of the sweets in his tea while Clara and Anna do the same. The old woman nods at Sadie, who sits, motioning for Caleb to do the same, as she slides a pocket-sized notepad and pencil over to him. He notices it's similar to the ones sitting in front of Jose, Anna, and Clara. Sadie makes eye contact with each of them, then, glancing down, opens her notebook and begins.

"Alright we've," she speaks, while scanning the first page, "got several items, starting with...this." Sadie holds up a large map of the island and unfolds it across the table.

Impressed with its size and detail, both boys lean over to get a better look. It's the first time they've seen it and obviously, it's something a lot of energy has been put into. Sadie begins detailing the routes they've been using between all of their places, how far radio contact reaches, and their hope to establish regular communication schedules. As she talks, the other ladies nod in approval, never saying a word.

Moving along, Sadie shifts to the areas each of them will cover. As the boys already know, Anna and Clara will return to the canyon. Jose's station will be at Anna's homestead, once all the prepared supplies have been relocated. Until then, he'll travel between the apartment and the cave, using the later as a base of operations for all the next moves.

"Caleb," Sadie says, looking at him.

Hearing himself mentioned for the first time, Caleb becomes anxious to learn what role Sadie wants him to fill.

"You'll split time between here and the cave...helpin' Jose, but..." she pauses, then finishes with an overprotective tone, "be smart...and careful...make sure you don't do too much and reinjure your ribs."

He likes knowing he'll be around Sadie's place, thinking it'll provide opportunities to spend time with her, but then she adds more.

"When all the supplies have been moved from here, we'll need you stationed at the cave."

Caleb's hopes instantly dwindle.

"From there, you'll travel back and forth to Anna's, helping Jose with the preparations and, of course, protecting the island's two points of entry." Sadie's focus turns to the map. "Here," she points out the landing site, "and here," she motions over the boats cove, "are the only ways in." Then, under her breath, adds, "that we're aware of."

Something about the comment alerts Caleb, but there isn't time to dwell on it, because Sadie continues talking.

"Keeping them secure and guarded is priority." Still looking at the map, she shakes her head up and down. "Leaving them unattended has been risky. They should be guarded...at all times."

Sadie sips her tea, while the other ladies sit quietly, already knowledgeable, and in full agreement with all she's said. As Sadie sets down her cup, Caleb breaks the silence.

"So...you've told us where everyone will be...except...you," he says.

Looking at him, then referencing the map, Sadie responds. "I'll travel between all of you until...closer to spring, then...I'll also stay at Anna's."

Caleb's eyes light up, but only Clara notices, as everyone else is focused on Sadie's finger as it traces the circuit she'll travel. Then, she outlines specific goods she'll move between them and lists what each site is responsible for. Jose jots a few notes, making Caleb realize he should do the same.

"Jose, when you settle on the homestead, your work truly begins." Sadie says.

Serious and astute, Jose holds his pencil posed to write. Sadie unrolls a clear film over the map. Dashed lines, in two different colors, represent the old and new sections of roads. She switches writing utensils and uses a marker to carefully detail what remaining roadwork needs done. She includes Caleb, hoping that he and Jose can complete the project in a couple of weeks. Feeling confident, Jose nods repeatedly, asks clarifying questions, and scribbles a few additional notes. Sadie interjects a couple of last details and when they're ready, she introduces a major component of the plan.

"While all this is goin' on...track tides" she says, looking at Jose, "and the ocean conditions..." she pauses to emphasize her next statement, "and...get the Intrepid II prepared for a trip around the island."

The boys, shocked, are spellbound and unable to comment.

Sadie notices their surprise, but continues providing additional information. "It'll be a test run. We'd like to confirm its capabilities... inspect the coastline and...make sure it's a viable back-up plan."

"Back-up plan? What?" Jose thinks it, but it's Caleb who asks.

Sadie reaches the segment of their plan that worries her and Clara the most. The old woman tries to ignore the uncomfortable feeling growing in her stomach, but as Sadie talks, her distress strengthens.

"When...or...if Gus returns...I'm planning on leaving for the colony." She looks directly into Caleb's eyes. "With you."

Caleb, remembering the intensity of all their one-sided discussion sessions, understands how everything he communicated and she asked, led Sadie to this conclusion.

"But...if somethin' goes wrong," Sadie shakes her head side-to-side, "I don't wanna get stuck...away from home. So...the boat's...our contingency plan." She looks at Jose, who's battling an extreme sense of worry and utter excitement. "If stranded...I'll need you to come and get me."

The boy swallows, feeling the severity of the task and hoping it doesn't ever come to that. For the first time, Caleb's doubts creep in, and he's unable to just listen.

"No way," Caleb bluntly states.

Sadie shoots him a look.

"There's no way I'll let you take that trip alone." Caleb turns to Jose, "If you have to come," he turns back to Sadie, "then you're pickin' up the two of us. No way I'm risking somethin' happening… to either of you."

His reaction is intense, heartfelt, and adamant. Sadie doesn't want an argument, understands his logic, and admits, having another person would add additional security. What she doesn't share is the possibility of also transporting colony members back here on the boat. That particular aspect might be too far ahead in the planning to be shared, and it may not even become a reality.

Clara lays a hand atop Sadie's, and they share a brief silent conversation. Sadie, suddenly feeling tired, realizes it's getting late and all of them have a heavy travel day ahead. She flips through her notebook, feeling good about how much they've accomplished and confident in the people surrounding her. Closing it signals the end of official business and the group collectively relaxes. Sadie thanks the guys for everything they've done and the roles they're filling.

"We couldn't do any of this without you…" pausing, Sadie glances at Clara before adding more, "the three of us," Sadie gestures towards Anna and Clara, "want to make sure you know how much… we appreciate what you two bring."

Anna smiles at Jose, slightly embarrassing him. He turns to Clara, who also has a huge grin across her face.

The old woman maintains eye contact with Jose, reaches a hand over to his, and takes a turn speaking. "We're family now," she reaches her other hand over to Caleb, "and this…is home." Specifically for Caleb, she adds a footnote, "If you want it to be."

Caleb wondered if talk about him coming back to live on the island would ever happen. His previous discussions with Sadie focused solely on Gus's arrival, the colony, and the people living there. They never broached the subject of a return journey and several times, he almost mentioned it, but always felt it'd be too much to ask—especially, after everything Sadie's already done for him. Besides, even now, he still isn't exactly sure how she feels about it. Obviously, the ladies talked in depth and came to some type of agreement, but Sadie's hard to read.

Looking at her now, Caleb searches for any clues. She hasn't made eye contact, and Sadie can desperately sense he needs some type of affirmation, but she's hesitant. Her gut instinct says there's a reason they've crossed paths again after all these years, but—she pushes those thoughts aside. Clara's the only one Sadie can't fool. The old woman senses Sadie's discomfort as she tries to remain nonchalant in Caleb's presence.

Caleb graciously thanks Clara, then Anna, and lastly, turns to Sadie. As he begins to speak, Sadie meets his gaze and forces herself to hold eye contact. It's unnerving, her pulse quickens, and she grows embarrassed by her body's struggle to maintain control. Caleb sincerely, and with a humbling gratitude, thanks Sadie. He really wants to know how she feels about his possibly living with them, but fearing her answer, Caleb doesn't ask. Instead, not wanting to lose the opportunity, he simply stands up, offering another round of thanks before excusing himself and the boy.

FORTY-ONE

Closing the cave door, Sadie drops her things and immediately strips for a quick rinse before sleeping. Tired, she crawls into her bedding, thankful for the emptiness that surrounds her. She finds peacefulness in solitude and it's a strange observation after so many years of forced isolation. She hasn't spent a night alone in her hideout for quite some time and she relishes the privacy while drifting off to sleep.

Sadie doesn't wake until late, which is a luxury she doesn't often take, but this morning she's planned for it. Looking forward to a slow day, Sadie lies comfortably in bed. When she eventually gets up and makes tea, her day finally begins. She moves about, warming up, takes a few more hot sips from her mug, and begins a yoga routine. Thirty minutes into her workout, a sweat covers Sadie's brow and her body begins to respond. Her practice is long and thorough—as today—she's taking as long as she pleases.

During a particularly difficult sequence, Sadie detects movement outside. Pausing, she strains her ears, listening closely as the noise grows louder. When the door latch slowly begins to turn Sadie ducks into a roll, grabs her crossbow, and lands crouched in a quick arrow load. With the bow posed toward the figure about to enter, Sadie hears her name being whispered, then a second time, only louder.

"Caleb?"

Sadie's response encourages his entrance. He opens the door further, sticking his head and torso in, only to freeze at the sight of Sadie. It's not just the loaded weapon pointed directly at his chest that causes him to stop short.

"Excuse me!" Sadie's anger soars, watching his eyes travel over her body.

His eyes rise to hers and his checks redden, "Sorry." He averts his eyes as Sadie stands and pulls a sweatshirt over her head. The image of her nearly naked burns through his mind.

"What are you doing here?!" Sadie snaps, frustrated by the intrusion and invasion of her privacy.

Caleb, still visualizing her barely clothed body, fails to respond. Instead, his mind travels over what little material Sadie did have on.

Catching the full intensity of her glare, Caleb knows he should feel bad about invading her space, but a part of him is glad he did. His thought is accompanied by a grin that upsets Sadie further. Trying to hold back his amusement, Caleb fights hard not to chuckle, and it agitates her intensely. Seeing her reaction, Caleb quickly recovers trying to prevent an utter disaster.

"I'm sorry. I should have radioed first. But...I didn't want you to leave before I arrived." His grin still lingers. "And...I expected you to be up...and about...especially this late in the day. Not..." he pauses, trying to choose his words wisely.

Sadie narrows her eyes. Unable neither to contain his joy nor hold back his thoughts, Caleb switches tactics. His eyes leave hers and travel down over her bare legs as he speaks.

"I'm sorry for barging in like this, but...damn! I mean, come on. You can't expect me to ignore...your...physique. I know I should feel bad about intruding like this, but...I'm glad I did," Caleb says, smiling.

His amusement isn't helping and Sadie doesn't appreciate any of the compliments. Sliding on a pair of pants, she covers up completely, but he doesn't stop.

"No please...don't let me stop you. Whatever you were doing, go ahead. Here...I'll move to the other side...I'll give you plenty of space." He moves around Sadie and sits facing her. "You won't even know I'm here. Please...continue."

Sadie, still pissed, holds her stance.

Caleb, feeling light-hearted about the whole thing, keeps smiling. "Maybe it'd help if you took your clothes back off."

Sadie picks up her shoe lying nearby and throws it at him. He catches it, but the second hits him across the chest.

For the first time Sadie's mood begins to lighten. "I was doing yoga."

"Sexy. Please...continue."

His honesty and attempts at cuteness are working, but Sadie doesn't let him know.

"I've a better idea," she says—this time, tossing both his shoes at him, "You head out on patrol...the long version...and I'll finish my practice."

Caleb can see a hint of enjoyment in her eyes, but understands the seriousness of the request. She wants to be alone.

"Alright," he responds, sounding overly downtrodden, still acting, for her benefit. He puts on his shoes, heads to the door and pauses. "You sure…you don't wanna take your clothes off before I leave?"

Sadie chucks another item in his direction and he ducks through the door just in time as it misses. Whatever was thrown hits the door behind him, causing Caleb to laugh as he hikes away. Inside, Sadie, too, is finding some humor. Shaking her head, she appreciates his compliments, now that he's away.

It takes a little effort, but she gets back to her routine—only, this time, she remains fully clothed. When finished, she goes about preparing a meal, eats alone, and curls up in bed with a book before drifting off into a nap. It's the sound of the door opening that wakes her. Caleb, seeing she's in bed, tries to move about quietly and not disturb her.

"It's alright, I'm awake." Sadie says, sitting up and stretching overhead. "If you're hungry, there's leftover red beans and rice."

Caleb thanks her and sits down as Sadie puts on the teakettle and joins him. He pauses between bites to drink from his canteen, feeling an awkward silence develop between them. He's not sure what to say, but Sadie does.

"Alright, Caleb…why…are you here…and not helpin' Jose?"

He chews his last mouthful before answering. "We finished the last section of road ahead of schedule…so…we're changin' things up. Both of us needed a break from the tractor. Jose's using the extra time to work on the boat…I'm here to retrieve another load of goods."

Sadie tilts her head slightly to the side, giving him an inquisitive look. She knows there's more to his being here, but doesn't have to ask, as, seeing she's not satisfied, he continues.

"This batch," he points to the stack of goods in the corner, "is the last of the supplies. I thought I'd finish movin' 'em to the homestead, so…officially, our task's complete."

Sadie maintains her same look, forcing Caleb to add more.

"And…" he pauses briefly, building his courage, "I wanted to see you. I thought it'd be nice to spend a day together." His honesty embarrasses him, and Caleb grows quiet.

Sadie, too, isn't sure how to respond and feeling a little trapped, thinks of something.

"Caleb, my plan for the day is to catch up on some sleep and rest. We've got a lot left to do...and before we know it...Gus could be arriving."

Hoping to get Sadie's focus away from work, Caleb gets up, cleans the dishes, and retrieves an item from the back shelf.

"Feel like a game?" he asks, setting a backgammon board between them.

Sadie hesitates, wants to dismiss him, but playing sounds like fun.

"Sure," she finally responds.

They spend the first few minutes checking they've set up the board correctly. It's been a long time since either of them has played, and they use the first game as a refresher. After that, it's the best out of three. They talk, laugh, and enjoy one another's company. Nearing the end of their match, Sadie makes another pot of tea and grabs a second board from the shelf.

"After I finish beating you," she says, teasingly, "let's switch." She sets the Scrabble box on the table for Caleb to see.

He nods in affirmation and, rolling his dice, hopes for doubles. Instead, he rolls an ace-deuce, making Sadie giggle. Taking a last turn, Sadie removes two pieces from the board, completing her victory.

"How 'bout...the loser makes dinner and cleans up?" Caleb suggests, opening the Scrabble game.

Sadie likes the idea, and agrees to the proposition, while pulling a tile. The game moves slowly, and Caleb can't believe the level of play she displays. He challenges her twice, only to lose both times when the words are found in the dictionary. With the last tiles out, Caleb knows there's no hope of winning, but he doesn't mind. His victory is in the fact that he's getting the chance to spend time with Sadie.

After their game, Sadie puts things away and heads out for a short hike while Caleb makes dinner. He digs through all the food supplies, trying to determine what would make the best meal. With food cooking, he briefly exits the cave to gather some fresh foliage for a centerpiece. Back inside, he cuts the delicate fern fronds to accentuate one large trillium. Three prehistoric-appearing leaves, rich in texture, with intricate vein patterns, join together in a trilogy of green strength. At the stem, where the leaves meet, an imposing—but closed—bulb hangs. Hints of purple and white petals surround its stout-looking structure, complete with their own tiny accents.

The centerpiece sits in an oversized mason jar partially filled with water. On both sides of it, a variety of candles reflect their soft light. The entire cave is lit with candles placed subtlety around the space. "No rechargeable electricity tonight," Caleb thinks, while finishing up dinner and turning off the burners. He finishes as Sadie enters. She sets down her bow and takes off her shoes, gazing around the entire time.

"Think you're burnin' enough candles?" Sadie casually jokes.

Looking straight at her, he responds, "I thought...for...just this once...for a brief bit of time...it'd be nice and...not too wasteful."

Removing her jacket and using it as an excuse to look away, Sadie breaks eye contact. She hangs it up and washes her hands and face. Things smell and look like they were prepared with the utmost of care. The spread's impressive and attempting to decipher Caleb's intent, she decides not to put forth the energy to think about it. In fact, Sadie doesn't want to think about anything. It's her day off, and that includes resting from all forms of mental anguish, preparation, thoughts, plans, and her constant attention to detail.

Now, all she wants is to eat, relax, and then curl up back in bed. Even though she's slept more today than normally, Sadie's body could use more. She's charging for the final push and the shift to Anna's, where she'll live between the homestead and the helicopter clearing. Catching herself mentally organizing, she blinks and purposely shifts her attention to the food, ready for whatever smells so good.

The meal and the company are both relaxing and enjoyable. Caleb tells several amusing childhood tales and Sadie enjoys simply listening and not having to respond. Genuine laughter erupts between them and as it subsides, Caleb gets up, clearing the table. He charges a burner for tea and cleans up their mess. It doesn't take long, and soon he returns with steaming mugs—the perfect ending for the day.

Sipping hers, Sadie's content. They sit in a comfortable silence, letting the meal digest and allowing the hot liquid to keep them warm. When Sadie gets up to retrieve a blanket, Caleb watches her every move. She wraps it over both shoulders and sits on her bedding. Still cradling the steaming mug, she leans her head against the wall, realizing she's nearly ready to sleep. Caleb, wanting to join her, hesitates, blows out most of the candles, and then chooses his bedding instead. As they sit across from one another, Caleb's glad Sadie allowed him to stay and feels grateful for the evening they've shared.

"This was nice," he says, looking at her and referring to their time together.

Sadie nods in agreement, sets her empty mug nearby, and discretely removes her outer layers of clothing before crawling under the covers.

Watching her add an extra blanket, he can't help himself, "If you're cold, I could…come over there and…keep you warm."

Sadie, without looking at him, and while settling into a comfortable position, rejects the offer.

"Yoooouuuuuu sure?" He asks, teasingly.

An answer hits him, literally, upside the head. When Sadie hears the thud of the shoe, she giggles uncontrollably, making Caleb laugh, too. She's still laughing as she blows out the last candle near her. When it finally quiets, she wishes him a good night and falls asleep grinning.

FORTY-TWO

Sadie's pace is demanding. Her day-in and day-out schedule is relentless, starting before sun up and ending long after sundown. The boys are amazed at her output and at how quickly things shape up. The helicopter site is finished, stocked, and ready for Gus's arrival. They have access roads cut throughout the entire area, and the Intrepid II's ready for departure. Even Clara and Anna have arrived, all set to keep an eye on the harbor and station the homestead's radio in preparation for the journey around the island.

Tonight, Clara and Anna will be alone as Sadie leaves to sleep on the boat with the boys, where they'll begin the tedious task of drifting out with the rising tide. It'll take diligence on their part, along with precise manipulation with the anchor. Jose is anxious to test a few new pieces of equipment he's designed specifically for the process. As they finalize all departure checks, Caleb unties the watercraft, while Sadie uses one of the new pole tools to push it away from the cliff's edge.

The former Coast Guard lifeboat seems to grow in stature as it slowly drifts further from shore, regaining a long-lost pride, setting out with good intent, as was its original purpose, and Jose beams with pride. Unfortunately, he witnessed years of wrongdoing and countless hardships the boat was forced to deliver upon others. In his heart, the boy always knew the ship deserved better, and now, as it's captain, he can make it so once again. From now on, it'll be a vessel of hope serving those in need.

It takes until near sunset for them to manipulate the craft out of the narrow mouth and into open waters. As the giant sea stack blocking the sight of the cove's entrance fades into the distance, they cautiously travel east, keeping the shoreline within view. By the time it grows dark, they've turned south, and the waters calm. After a simple dinner, the sky clears enough for them to see stars and the rising half-moon. The reflections across the ocean's still surface are an amazing sight and each of them appreciates their beauty. Sitting in silence, they pass time staring into the night, lost in their own thoughts and dreams. Eventually, Sadie directs them back to task.

"Okay…I'll take the first shift." She stands up, tells Jose he'll go last, and then turns to Caleb. "Relieve me in…three hours."

Jose, already beginning to descend below, passes Caleb, who still hasn't gotten up. Sadie, sensing Caleb's hesitation, quickly addresses him.

"Go on. I'll wake you when it's your turn."

Caleb, nodding, leaves even though he wants to spend time alone with her. He heads below, attempts to empty his mind, filled with thoughts of Sadie, and eventually falls asleep. When she does return hours later, he hears her approach but lies still even as she whispers his name. Putting a hand on his arm, she lightly shakes him, and without opening his eyes, Caleb covers Sadie's hand with his and mutters a soft hello. His thumb gently caresses her hand before she pulls it away and leaves him.

As he moves towards the deck above, Sadie crawls into bed and falls fast asleep. She sleeps soundly and once awake, Sadie notices Jose is still in bed and Caleb's not. She bolts upright, looking about, thinking something's wrong. There's barely a hint of light, but it's enough for Sadie to know that morning is on the horizon. Cautiously, she makes her way above and before emerging, takes several deep breaths, and then chances a quick look.

Finding Caleb standing with his back to her, she observes him unnoticed. His hat is pulled down tight, and Sadie sees the effort he's putting into keeping his hands warm, as each of his breaths are visible in the chilly morning air. When he turns, she ducks, out of instinct, feeling her pulse quicken. It's a curious reaction and waiting a moment before moving, she heads back down before returning with two steaming mugs. This time, she heads directly to Caleb and hands him one.

"Thanks," he says, holding it between his hands and blowing on the hot liquid before taking a warming sip.

Sadie, curious about why he worked a longer shift, asks.

Caleb shrugs his shoulders and responds, "I thought the kid could use a little extra sleep. He's been workin' so hard and today's gonna be a long haul."

Sadie smiles at his thoughtfulness and turns, hearing Jose. She woke him up when returning below so he'd be ready for an early departure. He's also holding a steaming mug, but his doesn't contain tea. The boy takes a drink, smiles, and then takes another. When he nears Caleb, Jose shows him what's he has.

"Hot chocolate!" Caleb exclaims, looking back at Sadie.

She simply smiles a reply. Caleb's not the only one who thought the kid deserved a little something for all his efforts. As they prepare for the day ahead, the sky grows lighter. The horizon is a patchwork of clouds and as the sun rises, they catch the dramatic explosions of color that suddenly appear. It's a weird sensation watching the sunrise over the Pacific. For all its beauty, it still serves as a reminder of how much the world's changed. The colors fade as fast as they appeared, and soon the cloudy overcast weather returns. Jose fires up the engine and they continue south. Along the way, Sadie and Caleb scan the shoreline and scout ahead, weary of the looming sea stacks that dot their path.

Approaching what Sadie terms the tail of the island, she knows they're already past Clara's canyon. Following the tail's shoreline, they spot the area where the break in the land exists, creating a separate island, as Sadie recalls first discovering it and trapping herself on the narrow peninsula. This particular part of the island is of great interest for Sadie and she looks forward to inspecting its layout. Amazingly, a short distance further, another larger break in the land appears and they discover there's a third island. The space between the landmasses appears big enough to squeeze the boat through, but without knowing the risks of submerged dangers, accompanied with an outgoing tide, they keep a safe distance.

The third island is much larger than the second and keeping a constant slow speed, they travel cautiously as the fog thickens. Reaching the tip of the peninsula and the furthest point south feels like an accomplishment. As they turn course, Sadie asks Jose to slow even more while she scans the cliff tops. Caleb notices a slight change in Sadie's demeanor while searching and inquires about it.

"I thought...I saw somethin', but..." Sadie lowers her binoculars and gestures at the fog hindering the view, "maybe not."

Soon, the fog's too thick to move safely, and they're forced to kill the engine and drop anchor. It's disappointing having to stop, but safety is priority. They gather in the closed bridge, and Sadie opens her map, reviewing the recently added details. She's recorded shoreline features, sea stacks, and where the second and third islands are located. Her notes include the speed they've traveled between each landmark, along with the length of time it took to move from one to the next.

As Sadie and Jose make calculations, Caleb loses interest and feeling the lack of sleep, excuses himself to go lie down. Engrossed in their task, the two barely notice and together, they finish detailing what they've observed. As they work, static comes across the radio. It fades in and out and as Jose adjusts the dials, it begins to take some form. A broken transmission, too jumbled to make any sense of, comes through, and then it ends abruptly.

For the next hour, they scan the channel and others without any luck, but at least the fog thins, and they're able to move forward. Sadie sends Jose to wake Caleb, and before he joins them, the boat's already on its way. Sadie hands Caleb a pair of binoculars and he scans the shoreline alongside her. There are only a few sea stacks to circumvent and then it becomes easier to navigate, but they slow considerably, finally reaching the gap between the second and third islands. Letting the boat drift by, a huge boil—hinting at what sits just under the surface—attracts their attention.

Leaving the area, they keep an eye out for any submerged obstacles and continue up the coastline. Almost missing the last gap between the main island and the smaller second, Sadie asks Jose to adjust course. They've kept a safe distance from shore, but without signs of hazards, Jose's comfortable moving closer. When the landscape shifts and becomes familiar to Sadie, she takes a deep breath and relaxes just a touch, intrigued by the effect of seeing it.

Jose increases speed and they travel with the sun in their eyes. Nearing the southwest point, the conditions change as the wind picks up and the water turns choppy. They expected the western side of the island to have rougher waters, since it's fully exposed to open ocean, but it's even rougher than thought. Veering north, they catch the full force of the wind and a five-to-six-foot swell that's rolling the sea. Jose makes adjustments, mandates lifejackets, and assigns both Sadie and Caleb emergency tasks. They scramble around, securing latches and equipment before returning.

Even though all the boat's gauges display normalcies, and his confidence in how the vessel responds grows, a bit of nervousness develops within Jose. At his direction, they stay alert, keeping watch while talking about possible options: either they continue or turn around. Realizing they may need to return south and anchor near the tail for another night, they weigh the pros and cons.

Continuing could mean risking worse conditions and arriving later, in possible darkness, in waters rough for negotiating the coves tricky entrance. On the other hand, staying on course could be the only window to arrive home safely before it gets worse, since, the swell may be building. Because there's plenty of daylight left, the conditions don't seem to be worsening, and a rising tide favors them, they decide to continue, at least for another hour. Any longer than that will put them past the halfway mark and then their only option will be to force the vessel ahead.

Traveling, while wrestling with the decision, is nerve racking and each of them second-guesses the choice, especially as the ship crests a larger wave. It's eerily quiet between them, except for an occasional utterance of checks as they monitor gauges and conditions. Sadie operates the radio, trying to contact the ladies on the homestead who should be within range. The lack of response only adds to their anxiety as Caleb points out a rogue wave while scouting ahead. Jose, nervous, maintains his composure, reassured by his vessel's capabilities. He knows she's designed to handle much worse, and—up to this point—there haven't been any real problems.

When a transmission from Clara comes over the radio, Sadie quickly responds, reports their status, and requests an update on conditions near the homestead and cove. The old woman sends Anna out to check and by the time the girl returns, the sea has calmed slightly and the crew's decision to push on is unanimous. As the sun sits lower on the horizon, the ship reaches the northwest point of the island where the ocean, still wind-blown and rough, becomes difficult to navigate. The swell's direction hits the boat portside, causing Jose to continually adjust the bow to take the waves head-on.

Nearing the sea stack at their cove, they discuss strategies and how to safely time entry with the crashing waves. The final push will put the waves at their backs, making it difficult to monitor the sets. A wave could catch the boat and send it into the jagged, rocky sea stack or the massive cliffs, that soon will nearly surround them. Making their situation even more hair-raising is the fog that starts drifting in. Sadie, who's been timing each set and counting waves, waits for a lull and then gives the go-ahead. Jose maneuvers and adjusts the boat's speed as Sadie and Caleb take their stations. Their timing is going to have to be near perfect and if they don't get it on the first attempt, they're not guaranteed a second.

Taking the current and tides into account, Jose slows, briefly reverses the engine, and then idles the boat. The ship's angle, possibly off, causes Sadie and Caleb to tighten grips on their pole tools as the sea stack nears. The two are tied in with safety harnesses that are getting their first real field test. The vessel adjusts, barely missing a jagged section, and Jose can feel his breath quicken. As the Intrepid II drifts, he gives it a three-second burst of propulsion so the boat's angle aligns properly. As the ship gets positioned between the stack and the opposite cliff, the first wave of a set catches them.

Jose, prepared, feels the push and reverses the engine again. He does it again with the second wave and then quickly drops anchor. The maneuver stops them from smashing upon the cliffs as the wave's energy catches and spins the vessel about. He yells, and they drop a secondary anchor. As the boat stabilizes, it sits almost directly behind the stack and inside the cove.

"That was gnarly!" Caleb exclaims, unhooking his harness and hurrying to rejoin the kid. "Nice job!"

With adrenaline still coursing through their veins, they wave to Clara and Anna on shore and cheer, celebrating the success. When it wears off, the reality of not being able to get ashore takes hold. They're confined until the boat can be moored safely, which requires constant manipulation and possibly calmer waters. Waves, curling around the stack, keep rippling through the cove impeding the vessel's progress, and soon, it becomes obvious, they'll be forced to spend another night aboard. When it grows too dark to see, they settle below, hoping tomorrow, getting to shore won't take too long.

Keeping the mood celebratory, Sadie makes dinner, and afterwards, surprises them yet again. She's planned for success and brought something else along, just in case. Relishing the rich, earthy aroma, Sadie closes her eyes while passing it under her nose. She cuts off an end, strikes a match, and takes several strong, controlled puffs. With the cigar lit, she passes it first to Caleb, who sits dumbfounded.

"When did you start smoking these?" he asks, before taking a puff.

Sadie laughs and shrugs her shoulders. Getting the cigar back, she takes another drag.

"Ohhh," she replies exhaling, "only on special occasions," she looks at Jose, "very special occasions." She hands the stogie over to Jose. "And this, is definitely special." Finishing her sentiment, she adds, "Congratulations...Captain."

His eyes shoot up to Sadie's and then back to the cigar. He's never smoked anything before, but between being called captain and holding the cigar, he begins to feel grown-up. The feeling fades quickly, as Jose nearly chokes on the smoke. Coughing furiously, both Sadie and Caleb laugh hysterically.

When Jose's able, he joins in on the laughter and tries again—only, this time much more cautiously. He pulls gently and lets the smoke waft around his tongue and out of his mouth. After another puff, the effects go straight to his brain, making Jose feel light-headed. Looking a little pale, he sits down and passes it back to Sadie, who offers some insight.

"It's an acquired taste," she says, taking another puff. "Hopefully..." she pauses, "we'll have more celebrations to help with that."

FORTY-THREE

When the Intrepid II returns safely, a huge relief washes over Clara and Anna. However, with the success of the trip, come new worries. Sadie, challenging Jose, pushes his abilities by drilling and practicing for an entire week aboard the boat. She's adamant about his ability to operate the vessel completely solo, including safely departing and returning to the cove. There's improvement with each of his attempts and when it finally happens, the empowerment fuels Jose; but the celebration is brief, and unfortunately, serves only as a reminder of the seriousness of what could lie ahead. With time concerns pushing her, Sadie transitions everyone to the next phase of the plan and departs with the boys for final preparations.

With them gone, Clara and Anna continue cleaning, organizing, and planning. Anna's home is getting a thorough makeover, one room at a time, as the young girl decides the extent of change she's ready to handle. Building courage, she leaves her parents' room for last. Opening the door, Anna steps in, deeply inhaling their lingering scents, making it even more emotional for her. Remaining motionless, she sits on their bed and after some time, decides to start with the dresser.

By the time Clara checks, the girl has everything in the room sorted into various piles. For the rest of the day, Anna makes trips carrying items between her own bedroom and her parents'. While moving things back and forth, Clara inventories and organizes all the supplies recently brought to the homestead. The old woman, impressed with the quantity of goods, sorts through everything carefully.

For both, working helps keep their minds off the looming absence of the others. It's difficult enough for Anna, struggling with the loss of her parents, let alone, with the additional new worries of potentially losing those now close to her. The anticipation of Gus's arrival, accompanied with the knowledge that Sadie and Caleb plan to leave, adds even more stress. Anxiousness gnaws on Clara's and Anna's insides, but they recognize that, at least, they're together, providing support and helping alleviate some of each other's worry.

At the clearing, there's also an underlying hint of anxiety, accompanying the daily grind of work and preparations. Jose, grateful for every task Sadie assigns, battles his nervousness when too idle. The boy's responsibilities are tremendous. He listens intently and each night, as Sadie updates work details and reviews strategies, Jose grows a little more comfortable. Tonight, however, Sadie has something different organized, and the boy looks on with curiosity while trying to control his nerves.

Opening a small crate, Sadie puts on display a small arsenal of weapons, talking about each while doing so. On the underside of the lid, she roughly sketches the clearing and points out locations where each of them will be stationed if Gus lands. They're already familiar with what she's saying, but they're mesmerized by the newest additions, especially since they helped moved the crate without ever knowing what it contained. Looking up, she freezes mid-sentence. Both boys haven't spoken or taken their eyes off the guns.

"How'd...you get all of these?" Caleb asks, breaking their silence.

"My dad's...buddy owned a military surplus business," Sadie answers.

Caleb knows most of the items couldn't have been bought in any store of old. Tilting his head, Sadie reads his expression and goes into further explanations.

"The two of 'em, spent a lot of time together, trackin' down...specialty items. At the time, I thought it was a therapy of sorts. A hobby... they both needed. I didn't know until later...when the Splitters..." Sadie trails off, then aggressively adds more, "When those bastards invaded, I got to see what my dad and him stockpiled, and...exactly what they'd been up too. There was more than enough firepower to take 'em down...and...we did."

While the boys examine the guns, Sadie grows quiet. Seeing the assortment of killing tools reminds her of those days and of the loss of her father. Forcing the painful memories away and returning to the task at hand, she's adamant about not being caught off guard, ever again. The plan is to keep everyone safe while taking whatever measures necessary to do so. With the focus back on their defense strategies, she shares her plan, until getting interrupted.

"Sadie. Is...all this...really needed? I mean...we know Gus is friendly," Caleb says.

"Yeah, but we don't know what's changed," she says, without hesitating. "What if it isn't Gus who lands, or...he's under someone else's control? We're gonna plan for all possible situations and…be prepared for whatever may come."

For the next couple of days, Sadie drills them for various scenarios. Each of them has their own responsibilities, depending upon how things play out. As they become accustomed to their roles and more confident handling each weapon, Caleb and Jose see Sadie's wisdom. She's meticulous and covers everything, making safety their ultimate priority; yet, with each passing day, they still grow anxious. The helicopter's arrival is expected, and not knowing for sure which night holds the full moon, means they're not sure which morning the arranged extraction date will fall upon.

Each evening they hope for clear skies, but the ever-looming fog prevents a moon sighting, and there's even the possibility Gus's arrival could be an entire month later. All they know is the window for Caleb's extraction is open. On high alert, they concentrate for any hint of the copter. Each morning, the routine becomes one of expectance—of constantly straining their ears and looking skyward. Taking a break to eat, the boys laugh and joke with one another. Sadie quiets them and standing with her head tilted, they see her seriousness.

Hearing what she does, all three of them disperse, scrambling to initiate the first protocol. At each corner of the landing area, they ignite small signal fires and take their places. As the noise grows, it intensifies, seemingly, in unison with their accelerated heart rates. Caleb hesitates and when Sadie signals, he strikes a flare. When it doesn't ignite, he grabs another, it sparks to life, and carefully, the burning stick is waved.

When the wind suddenly gusts downward, they get their first glimpse of the helicopter, and suddenly, things get very real. Jose, feeling his grip tighten and palms sweat, consciously relaxes both hands, steadies his breathing, and takes his practiced sniper position. Lying on his stomach, the boy carefully sites his rifle and controls the panic attempting to overcome him. As the copter lowers, two people are visible, which, according to the plan, requires him to move. Building his courage, Jose gets up and runs to his alternate station. Arriving quickly, he sets back up; keeping a disciplined eye trained where he was drilled to watch.

Sadie, seeing Jose make the correct adjustment, nods. So far, so good, everyone's in position, and still, only Caleb's visible as the bird touches down. As Caleb slowly approaches, the pilot loosens his restraints and leans out the open door. It's obvious he doesn't want to turn off the engine, and Caleb, barely able to hear, is forced to move closer. He's excited to see Gus and curious as to whom joins him inside. When he's within a few yards, Caleb yells, telling him to shut down. Caleb tries calling out, repeatedly, getting louder with each attempt, while cautiously closing the gap, until finally getting an audible response.

"Sorry, partner, no can do...got just enough fuel to get us back!" Gus hollers, then, looking around, begins to ask, "Where's ..."

He doesn't have to finish the question. Caleb's downtrodden expression and quick head gesture is enough to convey the fact that only he made it. Gus hates knowing they lost another, but at least Caleb appears well—the man's cleaned up and sporting a new haircut.

"THERE'S...MORE...FUEL!" Caleb yells fiercely. "SHUT... DOWN!"

Intrigued, Gus hesitates, and then finally does so. As the blades slow, the noise and wind decrease until once again, the forest regains its peacefulness. When the two men emerge, Sadie stiffens. The co-pilot is carrying a gun.

"Oh, shit," Caleb mumbles under his breath as Gus approaches.

Knowing Sadie's armed-response time, Caleb's immediate task is to disarm the man. He shakes Gus's hand in a warm greeting and then quickly turns to the other guy. Caleb vaguely recalls meeting him once at the colony, but doesn't remember his name.

As they shake, Gus acquaints them once again, "Caleb...Hank. Hank...Caleb."

"Think we met...before you left for here." Hank says.

"Yeah." Caleb nods in agreement. "Listen...I need somethin' and fast."

Hank, looking skeptical, stands nearly motionless.

"I need you to put down your weapon." Caleb says, non-confrontationally.

"Huh?" Hank's actions become guarded.

While Hank nonchalantly raises the gun, Caleb reacts, warning caution. Hank freezes, looks at Caleb, and then turns to Gus.

"You got, maybe..." Caleb, growing worried, keeps calm, "another thirty seconds or so. Just set it down...slowly. Please."

Hank, still suspicious of the circumstances, hesitates. When he takes a step closer to Caleb an arrow strikes the ground right next to his foot. He flinches, instinctively pulling back his leg.

Caleb warns, "The next one won't miss. But…it's okay. Just…set it down, carefully…then we can talk."

Slowly setting the firearm on the ground, Hank looks to where the arrow might have come from.

"There are…others…livin' here and safety is their main priority," Caleb begins explaining while picking up the gun, "that means…no weapons for visitors. Sorry." He turns to Gus. "That means you, too, buddy."

They both know there's a handgun tucked in the back of his pants. Gus, pausing longer than expected, makes Caleb nervous, but knowing Caleb's trustworthy and not sensing a trap, the pilot obliges. As Gus hands his over, he too scans the area, looking for who shot the arrow. As they look along the tree line, Sadie steps out from the opposite direction, shocking the visitors.

"Sorry gentlemen for the…less than cordial welcome," Sadie addresses them, carrying her loaded crossbow and stepping closer, "but…I'm sure you can understand our precautions." The men are stunned silent. "Any chance…either of you are still carrying somethin' that…we'd prefer be put aside?"

There's a prolonged silence, then Gus nods to Hank, who confirms his carrying a second gun. Without taking her eyes off the men, Sadie asks Caleb to retrieve it. While raising one foot slightly off the ground, Hank motions towards his leg. Caleb finds the hidden piece in his boot and sets it with the others.

Sadie, still focused on the men, gives another directive. "I appreciate your cooperation, but we'll need to verify your…honesty." She nods to Caleb before continuing. "So, please…hands on the back of your heads."

Uncomfortably, they follow her order as Caleb apologizes while frisking them; then, he confirms they're good. Sadie lowers her crossbow and steps closer for an introduction. She's already given quite a first impression, and both men are flabbergasted by her appearance and beauty. As Sadie reaches out to shake hands, her demeanor demands respect, and they humbly give it. Sadie motions for the men to move before retrieving her arrow sticking in the ground. Wiping away the dirt, she returns it to her sheath, and then Sadie directs them to a large canvas tent, set up solely to accommodate them.

Before briefing the visitors, Sadie asks Caleb to check on the others without divulging the fact it's only Jose who still sits on watch. The boy, along with Anna and Clara, will remain unknown to their guests until Sadie decides what information needs to be shared. As Caleb walks away, Sadie sits at a makeshift table with the men and begins her carefully thought out order of business. When Caleb returns, Hank is asked to go with him so Sadie can talk privately with Gus.

Outside, Hank and Caleb get the chance to talk. Hank's first line of questions all concern Sadie and Caleb grows uncomfortable with the newcomer's level of interest. Hiding his jealousy and answering what's possible to share, Caleb makes several attempts at changing the topic. By the time Gus emerges, he appears relieved to leave the bargaining table with Sadie.

"Jesus Christ, Mary, and Joseph!" are Gus's greeting words. He runs a hand over his stubbly hair, fighting a combination of awe and excitement. He turns to Caleb. "Only you'd find a woman like that. I'm positive she's gotten everything she wants…and I get the feelin'… I'm strictly on a need-to-know basis here."

Caleb, patting Gus on the back, chuckles, understanding the feeling, and in her absence, the men talk further about Sadie. She's disappeared to update Jose and giving him his next set of instructions, she sends the boy to the homestead to share news with Clara and Anna and then to man the Intrepid II's radio. Establishing communication between the boat and the helicopter before they depart is the next priority. As the boy leaves, Sadie joins the men as Caleb serves dinner. They grow silent as she approaches, making Sadie sense she's been the topic of discussion. Conversation is minimal while they eat, and afterwards, they get back to business.

With dark approaching, they've refueled the helicopter from the barrels stored nearby and have nearly completed loading all the supplies. Gus, sitting at the radio, establishes communication with Jose, then, he confirms the route they plan on using to travel back to the colony. The boy grows nervous, knowing they'll lift off early the next morning and he's their only link back to the island. If something goes wrong, he may have to ship out to retrieve them.

At the clearing, the visitors retreat to their tent to talk amongst themselves and turn in for the evening. As Sadie and Caleb watch the fire burn out, a comfortable silence settles between them. It's been a busy day, and everything went smoothly, without hassle. Both look forward to rest, but the anticipation of tomorrow's journey won't allow it. Sadie's extracted as much information as possible from Caleb with regard to the colony, but still, she's not sure what to fully expect. Her biggest fear is not being able to return home. Even with all the careful planning and preparations, doubts about leaving creep in, making Sadie second-guess herself. She knows the dangers of thinking this way and forces herself to stop.

As the last of the embers cast their glow, Sadie says goodnight and heads over to the nearly empty storage shack while Caleb watches her. Fighting the urge to join her, he retreats in the opposite direction. In his lean-to, he tries to find comfort, but tosses and turns, thinking only about Sadie and what lies ahead. He's the last to wake in the morning and when he emerges, the other two men are sitting with Sadie.

Joining the group, Caleb serves himself a helping of last night's leftovers while Sadie pours him tea. The talk revolves around leaving as soon as possible, and Gus and Hank begin their pre-flight checks as butterflies flutter in Sadie's stomach. She's never ridden in a helicopter before and leaving the island's sanctuary feels unsettling. She fights the gnawing fear of not being able to return and climbs in.

Packed full of supplies and extra fuel, space is confined in the heavier than normal helicopter, and Gus feels the strain on lift-off. Taking a slow circle of the area, they turn south, as per Sadie's negotiations. She wants to fly around the tail area to inspect it from the air before heading to the colony, but as usual the fog doesn't cooperate. Satisfied with the attempt, she gives Gus the go-ahead and the helicopter banks, setting a course back to what remains of the mainland.

FORTY-FOUR

Sadie's dumfounded by the landscape changes. It's difficult grasping the once picturesque national park is nothing more than a dying wasteland, sitting along the shoreline of a bloated Pacific. Most of the giant sequoias have fallen, the waterfalls, long dry, aren't recognizable, and barren patches of hardened dirt replace the once expansive meadows. The sight is unnerving and the further they fly into the Yosemite Valley, the more difficult it becomes to witness.

Upon their arrival at the colony, a small group gathers as the helicopter appears. Peering down, Sadie battles a mixture of emotions. She's grateful for a safe arrival, curious as to what Yosemite offers, and suddenly, hesitant about interacting with so many new faces. By the time she emerges, the group's grown and surrounds Gus, Hank, and Caleb. The mood is especially celebratory, since one of their own has safely returned. Feeling out of place, Sadie stands near the copter, observing everyone. It's Caleb who breaks from the pack to start introducing her.

"Everyone...this...is Sadie. And, Sadie...this is, well...just about everyone." He laughs as the group turns their attention to the newest arrival.

One-by-one, they introduce themselves. Assaulted by their intense body odors and filth, Sadie does her best to stay genuine and not react poorly, but it's not what she envisioned. They're dirty, undernourished, and poorly clothed. Seeing them makes her appreciate all she has even more, and encouraged by their seemingly good nature and gracious welcome, Sadie retrieves a small box purposely placed within reach.

"I've brought a few things...to share...and later...maybe...do some trading." Sadie observes their reactions. "But these," she holds up the package, "are gifts. Thank you for such a warm welcome."

The group, intrigued, squeezes closer. As Sadie opens the box, a low murmur spreads amongst them, growing louder as small, travel-sized sets of toothbrushes and toothpaste get handed out. Each person, genuinely thankful, accepts the gift, and the crowd slowly disperses. Straggling behind the adults, a small child catches Sadie's attention. Between the child's indiscriminate hand-stitched clothing and long dirty dreads it's difficult to tell if it's a young girl or boy. Sadie kneels, lowering the box, and the youngster, even more curious, peers into it.

"What color would you like?" Sadie asks softly.

"Dis one," the child timidly responds, pointing to a yellow one.

Sadie lifts it out of the box while asking a second question. "What's your name?"

"Luna."

"Well then...here you go, Luna," Sadie says, giving it to the girl.

Turning it over in her tiny hands, Luna's amazed by the crinkling of the plastic wrap. She's never seen anything like it. Sadie, captivated by the youngster's reaction, takes a moment before realizing the child has no idea what she's holding.

"It's a toothbrush...for your teeth," Sadie says, ripping another open and removing the small box of toothpaste and collapsible brush.

She shows Luna how the brush opens and snaps into its plastic square cover. Opening the tube of paste, Sadie demonstrates how to squeeze it out, while talking about the importance of cleaning your teeth. Luna, memorized, follows Sadie's every word and action. As Sadie returns the unused brush, Luna makes a shy inquiry.

"Whaa 'bout da others? Do dey git one?"

"Of course..." Sadie begins, "How many do you think didn't get one?"

Luna, without hesitating, answers in detail, using her fingers to keep track as she lists names. Sadie, impressed, hands Luna the box and asks her to be in charge of making sure they all get one. The girl's eyes light up, and her grin widens.

Sadie adds more. "After everyone gets their gift...I want you to check back with me. Okay?"

"Okay!" Luna exclaims, excitedly holding the box and running ahead.

Both Caleb and Gus share smiles with Sadie. They've joyfully watched the entire interaction, but ready to move, Sadie grabs her pack and crossbow, then helps pull the camouflaged cover over the helicopter. Still a little uncomfortable about leaving all the goods she's packed, Sadie hesitates, and Gus notices.

"Don't worry, everything's safe. First thing tomorrow, we'll unload it," he reassures her.

Sadie, sensing his trustworthy integrity, shoulders her pack and nods. Gus leads the way along a well-worn trail leading toward the colony and through the remnants of the once world-renowned park. Any surviving structures serve a purpose and along the entire way, Caleb talks about each. His only pause comes when Gus explains some of the recent destruction they encounter en route, promising later to share the detailed story of fighting off a Splitter raid. When they stop, it's at an old ranger station, serving as the colony's headquarters and doubling as Gus's lodging. Inside, the colony leader opens one of the adjacent rooms, offering the space to Sadie.

"You can store your supplies here," he says, then nods towards a folded cot, "and you're more than welcome…to bunk here…" Gus trails off, looking between Sadie and Caleb, unsure if their sleeping arrangements are together or separate.

"You wanna leave your stuff and finish the tour?" Caleb quickly interjects, turning to Sadie. "I'll show you around…and we'll wrap up in time for dinner." He turns to Gus. "We'll meet you there…and hear the rest of that story you promised."

Gus nods, affirming the plan, as does Sadie.

"Just give me a few minutes," Sadie says, entering the room and shutting the door.

True to her estimate of time, Sadie returns, carrying a daypack with her crossbow also slung across her back. She proceeds directly to Gus, who's taken a seat behind his desk.

"I'm not sure what colony policy is," Sadie motions to her bow, "and nothin' was mentioned while walking here, but…with your approval, I'd like to keep it with me. The recent attacks on the colony, along with the security measures you've pointed out…lead me to believe…safety is of the utmost concern." She pauses, letting her words take hold. "I like to be prepared and…if needed, offer my services…may they never be needed, but…despite the unlikelihood of another attack…I can be of assistance, if you need it. You have my word."

Gus doesn't doubt for a second that Sadie could ever be prevented from protecting herself or those around. The icy calm in her eyes speaks more than words. She's no stranger to the evils unleashed by the world's destruction, and besides, her logic's sound. If attacked, they could use the help, and knowing she'd be a powerful ally, Gus extends a hand to shake on it.

"I accept…and officially declare you on emergency security detail, but…as you said…may it never come to that."

As they part company, Gus chuckles under his breath. Once again, Sadie's gotten her way and has done so in a manner that makes him feel good about it. Caleb sticks close to Sadie as he introduces her to everyone they pass, even the ones she's already met. With each greeting, Caleb becomes more comfortable establishing a connection with his gorgeous companion, who draws endless attention. Several men don't take Caleb's subtle hints and offer Sadie their places, if she needs somewhere to stay. Each time, without answering, she graciously thanks them, and by the time they reach the medical facility, Sadie's a little uncomfortable and realizes staying anonymous is not a realistic notion.

Entering the structure, it's clearly obvious it used to be a gift shop. Faded Yosemite postcards and posters of Half Dome and El Capitan still line one of the walls and display shelves have been rearranged to store what little supplies the colonists possess. A few cots, scattered across an open floor space, serve their sick, but currently, the only occupant is an elderly man. Adjacent to the building sits an outdoor kitchen with an accompanying mess hall that consists of picnic tables arranged in two long rows under a large pavilion. Like many of the colony's other structures, the area's covered in a homespun version of camouflaged netting in an attempt to hide its existence.

There's plenty of activity in preparation of the evening meal and as others begin to gather, each person makes an effort to talk with Sadie or wave to her. When the line begins to form, Gus, who asks Sadie her thoughts about the colony, joins them. She gives detailed accounts of her observations, shares amazement at their ingenuity with the workstations and converting the park's campground into living quarters, and in turn, asks specifics about the garden's productivity, livestock management, and desalinating the ocean's water. As the line moves, Gus answers all she asks and when they reach the front, the conversation shifts to the meal being served.

Each person receives a single bowl of chicken soup, accompanied by a chunk of Native American style fry bread and a glass of water. It's meager, at best, but provides some relief to the hunger that plagues the colony. There's enough for all, but none ever get as much as they'd like. Throughout dinner, small talk travels across the table, until near the end, when Caleb begins asking about the recent Splitter attack.

Gus slurps the last of his soup, then responds. "Not long after you left, a small troop overtook one of the lookouts. A patrol scout managed a few warning shots...so at least we weren't caught completely off guard. They attacked, firing heavily and torching buildings, but luckily they were unorganized...and we surrounded 'em."

A flourish of visuals assaults the forefront of Gus's mind, but pushing them aside and wishing he could forget, he shares more. "We suffered...eleven causalities and afterwards, we discovered some of the Splitters were camped 'bout a day out...hidden up in the higher elevations. We caught 'em by surprise and...ended it quickly...but...it wasn't all our doin'." Gus nods in the direction of a lone female sitting at the end of a far table.

She arrived much later for the meal than everyone else and sat separately from those remaining. Sensing their attention, she downs her soup, returns the dish, and leaves. When she's out of sight, Gus speaks again.

"They had women with 'em...who fought alongside the men, but she didn't. She helped us...actually...she ended it." Her rampage tears across Gus's mind. One dropped gun and opportune moment had given her the chance she'd been waiting for.

Gus returns to describing it for the others. "She eliminated the last of 'em...and then dropped her weapon, raised both arms, and asked to speak with our leader...which, after some pause...I allowed. We negotiated and...eventually, came to an agreement. I offered asylum in exchange for intel on the Nation. She's shared what she knows, and...any time I have questions, she cooperates, but...as per the terms, she answers only to me, and she's never pressured to speak or interact with anyone else. She keeps to herself...and...after our conversations...I understand and respect her privacy. That girl's been through a lot and deserves sanctuary."

Refocusing, Gus talks specifically about the Nation and shares what's been learned, confirming the militant force is on the prowl. They're vacating Tahoe in small units, searching for new refuge and any remaining resources. Between the depletion of their water supply and the severe in-fighting that's erupted, their leadership brutally enforced a re-organization. Units are systematically being sent out, traveling by land and sea. Assigning long-term scouting missions to a vast number of their troops reduces the demand on the Nation's remaining resources and keeps them from killing one another. They're traveling on meager rations, basically fending for themselves and leaving behind a swath of destruction.

Gus's information paints a clearer image, making sense as to why Splitters arrived here and on Sadie's island. Even though they both managed to wipe out the ones sent in their directions, the news is still unsettling. Knowing that others may follow, or, scouting Splitters may return to report their findings back in Tahoe worries Sadie deeply. As Gus wraps up, they transition to an old outdoor amphitheater where a gathering's been called. One takes place anytime there's a new arrival, someone returns, or there's news to be shared.

As the log slab benches fill, Sadie notices only adults are present. Two fire pits, located on opposite sides of a small raised platform, cast flickering light upon the front area where Gus stands, address-ing the group. Sadie and Caleb, sitting in the front row, listen as he gives a brief synopsis of the events leading to tonight's meeting. A few colony members make inquires that he easily answers, but when one asks specifically about the island Caleb's returned from and what's it called, he stammers.

"Aaaahh…well…I guess, its Sadie's home so…" Gus trails off, looking to Sadie.

Caleb turns and seeing she's got nothing, blurts, "Three Sisters."

"Three Sisters?" questions one of the men in attendance, "Sadie, if you got sisters…I'd like to meet 'em."

A chuckle spreads among the men, but many seriously hope there are more women like Sadie. The lightness of the mood and the pause give Sadie just enough time to respond.

"Sorry, boys, hate to disappoint, but…I don't have any sisters." They appreciate her jovial response and Sadie's decisive with what she shares next, "It's called Three Sisters because…it's actually three islands…mainly only one that's inhabitable, but there're two smaller extensions to the southeast."

Sadie knows Caleb was referring to her, Clara, and Ana, but that's not information she wants to divulge. Caleb understandingly nods and appreciating Sadie's uncanny ability to think rationally in terms of safety, finds her explanation plausible. Gus, directing the gathering back to their main focus, asks Caleb to speak. Standing, he tells his version of the expedition in which he nearly died, keeping it brief and to the point. He talks about the loss of his friend, and their comrade, and shares details establishing Sadie's role in both his survival and the final elimination of the Splitters remaining on Three Sisters.

He reiterates his mission was to search out possible relocation sites and then turns things over to Sadie. She's careful with her word choice and remains vague regarding how many people actually live on the island. Sadie informs them she's been designated as the spokesperson for Three Sisters and before she left, it was determined how many more people could possibly be accommodated there. She offers very few specifics about the island's resources, but states safety and sustainability are of utmost priority.

Without getting too detailed, Sadie announces her plan to meet with those interested in leaving the colony to determine, who, and how many, can return with her. Sadie's statement kicks off a flurry of concerns, frustrations, and emotional responses. Several colony members argue about her authority and want to know what right she has to limit and decide who gets the opportunity to leave. Caleb, growing upset at their reactions, argues back, defending Sadie. His frustrations, along with those of the colony members around him, continue to escalate as Sadie continues to remain silent. As the discussion shifts to a heated yelling match, she steps forward, calmly raising both arms. When the crowd quiets, she speaks.

"Folks, I feel your concerns and…more than understand your reaction. I came here simply to offer what help I can. We're faced with enough challenges…and together, we'll figure out ways to overcome 'em." Seeing the tension still hasn't eased, Sadie continues speaking in a calm, methodical manner, "Three Sisters," (she finds it odd referring to her home's new name, but nonetheless, there's a point needing made) "isn't capable of supporting everyone here. We killed our planet and…we don't want to make those same mistakes again… nor risk destroying my home, but…I hope some of you will be able to help…and, together…we'll find ways to secure the livelihood of everyone who needs…and deserves it."

Several of the colony members return to their seats, and Sadie knows her words are beginning to have a positive effect. Not wanting to lose the momentum of their acceptance, she keeps the same mannerisms and reveals more of what she intended to share in the first place.

"I realize you don't know me or my intentions. We've all suffered...lost, and had to fight to survive. But...I think...if a few of you are willing to trust...and work with me...we can find a way to help us all. My hope is...together...we can develop sustainable ways of living that'll support more of us...and provide opportunities for everyone." Sadie pauses long enough to make eye contact with everyone as she scans the crowd. "I've brought what goods I can share, and trade...in hopes of creating a system to ensure our mutual survival. I'd like the chance to talk individually with you, to...determine who's interested and...who's willing to try to contribute to the efforts."

Gus gets up, stands near Sadie, and addressing the group, suggests they sleep on it, while reiterating the positive outcomes—they've finally discovered a place where some of them can safely relocate. And hopefully, those that do leave can work on making it possible for others to follow. He closes the meeting with more uplifting comments, and Sadie appreciates his tact and leadership.

A low murmur of chatter spreads among the group as they leave. As the last person disperses, only Gus and Caleb remain with Sadie. They leave together and head back to headquarters, where she's decided to sleep. Along the way, Gus suggests using the headquarters' office to conduct her interviews and asks what the needs are for increasing Three Sisters' productivity. When they reach the structure, Gus departs their company, leaving Sadie and Caleb alone. It's been a long day, and Sadie, appreciating Caleb's support in the meeting, thanks him, then asks if he's available to help move supplies in the morning.

"Sadie, you don't need to ask. I'll be here first thing in the morning unless..." his eyes take on a sensual look and Sadie senses what's coming, "you'd rather I stay here...with you tonight."

Seeing his joking, yet seriously-hopeful comment didn't have the effect he wanted, Caleb stammers a quick goodnight as Sadie turns to leave.

FORTY-FIVE

Early the next day, Sadie wakes all sweaty and sticky. Even at night, it didn't cool much, and she's yet to acclimatize to the different weather pattern and lack of moisture. Despite how nice the sunshine felt upon their arrival, Sadie knows the area's relentless heat will soon grow tiresome. The colony labors in it daily, fighting to scratch out an existence, and finding ways to sustain themselves. Sadie can already tell today's going to be a hot one and leaving the small room, she quietly slips out for a predawn walk. The silence outside gives Sadie a chance to organize her thoughts and contemplate the events arising from last night's gathering.

Walking deeper into the heart of the colony, Sadie loops through the lower campground, casually observing the people's homes. Several miniature posts display faded site numbers, and each place, with its own distinct character and makeshift living quarters, nestles snuggly near the allotted neighboring spaces. Some colony members live in actual campers and RVs, years beyond being mobile, but serving instead as permanent residences. The most basic of quarters are nothing more than patchworks of tarps, keeping their owners sheltered from the elements.

At the entrance of a second loop, a faded sign reading Upper Pines still stands. It conjures images of a family vacation Sadie remembers from childhood. The area no longer has the same majestic beauty nor the huge expanses of forest, but walking among the campsites and the fallen giants, Sadie recalls the trip and the excitement she felt exploring the wilderness and hiking the park's trails. Finishing the circuit amongst thoughts of times past and current, Sadie's grateful for the fond memories and the life she's now experiencing.

Nearing the mess hall, she hears movement and notices a small group of ladies preparing the breakfast meal. Sadie wanders over, saying good morning, and inquires about the food rationing and meal choices. At first, their kitchen manager is defensive and unsure of the intent behind Sadie's questions, but as the conversation continues, things become more comfortable. By the end of it, the woman is thanking Sadie and looking forward to the promised goods. Walking away, Sadie's satisfied and feels validated with the food she's packed.

Returning to Gus's office, Sadie is greeted by Caleb. He smiles upon seeing her approach and then speaks of the volunteers he's found to help unload the copter. They'll meet up with them after the morning meal, which Sadie thinks is perfect timing. She turns to Gus, standing nearby, and asks if he'd be willing to hang back a bit, but before he replies, Sadie makes the request more enticing.

"Tell you what," Sadie begins, "you stay, and breakfast is on me."

Gus can't refuse the offer. There's barely enough food for the colony and every chance to find an alternative source for a meal is a blessing. Besides, it'll give him the opportunity to learn more about this mysterious woman, who's suddenly playing a vital role in the colony's longevity.

"Okay, you gotta deal," he says.

Sadie tells Caleb to go on ahead, assuring him she'll see him afterwards. He hoped to be invited, too, but seeing Sadie pull out a notebook, he thinks differently. Remembering the barrage of questioning he faced, Caleb looks at Gus, exchanging a quick, yet knowing glance. Gus, seeing the subtle change in Caleb's facial expression, second-guesses his decision and wonders what he may be getting into. Sadie doesn't fail to notice, either.

"Don't worry...I've only got three questions...at least...for now," she says, with a widening smile.

As Caleb leaves, she retrieves everything needed for breakfast and gets a batch of oats cooking.

"All right...when we first talked, I asked about the colony's population. Did that number include everyone? Or...were the lookouts patrolling along the perimeters excluded?" Sadie asks, while they wait for the food to cook.

"No...I included 'em," he answers casually.

Sadie thought so, and with confirmation, she gets to the heart of it. "Okay, then...what I need...is names. Who should stay?"

Gus hesitates long enough in answering that Sadie rephrases the question.

"Whose absence would...be detrimental to the colony's survival?" she asks, trying again.

Gus, wrestling with how to answer, isn't sure he wants to exclude anyone. It's not an easily answered question, and thought needs to be put into it. While he contemplates how to respond, Sadie adds her last inquiry.

"While you're thinking, I'd also like suggestions on who to take... who are the best candidates...people that'd do well...working with me, on a team." Sadie gets up, letting him ponder her requests and returns with breakfast.

Setting down a bowl, she understands the dilemma Gus faces and doesn't push the matter. Instead, taking a few bites, Sadie waits patiently. He lets the hearty meal nourish his body and mind before attempting any response.

"I'm not sure...I'm comfortable sayin' who should stay...and who should go," Gus begins, "and...I know my opinion's an obvious place to start, but...this is gonna take a lot of consideration...I need to let it simmer. In the meantime, let's get you talkin' with folks...start gettin' a feel for the ones that might fit. Tomorrow, you can set up here...it'll be easy to spread word at dinner."

Sadie nods politely, appreciating the wisdom of his response and thanks Gus for his offer of using the office. Letting him know, she's still contemplating what approach to take, Sadie suggests not making any announcement yet. First, she wants to focus on unloading and organizing the goods still in the helicopter. Sadie knows, getting a feel for the colony members is going to take time and a little delay may help with the monumental decisions that face her.

Cleaning up their meal, Sadie hears Caleb approach. Three men follow him, and suddenly, she's very aware of their masculinity. One's wearing a thin, tight-fitted t-shirt, another sports a sleeveless buckskin garment, and the third is completely bare-chested. Obviously, they're the local muscle and Sadie finds that her chores just became a little more enjoyable. She shakes each of their hands, and Caleb notices Sadie's subtle body language revealing her appreciation of the men's physiques. Growing self-conscious of his still weakened frame, Caleb realizes the best men for the job may have been the wrong choice. He picked strong workers, not thinking of them as potential competition. Trying to hide his jealousy and pushing away any negative connotations, Caleb leads the way.

Along the trail, the men make small talk with Sadie, enjoying her company and genuinely interested to see what the new girl has brought. The trio calls themselves Delta Force, since all three have names starting with D, and they work together as a perimeter patrol unit. Off rotation now, they normally spend their time away, making sure no one breaches the territory. Sadie—very interested in their protocols, where they patrol, and the resources available—asks very precise questions. The men not only enjoy the attention but are intrigued by her line of questioning and the knowledge she obviously possesses.

By the time they reach the copter, Sadie's learned a great deal and the men are smitten with such an intelligent and attractive woman. Caleb, who's remained silent for the entire walk, feels left out and looks forward to a change in conversation as they pull back the camo netting and open the helicopter's door.

"Alright, boss...where ya wanna begin?" Caleb says.

Sadie smiles at Caleb, making him immediately feel better, then, she turns businesslike, directing each of them with specific tasks. Among the five of them, they're able to unload the supplies rather quickly, getting everything out and organized into piles that only Sadie understands. The Delta men, astonished with what Sadie's brought, can't believe it all fit in the bird.

"Okay...this pile," Sadie pats a stack of food bags, "goes to Marla at mess...she's waitin' and has a cart we can use. You think you boys can handle these?"

The trio's machismo takes over and they joke amongst themselves about who can carry the most. They start by shouldering four sacks, two on each side that Sadie checks, making sure their loads are balanced. Then, Sadie hands a box to Caleb and sets a second on top. He nods before she even asks. The other men left, carrying well over a hundred pounds apiece and all he has is the light load, which he knows she saved for him.

Understanding Sadie's caution and his recovery process, Caleb tries not taking it personally or as a challenge to his manhood, but once again, he's left feeling inadequate. Caleb makes sure Sadie doesn't see his embarrassment, as, so far, the day hasn't gone exactly the way he envisioned it. With the men gone, Sadie opens a few packages, reminded about how much work Jose did to help make all this happen. Thinking about him also brings up thoughts of Clara and Anna, and she hopes all is well back home.

It doesn't take long before the Delta boys appear again, with Caleb following, pulling the cart. They're all sweaty and Sadie mixes a batch of electrolyte orange drink and offers it to them. They down it quickly before savoring the second serving, while Sadie looks over the wooden cart, deciding how much weight it can support.

"Marla said you could use it for as long as you need," one of the Deltas shares. "She was ecstatic...we've never seen her so happy. Said it was even more than you promised!"

Sadie, glad to hear it, begins moving items around. The men immediately get up, eager to assist. They manage transporting the last of it to the ranger station in the heat of the day, and afterwards, Sadie makes another batch of drinks and invites them to stay for lunch, which they accept. She pulls out three separate food buckets, asking the Deltas which meal they'd like, and removes only one pouch from each container as they pick. When she gets to Caleb, Sadie opens a different container, already knowing his favorite. While eating, they share more about themselves and Sadie never seems to run out of questions. The men happily answer and at the end, Sadie presents them with the buckets they picked from. The trio balks at the gift.

"No...it's too much. We didn't help so we could...get somethin' in return," one of the Deltas says, while the others nod in agreement.

"I know. That's why it means even more," Sadie responds.

"Sadie...really...we can't."

"Yes...you can...and...you will," Sadie states very matter-of-factly through a huge grin. Before they try to refute her again, Sadie continues, "You boys spend most of your time away from the colony makin' sure it's safe. I know living off the land...especially 'round here, can be challenging." She looks slowly at each one of them. "A day may come when you need these rations, and...if it does, you'll be glad they're there. Take 'em on your next perimeter duty...build three caches... spaced strategically along your routes..." she pauses, making certain they follow, "and let the others know where they're hidden. I want to contribute to Yosemite's safety...and the first line of defense is you patrollers. They could make the vital difference...and everyone here... depends on that difference."

Her logic is too sound to refute, and the team accepts the supplies.

"Good, with that settled…we can move on…Here," she opens a parcel and hands them enough new clothing to outfit each from head to toe.

It's quality outdoor gear, designed for both comfort and for surviving the elements.

"I thought Delta Force could use some upgrades," Sadie says.

"Okay…now this…is too much," one Delta says, attempting to hand things back.

Sadie's look amuses Caleb. He knows she's getting ready to get her way while simultaneously making them feel good about it. He listens as she works her charm and logic on the team. By the end, they've not only accepted the new gear, but have tried most of it on, making sure they've gotten the correct sizes. Caleb gives Sadie a sly look.

"What?" she says, in a near chuckle.

"You know what," Caleb says, shaking his head.

She laughs and the sound is music for his soul. As the men gather their gifts, Sadie offers another thanks and sends them on their way. In their absence, Caleb cleans up, stalling his own departure, hoping to spend as much time with Sadie as she'll allow. While he finishes, Sadie checks her inventory list, making notations in the margins. Lost in thought, she fails to notice Caleb watching her. Eventually, Sadie looks up, sees him, and decides it's time to move.

"How 'bout…you take me to see the animals?" she asks.

His smile is enough of an answer, and along the way, Sadie has a few more questions for him. She keeps things fairly light and Caleb doesn't mind. When they make a stop at the medical facility so she can talk at length with whoever's working, Caleb grows bored, quits listening, and wanders about, looking at the old photos and posters. When Sadie calls to him, they once again depart.

As they near the animal pens, a worker appears, and Caleb introduces Sadie. Her attention is focused on what the farmer shares and the details regarding the colony's livestock management. As the conversation transitions to in-depth specifics, Caleb once again loses interest. Sadie's appetite for information is endless and her inquiries spark excitement among the additional workers joining the conversation. Sadie, noticing Caleb lagging behind, tells him she'll catch back up with him at dinner. He nods, and while leaving, Caleb overhears a fading conversation about chickens that makes him smile.

FORTY-SIX

Settling into a routine, Sadie slips out for a predawn walk. It's her third morning in the colony, and so far, things are going rather smoothly. She eats breakfast and lunch from her personal supplies and joins the others only for the evening meal, where she casually interacts with various people. Sadie has yet to barter any goods but has given away plenty. Besides the food stores, she's provided medical supplies and an assortment of seeds that will hopefully sustain the colony even longer. Everyone she's interacted with has been pleasant and her generosity hasn't gone unnoticed.

Nearing the campsites, Sadie makes a decision. She's ready to talk with candidates interested in relocating and believes visiting people in their homes is the best way to go about it. In the comfort of their own surroundings, they'll be more relaxed, allowing Sadie a better chance to gauge their personalities. She'll make an announcement at dinner and her instinct about this feels good. As she nears an outhouse, its door opens and Luna emerges. The child looks up, and seeing Sadie, runs the distance between them.

"Good morning Luna, you're up early," Sadie says softly.

"I had ta go potty."

Sadie smiles and asks the child if she wants company walking back home. Luna giggles, points, and Sadie smiles at the proximity. It's literally next-door and the nearest place. It's a structure Sadie hasn't failed to notice, and wondering about it, she asks the little girl how many people stay there.

"All us kids, wit' no mommies and daddies...we stay here. Com'on," Luna's volume increases, "I'll show ya!"

"That's okay. We don't want to wake everyone...how 'bout another time?" Sadie suggests, trying to lower the volume of their conversation.

Luna nods, doesn't move and stands staring at Sadie. The girl glances back to the ramshackle orphanage, then quickly turns back to Sadie. It doesn't take but a second before the tiny girl explodes with information.

"I finish wit my job...Eber' buddy's got ah toot brush...'cept sum of da patrollers...cuz thur not here...same wit da wader workers, by the ocean, they don't got one either, but...when dey cum visit...I'll give 'em one. I got 'em...still in da box!"

The child beams with pride at accomplishing her task, making Sadie's heart swell. She's so cute and incredibly young that Sadie can't help but encourage her.

"Good work, Luna! I knew you were perfect for the job." Sadie squats to be at eye level before continuing, "You keep that box, and when all those people get their toothbrush..." Luna hangs on Sadie's every word, "you pick another...and keep it...for when you're older."

Luna's eyes open wide as her smile grows.

"How old are you?" Sadie asks.

The girl holds up one hand. "I'm tis many...five sumners, but... I'm a'most six sumners."

"Almost six summers," Sadie echoes, "well, then...I think you're old enough for an even a bigger job."

Luna, fidgety with anticipation of an added responsibility, can barely control herself.

"Every time someone new comes to the colony..." Sadie smiles watching Luna, "you make sure they get one, too. Okay?"

"OKAY!" Luna answers so loudly that others sleeping nearby had to have heard.

Confirming her thoughts, a woman steps outside the makeshift housing. Luna hears the door open and turns.

"Auntie T!" the child exclaims.

The woman, who teaches the children, walks over, quietly reminds Luna that others are still sleeping, and makes her introduction. She's very aware of Sadie's arrival, has heard non-stop chatter from Luna, and finds it nice to finally meet her. Auntie T sends Luna back so she can talk privately with Sadie. Their conversation, although brief, gives Sadie an insight into Luna's story, along with some of the difficulties the orphanage faces. Sadie makes a few inquiries about the others working with the children and the educational curriculum they provide.

Before leaving, Sadie agrees to visit soon to meet the rest of the kids and learn more. Parting ways, Sadie can't help but think about the things she has back home that could benefit the children, but her thoughts are interrupted as the Delta Team exits a nearby site. Seeing Sadie, they excitedly walk over, dressed in their new gear, and she can't help but smile.

"Good morning," the three men say, almost in unison.

Sadie returns the pleasantry.

"Perfect timing, Sadie," says one of them.

"Yeah…we're on our way to meet Gus…and hoped to see you," says another.

"Our rec time's over and we're headin' back to duty," the third in the trio chimes in. "We thought, maybe…you'd like to join us. We're going towards the ocean and…we know you want…to meet…the pro-fess-sor. And see the de-sal…oper-ation."

His words and teasing tone force Sadie's head sideways in a quizzical expression. The Delta's let out a soft chuckle.

"We've heard 'bout your visits…the med clinic…the animals. The whole colony's buzzin' about the seeds and everything else you've given away. Talk is…there's gonna be some new food." He stops as his buddy chimes in.

"Yeah, word around here travels fast…and…everyone's talkin' 'bout you."

"We know you wanna go out there…so join us," the last one adds, almost pleading.

Sadie's cheeks flush. She's slightly embarrassed, slightly honored, and keeps her reply simple. "Thanks, I think…I will."

"Good…hopefully we can escort you all the way. We're asking permission to change protocol. Patrol units always start at the Mid Valley checkpoint. Then, on arrival, the crew there rotates to Oceanside, whose crew then sends their patrollers ahead…and so on, until each unit moves to the next assignment and the last group returns to the colony."

"Only one rest cycle, cuz the added patrol…right?" Sadie says, recollecting a past conversation with them.

"Yep," the same Delta answers, "since the Splitter attack we've added an additional patrol…used to be two teams at a time here, but…to ensure better coverage and…ultimately the colony's safety… we changed it."

"Makes sense," Sadie says, endorsing the decision.

All the Delta men nod in agreement. The further they walk, the deeper into discussion they become as Sadie probes for more details concerning their work. She gets them to share their concerns, talk additional measures, and explain the limitations they're faced with. The conversation abruptly stops as they near Gus's place and the sound of approaching footsteps gains their attention. Turning around, they see Caleb catching up.

A couple of nods are all that's shared with Caleb before the group hastily returns to chatting, in order to finish talking before entering the station. Inside, the Delta patrollers meet with Gus who's already in the company of two senior advisors while Sadie offers Caleb a quick breakfast. She tosses him an energy bar while talking about needing to pack for the coast. Realizing immediately, Caleb wants to join her, Sadie thinks it's a great idea, and invites him.

When Caleb returns, packed for the journey, Sadie's standing among the men and looking over a map of the area. Gus is explaining the patrol routes and providing Sadie with detailed information. The colony leader answers what she asks, and occasionally, one of the other councilmen chimes in with more. Caleb can't believe how quickly she's become a trusted member of leadership. She's standing shoulder-to-shoulder with the colony's top leaders and the best patrol unit they've got.

"I think...reinforcements for Mid Valley...and at Oceanside would help." Sadie says, before excusing herself briefly and returning from her small room with a crate and two ammunition boxes.

Two of the Deltas rush to help and each grabs a box.

Offering a brief explanation, Sadie talks while using a small pry tool to open the crate, "My dad's friend ran a military surplus store and...collected more than...the usually inventory. When the floods hit...all his goods were already moved to higher ground."

As she lifts the lid, all the men simultaneously lean forward to peer in, while letting out a collective gasp. Sadie, lifting one of the semi-automatic weapons, hands it over to Gus, while fighting back the images she starts seeing of burning bodies falling to the ground amongst a storm of bullets from the very assault rifles she's gifting. Holding the gun, Gus is astonished by her generosity and even more so with the amount of ammunition accompanying it. The men are speechless and amazed even further as Sadie opens the ammo boxes.

"Each of these...contains six grenades." Sadie sets one of the explosives on the table.

Gus nods while replying, "These will definitely beef up security."

As he carefully puts the grenade back, one of the other council members—who has yet to speak—finally says something. "Exactly... how big...of an arsenal do you have back on Three Sisters?" he asks.

"That, sir," Sadie begins, keeping her response vague and light-hearted, "I'm afraid, is classified."

Caleb and the Deltas laugh, Gus shakes his head, and the other two men aren't exactly sure what to think, but obviously, Sadie isn't going to divulge any further details. The conversation shifts to the best way to implement these new defenses and it's decided that Delta Force will transport the new equipment. Delta's instructed to ensure the new defense strategies are put into place and they're also given permission to escort Sadie for the entire route. Each of the Delta men, in his own unique way, nonverbally communicates his delight. Their reactions amuse Sadie, which, in part, was their intent.

Since getting to the coast takes two full days of hiking, Sadie realizes she'll have to put off talking with those interested in relocating. Before leaving, Sadie asks Gus to announce the meetings with potential candidates will start when she returns. With everything settled, the group heads out to begin the long, hot journey. Along the way, Sadie sips from her canteen, but by the time they stop to break she's completely drenched in sweat and can't seem to drink enough. Taking off her pack and wiping her brow, Sadie's thankful for the bit of shade they've stopped under.

Upon reaching the Mid Valley checkpoint, Delta Force inquires about the absence of the water transport. The goat cart pulling the colony's water supply should have already passed. They're informed of the problems at the de-sal operation, the repairs that are under way, and since the delivery's been late the past couple of days, the assumption is nothing's wrong. But, according to protocol, if nothing arrives by nightfall, then at first light, a security check is mandated.

The Mid Valley patrol group had been discussing which one of them would make the hike to check, but with Delta Force's arrival, now their entire unit can remain together, rotate stations, and check into the failed arrival. Exchanging questionable glances and silently determining who will be the bearer of the news, it's quickly decided as one of the Deltas speaks up.

"Actually...orders changed. We're going straight to Oceanside, introducing and training on new procedures and...equipment." The Delta leader says.

One of his teammates holds up the semi-automatic while the other lifts the ammo boxes. Before any of the Deltas gets in another word, a Mid Valley patroller pipes up.

"Wha d'yah mean you guys get to skip ahead! What the hell!" he says, pissed.

Quickly avoiding any turbulence between the two work teams, the Delta crew explains the upgraded security measures and their role of getting them implemented at each station. As they talk weapons, implications for use, and training with the new equipment Sadie approaches. She's been scouting a campsite with Caleb and after finding a suitable location, has come to check in.

All the men stop talking as introductions begin, "Guys, this is Sadie. Sadie this is..."

"Alpha pack," Sadie finishes, interrupting the Delta lead and reaching to shake each of their hands.

The men, already a little edgy with their change of work detail, are taken aback by her knowledge.

Seeing their reactions and reading their body language, Sadie addresses them. "Sorry, guys...I've been brought to speed on patrol units, the rotations you normally keep, and most of the procedures you adhere to. I know it's a bummer...learnin' you've been assigned an extra duty, but..." she pauses long enough to remove the sack slung over her shoulder, "I thought maybe this...would make up for it." Sadie says, pulling out a six-pack of beer.

"No way! I thought those were extinct!" one of the patrollers exclaims.

Alpha pack—finding themselves in a totally different state of mind—lean closer to Sadie as she speaks.

"They're old, and obviously not cold, but...I thought your unit deserved a little somethin'. There's two for each of you." As one of them begins to reach for the beer, Sadie casually sets them back in the sack, while talking, "But, first...weapons training."

Even more shocked by this mysterious new girl, the men look to Delta crew, who nod and follow her. She's the only one amongst them with any experience firing the weapon. Tactfully and with authority,

Sadie teaches its safety, operation, and maintenance. As she moves to the grenades, the lessons are quick and simple, and—by the end—Sadie feels confident in their progress and abilities. After wrapping up, Sadie tells the Alpha guys they've been given the evening off and hands over the beer. She and Delta Force will cover the evening's patrol duties. As a sign of understanding and appreciation, the sound of three cans opening greets their ears.

"Would you care to share a beer?" One of the men says, pausing before his first drink to offer it to Sadie.

Sadie, appreciating the offer, declines, stating she's on duty. He quickly offers to wait till she's off, as the other two Alpha guys wish they'd thought of it first. Still, she politely declines.

FORTY-SEVEN

While hiking, Delta Force continues answering Sadie's questions, filling her in on all aspects of the Oceanside camp and the desalination efforts that currently sustain the colony's water needs. Particularly interested in the Professor, she listens intently as the men provide what information they know, making the passing hours of the long trek more enjoyable. It's another hot day and the sun wilts Sadie, even though she keeps covered from head to toe, making sure to protect her unaccustomed skin to the burning rays.

The Professor, who once taught at Berkeley, survived the Tri-nami and the Global Flood that followed because he happened to be on his annual Yosemite camping trip with his grad assistants. He, along with most of his students, stayed in the park and played key roles in the colony's success. As the valley's lakes and streams dried up, the Professor devised a solution and set up camp along the coast in an effort to remove salt from the ocean and provide clean drinking water to Yosemite's population. He rarely returns to the colony, his work ethic and knowledge are unsurpassable, and Sadie's warned about his unsocial manners.

Coming out of a bend in the trail, Sadie halts, causing the Deltas to do the same. They smell it too and after the next bend, they see smoke that appears to be coming from the camp. Sensing wrongdoings, Sadie confirms with the patrol unit that this isn't normal and the group picks up the pace, alert for what could lie ahead. When Sadie halts again, it's to give quick instructions and split them into three groups. One of the Delta crew stays with her, one accompanies Caleb in the opposite direction, and the third stays near the trail.

As a noise becomes clearly audible, everyone settles into position. When the water cart from camp approaches, it's evident there's a problem. The two women accompanying it keep looking back over their shoulders and forcing the goats to move quicker than they want to. Two of the animals pull a partially filled water container, while several other goats are tied behind the cart. When they see the lone Delta patroller, the woman rush ahead, frantically speaking and gesturing.

Sadie holds her position, signals to Caleb to do the same, and sends one of the Deltas to check. He returns quickly, reports the terrible news, and returns to his position just as two trailing men come into view. A pair of Splitters, seeing the cart ahead, stop to take aim, failing to realize, they've walked right into an ambush. Before the militants can fire, both their bodies fall to the ground with arrows piercing their hearts. Verifying both men are dead and retrieving her arrows, Sadie collects the Splitter's weapons as the group reunites to talk strategy and get further details from the fleeing women.

Impressed with the success of her strategy and shooting skills, the men continue to defer to Sadie. First, she sends the water cart and escapees ahead to report to Mid Valley and then to the colony. Knowing they can reach camp undetected, Sadie gets the rest of them moving quickly in hopes of saving any other survivors and preventing the invading Splitters from continuing into the colony.

By late afternoon, her group reaches the outskirts of camp, feeling encouraged that their presence is still unknown. This time, Sadie divides them into two recon units. They'll use last light to gather what information they can on the invaders, and then, devise an attack under the cover of darkness. They hide most of their belongings and packs before splitting into different directions and cautiously proceeding. As each group moves around the terrain, finding cover, things don't look too promising. Two yachts are anchored offshore and two zodiacs are beached on the short stretch of sand that serves as a water collection site. The few outbuildings used to house the workers and goats have been reduced to nothing but smoking embers. Scattered around are the bodies of several Oceanside members that have been left where they fell.

Sadie's group finds a location to safely observe from, and they take turns sharing her binoculars. As the sun sets, the plan is to regroup and figure out whether—and how—to best strike. Preparing to leave, a commotion draws Sadie's attention. Screams fill the air as they witness, from a distance, a woman being dragged by her hair and forced upon one of the zodiacs. She kicks and fights valiantly until one of the men strikes her with the butt of his rifle. Her body crumbles and falls motionless as the zodiac speeds off toward one of the anchored vessels.

While watching, Sadie battles the urge to use Caleb's rifle to stop them. The only thing preventing her response is the knowledge that firing would expose them and eliminate their only advantage. Still, Sadie has trouble stomaching what will more than likely be the poor woman's fate. As they continue watching the zodiac, the men aboard unload their unconscious victim, exchange words with two other men aboard, and then they return to shore.

In the last hints of light, Sadie, Caleb, and the Delta men observe where the two Splitters return, making sure to take notice of the intruders' accommodations for the evening. In darkness, all but one of Sadie's two groups rendezvous to share intel. A lone Delta remains behind, continuing to keep watch so Splitters don't happen upon the rest of the team. Sadie, remaining in lead, estimates the number they're up against and the men nod in confirmation. From what they've been able to gather, there are five men ashore and at least two aboard the boat where the woman was taken. As for the second yacht, they haven't seen any signs of movement, but being cautious they assume its crew is aboard.

Sadie collects a few random objects lying around and under the moon's light, she uses rocks and sticks to recreate the locations of the Splitters and what remains of the camp. Each item she places is accompanied by an explanation of what it represents, and when the model is complete, Sadie straightens up from a kneeling position and speaks to the men.

"It boils down to two options. Hang back, wait for back-up, and hope in the morning these bastards don't leave, searchin' for their two companions chasing the cart...or..." using a stick as she speaks, Sadie starts outlining a plan of attack.

Her instructions are precise, well thought out, and organized in a manner to maintain the element of surprise—that is—if all goes as planned. It's agreed that catching the Splitters off-guard is the colony's best scenario for defending itself. Even so, the plan calls for actions that aren't easily forgotten and could be difficult to live with. Sadie looks each man in the eye and makes sure to address exactly what it will entail.

"Doing this...means each of us...will have blood on our hands. It'll be up close and personal, making it...even harder to handle." Sadie pauses. "If anyone feels strongly against it, or...not sure...if... when the time comes, you can go through with it...then none of us will judge. But, you've gotta speak now...because any hesitation on your part could kill us all."

A silence settles over the group, but one-by-one the men look at Sadie and nod. When everyone's in, Sadie goes over the plan for a second and then a third time. If things go accordingly, they'll regroup and then discuss how to best approach the boats, but first, they head out to reconnect with their missing teammate—who is still on watch—to learn if he's observed anything new. When they reunite with the lone Delta, it's not in his original location. He's captured one of the Splitters and has him bound and gagged. Upon closer inspection, they learn it's a young kid, probably just out of his teens, who's semi-unconscious. Sadie checks his eyes, waves a few fingers in front of them, and quizically looks at the embarrassed Delta.

"I didn't realize he was only a kid. He wandered over to pee and...I struck before I saw his face. When he didn't get up, well...you can see," the Delta says.

Sadie returns to checking and asking the captive if he understands her words. The young Splitter nods once, closes his eyes, and feels a wave of nausea hit him. Sadie, recognizing the signs, loosens his gag as he leans over, vomiting.

When he stops, she straightens him up and talks slowly, "You've... got...a...con-cussion and...it's...severe."

His eyes close again and his head begins to slump.

Sadie commands him to focus, then gives him a reason why. "If... you fall asleep, you could slip...into a coma...and...you may...never wake. Do you...under-stand?"

He faintly nods yes.

"Good. We'll help keep you awake...and...make sure...you're able to respond...okay?" He confirms with another barely detectable nod, as Sadie asks, "What's your name? Can you...speak?"

His eyes focus in and out as the hurt behind them grows. He nods yes, then, licks his lips, attempting to form a response, which takes a huge amount of effort. He manages two syllables, "Aaaaaa-dom."

"Adam?" Sadie repeats.

He nods yes, barely moving his head. Sadie, taking advantage of his feeble state of mind, slowly asks more questions, all simple, easy to answer, and gradually leading him into revealing things he may not have normally shared. They learn tidbits about the boats' crews, and by the end of her questions, she has a better idea of exactly how many Splitters to expect. As the night grows later, Sadie knows it's time to move and instructs the same Delta member to remain with his captive. He's to continue asking questions in order to keep him awake and to probe for whatever else he can get.

As the team sneaks into position, Sadie signals, and she and Caleb go first, followed closely by two of the Deltas. They creep into a clearing where the four remaining Splitters lay sprawled around the embers of a dying fire. The unaware men arrogantly camp unprotected and as they step closer, the guy nearest Sadie rolls over and partially opens his eyes. Sadie reacts, initiating the attack, making sure the man will never get up again. She steps away from her target, making sure the others have also been eliminated. All four Splitters, now unable to sound any alarm, and bleeding profusely from ear to ear, die quickly.

They relocate the bodies, making sure to stay hidden from the yacht's view while confiscating what goods the invaders had. Besides the enemy's weapons, Sadie takes clothing off the bodies and gathers what's been tossed aside. Regrouping, their mood is remorseful, and yet, oddly celebratory. With their success comes consequences that will accompany them for life, but Sadie can only think about what's next. No new information has been extracted from the kid, who barely remains conscious. After checking him over one last time, she keeps the same Delta on watch and moves the rest of the team, ready to explain part two.

"NO! NO WAY!" Caleb says, struggling to keep his voice low, but this time, he refuses to remain silent.

During this whole journey and plan, he's felt like a tag-along nearly forgotten. But this is too much.

"Sadie, we're not using you as bait! I don't care how good a plan the rest of you think this is. I'm not okay with it...and I never will be!" As his emotions begin to overwhelm him, Caleb walks away.

He takes a deep breath, tries thinking it through, and soon, is joined by Sadie, who's been watching him. When he makes eye contact with her, she knows, even in the darkness, how much he cares about her.

"Caleb...we don't have much time. The strategy's sound...you got a better idea?" she asks.

He wishes he did, and desperately, he keeps trying to think of one.

Sadie moves closer, lowering her voice, "We have to get on that boat. I wish there was another way, but...it'll work." She pauses, and then adds, "You have to go with...please."

He wants to object, but he can't refuse Sadie. Still not happy, he rejoins the others, and under protest, Caleb agrees to what Sadie asks. Caleb and one of the Deltas change into the confiscated clothes and make changes to their appearances by copying the looks of the two Splitters who brought the last victim out to the yacht. Fearing if they walk any farther they could be seen, Sadie stops, takes a deep breath, and says a silent prayer, while unbuttoning her top layer. Undoing her braid, Sadie shakes loose her long hair and strips down to a skimpy tank top and a very short pair of dry-fit compression shorts that accentuate her figure perfectly. The men, trying not to get distracted, instantly realize how correct Sadie was with devising this part of the plan.

"I'm ready," Sadie says, stepping in front of Caleb with her hands held together.

"You sure 'bout this?" he asks, still not happy.

She nods and he loosely binds her hands before carefully placing a gag in her mouth. They take a few more strides and then begin acting. In sight of the vessels, Caleb roughly grabs Sadie forcing her forward. She revolts and tries running, only to be tackled and then carried off. Sadie yells through the gag and puts on a believable show. They manage maneuvering Sadie onto the zodiac and sit her up front in immediate view. Caleb sits behind her with a gun pressed to her temple, an arm around her waist, and his face partially hidden by her hair.

The Delta sitting behind them and operating the boat, wears a hat pulled low. They circle the smaller vessel twice and when the two crew members, they'd seen before finally emerge—it's with frustrations of being woken up so early. But, when they see Sadie, who's all they focus on, sly smiles of enjoyment appear.

"Eewwww-eeee..." one of the crew excitedly yells as the zodiac slowly approaches the aft deck, "Da Cap is gonna like dis little mornin' surprise...'specially since da last one still ain't woke."

The zodiac eases forward as the sun appears for the first time. The men aboard the yacht squint as Sadie's heart flutters. As the two boats touch, the first man leans to grab Sadie, and when he does, the

Delta acts. He grabs Sadie's crossbow prepped at his feet, and shooting over his crew's heads, hits the second man on deck in the chest. Simultaneously, Sadie skillfully uses the knife hidden between her wrists and forearms to strike. Her target falls forward as she moves aside letting the body drop into the small dinghy. Hurriedly, they cover it with a tarp, secure the zodiac, and verify the Splitter on deck is also dead. Sadie hastily redresses and reclaims her bow as the men conceal the body.

Using hand signals to direct movement, they cautiously begin searching the yacht. Caleb and Sadie move together, leaving the lone Delta behind on watch. As they get deeper into the vessel, their hearts race in anticipation of what they may find. Nearing what looks like the main stateroom, Sadie hears a muffled voice from inside and they remain motionless, straining to detect any other sounds. Someone, moving about loudly, isn't aware of their presence and once again speaks. This time they can distinguish words and know it's a man.

"Oooohhh...look who's finally waking up. Come on sleepy... open your eyes. That's it...look...look what da Captain's got for ya," the voice from inside says.

The woman's eyes take a moment to focus and when they do, she's terrified.

The sounds of her struggling excite him further as he draws nearer. "It was hard waitin' all night, but...I'm soooo glad...I did."

Sadie turns the door handle and finding it locked, looks at Caleb. She sets her bow to the side, loosens her buttons, and unties the gag she wrapped in her hair. Placing it in her mouth, Caleb shakes his head vigorously no, which goes ignored as she retreats several steps. Following in protest, he falls right into her trap.

Sadie pulls him around, grabbing his knife hand while raising it to her neck. At the same moment, she loudly kicks the wall and makes struggling noises. Before he can fully recover, she pushes against Caleb, forcing them towards the closed door. As it opens, Sadie spins them around so she's facing a now present naked man. Standing with her hands hidden behind her back, Sadie forces Caleb into a role he doesn't want.

"Wha'da...oohhh...I see you've found me another playmate," the naked man leers, stroking himself.

Caleb, being evasive, keeps his face hidden while shoving Sadie forward. She pretends to stumble, and with his eyes on her, the Captain doesn't realize what's happening. Caleb strikes with his rifle butt and as the man falls, moaning in pain, Sadie permanently quiets him with her blade. Entering the room, Sadie reaches the bound woman first and talks while cutting her restraints. Sadie stays by her side while Caleb finishes checking the remaining cabin berths and verifying there's no one else aboard. When he returns, unsure of what's next, he finds Sadie searching the Captain's room.

"Now what?" he asks, pausing as she gut-wrenchingly searches among implements of cruelty and sexual deviance that surrounds them.

The room isn't just the Captain's quarters, but where he keeps his victims. One drawer holds nothing but women's underwear; another holds jewelry, trinkets, and personal belongings, all obviously female. Sadie halts, realizing they're trophies, and closes the drawer, while looking at the newly freed woman who's steadily becoming more cognizant and disturbed. Seeing panic and shock on the woman's face, Sadie returns to her side, then responds to Caleb.

"First…we get her out of here and back to the colony." Sadie leans over the lady, speaking clearly. "We're gettin' you outta here…and back to shore…okay?"

The woman nods, fighting back fear as Sadie directs Caleb. He gets assistance from the Delta, keeping watch, and they carefully go about their tasks. Their absence gives Sadie time to talk the woman calm and prep her on the rest of the rescue. When Caleb returns, he hands over the gathered items and waits outside the door as instructed. When he's finally called back in, the women's appearances have been altered. They wear the dirty Splitter uniforms he delivered, their faces are smudged darker, and both have their long hair tucked under hats.

Sadie makes small alterations, cuffing sleeves and pants so the clothes look better fitting. Up close, it's a dead give-away, but—from a distance—it'll work. If there are any Splitters aboard the second yacht, and if they happen to be watching, then the disguises will suffice. Turning to Caleb, Sadie checks for any other needed changes. He nods, but not with approval.

"Caleb, it'll be alright," she begins, seeing his obvious uneasiness, "we've secured the shore, and reinforcements are en route...I'll be back by first light."

He still doesn't like it, but that's never seemed to matter. Standing silently, he looks over Sadie, and using her hair as an excuse, touches her. He lightly tucks in a couple of loose strands and adjusts the angle of her hat. When she looks up, he's staring into her eyes, and Sadie forces herself to break from their hold.

"While I'm gone," Sadie says, turning away, "make sure the radio's monitored and keep eyes on that other boat."

Just by mentioning the other vessel, Sadie's gut responds. An eerie energy hangs about that vessel and she needs to know more before proceeding.

FORTY-EIGHT

Aboard the zodiac, both women struggle keeping their hats in place and hair covered as the wind picks up. Sadie clutches hers with one hand while maneuvering the small craft with the other. She beaches it, and together they drag the boat further up the sand, securing it next to the other. Looking back at the anchored yachts, Sadie senses being watched, she's just not sure whether it's Caleb or someone else. Not wasting time, the women move out and when the Delta guard intercepts them, Sadie speaks to her patrolman while removing her hat. With his recognition, he lowers his weapon.

Elated at seeing the rescued Oceanside member and excited to share news of the Mid Valley patrollers who have just joined them, he escorts the ladies back to where the captive's been moved. The prisoner sits bound and gagged, contemptuously eyeing the approaching group. Seeing Sadie and the trailing woman dressed in Splitter attire, gains his attention and curiosity. Adam reads the womens' body language while attempting to overhear what they discuss, hoping he can learn more and possibly discover what's to become of him. Not able to hear much, he simply watches as the rescued woman points in his direction while speaking to Sadie.

Struggling through a throbbing headache, sore eyes, and a weakened state, Adam does his best to follow their actions, occasionally picking up a few words and learning the groups' dynamics center around Sadie. He watches as she debriefs the new arrivals, gives orders, and dispatches them. Sadie, hoping to gather more intel, inquires by nodding towards the prisoner. The Delta who's been watching the captive, responds by shrugging his shoulders and frowning. The boy's nowhere near as cooperative as before and to prove it, he turns and loudly addresses Adam. The young man leers while raising his tied hands and clearly, gives them the finger.

"See what I mean," the Delta says, turning to Sadie.

Sadie's confident she'll be able to get better results, but first, she issues new commands, sending the Delta guard away. Left alone with the prisoner, Sadie slowly moves his way and looks over the kid. She raises her hands, motioning towards the gag and communicating her intentions. He remains still and Sadie unties it while speaking.

"You still look...ah bit...rough," she says, examining him closely, "Can you follow my finger?" He does and when Sadie asks if it hurts, he nods. "What about your head? It hurt, too?"

He nods again and she examines the lump just above his hairline along his left temple. It's rather large, but the swelling's stopped, and the discoloration is just beginning to show. Sadie offers him a drink and rips open a food ration. Slowly, she chews on a mouthful and offers him half. They eat in silence as both of them consider their situations. As Sadie swallows the last of her food, she begins addressing him.

"You're lucky...to still be here." She pauses, letting the tone of her voice serve its purpose. "I'm sure you noticed the woman I returned with...and...our clothes." Sadie looks over her attire, then his. "I've got news...that might be hard to take."

She looks Adam straight in the eyes and communicates with a preciseness and manner that resonates on multiple levels, "We've eliminated your comrades...first, the crew camping on shore, then...we took control of the Captain's boat." Sadie gauges his reactions. "The Captain was..." she hesitates, trying to verbalize a fitting description of a man who ceaselessly used cruelty and torture as a form of personal entertainment, "he was the type of man...I hope to never...encounter...again. Those poor women...what they...endured." Sadie lowers her eyes and voice while going on instinct, "When he finished...with 'em...were any left alive?"

She looks him straight in the eyes and holds her gaze. Adam's body language changes immediately. Both shoulders drop, as he shakes his head no, breaking eye contact. It wasn't just the Captain. He always got the ladies first and when he tired of one, she was turned over to the crew. Knowing it wasn't right, he'd taken no part in what followed, but he'd never done anything about it, and even worse, he delivered plenty of women to their doom.

Sadie, reading his reaction, takes a different approach. She leans in close, inquiring about his family. It's not what Adam expected and it catches him completely off guard. He slowly responds, and afterward, Sadie remains silent and doesn't ask another thing. Instead, she allows what's been shared to digest and lets Adam grow introspective.

As the day lengthens, she shares more water and food before trading places with the Delta returning to guard duty.

Sitting near the beach, Sadie watches the sunset while feeding a small fire. Keeping up the facade, she sits among the former Splitter camp contemplating their current predicament when suddenly, her head snaps up. Checking the smoke's direction, she casually stands, looking towards the anchored yacht. The wind, much lighter now, blows directly from it, verifying someone's aboard and cooking. Smells of grilling permeate the air, sending a chill along Sadie's spine and up the back of her scalp. Her stomach flutters and again, uneasiness creeps through her.

Checking the fire before venturing around one last time, Sadie lets all that's been gathered, discovered, and shared percolate. Putting everything together, she knows something's missing and whatever it is, it points to the mystery yacht. Three Oceanside members are unaccounted for—including the professor—and she assumes they must be aboard. Returning once again to trade out with the Delta on prisoner duty, Sadie uses the last of light to re-examine Adam.

"Is it safe...to sleep yet?" he says, speaking first.

"It'd be safer to wait," Sadie responds, surprised by his question, but not showing it.

It's not what Adam wants to hear and slumping his shoulders, he doesn't try to hide his disappointment. He's tired, sore, and everything aches. All he wants to do is lie down and rest. Between being stuck in the same position and fighting to stay awake, he's exhausted. Sadie, seeing an opportunity, tells him to stand and adjusts his restraints, making sure their secure as Adam acquires a new position. The blood flow returns to his legs as he alternately raises each foot, repeatedly, above the ground.

"Thanks," Adam says, appreciating the change.

Sadie nods and offers him a drink, which he accepts.

"Our missing men...on the other yacht," Adam's eyes dart to Sadie's, confirming her gut feeling, "You took 'em there?" she asks.

Sadie's question doesn't need a verbal response, as the answer's clearly evident. Adam doesn't even hear it as an inquiry, but as a statement of fact. Sadie—reading every detail of his expression—moves ahead, feeling more and more confident.

"Any chance they're still alive?" she asks, stepping closer and speaking just above a whisper.

Adam, looking genuinely uncertain, can't say for sure and doesn't know how to respond. No one's ever returned, once delivered there, and chances are—not good. He shrugs while noticing her changing demeanor and grows nervous. Sadie's eyes travel up and down his body making his discomfort grow. When she suddenly steps closer, his stomach lurches.

"We're goin' in to save 'em...and...you're helpin'," she blurts.

Adam's face drains of color as his terror at the mere thought of it grips him. Sadie's insides twist, watching Adam, and she wants to know what's causing such a reaction from him.

"I'm not goin' on dat boat!" he states loudly.

Sadie, surprised by such an adamant response and shocked by his interpretation, knows she's on the right track. Easing any tension, Sadie tactfully continues. "Adam, the people livin' here are good folks. They work hard...take care of one another...find ways to survive. It's not like living with," her voice softens, "the Nation." She doesn't hesitate but keeps a non-confrontational tone. "It couldn't have been easy...livin' with 'em. Especially...for a kid."

"I'm not a kid!" He glares at Sadie. "I'm twenty-three!"

Sadie, taken by his sudden fierceness, begins to see Adam in a whole new light. Mistaking his malnourished frame for youth, she realizes that years of near starvation have stunted his growth and slowed his development. Seeing the fight emanating from within Adam, she knows he's made it this far by not backing down. Reassured of the direction she's pursuing though, Sadie continues speaking in a hushed, relaxed tone.

"I'm sorry...all I'm sayin'...is...livin' the Splitter lifestyle can't...be easy, there are other ways to survive. And...the people here are doin' it, at least, until..." Sadie trails off, pausing with genuine concern for the missing men and the colony's safety. Turning her attention back to Adam, she reads his softening body language. "They don't deserve what awaits 'em out there."

Adam squirms, feeling Sadie can see right through him. He's not exactly sure of the extent of her knowledge, but she sure seems to have a handle on everything. Debating his options, Adam contemplates what choices he has. On one hand, if the Splitters that remain regain control, they'll go after him as a scapegoat for the losses they've suffered. However, fearing for more than the end of his life, he doesn't want to join the victims on the yacht. Just thinking about stepping aboard is terrifying. On the other hand, if the Nation doesn't regain control here, then his fate lies in the hands of his present captors. Looking into Sadie's eyes, he breaks contact.

She jumps at the opportunity. "Adam, I'm not takin' you to the boat. All I need to know…is…how you delivered 'em?"

His eyes dart back to hers and hold their ground. Suddenly, Sadie isn't too confident with the direction she's pushed and worries Adam may no longer be so cooperative. Sadie's body language shifts and she doesn't hide the weariness the recent activities have taken on her.

"Should…I make the attempt during daylight, or…at night?" she asks

Still debating his options, Adam stares at Sadie. He doesn't want to admit it, but inherently, he knows what's right and subconsciously stresses about the role he's played in so much wrongdoing. Unsure, he decides on a simple answer.

"Sunrise," is all he says.

Hearing such a specific response makes Sadie feel better, but she holds back any of her enthusiasm. Instead, Sadie stands and asks for his clothes. Surprised, Adam's not sure what to think and he hesitates.

"Come on…I need 'em. They'll fit me better than these," she points at the baggy outfit she's wearing. "I'm goin' out there…disguised…as you."

Pointing at his feet, she tells him to start there. With his shoes removed, Sadie unbuttons her pants as he stares in disbelief. Noticing, she commands him to do the same. With bound hands, it's a challenge, and while struggling, Adam contemplates asking Sadie for help. When he manages getting them undone and wiggled towards the ground, she finishes pulling them off. It takes a moment to figure out a way to remove his shirt without completely releasing his hands, but once it's done, Sadie's wardrobe change is complete.

With knife in hand, Sadie steps closer, making Adam suddenly very nervous. Momentarily, irrational fear grips him, and believing he's completely misread Sadie, Adam fears for his life. It passes with a flourish of heartbeats as she reaches for his hair, nearly identical to hers in color, and checks its length before shearing off her long, beautiful locks. As the last section of her hair falls away, Sadie rubs her hands through it, experiencing the oddity of its feel. Immediately, she changes, and it frightens Adam. When she looks up, cold-blooded determination emanates from her eyes, and it's like looking at an entirely different person.

"Why sunrise?" Her icy glare sends a chill up his spine.

Unable to break eye contact, he answers, "It's when dey go to sleep."

With confirmation of their nocturnal habits, Sadie keeps Adam thinking she knows more than she really does.

"All of 'em?" she asks.

He shakes his head no, Sadie lifts her eyebrows, and he offers more. "During da day...da giant faggot's on duty."

Sadie's briefly caught off guard as a myriad of thoughts bombard her brain. Even though she quickly recovers, Adam notices. He starts thinking maybe Sadie doesn't really know anything about what happens aboard. Before she speaks again, Adam interjects his thoughts.

"You have no idea 'bout dat boat...do you?" A faint flicker of a grin shows in his expression, and Sadie worries she's losing ground.

Continuing to bluff, she ignores his comment and goes on the offensive. "Maybe...I should take you out there and...leave you to 'em."

Sadie doesn't know who "them" is, but the scare tactic works and the response it elicits is obvious. He grows quiet and Sadie realizes she's near the end of getting info from Adam. From what she's gathered, there are at least three men aboard, most are nocturnal, and one stays on guard during the daylight hours. Contemplating her next steps, Sadie moves about letting Adam hang with the uncertainties of her inferences.

Sadie debates strategies, going back and forth over all the possible positive and negative outcomes, until interrupted by a faint noise. Confirming its direction and verifying it's one of the returning Deltas, she meets him part way, asking for any updates. Initially shocked by her changed appearance, he confirms that there's nocturnal activity aboard the vessel. Sadie outlines a plan, providing specific details, including what to share with the other Mid Valley patrollers and how to incorporate the colony reinforcements, who should be arriving sometime later.

"Make sure they know…when I return, I'd like to speak more with Adam." Sadie says.

He nods and keeps guard over the prisoner as Sadie heads towards the beach camp. She'll have just enough time and darkness. Making her way to the zodiac, she drags it into the water and quietly paddles towards the Captain's boat. The calm waters make it an easy trip and she's careful to remain unseen by the other vessel, as a surprised Caleb greets her.

Caleb speaks first, as he looks over her new disguise, "I didn't expect you yet…what's wrong?"

There isn't lots of time before sunrise and Sadie knows they must be efficient. She placates his concern, provides an overview of what's been learned, and asks for any new intel he may have gathered. He adds little and Sadie dives into her plan, not giving Caleb a chance to interrupt or protest. She warns of the timing, he relinquishes trying to stop her, and the two of them quietly return to shore, paddling in the last of the darkness. This time, it's Caleb who'll serve as bait, in what they hope will be the final elimination of these intruders.

FORTY-NINE

As the zodiac zooms towards the unknown, Sadie's gut screams caution. So far their tactics have been effective in keeping them safe and she prays it continues. As they near the huge yacht, Caleb's bound and gagged body bounces with the small chop across the ocean's surface. Between a light chill that looms over the morning and the uncertainty of their task, goose bumps cover his bare torso and arms. Uncomfortable in his role as bait, Caleb tries calming his nerves. Closing in on the vessel, they see faded red lettering, barely legible, which reveals the name Maji Wanga on its back.

Their approach doesn't go unnoticed, and before they reach the large watercraft, a behemoth of a black man appears on deck. Both are taken aback at his appearance, and Caleb immediately starts his routine, acting the part of a reluctant hostage. He struggles against his bindings, curses through the gag, and extends his bound legs to kick the zodiac away from the boat as it nears.

The man towering above them is dressed in nothing but a white butcher apron stained with blood. His long, black dreads are held back by colorful displays of beads and small oddities, exposing an equally dark face covered by a combination of tattoos and piercings, all accentuated by a small curved bone through his nose. As Sadie brings the zodiac closer, the man chuckles, while reaching down to grab Caleb with his huge arms, which are decorated with intricate scarification patterns and brands seared into the flesh.

In a thick Louisiana Creole accent, accompanied with flamboyant gestures, the giant addresses them, "Ewwww-eeeee, gots moin...ahh feisty won. Ennnnn...gooed wookin'...tey's gwunna luv you."

Caleb kicks again, landing a blow to the man's massive arm. Before the monstrous man regains his balance, Sadie uncovers her hidden crossbow and strikes. Her arrow pierces his chest and for a moment, the giant stares at it before attempting to remove it. As his hands clasp the shaft, Sadie fires another, this time, at his head. He falls to a knee as Caleb scrambles to board the vessel. Still dumbfounded by the attack, the man uses his last breath in an attempt to curse them.

"J'ai…faaaa…im…" he begins, before collapsing sideways in a crumpled heap of mass, exposing more of him than Sadie cares to see.

Once aboard, she can't help but notice his thick, muscular backside, along with how well-endowed he'd been. Sadie adjusts the apron to cover his nakedness as a shudder of fear runs through her. He's the first person she's seen that not only doesn't appear to be starving, but looks extremely well fed. It takes a considerable amount of calories to maintain that much mass, especially on such a large frame, and the sight is upsetting for Sadie, who knows his survival must have come at the detriment of many others.

It takes both Sadie's and Caleb's full effort to drag his body out of sight and hide it. Cautiously, the two proceed, as an unsettling eeriness builds within them. The yacht reeks, and the stench grows stronger until they find its source and where the now deceased man must have come from. In the galley, they're surrounded by unimaginable displays of voodoo, evildoings, and obvious cannibalism. Shocked by several of these sights, Sadie tries calming her heart as it threatens to rip out of her chest, but seeing butchered human flesh dangling from a meat grinder doesn't help. Neither does the array of shrunken heads hanging around. Even with their eyes stitched closed, the miniature wrinkled faces seem to follow Sadie and Caleb's movements, warning them of the terrors lurking aboard.

Seeing Sadie closely examining one, Caleb whispers, asking if she thinks they're real. She shrugs and grows wary of a suspicious-looking pot that draws both their attention. Overcome with an urge to remove the lid, Sadie does so, and it nearly falls from her hand. Seeing her reaction, Caleb can't help but look and is forced to turn away from the sight, fighting his gag reflex.

"Guess that answers your question," Sadie whispers while returning the lid.

Anxious to leave their current surroundings and even more disturbed, Caleb and Sadie quietly exit and creep deeper into the belly of the vessel. The hairs standing at the back of Sadie's neck cause her to doubt this part of her plan. Maybe she should have waited for the colony reinforcements and not put them into this situation. Step by cautious step, a tediously slow mantra of movement develops, dragging them forward.

At mid-ship, the interior changes, and each door presents a heart-thumping predicament. Open it or ignore it? With uncertain anticipation, they check each, mentally note the locked ones, and inspect what the others expose. With each door they check, Sadie knows the increasing odds they face of running into the other Splitters, and proceeding nearly overloads her sense of safety.

Suddenly, she freezes, as her stomach drops at the mere hint of movement ahead. After a lengthy pause, she signals, and they proceed, closing in on the muffled sounds. As they get close enough to distinguish a voice and exactly where it's coming from, they pause again. Unable to catch more than just a word or two and still uncertain of how many people lie ahead, Sadie halts.

She leans to peer through a door, left slightly ajar, then gradually signals them forward. Caleb follows and finds himself in an ornate sleeping chamber that accommodates two distinctly separate bedroom spaces on opposite sides of the large space. The room's layout provides cover for them to move close enough to hear what's being said from the adjoining stateroom.

"Gooed thang fa yah we's like ta play wit our food." A throaty chuckle follows and eventually fades into more talking, "En we's gonna play for a while…ain't we white boy?"

Muffled grunts and movements fill the void, as terror seizes them. Sadie moves to a location that offers a limited view into where the voice emanates. The further she leans, the more she's able to see, but it's not nearly enough to provide a visual on their targets. On hands and knees, she creeps forward as Caleb fills her vacated space. Hidden behind a curtained partition, Sadie catches glimpses of medical equipment and supplies. Looking through a gap in the fabric a horrendous view of bloody bandages, splattered operating equipment, and cutting tools can be seen.

Sadie adjusts her angle and braves more of the sickening sight. Shackled to the wall and nursing a recent amputation, a man hangs, nearly paralyzed with pain. Bandages around the stump, just below his shoulder, are soaked dark red, causing images of bloody flesh in a grinder to flash across Sadie's mind. The evilness emanating from everything, even the very air they breathe, frightens her. Forcing her body ahead to another hole in the material, she builds courage before taking a quick peek. Instinctively ducking at the verification of movement just on the other side, the struggling from there grows louder and Sadie's nerves jump at the sound of a man's voice.

"Yeh...ya like dat...don't ya?" his voice trails off, as more struggling can be heard.

Sadie, risking another look, peers through the small peephole and finally she's able to see the man behind the voice and to whom he's talking. It's hard to tear her eyes away from the disturbing image. A grossly overweight man, oddly colored, and dressed in women's lingerie, hovers over a naked man tied face down across an apparatus that's designed for just that intended purpose. In one hand, he's using a riding crop to caress his captive's body while the other stays busy fondling himself. The horrific sight has an uncomfortable, skin-crawling effect on Sadie.

As the tormentor gradually moves around his victim, Sadie realizes the oddity of his skin tone and hair color is actually from a lack of pigment. He's albino, and she's never seen one in person before and didn't even know it was possible for people of color. But it's the only explanation that fits—he's a mulatto albino—and as she continues to watch, he removes the feather boa from around his neck and runs it across the man's ass.

"Boy, jou and moins gonna have us ah gooed time," the ghastly man says, while groping his victim.

"Leave him be!"

Startled, Sadie's attention darts to the source of the unexpected outbreak.

So does the albinos. "Shut da fuck up ole mahn!" he yells.

From her limited range of vision, Sadie can just make out a figure that she assumes to be the Professor. A thick metal collar around his neck with an equally sturdy chain attached, keeps him detained. Both arms are tied behind his back and his legs are bound, but he's standing. One eye is swollen shut and lash marks streak across his chest.

"No! You don't treat us like this," the Professor boldly states.

"Aaaahhhh...is da fessor ready fa mo...ahh?" the albino teasingly waves his crop at the Professor. Putting it aside, he approaches a nearby rack and slowly makes a selection from the many implements hanging there. After picking one of his favorites, he returns to the chained man. "An eer I tought...we was done, 'specially...since da suns up nnn...I'm past due fa sum zeeees, but...fa you boys...I dink I'ms gonna make ahh...ception."

Caleb, anxiously waiting for feedback, listens, unsure of what's happening. When Sadie turns in his direction, she signals three friendlies and one hostile. He confirms, and while moving to a better position, sounds of pain fill the space, increasing the intensity of the moment. Sadie raises a single finger, and then pauses.

"Com'on prooo-fess-eerrr...were's all dat wader you make goin'?" the albino asks, pausing between the blows he's delivering.

The Professor, barely able to withstand the torture, shakes his head, refusing to divulge anything about the colony, knowing it's a no-win situation. This scenario already played out once before, and even though he gave up info about the desalination process, it hadn't mattered. They're only being kept alive long enough for the crew's sick and twisted pleasures before, eventually, being eaten limb by limb. His lack of response incurs a greater wrath and the torturous pace increases.

Sadie, moving to the edge of the partition, raises a second finger while getting her crossbow into position. As her count reaches three, she pushes aside the curtain and fires, completely missing the mark. Her arrow pierces the obese albino's flabby underarm as her hand stings with a burning sensation from the snap of his whip that turned towards her as she appeared. It caught Sadie by surprise, but in mid-backlash, she rushes forward on the offensive. Engaging in hand-to-hand combat with a man much taller and at least twice her weight isn't something she intended trying. Sadie ducks under his arm, removes her knife, and strikes.

The infliction isn't deadly, but it weakens her opponent and provides seconds of distraction for another strike, which lands across his back. Sadie sidesteps a massive elbow blow that nearly catches her in the chin and spins towards his front, as Caleb jumps into action. Choking the man from behind with his own whip, Caleb has to use his entire body weight and strength to keep control of the thrashing man. Strangulation is a horrible way to die and the brutality of it, mixed with the awful visual, makes Sadie's stomach lurch. Caleb and the man slowly slip to the floor as the last kick of life reverberates through the meaty flesh of the man's naked leg.

Out of breath, physically fatigued, and emotionally distraught, Caleb releases his death grip, letting the whip fall upon the floor. Standing, he stumbles with his first step before regaining balance. During the violent commotion, Sadie anticipated the possible arrival of anyone else aboard the vessel, but in the lengthening silence, she shifts focus and works to free the captives. Starting with the Professor, who's in shock at the sudden attack and rescue, she reminds Caleb to stay diligent and keep watch. Fiddling with her pick set, Sadie finds the implements that fit best and attempts unlocking the collar from around his neck. The professor regains composure, and as Sadie finds success, he finds his voice.

"Did you get the other one?!" the Professor asks.

Removing the rest of his bindings, Sadie informs the professor about the giant black guy they first encountered when coming aboard. Talking fast, she describes him and quickly recounts the events leading to his demise while working on releasing the other man. She starts with the ball gag in his mouth and as soon as it's out, he yells.

"No! There's two of these fat fuckers!" The man, freed from the confines of the torturous contraption, keeps repeating the same profanities over and over while kicking the body of his dead tormentor. "Fat...fucking...disgusting twins!"

The professor grabs him, making it stop, as Sadie picks the locks, releasing the one-armed man. He's pale and unconscious, but definitely still alive. With all three captives freed, Sadie wants specifics about the missing twin and whether they're aware of anyone else on the ship.

"We only know of three. The man you killed, this one, and his twin, who left with...ahhhhh...after...after they..." the Professor can't finish his sentence.

Instead, he nods to the man with the missing appendage and Sadie understands. She turns her attention to the one who lost control kicking the dead body. He's recovered his clothes and is in the process of dressing.

"You a patroller, or one of the Professor's workers?" Sadie asks, once he's clothed.

He stares blankly, looks at the Professor, and then back to Sadie before tentatively answering. "Patroller."

"Ok good...if were gonna make it outta here, were gonna need your help." He nods slowly, and Sadie continues, "First off, no more outbreaks. We can't risk being detected. You've made a commitment to the colony and so far we've managed keeping 'em safe. Our intentions are to keep it that way...understand?"

He nods in affirmation, and Sadie, hoping he's dependable, adds more. "We need to confirm the twin's the only one left and make sure no more Splitters are lurking about. You'll keep watch here...Caleb and I will scout the rest of the boat...some of the rooms were locked and he's gotta be in one of 'em. We end this now," she says with a bone-chilling authority.

Sadie, the Professor, and the patroller talk further as they provide what little information they can. She gives them her knife and checks on Caleb, who's been keeping watch. Seeing Sadie with the patroller, Caleb signals all-clear, and she updates him on the missing twin and what's intended.

"I thought these guys were nocturnal? Couldn't we just wait here...in ambush? This has to be where he'll return to sleep," Caleb says, clearly concerned.

Sadie agrees with his rationale and it reinforces keeping the patroller positioned here to protect the Professor and his unconscious worker. If the twin doesn't return, or worse, heard the commotion, he could be waiting for an opportunity to attack or use the radio to call for help. Caleb nods in understanding, and the two of them recheck each area they passed on their initial inspection.

One by one, they re-verify which rooms are locked and examine the ones that are not. After clearing all the accessible spaces, Sadie carefully picks a lock and when it clicks open, they both gasp. The remodeled utility room houses an arsenal of weapons. Before relocking it and moving to the next, they remove several firearms and better supply their recently freed comrades. Returning to where they left off, Sadie has trouble unlocking a door, and it takes longer than expected. Each failed attempt is accompanied by a slight clicking noise that echoes across their rattled nerves. When the locking mechanism finally succumbs, Sadie's hesitant.

Slowly manipulating the door to open reveals another round of upsetting images. The walls are completely covered with childish pictures, drawings, and coloring book pages. The furniture is miniature, and the shelves and surfaces are full of toys, games, and stuffed animals. Even though it's decorated as a place of comfort and safety, it has an opposite effect, giving Sadie a whole new series of goose bumps and bad feelings. There's another door to the side and unsure of what they'll find, Sadie opens it. The space houses several bunk-style sleeping beds each containing various constraints, but there are no occupants.

"This boat...should be...burned," Caleb says, exasperated by the sight.

Sadie nods—sickened to think of what occurs in these quarters—as they continue the search. There's only one more locked stateroom, and both anticipate finding the missing Splitter there. As Sadie takes a knee to begin work on the lock, it suddenly swings open, shocking both parties. From her vulnerable position, Sadie ducks sideways as the door slams shut. Caleb reacts with a violent kick, breaking it open, and with a raised weapon, he enters to see a flash of movement leaving through another door.

With racing hearts and adrenaline pumping, they follow in close pursuit. As they weave through the ship, Sadie and Caleb work as a unit while attempting to cut off the second twin. Afraid he's trying to get to the weapons stash, they force him upward until they find themselves maneuvering through the pilothouse and then out onto the bridge. The brightness of the sunlight affects the sensitivity of the nocturnal one's eyes, as he scrambles and takes cover behind stowed gear. Hearing the pump action of a shotgun from behind, Caleb and Sadie suddenly fear they've run into a trap. Turning, they're even more surprised at seeing the Professor.

"I thought I'd help," he says, in response to their looks.

Distracted momentarily by his presence, they fail to notice as the albino twin shifts positions to gain an advantage and suddenly pops up firing a handgun. Sadie instinctively reacts by pushing the Professor aside to safety. Caleb responds with his own barrage of bullets, hitting his mark and finally ending the stand-off. Feeling relieved and glad everything's finally over, he turns around, but his relief shifts to terror. He watches as Sadie stumbles and violently smacks her head while falling overboard, leaving a bloody trail behind. Her body strikes the water and slowly sinks into the depths of the sea as her vision—fades—to black.

ABOUT THE AUTHOR

Nikki Lewen was born and raised in the North, college-educated in the Midwest, earned her graduate degrees in the Deep South, then, after a short stint on the East Coast, she crisscrossed the county in a small RV, before finding a home near California's Pacific Ocean. A compulsive surfer, nature lover, and avid fitness buff, she spends countless hours up to her elbows in dirt and stone, re-shaping the land alongside her cabin in the towering redwoods.

As an up-and-coming author, she has been collecting writer's club memberships, finds fast food nauseating, and generally views privacy as a dwindling commodity in today's world of instant connectivity and digital documentation.

THANK YOU!

I hoped you enjoyed *Three Sisters*, the first book of the **Three Sisters Trilogy**, and you're eager to read more of Sadie's fate while doing your part to heal the damage, that unfortunately, we've already done to our poor Mother Earth.

It would be vastly helpful and much appreciated, if you could review this book on Amazon. It will provide valued feedback, improve future books, and help other authors and readers like yourself decide if the **Three Sisters Trilogy** is right for them.

Please tweet about this book and post to Facebook as well.

A huge thanks!
Nikki Lewen

Here's a preview of the second book in the Three Sisters Trilogy: *Return to Three Sisters*.

Slowly, using the blade almost teasingly, the Splitter warrior gently cuts away what little clothing remains on Sadie's body in a careful pursuit of any last hidden items that may be concealed. Stepping back, the Commander kicks away the pile of discarded items and returns to straddling the chair, feeling even more intrigued. She was prepared to handle a man, but the discovery of a female changes the game. Sadie, who has yet to speak, calmly watches as her captor's eyes follow the curves of her nakedness.

"Wow...you're...really...really.........fit," she finally states—admiringly—adding to Sadie's sensation of feeling like a piece of meat.

"You still look good, too," Sadie remarks in her normal voice.

Her comment has the effect she hoped for, and the Commander, although trying to hide it, doesn't avoid a shocked response.

"Sorry...might be that terrible haircut or...all ur bruises, but..."

Sadie, slowly shaking her head, interrupts. "No, Russo, we've never met."

At the mention of her long-ago name, the Commander stands. She hasn't been called that in years. The mysteriousness of this woman, along with the circumstances surrounding her, adds to the increasingly troublesome nagging in the fierce Splitter's stomach.

"Your hair's different...way sexier," Sadie adds, keeping her opponent off balance. "And you've gotten more ink, but you look..." Sadie trails off, looking over the impressive female figure standing before her, "really...bad ass." She smiles, watching as the Commander reels with uncertainty.

Russo takes a step closer and Sadie, appreciating the indication, continues with more flattery.

"You were incredible, a true champion...and, from the looks of you...still are."

Putting together the picture Sadie paints, the Commander regains a little ground. "You used to watch me fight?"

"A few times," Sadie casually replies, watching the former UFC fighter grow quiet in contemplation.

A long pause settles between the two ladies as Sadie anticipates the direction her adversary will take.

"You know 'bout me, but...what 'bout you?" The Commander asks, admiring Sadie's smooth and pale skin. "You obviously aren't exposed to the sun, so...you must live somewhere out here...in these outer islands."

Russo's accurate observation and the intrusive feeling it elicits serve as a reminder for Sadie of her opponent's intellect and the strange dynamic developing between them.

Sadie nods in confirmation. "What else can you tell?" she adds, encouragingly.

The Commander leans in close. "There's much to you, and this... is gonna take some time." Without any indication, she abruptly gets up and shuts the door.